I, MEDUSA

BY AYANA GRAY

Beasts of Prey
Beasts of Ruin
Beasts of War
I, Medusa

I, MEDUSA

A NOVEL

AYANA GRAY

ZAFFRE

First published in the UK in 2025 by
ZAFFRE
An imprint of Bonnier Books UK
5th Floor, HYLO, 105 Bunhill Row,
London, EC1Y 8LZ

A CIP catalogue record for this book is available from the British Library.

Hardback ISBN: 978-1-78530-682-2
Trade Paperback ISBN: 978-1-78530-683-9

Also available as an ebook and an audiobook

1 3 5 7 9 10 8 6 4 2

Typeset by IDSUK (Data Connection) Ltd
Title-page and part-title art: Vinap/Adobe Stock
Printed and bound by CPI (UK) Ltd, Croydon CR0 4YY

The authorised representative in the EEA is
Bonnier Books UK (Ireland) Limited.
Registered office address: Floor 3, Block 3, Miesian Plaza,
Dublin 2, D02 Y754, Ireland
compliance@bonnierbooks.ie
www.bonnierbooks.co.uk

For my sister:
I'd turn a thousand men to stone
to keep you safe.

Gods always behave like the people who make them.

—Zora Neale Hurston

Sometimes it seems that anger alone keeps me alive.

—Audre Lorde

NOTABLE NAMES AND PLACES

Aithiopia A large section of what is now referred to as sub-Saharan Africa; not to be confused with modern Ethiopia; sometimes spelled Aethiopia

Amphitrite Wife of Poseidon; daughter of Nereus; queen of the Sea Court

Athena Daughter of Zeus; goddess of wisdom, warfare, and craft

Athens A Greek city-state from the classical period known for its arts, sport, learning, and philosophy

Ceto Daughter of Pontus and Gaia; wife of Phorcys; mother of the Gorgons; goddess of perils at sea

Euryale Daughter of Phorcys and Ceto; sister of Stheno and Medusa; second-born of the three Gorgons

Gaia Mother of Ceto and Phorcys; grandmother of the Gorgons; a primordial goddess considered to be the mother of all life

Gigantomachy An infamous war of conflicting origin waged between the Giants and the Olympians; the Olympians were victorious (not to be confused with the Titanomachy).

Gorgons The collective name bestowed on three of Phorcys and Ceto's daughters, Stheno, Euryale, and Medusa; the Gorgons were known, in some interpretations, for having serpentine hair and the power to turn a person into stone with their lethal gaze.

Hermes Son of Zeus; god of travelers, speed, athletes, and messages

Medusa	Daughter of Phorcys and Ceto; sister of Stheno and Euryale; youngest of the three Gorgons
Nereids	Collective name for the daughters of Nereus; sea nymphs
Nereus	Father of the Nereids; a shape-shifting sea god
Olympians	The twelve ruling gods of the pantheon who live on Mount Olympus; traditionally, this includes Aphrodite, Apollo, Ares, Artemis, Athena, Demeter, Hephaestus, Hera, Hermes, Poseidon, Zeus, and, interchangeably, Dionysus or Hestia.
Phorcys	Son of Pontus and Gaia; husband of Ceto; father of the Gorgons
Pontus	Son and consort of Gaia; father of Ceto and Phorcys; grandfather of the Gorgons; a primordial sea god
Poseidon	Son of Cronus and Rhea; husband of Amphitrite; king of the Sea Court
Prometheus	One of the Titans and a god of fire
Sea Court	An informal collective of gods with an affinity for the sea
Stheno	Daughter of Phorcys and Ceto; sister of Euryale and Medusa; eldest of the three Gorgons
Zeus	Son of Cronus and Rhea; king of the gods

I, MEDUSA

AFTER

IT'S WELL PAST midnight when the woman finds the temple.

Her first thought, as her heels sink into the beach's wet sand, is that the place at which she has arrived is not at all what she was expecting. The holy sites she is accustomed to are grand and imposing marble complexes staffed by a retinue of dutiful priests or priestesses. The lone torch-lit building that looms before her in the dark, with its crumbling stone ramparts and visibly neglected grounds, is neither grand nor imposing. The woman notes that the place is, in fact, quite small, half obscured by the surrounding dunes, and unlikely to have other visitors this late in the night. The woman is not deterred as she diverts from the coastline to draw closer.

Tonight, a temple without visitors is auspicious.

A crude path lined with pebbles and driftwood leads her from the beach to the temple's only entrance. The moment she crosses its threshold, the smell of myrrh fills her lungs, drawing from her a dull ache, a long-buried grief. She ignores that ache, smothers the grief, then presses on.

Eventually, she finds the old priest alone in the temple's open courtyard. He's holding a broom, locked in fierce battle with the sand that litters the tile. His olive skin shines with perspiration, his gray tunic is modest and plain. He is a foreigner in these lands, just as she is. It takes several seconds before he looks up and notices her. He has cloudy, albeit kind, brown eyes and a decidedly paternal smile. That smile makes the woman think of her own father, what he'd think if he knew what she was about to do. She dismisses that thought quickly. Her father is a god, and if she knows anything about gods, it is that they care little for mortals and less for mortal plights. Instead, her attention returns to the priest. She offers him a low bow—a lingering habit from her time as a priestess. Then she speaks. Her voice is petal soft.

"I've come to ask for a blessing."

The priest sets his broom aside and laces his gnarled fingers. Silence stretches between them before he gives his answer.

"What do you offer in exchange?"

The woman bows her head, contrite. "I've no coin, nothing of value."

This is met with more silence.

"Please, I'm . . . I'm desperate." The woman waits a beat before lifting her gaze. When she does, she finds the priest's expression has changed. She knows what he sees: a young, dark-skinned woman wearing a simple white tunic and a simpler white head wrap. She knows that this is a game, that she has already made the first move. Now it is his turn.

"It is no matter," the priest says gently. "There are always other ways, other kinds of exchanges." He gives the woman a significant look— a look she has been anticipating—before he beckons. "Come, child."

The woman obeys, closing the small gap between them to accept his veiny hand. She does not shiver when he traces the pad of his thumb over her palm.

Then his grip tightens.

The woman does not object when the priest pulls her against him, nor when he crushes his wrinkled lips against hers. She does not protest when he lowers them both to the sand-swept floor, nor when he guides her to clumsily mount him. His body is bony and frail, but she feels it harden with desire between her thighs.

"I am untouched," she whispers. "I have never . . ."

"That is all right," says the priest. In the flicker of the torchlight, his once-kind eyes have grown wolfish. "I will show you what to do. But first, let me see you."

The woman hesitates, then unfastens the pins that hold her tunic together at the shoulders, so that the garment falls around her waist. A low, appreciative groan escapes the priest's lips.

"Tell me your name." His voice is scraped raw with lust.

A small smile touches the woman's face. "I could tell you who I am," she says. "But I think it better to show you *what* I am."

The old priest looks up from her bare breasts, confused, but the woman is already loosening her head wrap. She lets it slip to the floor, then blinks with newly yellow eyes. The priest's grow coin-wide with terror.

"*Abomination,*" he rasps. "You're a—" He does not finish his sentence. Already, his vital organs are calcifying to cold, gray stone, as is the rest of his body. His fingers curl inward as he claws at the air, grasping at something he'll never reach. All the while, the woman sits silently astride him, waiting. Some distant, detached part of her—the part of her that's remained human, perhaps—knows that she should feel *something*. Relief. Vindication. Horror.

The best she can manage is exhaustion.

The woman presses her fingertips to the priest's stone tunic as his fluttering heartbeat slows, then stills. Only when she's certain that he's dead does she rise. She reaches up as hissing fills the temple, and the ink-black serpents that sprout from her scalp in place of hair taste the salt air with eager forked tongues while they nuzzle her hand.

Vaguely, the woman wonders how long it will take to drag the statue of the priest down to the shoreline, how many hours might pass before his absence is noticed. She tallies how many men she has killed thus far and wonders how many more she will kill before the rage within her is sated, before it feels like enough.

As she douses the temple's torch and surrenders to the dark, Medusa thinks about monsters, and how easily she became one.

PART I

MORTAL

I

"MEDDY!"

I straighten at the sound of my name, doing my best to look attentive. The effort is entirely wasted on my mother. Her dark, glittering eyes are already fixed on me, and narrowed with familiar disapproval.

"You aren't paying attention," she accuses. "Do it again."

I stifle a whine as she ushers me, none too gently, to the center of our veranda. Once I am in the correct stance, she claps.

"Begin."

A slave seated nearby on a wooden stool starts to pluck a short-necked lute, filling the warm morning air with a sweet melody. On cue, I pivot, raising my arms and clapping in time with the music while attempting to ignore the stiff ache in my biceps. I focus on the heady scent of flowers in the distance, on the hard press of the tile against the ball of my foot. I try to lose myself in the song's rhythm, and when I close my eyes, I pretend I'm somewhere else, anywhere else. Barely a minute passes before my mother tuts. The music halts.

"Stop grimacing," she says irritably. "You're moving like you're in pain."

"I *am* in pain," I mutter. "I've done this dance a hundred times."

My mother remains unmoved. "You'll do it a hundred more times, if that's what it takes," she warns. "You must be perfect. The gods gracing our halls will expect nothing less."

This is a reminder I do not need.

Tomorrow night, my parents will host a feast under the guise of celebrating the start of spring, but I've spent enough time watching the
political games of gods to understand the real reason for the occasion.
My sisters and I are now all of age, which means it is time to see us made
useful. For my parents, this means married.

"The gods of the Sea Court won't be the only ones in attendance."
My mother speaks as though she were privy to my thoughts. "There
may very well be potential suitors present, men of high and noble birth
in search of a young bride. It's all the more reason for you to be at your
best."

"Do any of these men of high and noble birth come from an interesting place?" I ask.

My mother assesses me anew, suspicious. "They could."

"Do you suppose any of them might bring anything interesting with
him, like maps or scrolls from his homeland? I'd love something new to
read." As soon as the words leave my mouth, I know they are a mistake.
A young male slave sweeping at the other end of the veranda shakes his
head, visibly amused. The two female slaves flanking my mother with
sunshades exchange looks of uncertainty.

"Of course not," my mother snaps. "And I don't want to hear another
word about maps, scrolls, or any other nonsense. Start again."

I return to the dance's first position and wait for the lute player to
resume. This time, I stumble as I pivot, then trip on the hem of my tunic.
Behind me, there's a poorly disguised snort from one of my sisters. A
tingling heat that has nothing to do with the sun overhead creeps up my
neck.

"You're not trying hard enough," my mother scolds. "Each step should
appear light, effortless. I want you to try to move with more grace,
like—" She catches herself, but I finish her sentence in my mind.

Like Stheno and Euryale.

I turn to look at my older sisters, not far off, reclined on chaises in
the sunlight. Plenty of goddesses—our own mother included—prefer to
manipulate their appearances so as to seem ever young. But my sisters
truly are twenty-one and nineteen, only a few years older than me.

Stheno is like a gazelle—tall, supple, and fine-featured. Euryale is of a more petite build, but she has inherited our mother's round cheeks and dimpled smile. I don't like to imagine how I look when I stand next to them. My sisters and I share the same dark, sun-blazed skin. We all favor our parents, but there, our similarities end. At seventeen, I'm still skinny, devoid of any feminine softness about my hips, and I once overheard a slave call my wide-set brown eyes "owlish."

I sigh. In these moments, I feel like a common moth trying in vain to pass for a butterfly. A well-worn sense of defeat settles over me.

"Never mind," says my mother. "We'll continue later." She collapses onto a chair while her attendants lean in to fan her more vigorously. In the morning light, she looks like a shining daughter of the sun god Helios, but Ceto is a goddess of the sea through and through. Her rich brown skin stands in brilliant contrast to her yellow tunic and is complemented by the white cowrie shells braided into her black hair. To the untrained eye, she would appear only a few years older than my sisters and me, but that is all illusion. My mother is, in fact, thousands of years old.

"You, there!" She snaps her fingers at a passing slave. "Bring me my wine!"

The slave she beckons is a small, stooped woman, wrinkled and dark like a raisin. She stops what she's doing immediately and bows. "Yes, Goddess." She retrieves a silver goblet and pitcher from a nearby table and begins to pour.

My mother holds up a hand. "Not the red." She snatches the goblet away. "I want the white."

The old woman stiffens, as does every other slave in the vicinity.

"My apologies, Goddess," the woman says quietly, "but there is no more white wine left."

My mother's brows arch. "Where is it?"

"Gone." The old woman begins to tremble. "The last of it was finished yesterday."

"There's more somewhere, *find it*." My mother dismisses the woman with a wave, but agitation colors her voice.

The woman's trembling worsens, and that's when I know with certainty that there is no more white wine in our reserves. We do have a small vineyard on the island, but I suspect that our inventory has been significantly depleted by the preparations for tomorrow's feast. I also suspect that when my mother works all this out, someone will suffer for it. The muscles in my stomach begin to knot. My mother's mercurial moods can come on like a late spring storm, sudden and catastrophic. I search the veranda, desperate, then lock eyes with my older sisters. The plea I exchange with them is wordless, but I know they understand. Euryale steps forward, tactfully placing herself between the old woman and our mother.

"Mama," she says sweetly. "It's so early. Perhaps water—"

My mother strikes with the speed and precision of a viper. The goblet she's been holding hits my sister in the face, splashing dark red wine across her tunic's front before clattering to the tiled floor. Euryale cries out in pain. I start toward her, but Stheno rises to catch my arm and holds me back. We both watch as Euryale doubles over, a hand clapped over her mouth. When she straightens, I see that a bead of bright golden blood has bloomed at the center of her bottom lip. She stands there a moment, stunned, before dragging a bare arm across her mouth and smearing the blood like honey. Anger prickles hot against my skin.

"When I desire the counsel of children, I will ask for it." My mother's words are low, menacing. "Do you understand me, Euryale?"

"Yes, Mama." Euryale stares at the ground. "Forgive me."

My mother's face slowly changes. Her dark brown eyes grow shiny and wet; deep lines wrinkle the corners of her mouth, so that her divine façade of youth is momentarily lifted. She stares in horror at Euryale's bloodied lip, and I find myself wondering if she's thinking of our father, of how many times he's bloodied *her* lip. Abruptly, she pulls Euryale close and cups her face. At her touch, Euryale flinches.

"My beautiful girl." My mother thumbs away the golden blood, her voice suddenly warm and gentle. "I'm so sorry. You know I didn't mean to strike you so hard. It's only that the preparations for this feast have taxed me a great deal. You forgive me, don't you?"

"Of course, Mama." Euryale has not lifted her gaze. "I forgive you."

My mother smiles, and I watch as whatever piece of herself she has exposed reburies itself as though it were never there at all. She crosses the veranda and grasps the entire undrunk pitcher of wine the old woman tried to offer before. She holds it with both hands and drinks directly from its rim. I watch, slightly nauseated, as red wine dribbles from the corners of her mouth and down her neck, soiling her front. When she lowers the pitcher, her expression is slack, unfocused. She gathers up the hem of her tunic and saunters off the veranda in a flutter of yellow. Her attendants fall into step behind her, and after an uncomfortable pause, the lute player bows and excuses himself, too. In my mother's absence, the morning air seems to warm again, but a staleness lingers.

Euryale trudges back to her chaise and slumps onto it. Thanks to her immortal blood, the cut on her lip has already healed, but the white tunic—one of her favorites—is ruined. She looks down at herself, then at Stheno and me. There's a terrible helplessness in that look, and the anger I felt before reignites. Blood rushes to my face, and I clench my fists so tight my fingernails leave tiny red crescents in the meat of my palm. I eye the abandoned goblet still on the ground and fight a reckless impulse to go after my mother and hurl it at *her,* to let her have a taste of the pain she has caused. When Euryale's face crumples, Stheno and I quickly move to the chaise to sit on either side of her.

"I *hate* her." A tear rolls down Euryale's cheek.

"Don't cry," Stheno whispers fiercely. "She doesn't deserve your tears." She squeezes one of Euryale's hands hard. I clasp the other, but more gently. Stheno begins to hum a nameless tune, and I join her. We hum together until Euryale calms.

I don't remember how old I was when I realized I was different from my sisters, that their blood was golden while mine ran red; that the threads of their lives, and my parents' lives, would extend for all eternity while mine would eventually be cut. It is a quiet but unavoidable truth, one that has always set me apart from the rest of my family. In these moments, though, I know my sisters and I are still bound together—by the confines of our home, by the expectations of our ambitious father, by the shared fear of our erratic mother.

"I *will* marry," Euryale vows. There's a new steel in her dark brown eyes. "And then I will leave this island forever."

I tense. I cannot fault Euryale for wanting to leave home. For as long as I can remember, I've wanted the same thing. I've yearned to leave our island and see the world I know only from the odd trinkets that occasionally wash up on our shores. But alongside that yearning is a very real fear. I am the youngest, and I worry that, someday, my sisters will leave me behind. My gaze wanders past our veranda to the jagged coast below, then to the calm, boundless sea that betrays nothing of the lands and life I know must exist beyond it. I close my eyes and swear a quiet oath.

Someday, I will leave this island, too.

I squeeze Euryale's hand a little tighter, and I'm glad when none of us speak again. Eventually, my sisters go inside, but I stay out on the chaise awhile, hugging my knees to my chest. I breathe in the smell of wet sand, listen to the endless roar of the waves below. It's beautiful, peaceful, and maddeningly familiar. A sigh escapes me unbidden.

"Honestly, Meddy," says a low, teasing voice behind me. "Maps and scrolls?"

Despite myself, I allow a smile to tug at my lips. I don't have to turn around to know the owner of that particular voice, but I do anyway. The young male slave from before—the one who'd been sweeping—now stands a few feet away, wearing a wry smile of his own.

I shrug. "It was worth asking."

Theo snorts and settles beside me. He pulls a small block of wood and a carving knife from his tunic's pocket and begins to whittle away. At once, a calm washes over me like a wave, and the remnants of my earlier anger dissipate. That's the effect Theo usually has on me. He always smells of the garden where we first met when we were small—earthy, slightly floral. We became friends years before, when I accidentally cut my finger on a rose prickle and he valiantly tore a strip from his own tunic to bandage the wound. He's grown taller since that fateful day in the garden, but little else about him has changed. His black hair is still a mass of short, tight curls; his skin is still as dark as mine; and he still manages to hold a light about his person, as though he's stolen some piece of the sun and locked it deep in his chest. We lean into each other as he works, shoulder to shoulder, and for a moment we're content that way.

"Are you ready for tomorrow night?" he asks.

I sit up, the spell broken. "I'm ready for my mother to stop talking about it, if that's what you mean."

Theo's brow furrows the way it always does when he's thinking. He stops whittling. "She mentioned suitors might come," he says. "Do you think any of them will actually make offers of marriage?"

I pause, and an uneasiness nestles inside my rib cage. "I can't be sure," I admit, "but even if one did, I doubt I'd be the one asked."

"What makes you say that?" I'm touched by the defensiveness in my friend's voice.

"Stheno and Euryale are immortal," I say patiently. "I'm not. Any suitor in his right mind would pick one of them before me." The words aren't as hard to say aloud as they used to be. Seventeen years has given me ample time to come to grips with some truths. I understand that, for gods, marriage is a tool. In the eyes of most, my mortality would ensure only a brief political alliance.

"Then those suitors are fools." Theo grins. "It *would* be good, though, if one of them brought some new maps for us to look at."

I smile. There is an endless number of things I admire about Theo, but I know that what binds us most tightly are the things we share—mortality, a constant awareness of the passing of time, and a desire to leave this island and see *more*.

I resettle against him, resting my head on his shoulder. He continues his work on the small block of wood, and I find there's something peaceful about the slow, constant rhythm of the work.

"One day, we'll leave this island," I whisper. "We'll build our boat and gather our supplies, and then we'll leave, together." It is an unlikely dream, impossible even, but the words are still sweet said aloud.

"Together," Theo echoes softly. "You and I will go, together."

In the silence, I try to memorize every detail of this moment—the soft crash of the waves below, the sun-kissed warmth of Theo's skin on mine. Today, all is well.

Tomorrow, the gods descend.

II

MY FATHER, PHORCYS, is no king.

That doesn't stop him from pretending as much as my sisters and I enter our great hall the next evening and settle at the table alongside him and our mother. He sits in a chair fashioned like a throne, lording over all of us. The sun has barely set on our island, but already his dark eyes are glazed and unfocused, a sure sign of wine-fueled indulgence. Objectively, I suppose his chosen form is a handsome one. His skin is dark like mahogany wood, and his kinky hair—white and thick—reminds me of the sea-foam that sometimes gathers at our island's shores. I note that, tonight, he has donned a tunic dyed a rich purple, and each one of his long brown fingers is furnished with a golden ring. I know it is all for show, a reminder to those present that he used to be the primordial sea god of hidden dangers in the deep, a sort of king in his own right. He used to control vast leagues of the open sea; thousands prayed and offered tribute to him. But my father is only a shadow of that ancient and powerful being now. Sometimes, secretly, I pity him.

The five of us remain seated at the host table while slaves scurry about like ants turned out from their mound. Our great hall is always elegant. Tonight, though, its white marble floors have been scrubbed and polished to a high shine. Garlands thick with fresh lilies and irises have been strewn about the interior stone pillars, and my nose fills with the savory aromas of roasted lamb, seasoned legumes, and baked bread. My eyes search for Theo among the slaves, to no avail. With a pang, I wish he were here, that I could talk to him.

The minutes stretch without the arrival of our first guests, and I begin to wonder if the tension hanging thick in the air is real, or simply my imagination at work. Several seats down, my mother pours her second drink to the brim without bothering to ask a slave, while my father impatiently drums those ringed fingers along the table's edge. Stheno, Euryale, and I exchange looks, but none of us dare speak. I know my sisters are thinking the same thing I am. A poorly attended feast would be fodder for light gossip among gods, a feast with no guests at all would be considered a sound failure. I swallow.

After all my mother's planning and preparation, is it possible no one will even come?

As if in answer, the main doors to our hall suddenly open with a low groan. My breathing eases as, one by one, familiar faces begin to appear.

At last, the gods of the Sea Court have arrived.

First, my aunt Eurybia, a buxom, green-haired sea goddess, traipses in wearing a tunic of shimmering white. She strides right up to our table to plant salty kisses on each of our cheeks. My more subdued uncle Thaumas files in after her with less pomp, but he offers each of us a low, chivalrous bow. Other members of my complicated family tree arrive over the next hour, but my attention wanes. All too soon, the hall is full and noisy.

Euryale nudges me. "It's time," she whispers.

I wasn't nervous before. Now my mind seems to detach itself from the rest of my body as she, Stheno, and I rise and head for the center of the hall, where there's an empty space. My heart rabbits inside my chest as the lute player takes his seat and signals to us with a nod. I assume my starting position alongside my sisters and wait while a whole century seems to pass.

Then the first chords of the lute fill the air, and I begin to move.

I have practiced this dance on our veranda a thousand times—the movements are more a thing of muscle memory than anything else—but tonight, in front of so many gods, I'm intensely conscious of every step. I press my foot into the polished marble, praying with all my might that

I won't stumble or trip. To my surprise, I do neither. I kick out a leg and arch my back so that my black locs fly out behind me. Several of the gods murmur in appreciation, and something within me takes triumphant flight.

Each of my locs is as thick as my smallest finger, and they nearly reach my shoulders. I am not ever going to be as beautiful as my sisters, but my hair is something that, I know without a doubt, people truly admire. My locs are my pride, perhaps my dearest physical possession.

The lute player's plucking quickens, and my sisters and I match the new cadence. We clasp hands as we form a tight circle, moving faster and faster in time with the song while our feet move in perfect tandem. Then—

The music stops.

At first, I think I'm imagining it, the new and sudden silence. Stheno is looking over my shoulder, frowning, and when I follow her gaze, I realize that everyone in the hall has turned their heads in the direction of something. *Someone.*

The crowd begins to buzz, low at first, but gradually they become more animated and excited as gods press in to see the newcomer. In their midst, I make out a head of glossy black hair and rise to my toes, curious. Finally, the gods and goddesses part, and I'm able to see what has flustered them so.

That is the first time I lay eyes on Poseidon.

Like most of the newer gods, the king of the sea is tall, slender, and lean. His skin is not as dark as mine or my sisters', but it is still sun-bronzed, the clearest indication of an immortal life spent among the tides. There is nothing soft about his person; he is sharp and muscled, angular in the extreme. His wavy hair is so dark that it looks blue in our hall's flickering candlelight. In contrast, his toga is so white that I can barely look at it without squinting.

"He came." Euryale's bewildered whisper is so low I barely hear it. "I didn't think he would."

In truth, I didn't think he would, either. My mother had certainly mentioned that she and my father had invited the sea king to this feast, but his attendance had always seemed unlikely. The new gods—the

Olympians—don't usually fraternize with the old gods, who are considered inferior. Now I watch as Poseidon moves among our guests, looking genial but decidedly reserved. There's a natural lure about his person, something that seems to draw everyone closer, and the regal distance he maintains only seems to strengthen that lure. His unhurried strides remind me of a panther stalking through a jungle.

He even walks like a king, I realize. I remind myself that he should. Zeus, ruler of the Olympians, may serve as king of the gods, but his brother rules over every god in the Sea Court. At present, Poseidon is the most powerful being in this hall.

For a moment, I think he's going to look our way, but then he's swallowed up by the crowd again. I feel the slightest twinge of disappointment. The feast's normal din eventually returns, but we remain standing in the middle of the hall.

"What should we do?" Euryale asks under her breath.

"We keep dancing," says Stheno. She is always surest. "We finish."

I barely have time to register what's happening before the lute's chords resume, and I am moving again. Around us, some of the gods are still distracted, but plenty turn back to watch us. Nothing has changed, really: My steps are still instinctual and easy, but it all seems different now. I feel the press of each god's eyes more keenly, and though I can't be certain, one set of eyes seems to burn into me more intensely than the rest. I know it is the sea king's, but I can't find him as I twirl and leap, and eventually I give up trying. There is great applause when we finish and take our collective bow; several of the nearby goddesses audibly commend our mother. Within seconds, my father has pushed through the crowd and taken hold of Stheno's arm.

"Come," he commands. He leads the three of us to the back of the hall, where other gods are already jostling around someone. I know what's about to happen, but I still suck in a sharp breath as those gods move aside and we find ourselves face-to-face with the person everyone has been clamoring to see.

"My king." My father's voice is grand as he bows. "May I present my three daughters: Stheno, Euryale, and Medusa."

From the moment he entered our hall, I wanted the sea king to notice us, but nothing has prepared me for the moment he does. Poseidon turns to us slowly, and the first thing I note is that, up close, his irises are an unnaturally bright sea-foam green, rimmed with gold around their edges. He has a long nose, a dusting of dark stubble along his jaw, and lips that remind me of an archer's bow. One corner of those lips quirks as he briefly looks us over the same way I've skimmed over vaguely interesting scrolls. My bones hum under his gaze.

"Your daughters are beautiful, Phorcys." The sea king's voice is crisp and baritone, touched by a slight but detectable Olympian drawl. "Surely they are the envy of all the Sea Court."

Beautiful? The compliment startles me. I'm used to Stheno's and Euryale's looks being complimented, but I'm not usually included in that praise. I feel as though someone has let loose a hundred hummingbirds inside my chest.

"They are not sons." My father shrugs. "But they are old enough for marriage." He smiles pointedly. "Of course, if any of *your* sons is in search of a bride . . . ?"

I start. It's jarring to remember that Poseidon is old enough to have sons of marrying age. Like my parents, he is thousands of years my elder, but tonight, he looks like a young man of twenty or thirty years at most. Without warning, his eyes fix on me. I can read nothing from his expression.

"And which of Phorcys's daughters are you?" he asks.

I curtsy. "Medusa, my king."

Poseidon smiles, then turns back to my father to begin a different conversation. Our audience with him is over. Stheno and Euryale loop their arms through mine, and the three of us duck back into the crowd again.

As soon as Poseidon is out of sight, I exhale.

"I think the sea king liked you best," Euryale teases under her breath. "He *smiled* at you."

My cheeks warm. "Don't be silly," I mutter. "He smiled at all of us." I say the words aloud, but the imaginary hummingbirds are still fluttering madly about my rib cage. For a moment, I let myself entertain Euryale's words. I let myself believe that maybe she's right, that maybe Poseidon *did* like me best. After all, I was the only one he addressed directly. Just as quickly, reason prevails. *No.* That would be absurd. Poseidon is not just a god, he's an Olympian, the *king of the sea.* He has power and prestige well beyond anything I could ever hope to attain. And who am I, in the face of all that? The mortal daughter of two minor sea gods in his vast and sparkling court. He will, I know deep down, forget me. It is likely he already has.

"Meddy!"

My mother has not raised her voice, but it still carries over the hall's din. My sisters offer sympathetic looks before tactfully uncoupling from me and continuing to a table full of food. I sigh and change direction, returning to the front of the hall to join my mother at our table. She is holding another golden goblet full to the brim with red wine, and even from several paces away, I can smell it on her breath. That isn't what slows my steps, though; it's the man seated beside her. I've never seen him before. He appears to be in his forties—though, among gods, one can never be certain—and has skin the color of wet clay, set off by thick, wavy black hair that has only just begun to gray at the temples. As I reach the table, he stands and offers a courteous bow, sparing me only a fleeting smile. My mother is now beaming, and I can't entirely temper the prickle of unease I feel as the man disappears back into the crowd.

"Come. Sit with me," my mother orders, indicating the seat on her other side. I want to ask her about the mysterious man, who he is and what he wanted, but before I can, my mother gestures. "It's a magnificent feast, isn't it? Nearly every god in the Sea Court is here." Her smile turns smug. "You know, your aunt Tethys hosted a feast some time ago, but it wasn't nearly so grand as all this. I can't wait to see her face when she learns that *we* were graced by the sea king."

Like my father, my mother was once great and powerful. She was goddess of all the ocean's monsters and notorious for her collection of murderous sea pets. Sometimes, I grieve for the goddess she used to be, the goddess I've never known. Sometimes, I pity the petty woman she has become.

"Did you see your uncle Nereus?" My mother has already moved on. She points. "It seems he's brought his entire brood tonight. I certainly hope we have enough food . . ."

I follow her gaze to several young women clustered in one of the hall's back corners. I must have missed their arrival. There are a great number of them, and even from a distance, it's clear they're all of the same kin. Most of them are brown-skinned, but a few have more curious features—kelp-green hair, unnaturally long webbed fingers, and scaly appendages that shimmer in the light.

I have heard of my cousins, the Nereids, though I've never seen them before. They are sea nymphs, widely famed among gods old and new for their familial beauty. In their midst, I spot an ancient-looking man with umber skin and thin gray hair.

That is my uncle Nereus, their father and namesake.

My eyes stop on a young woman posted at his side like a sentinel. She favors him, so I know she must be a sea nymph, too, but she stands especially tall, and holds herself with an austerity that sets her apart from the rest of her sisters. She also wears a diadem made from pale pink coral.

"Who's that?" I ask.

"Hm?" My mother looks up. "Ah, that's Amphitrite, Poseidon's wife. They must not have come together." She chuckles, as though enjoying a private joke. "*That's* not unusual."

I have heard plenty about the king of the sea; I know startlingly little about its queen. To my surprise, Amphitrite wears her black hair in locs like mine, though hers are far longer and fall to her waist. She has rich oak-brown skin, full lips, and high cheekbones that might make her striking in a certain light, but her beauty is marred by the scowl twisting her features. Like most gods, she appears to be young, a woman in her mid-twenties, but something in her countenance betrays her true age. Her obsidian eyes dart back and forth, cool and flat. I fight a sudden chill, despite the room's warmth.

"She looks angry," I whisper.

My mother waves a dismissive hand. "That is just her face, darling."

I look between the sea king and the sea queen, positioned on opposite ends of our hall. The contrast between them could not be more pronounced. Poseidon, still standing beside my father, has attracted a growing crowd of admirers. He is laughing, and a charismatic aura seems to emanate from his very being, even at a distance. By comparison, Amphitrite stands near motionless, silent and glacial. I cannot understand how two people so seemingly different could marry, and I find myself wondering if perhaps their union was arranged. Without warning, the queen turns, and her imperial gaze pierces me with the precision of a sailor's harpoon. I recoil, as though I've been struck. Then, to my horror, she starts in our direction.

"She's—" The words die on my tongue as the sea queen reaches our table with inhuman speed and stops before us. I'm grateful that, even in my terror, I have the sense to stand at the same time my mother does.

"Ceto." The queen's voice is low and dulcet. "I did not have the opportunity to greet you when I arrived. Forgive me."

"Queen Amphitrite." My mother bows low in a rare show of genuine deference. "No apology is required. Your presence honors us."

The queen returns her attention to me. "And who might you be, girl?"

"I—"

"Medusa is my daughter." My mother answers for me. "She's my youngest."

When I met the sea king earlier, it seemed he barely noticed me. The opposite is true of the sea queen. She seems to take in all of me at once. In particular, she studies my hair with keen interest.

"How old are you, child?"

"Seventeen, my queen."

"A perfect age to begin entertaining suitors for marriage," my mother cuts in again. "Wouldn't you agree, Your Grace?"

Amphitrite does not answer my mother or even look her way. Instead, her gaze stays trained on me. "Is it your wish to marry, Medusa?"

"I . . ." My eyes flick to my mother, who nods encouragingly. "Yes, my queen. I hope to honor my family by finding a good husband."

This seems to amuse Amphitrite, because a small smile touches her lips. "And what qualities, in your view, make for a good husband?"

I stiffen as a new panic grips me. This was not a question my mother prepared me for. I take a deep breath before I answer. "I would hope to marry someone kind," I say carefully. "Someone intelligent, brave, and . . ." I steal an involuntary glance at the sea king across the room. It's a fleeting look, but I know at once that the sea queen notices. Her dark eyes narrow.

"And handsome?" she adds.

"Y-yes, my queen." My eyes drop to the floor. When I dare look up again, the queen's expression has changed. It's hard to know exactly how to interpret the look she's giving me, but I see recognition, anger, and then . . . something that looks almost like pity.

"I hope you find just what you're looking for, Medusa," she murmurs. She turns to my mother and gives her a final parting nod before returning to stand with her own father and sisters.

My mother waits until the queen is out of earshot before she leans in. "Well done," she whispers in my ear. It appears she did not notice the final look the queen gave me.

"Excuse me, Mother." I step back. "I need air."

I waste no time slipping from the hall and putting as much distance between myself and Amphitrite as possible. Once I'm far enough away, I lean against a wall, pressing my head against the cool stone. The panic I felt before intensifies as I turn the encounter over and over in my mind. Why did Amphitrite notice *me*? Why did she ask me what qualities I thought made for a good husband? And at the end, why did she look at me like that, like she was angry? Was it because I'd looked at Poseidon? I'd looked at him for only a second, I hadn't meant to do it, but . . .

I sink to the floor and bury my face in my hands.

"Meddy?"

I look up, surprised, and feel the tension in my shoulders ease slightly as Theo's familiar voice finds me in the hall's dark. My friend is holding an empty silver tray under one arm, smiling as he draws nearer. That smile fades as he takes in the look on my face.

"Meddy, what's wrong?"

"I . . . I think I've just made a terrible mistake."

Theo frowns. "How?"

My words are halting at first, but slowly I tell him about my encounters with both the sea king and the sea queen. When I finish, Theo shakes his head.

"You didn't do or say anything wrong, Meddy," he assures me. "So what if you looked at Poseidon? He's the king. I'm sure lots of people look at him. And maybe the queen was unhappy about something else. It doesn't mean she was angry with you."

I tell myself that maybe Theo's right, that maybe I haven't done anything wrong, but the uneasiness coiling in my stomach doesn't go away.

"Come on." Theo props the serving tray against the wall, then throws an arm over my shoulders. The weight of it grounds me and makes me feel a little better. "Let's go for a walk."

My mother's gardens have always been my favorite place on the island.

During the day, the blazing sunlight often forces me to find refuge in the shade of their trees; tonight, though, the air is temperate. It seems every leaf, branch, and flower here is dappled with ethereal silver moonlight. Theo falls into step beside me as we wander the gardens' winding paths in silence for at least an hour, past long dirt rows of asters and trickling stone fountains. I take in the sweet scent of honeysuckle as we head toward a section of the gardens bordered by a wall of cypress trees and walk along its edge. In the quiet, some of my uneasiness is allayed, and I breathe easier.

"I watched earlier, when you danced with your sisters," Theo says. "You did really well."

I swell with pride. Until Theo spoke, I hadn't realized just how much I'd needed that praise. A smile tugs at my lips, and I nudge him. "Thank you."

"No, thank *you*." It's Theo's turn to smile, but now I detect a hint of mischief in it. "You got me away from the kitchens just in time. Hanna was bothering me again, kept pretending she was drunk and trying to kiss me."

I snort. Recently, Hanna, one of my mother's attendants, has been less and less subtle about her attraction to Theo. I raise my brow. "Perhaps you should let her kiss you," I tease.

Theo rolls his eyes. "I don't want to kiss her."

"Why not?" I elbow him in the ribs as we near the end of the cypresses. "Don't tell me she's not pretty enough—"

"Wait." Abruptly Theo looks up, frowning.

"What?"

He holds a finger to his lips to silence me before taking a few steps forward and peeking around the last cypress tree bordering the gardens. I know that, on the other side, there's nothing but a small open lawn. When he turns to face me again, his expression is stricken. I quietly pad over to join him.

"What's—?" I look over his shoulder, then fall silent.

It takes me a moment to understand what I am seeing. On the garden's open lawn, in the exact place where Theo and I have sat countless times, they are only two indistinct figures at first. Slowly, though, my vision focuses.

It is one of the sea nymphs.

I know it instantly. She's dark-skinned, inhumanly beautiful. Her short, curly locs are colored the brilliant blue of the ocean under sunlight, fanned out around her head in a halo. She is clearly another one of Nereus's many daughters, though I don't know her name.

I do, however, recognize the god pressing her into the grass, even with his face bent into the crook of her neck.

Poseidon's dark hair is silhouetted in the moonlight, and a breathy sound escapes the sea nymph as she rakes her fingers through it before they kiss. One of his hands snakes down her side, then disappears between her thighs. I cannot see, but I know he is touching her in a private place. That strikes me as odd. She doesn't seem to mind, but I don't understand why. Blood roars in my ears as I stand half hidden by the trees, transfixed. The two of them are utterly consumed by what they're doing; they haven't even noticed us. Some part of me knows we should leave before that changes, but I find my feet have rooted themselves into the grass, anchoring me there. I watch as Poseidon moves the hand between the nymph's thighs faster, and she begins to moan, arching her back as she grips his shoulders and squirms with apparent pleasure. I try to swallow, but my mouth is dry, and there's a new, hard lump in my throat. I don't know exactly what the two of them are doing, but I find that the longer I watch, the harder it is to look away. Some deep, innate instinct tells me that I'm seeing something I shouldn't be, something mysterious and utterly adult, but even that isn't enough to make me stop watching. Strange new sensations begin to surge through my body—heat pools low in my stomach; there's a pleasant, peculiar tightness between my own legs. Suddenly, the nymph cries out, and a shudder trembles through my whole body.

"Meddy."

I jump. Had he not touched my arm, I would have forgotten Theo was there. It's impossible to know what my friend is thinking; his face is inscrutable. At once, I'm embarrassed. Had he been watching Poseidon and the nymph, too, or had he been watching me? I find myself wondering what I must look like, if my thoughts are written all over my face. Slowly, we withdraw until we are hidden completely by the cypress trees again.

"We should go," Theo whispers.

I open my mouth, but he turns and begins walking away quickly before a single word leaves it. I glance over my shoulder a final time, then I follow.

III

"HOLD *STILL.*"

I wince as Stheno pulls my locs tighter, but she pointedly ignores me and continues her work. She sits on a stool, and I sit between her knees. When she tugs at a particularly tender part of my head, I turn and glower.

"You're going to pull my hair out!"

"It'll grow back." She shrugs. "Now turn around."

I obey, but grudgingly. I know that, for the most part, Stheno is only teasing. All my life, my sisters have taken turns doing my hair, and they do try to be gentle. They were the ones who twisted my hair into locs like theirs when I was small. Euryale often massaged my scalp with diluted coconut oil, while Stheno showed me where to find the island's best freshwater pools to wash my locs. They are my dearest physical possession, and in many ways they are also a constant reminder of my sisters' love. I pinch one between my forefinger and thumb now, remembering when I once complained that they were too short.

They'll grow longer with time, Euryale reminded me then, laughing when I pointed out how long hers already were. *You just have to be patient.*

They'll grow to be even more beautiful than they are now, Stheno added, rolling her eyes. *Then you'll be absolutely insufferable, and we'll have to toss you into the sea.*

I smile at that old memory now. In the end, Stheno was right. My locs have grown to be as beautiful as she promised, and she teases me mercilessly every time she catches me absently playing with them. That is my eldest sister's kind of love. It is never honeyed, but I still find hidden sweetness in it. Perhaps it's because I know, deep down, that Stheno's natural tendency for candor means I can always trust her. I know she'd never lie to me, even if the truth hurt.

I'd certainly be glad for some of that candor now as she continues retwisting my roots, but today Stheno stays quiet. I feel the tension in her fingers as she gathers up my locs to arrange them in an elaborate half bun atop my head, then pin it with golden helichrysums. That tension seeps into my scalp and needles down my spine, leaving me fidgety. Neither of us says it, but we both know the source of this tension.

Today, the prince arrives.

My mother was right about one thing: By all accounts, the gods and goddesses of the Sea Court talked about our spring celebration feast for many weeks. Some even talked about how beautiful Phorcys's three daughters had become. Unfortunately, *talk* had not yielded much in the way of viable suitors for my sisters and me. As the days turned to weeks, then a month, the anxiety in our household grew as thick as the early summer's stifling heat. I suspect that is why my father responded with great enthusiasm when he finally received a message from Prince Maheer only a fortnight ago, asking if he could pay us a visit. Before, talk of marriage had been nebulous and vague, a thing of some distant, opaque future. Now there is no uncertainty as to what is about to happen.

Today, one of us will become the prince's betrothed.

"Did you know he's a demigod?" Across her opulent bedchamber, my mother seems unable to stop herself from constantly tugging at and adjusting Euryale's tunic. Her hands fly about like frantic sparrows, and the excitement in her voice is offset by another emotion I can't quite name. "He's a bastard of Ares, but his mother is a mortal princess," she continues. "Through her, he stands to inherit a small but wealthy kingdom in the lands they call Aithiopia. His wife will also be entitled to that wealth." She looks up and lets her gaze linger over each of us in turn. "It is of great importance that a match be made today. Do you understand?"

I have never taken much interest in the complicated hierarchy by which gods arrange themselves, but that doesn't mean I'm not aware of it. As daughters of minor sea gods, it would be improbable for my sisters and me to wed the legitimate children of the more illustrious Olympians, but a *bastard* child is different. The bastard of an Olympian is both suitable for our station and an undeniable link to higher status and prestige. To be sure, gods enjoy flaunting their wealth, but what they covet most jealously is the inimitable currency that comes with power. I know power is what my father craves most of all, just as I know that he will use us to take as much of it as he can.

"I suppose we should go." My mother stops her fussing and gestures for the three of us to line up before her, giving us each a final inspection. We've all had new tunics made for this occasion. Stheno's is dyed lavender, Euryale's is yellow. My tunic is a pale spring green. The curtains in my mother's room are drawn back, but the summer air is still heavy with the scent of the marjoram oil we've dabbed onto our arms and necks. I hold my breath as she looks me over last, then nods with rare approval. I can tell, even at a glance, that she hasn't been drinking today; strangely, it makes her seem younger, like she could be our fourth and eldest sister. She takes a deep breath, steadying herself. "One day, the last of you will marry and leave me." A soft laugh escapes her, but the smile doesn't reach her eyes. "Then I'll be on this island all alone."

My sisters and I shift uncomfortably where we stand. In truth, my mother's words bite into a soft part of me I didn't know I'd left exposed. Growing up, I rarely felt the kind of bond with her I knew daughters were expected to, but in that moment, I know without a doubt that my mother and I *are* bonded by something. I know because in her eyes I see a wistfulness I've seen mirrored in my own, a bone-deep longing to leave this place. My mother is eons old, but I find myself wondering who she was at seventeen, before she was a wife, a mother. I know little of her past, but I do know that she and my father were not born on this island, as we were. I'm not sure what's worse: to never know a world beyond this one, or to know it and still be confined. My mother and I lock eyes for just a second before she raises her chin imperiously.

"Come," she orders. "The prince is waiting."

. . .

Our gardens have been transformed.

They are lovely any day of the year, but as my sisters and I follow our mother through the neatly raked dirt paths and corridors of perfectly trimmed hedges, I can tell that more care than usual has been taken to make them look magnificent for the prince's arrival. When we reach the open lawn where my father's already sitting, he offers only a cursory nod as we take our seats beside him. Stheno and Euryale are like my mother, cool and elegant despite the blistering sun overhead. I am, as usual, less so. Inside, the air was sweltering; outside, it is oppressive. One look at the slaves posted in a line by the edge of the lawn tells me I'm not the only one uncomfortable in this heat, but of course my parents and sisters would not notice. As immortals, they are far more tolerant of the elements than I'll ever be. To distract myself, I look around the lawn. Only then do I realize its significance.

It's been almost two months since Theo and I accidentally stumbled upon Poseidon and the sea nymph together on this very grass. In the days following the feast, I tried to bury what I'd seen, but the memory took root within me and grew like a stubborn weed. Even now, I find that I can still picture everything I witnessed with perfect clarity: the way Poseidon traced a knuckle down the hollow of the sea nymph's neck before venturing lower, the way the sea nymph's tunic was pulled up around her waist, how her bare brown legs looked under the glittering starlight. I went to sleep that night full of questions, but in the morning, I found no one to answer them. I'd always been able to talk to Stheno and Euryale about anything, but for the first time I wasn't able to. I wondered if my sisters would know what Poseidon and the nymph had been doing. I wondered if they'd scold me for watching or, worse, tease me. In the end, I decided that I didn't want them to do either, and so I said nothing. As for Theo, he all but pretended it had never happened.

I look up now, hoping to find my friend among the other slaves standing at attention, but to my disappointment, Theo is nowhere in sight. I shift in my seat, considering what the consequences of asking for water or a fan might be.

Then the quiet is shattered by a snarl.

It is a raw, guttural sound that sets my teeth on edge. Every one of the slaves jolts as though they've been struck, and though my parents and sisters are subtler, I notice that even they tense in surprise and confusion. There is a pregnant pause, a moment in which it seems the whole lawn has stilled. Then I hear a new sound, the distinct metallic clinking of chains drawing nearer. A second later, the source of both noises becomes clear.

A pair of large, muscled men wearing neat white tunics rounds the line of cypresses. I suspect they are slaves, too, but I spare them only a glance. I'm much more fascinated—and terrified—by what walks between them: the creature responsible for that hideous snarl.

The lion being led onto our lawn is enormous; it would tower over me if I stood before it. Its mane is coarse and matted, deep brown except for a golden patch near its face. Mud crusts its massive paws, and I shiver as I watch its hooked white claws puncture the dirt with each step. Its mouth is bound with rope, and an iron collar attached to two long chains is fastened around its neck. I'm certain that this is the only reason it hasn't attacked its handlers. So distracted by the beast am I that I don't immediately notice the man who trails in breezily behind it, flanked by several more slaves clad in white, who throw flower petals in his wake. When I finally tear my eyes from the lion to look at him, I start.

It's the man from our spring feast, the one I saw speaking to my mother.

I have never seen the bastard prince's father—Ares, the Olympian god of war—but I suspect the prince has inherited his looks from his mortal mother. His dark hair and brown skin are as I remember, but in proper daylight, I take in more. The prince is a man of short stature, barely taller than me. I note that the black cotton tunic he has donned, embroidered with intricate gold thread, is finely made but ill-suited for our island's tropical climate. Already, beads of sweat dapple his forehead in a glittering crown. I imagine he might once have been of a more athletic build, but age has thickened his middle and added a softness around his neck and chin. As he draws closer, I discern that his eyes are a light brown.

Those eyes study Stheno, Euryale, then me before he turns to address the lion's handlers.

"Remove its muzzle," he says in a reedy voice.

My pulse quickens at the same time the two handlers exchange wary looks, then approach the lion slowly from either side. The lion snarls again, and they pause, uncertain. It occurs to me that neither of them is willing to get close enough to the beast to remove the ropes binding its mouth shut. After a moment, the prince makes a sound of irritation.

"Stand aside," he commands. My whole body seizes as he unsheathes a dagger from his belt and approaches the lion himself. A growl rumbles from deep inside the creature's throat.

He's going to be mauled. My fists clench as the prince comes within mere feet of the lion. *He's going to be mauled, and it's going to be bloody.*

The prince first takes the chain serving as the lion's leash, then stops before the beast. He is much smaller, but somehow he still manages to look down his nose at it.

"Down," he orders, raising a fist.

I wait for the inevitable violence. To my shock, the lion's golden eyes seem to flash with understanding. It lowers itself to the ground.

"Be still." The prince raises his dagger and slowly slices at the ropes so that they fall in a heap.

The now-freed lion only licks its black lips and yawns.

I'm already stunned, but the prince isn't finished. "Come," he commands, yanking hard on the lion's chain.

Slowly, the lion rises again and walks beside the prince in small circles.

After its third lap, the prince faces us again, grinning as he sheathes his dagger.

"Phorcys, great god of the sea." He stands taller as he addresses my father. "I am Maheer, mortal son of the god Ares, who is son of the sovereign god-king Zeus. I come to you this day to take one of your daughters for marriage and make her my queen, if it please you. As a token of my respect, I also present to you this gift." The prince gestures toward the lion still standing behind him. "I captured this beast from a distant land and trained it myself. It is yours to do with what you wish."

I steal a glance at my father and don't miss the way his lips have pursed. He is doing his best not to let his face betray his thoughts, but I can imagine they are the same as mine. It would be no small feat, capturing a lion of this size and ferocity, and braver still to teach it obedience. This prince did not impress me initially; now I wonder if my judgment of him might have been premature.

After a moment of what seems like deliberation, my father stands. "Prince Maheer, we thank you for this gift." He is using his deeper, godly voice now, the one that rings with an authority he no longer possesses. "It would please us for you to wed one of our daughters. All three of them are healthy, of respectable lineage, and fertile."

I have enough time to resent the fact that my father's description of us would also aptly describe a trio of nanny goats before he turns to my sisters and me. The smile on his lips is placid, but it doesn't quite reach his eyes. I hear the unspoken threat behind it.

Disgrace me, and you will suffer.

My mother nods, and at once, the three of us stand. I have known this moment was coming for days, weeks, but I am still unprepared when it arrives at last. The scorching sun overhead seems to fade, and though the garden is full of people, the only ones I'm aware of now are my sisters, the prince, and myself. Time seems to slow as Prince Maheer approaches us, looking equal parts assessing and intrigued. His perfume reaches me first, and when I inhale, I smell something sharp and spiced. He walks back and forth among us, pensive, and I do my best to stand absolutely still. I'm intensely conscious of the blades of grass pricking the soles of my feet, of the places where my tunic has grown damp and sticky from sweat. A single one of my locs suddenly falls from its bun, swinging before my eyes. I try to tuck it quickly behind my ear, but the movement catches the prince's attention. He approaches and looks me over before pinching that loc between his fingers.

"How curious," he murmurs.

I don't breathe, I don't move, and on either side of me, I feel my sisters both stiffen. All our lives, we have been three parts of one whole. Now, for the first time, we are being singled out and held apart. I lower my gaze as the prince continues to study me, and a thousand thoughts fly through my mind like loosed arrows.

What if it's me? What if the prince picks me *for his bride?*

What if this is my chance? A chance to leave this island?

What about Stheno and Euryale? What about Theo?

The prince steps back and nods to my father. "I have made my choice."

Even the garden's surrounding trees and flowers seem to hold their breath.

"Her." The prince points to my right, to Euryale. "I choose her."

The world around me has taken on a strange new haze, but when I turn to look at Euryale, there's no mistaking the mix of surprise and delight on her face. My mother is pressing a tender hand to her chest, on the verge of joyful tears, but it is my father who looks happiest of all. He's beaming.

"She is yours," he says, his voice full of new warmth. To one of his attendants, he says, "Prepare invitations for every god in the Sea Court, the Olympians, too. We will begin plans for a wedding at once, a grand celebration befitting Prince Maheer's noble lineage."

Soon to be our joined *lineage,* I think.

Around me, some of the slaves of our household have broken from their usual discipline to cheer. In seconds, Euryale is surrounded, and I stare at my feet, mostly because I don't know where else to look. A tight snarl of emotions is knotted in my chest—muddled and contradictory and confusing.

I thought, a mere hour ago, that I wouldn't care if the prince didn't choose me. I thought I'd feel relief when it was all over, when he inevitably picked one of my prettier, immortal sisters. That doesn't explain why the sensation burrowing itself beneath my skin feels very much like disappointment. At once, guilt pricks me. I should be happy for Euryale, I *am* happy for her, but . . . I remember the way the prince looked at me. I thought, for the briefest moment, that perhaps he'd pick me, that *I* would be the bride. Marrying Prince Maheer would have meant leaving my family, but perhaps it would also have given me a chance at the thing I've always wanted most of all: to leave this island.

For just one moment, that perpetual fear of my sisters leaving me behind was quelled.

I blink hard, embarrassed to feel more than one tear slide down my cheek, and brush them away quickly. More than anything in this moment, I wish I could find Theo.

I lift my gaze and am surveying the lawn for the easiest way to slip out when I realize that Stheno is still beside me, perfectly silent. Unlike nearly everyone else in the garden, she isn't looking at Euryale or the prince, and there is no love or affection in her dark brown eyes. Instead, her gaze is trained on the lion. In the midst of the celebration, it seems the beast has been all but forgotten and now lies contently, curled up in the sun like a common cat. I look from the lion to her, and though she doesn't acknowledge me, she speaks in a voice only I can hear.

"I'll be the first to admit I know little about the training of wild beasts." She says the words aloud, as though she's musing. "But I do find it curious."

This catches my attention. "Curious?"

Stheno gestures to the lion. "Prince Maheer has traveled to our island from some distance, almost entirely by sea," she says. "I have to imagine that a lion of that size would need substantial amounts of food to remain nourished, far more than a single ship could carry. I don't think a diet of fish would sate it, either."

I frown. I don't understand what my sister is getting at.

"He couldn't have butchered all the meat beforehand," Stheno continues. It's still as though she's talking to herself. "It would have spoiled before it could be consumed. Livestock might work, but then you'd have to bring additional food to keep them fat, which takes up precious cargo space and produces waste." For the first time, my sister turns to look at me directly. "But if you had *another* source of food for your pet, if you brought more slaves than you'd ever need . . ." She shrugs. "I suppose there's little difference between a trained lion and a well-fed one."

The insinuation behind my sister's words takes root, and my blood runs cold. "Stheno." My voice trembles more than I want it to. "You're not saying that Prince Maheer . . . ?"

"Do you want to know the surest way to assess the measure of a man?" Stheno blinks, unnervingly calm. "You look at those who serve him." She leans in. "So, *look.*"

I obey, albeit slowly. It doesn't take long for me to pick out the prince's slaves. While everyone else on the lawn is smiling and clearly at ease, they are gathered close together like pack animals. Most of them are warily eyeing the prince, but a few of them steal glances at the resting lion. I realize now that I'd been so taken by Prince Maheer's impressive entrance that I hadn't bothered to pay attention to those who entered *with* him. The most fortunate of the prince's slaves bear shallow cuts and crudely dressed wounds; others sport more grievous injuries—a gouged eye, nubbed fingers, and missing limbs. I turn to Stheno, horrified.

"I thought he'd trained that lion," I whisper. "I . . . I believed him."

"Of course you did," Stheno says. She doesn't sound surprised. "Prince Maheer is a man with power, and men with power are always the first to be believed."

I shake my head. "Stheno, what kind of man could do something like that?"

"A cruel one," she says simply. "Then again, I've learned that most men are cruel. Some are just better at hiding it."

A new thought grips me, blade-sharp and acute. "Do you think the prince would be cruel to Eury?"

The look Stheno gives me then is worse than any spoken answer. Just an hour ago, I was grateful for my eldest sister's natural candor. Now I wish I didn't see the truth in her eyes. Fresh tears well in my own. This time when they fall, I don't bother to wipe them.

"There has to be something we can do," I whisper. "Can't we stop the marriage?"

Stheno shakes her head. "The prince has selected his bride, and Father has accepted his choice."

"*Euryale* didn't accept it!"

Stheno's expression hardens. "Nor would she be permitted to. Euryale is a woman."

We both look to our father then. He's standing with Prince Maheer, shaking his hand and looking supremely pleased. I know then that my sister is right.

"Prince Maheer may be mortal, but he is also a son of Ares, and a grandson of Zeus himself," says Stheno. "Euryale's marriage to him represents an opportunity to significantly elevate our family's standing. Father won't relinquish that opportunity willingly." For the first time, her expression turns wary. "Nor will he abide anyone who threatens it."

Our father didn't say a word to us before the prince's arrival about the conduct he expected from us because he didn't have to. My sisters and I have seen who my father can be when he loses his temper. I flinch. Jeopardizing Euryale's marriage to Prince Maheer almost certainly risks provoking my father's wrath, but . . .

"There has to be something we can do," I repeat. "Marriage is a lifelong commitment, permanent."

Stheno arches a brow. "Euryale and I are immortal, Meddy. For us, nothing is permanent."

The words smart more than they should. Stheno doesn't often remind me of my mortality. As if she realizes what she's inadvertently done, she softens her expression.

"At best, she will only have to be his wife for the duration of *his* life," she says more gently. "It won't be like Father and Mother. It won't be forever."

"What about after?" I ask quietly. "What happens after he dies? Will Eury be free then?"

Again, Stheno's somber expression is answer enough.

I hold her gaze. "She's our sister."

Something behind Stheno's eyes gives, and for a moment I see the pain I know she must see in mine. Just as quickly, it's gone. "She *was* our sister," she corrects me flatly. "Now she is Prince Maheer's bride-to-be."

Then, without another word, my sister rises, gathers the delicate folds of her lavender tunic, and leaves me in the garden.

IV

THAT NIGHT, MY dreams are violent.

In the first, I find my father in our great hall, though I realize at once that it is not a version of him I've seen before. The god that sits before me on a pale driftwood throne has scaly gray skin and eyes that burn a lurid yellow. His long white beard is tangled, his tattered robes sewn from dried green kelp. Though he is inert, there is a frightening wildness about his person. I understand that this primordial creature is what my father was before he altered his true likeness to make himself more palatable for human worship. He does not speak as he surveys me, but I need no words to know that he is full of ancient rage and power, more than capable of hurting me. When he rises, I do not hesitate. I turn on my heel and run until I reach an empty corridor.

At its other end stands Maheer.

The prince is dressed in that same fine black tunic, still smiling with too many teeth as he assesses me. He looks me over, and his expression turns mocking.

I would never have picked you. I hear his voice in my head, though his lips never move. *No one would ever pick you.*

I turn away from him quickly, screwing my eyes shut. When they re-open, the corridor is gone and I'm standing on the shores of the island, mere inches from the water's edge.

"Meddy!"

Even in my dreams, Euryale is lovely. I'm surprised to find, as she approaches me across the sand dunes, that the copper crown atop her locs suits her. She is a true queen, smiling at me, her expression full of painfully bright hope. She does not see the lion trailing in her wake, its bone-white teeth bared.

Run. I feel the shape of the word in my mouth, but it lodges there. Panic swells in my chest as the lion draws closer. I try to point, to warn my sister, but Euryale takes no notice.

Run, I want to shout. *Run.*

My sister is still smiling at me when the lion attacks. Her body crumples instantly beneath its weight. I watch as her neck snaps, as the beast tears at her body while my own is rendered immobile. A terrible grief grips me as I watch my sister die, then beneath my anguish comes a white-hot rage—rage because I can do nothing; rage because I am helpless; rage because I've always been helpless. Whatever power holding me firm loosens its grip, and a scream tears from my throat, long and raw.

The last thing I see as my vision fades is the lion, staring back at me with something in its goldenrod eyes that looks like pity.

I DON'T REMEMBER how old I was when I first started walking along the shores of the island.

What I do know, when I wake the next morning in a sweaty tangle of blankets and bedsheets, is that the urge to head for those shores feels less like a conscious decision than an old instinct. The muscles in my shoulders relax as I slowly follow an invisible line along the coast, focusing on the press of my toes against the cold, wet sand. The incoming tide laps at my ankles, and my gaze drifts east, past the wave breaks, to the place where the sea turns a deep, abiding blue. It isn't the first time I've stared into those depths, wondering how far I might swim before fatigue found me. I'm so occupied by that reverie that I don't realize when I'm no longer alone.

"I might have expected to find you here."

I turn, then tense. Euryale is making her way toward me across the sand dunes, her black locs lifting slightly as a breeze ripples through them. She isn't wearing a copper crown, as she was in my dream, but the sight of her on the beach now is so strikingly similar that I actually glance behind her, half expecting to see a lion. She misinterprets the anxiety on my face, and her smile turns rueful as she stops before me.

"Don't look so surprised," she says, pursing her lips. "You're not the only one who likes to walk this beach."

It's true. I may not remember how old I was when I first started walking along the shores of our island, but I do remember that Stheno and Euryale always walked with me in those days. They were the ones who showed me where to find the seahorses hiding in the tide pools, where to look for blue crabs and pebbles of sea glass. As if she's privy to my thoughts, Euryale gives me a self-satisfied nod before settling on the ground and patting a spot beside her.

"You know, the first time Stheno and I let you walk with us here, it was because we had to." She stares out into the open sea as I sit down next to her. "Mother was having one of her 'headaches,' and you were being a terror, so she told us to keep you occupied. We brought you to this beach and decided we'd teach you how to swim."

"How inspired." I roll my eyes, then smile. "What could possibly have gone wrong?"

"We were children, too," Euryale says defensively. "And it seemed like a perfectly reasonable idea, at the time."

I turn to her, brow raised. "So, how exactly did you go about it?"

"Oh, Stheno tossed you right into the sea," Euryale recalls cheerfully. "That was the way we'd learned."

I frown.

"You did well at first," Euryale goes on. "There was a great deal of kicking and some rather gratuitous splashing, but you steadied. Stheno and I were quite impressed, actually." Her smile fades. "But then you got caught in one of the currents, you were pulled too far out to sea. We didn't really understand that you were mortal then; we thought you were only playing when you cried out for help. If Stheno hadn't figured it out and gone in after you just in time . . ." She looks down, ashamed. "That was when I realized you weren't entirely like us, that we had to be more careful with you."

I gnaw on my bottom lip, discomforted. I've never heard this particular story before, but I can recall plenty of others like it. All our lives, my sisters have taken great care to make me feel included, as if my mortality were only a superficial difference between us. Sometimes, though, that difference becomes impossible to ignore.

I study the clouds overhead, looking for a way to change the subject. "I didn't get to speak to you yesterday, after your official proposal from Prince Maheer," I say carefully. "Congratulations."

"Thank you." I don't know if I'm imagining it, but something in Euryale's affect seems to change slightly. She's still sitting up with perfect posture, regal and poised like the queen she'll soon become, but some unnamed emotion lingers in her eyes. When she offers nothing else, I try again.

"A few months ago, you said you couldn't wait to be married. Are you excited to marry Maheer?"

"I'm excited to leave this island," Euryale says with a pealing laugh. It's only because I've known her my whole life that I can tell it's not her real one. Something about it is forced.

"But surely you'll be happy as a queen, too," I press. "Isn't that what you wanted?"

My sister's face grows impassive. "I suppose."

"Eury." My voice is soft. "If you don't want to marry the prince—"

"What I want doesn't matter, Meddy." Euryale sets her mouth in a firm line. "It's decided. Prince Maheer is a good match for me, and this marriage is good for our family. I should count myself fortunate that he chose me to be his bride."

"But—"

"I don't want to talk about it anymore." Her dark eyes flash, and for one breathtaking moment she is the exact image of our mother. I reach for her, but then my eye catches on something. The tear in the neckline of my sister's light blue tunic is small, almost negligible, but I peer closer when I note the unmistakable flecks of gold dried near my sister's shoulder, on her jaw.

"Eury . . . is that blood?"

My sister's eyes widen at once as she registers what I've seen. She stands, hugging her arms around her middle and turning so that both the blood and the tear in her tunic are out of view. "No. It's nothing."

I wince. Euryale has always been a terrible liar. "Was it Mama?" My anger builds as I stand, too. "Was she drinking? Did she—?"

Euryale only scowls at me. "I said it's nothing."

I draw myself up to my full height, so that my sister is forced to meet my eyes. "If you don't tell me, I'll go to Stheno."

She studies me for a long moment, and I imagine she's assessing how seriously to take my threat. Abruptly, though, her bravado seems to abandon her, and her shoulders slump. She doesn't look at me. "It wasn't Mother."

"Was it Father?"

Euryale shakes her head. "Prince Maheer found me, late last night. He'd been drinking. He asked me to come to his chamber, and I declined. I didn't think it was appropriate to be alone with him before we were married." She pauses. "He . . . didn't like that."

I hear Stheno's voice reminding me that most men are cruel, reminding me that some men are just better at hiding it, but I still stare at Euryale in disbelief. "He hit you for that? Tore your dress?"

"He only hit me once," she murmurs. "And he immediately apologized. I don't think he really meant to. And he's promised to have new dresses made for me, once we return home to his—*our*—kingdom."

I gape at my sister as a terrible truth sets in. Euryale is immortal, ever young, ever perfect. I've seen with my own eyes what happened when my mother threw a goblet at her. I watched her split lip heal itself within seconds, leaving no trace of either the wound or the violence that caused it. I see now exactly what life awaits my sister. If Prince Maheer dares hit her now, before they are even wed, I know it will only worsen. I know he will hit her many more times and that my sister's face will never betray so much as a hint of his barbarity. He is mortal and will eventually die, but the idea of my sister suffering that kind of treatment for even a few decades makes my fists involuntarily clench at my sides. The anger that ignited in me before courses hot through my veins until my whole body is warmed. I imagine finding Prince Maheer and punching him in his own face as hard as I can before realizing that it would change nothing. Once again, there is nothing I can do. Once again, I am helpless, and so is Euryale.

"You can't marry him," I say in a low voice. "You can't marry a man who hits you, Eury. If Mother and Father knew, surely they would—"

"They would do nothing." Euryale says the words evenly, but there's a savage bitterness in her voice. "Do you honestly think Father cares at all about what Maheer will do to me once we're married? Do you think he would allow anything to stop this union?" She shakes her head. "When Maheer picked me, I'd hoped that I might be marrying someone kind, but if he can't be that . . ." She sighs. "Marriage still gets me off this loathsome island."

I've sometimes thought that Euryale, with her soft voice and easy laugh, was the gentlest of us three. Now I think she might be the strongest. She takes me by both shoulders, so that I'm forced to hold her gaze.

"Be happy for me," she says. "That's all I ask. Please."

I glance at the tear in my sister's tunic, at the golden blood speckling it, then I look into her eyes again. There's an acute desperation in them that I recognize because I've felt that very same desperation myself. Euryale has weighed the price of freedom from this place and deemed it one worth paying.

I wonder what price *I* would pay, for that same freedom.

"Please, Meddy," Euryale whispers. "I'll be all right. I promise. Once Maheer and I are married and I've given him a few sons, I'm sure I won't have to see him much. Just look at Mother and Father; they barely see each other at all."

Those words give me little comfort.

"I'll be a queen." She adds that last bit with a smile, as though she's trying to cheer herself up. "I'll have my own palace to do with what I please. Mother won't be there to bother me, and I can drink wine and eat honey cakes all day if I want."

I raise a brow. "Don't you already do both those things here?"

She swats at me, laughs, then pulls me into a hug so tight it leaves me breathless.

"You'll visit me," she whispers into my locs, "won't you?"

"Of course. If Mother and Father allow it."

She squeezes tighter, so I wrap my arms around her and hold on.

I know, in my heart of hearts, that what Euryale says is true. I know that everything *will* be all right.

Just as I know, in my heart of hearts, that I will do everything in my power to stop my sister's marriage.

V

THE HALLS OF our palace are quiet and still as I make my way to Prince Maheer's bedchamber that night.

It's late, the air humid and thick with the promise of a summer storm. Every few steps, I falter, expecting to run into a slave, but the halls are all empty. I am alone. I inhale and exhale slowly, trying to keep calm as a small cloth sack thuds against my hip. I've gone over my plan more than once, practiced my words a dozen times, but that does nothing to stop the trembling in my legs or the sweat gathering at the nape of my neck. I swallow hard, remind myself why I'm doing this.

For Eury. For her, you can do this.

I reach the door to Maheer's chamber and knock softly. My pulse leaps as the door opens seconds later and the prince himself appears in its frame.

"What's this?" His eyes drop to me. "I didn't call for a slave."

He does not recognize me, I realize. In a way, it makes sense. Tonight, I'm wearing only a modest calf-length tunic, and my locs are loose about my shoulders. From the smell of him, I gather that the prince has been drinking.

I bow. "I am the sister of your betrothed," I murmur. "I've come to speak with you, in private." I look up and see recognition. The prince smiles.

"Ah yes, of course. Please, come in."

My father has designated the third-largest wing of our home for Prince Maheer, a collection of rooms decorated with fine silk linens and thick animal pelts spread about the marble floor. I follow the prince inside, watching as he collapses onto one of the chaises and stretches like a cat. I note that there's an almost full pitcher of wine on a nearby table.

"Sit," the prince commands, gesturing toward the settee across from him. I obey, and he offers a lazy smile.

"I've brought a gift," I begin. "It's—"

"I hope it's better wine," he says. "The stuff the last slave brought in tastes like fermented piss."

I do my best to hide my surprise. Now that the marriage between him and my sister is confirmed, it seems the prince has utterly abandoned any façade of chivalry. I keep my expression composed, my head lowered.

"I have no wine, my prince, but I do bring something else." I have to work to keep my hands from shaking as I withdraw the purse from my sack. Prince Maheer's eyes snap to it with interest, then widen as I pull out a single blue sapphire. It's the size of a grape and sparkles brilliantly in the candlelight.

The prince gapes. "Gods," he says softly. "That's magnificent. Where on earth did you acquire it?"

"Trinkets wash up onshore all the time. I collect them."

This is only a half lie. I *do* collect the odd objects that occasionally wash up on the island's coast, but that's not where I procured the gems I've brought with me tonight. In truth, I stole them all from my mother's overflowing trove, confident that she would not miss them among the many she possesses from centuries of hoarding. The prince seems to believe me, though, because he's still studying the sapphire.

"I can give you more," I say quickly, taking advantage of his keen attention. "But I would need you to do something for me."

The prince tears his gaze from the sapphire to look at me again. I'm disheartened to find that he now looks entertained. "And what might that be?"

I take a deep breath before answering. "You must rescind your marriage offer to my sister."

I'm pleased to see at least a flicker of surprise on the prince's face. It's clear that whatever he might have expected me to say, it wasn't this.

He sits up, frowning. "Why would I do that?"

Because you are a wretched, monstrous man. I bow my head, feigning sadness. "Because I love my sister. If you marry her, she'll be taken far away. I fear I may never see her again." When I look up, a hint of mirth has touched the prince's eyes. He looks pitying, which makes me hate him all the more.

"Your love for Euryale is touching," he says. "But marriage is a woman's sacred duty, second only to motherhood. Would you truly deny your sister that?"

Not for the first time, I feel a pang of guilt. However repugnant I might find Prince Maheer to be, I know a part of him is right. If I am successful tonight, I will be denying Euryale something I know she wants, at least in part. I don't want to imagine what she'll say if she ever finds out I was here, if she ever learns what I'm trying to do.

It's for her own good, I tell myself. *It's to keep her safe.*

I temper my guilt and look up at Prince Maheer. "I just want her to stay here a little longer. I just need a little more time." *And perhaps, with more time, Euryale will receive a better marriage offer.*

"Don't we all?" the prince murmurs.

I hold up the sapphire again. "Will you take it, then, and tell my father that you no longer wish to marry her?"

Instead of answering, Prince Maheer leans forward and plucks the gem from my palm to examine it more closely. A smile tugs at the corner of his lips. "This is less a gift than it is a bribe," he muses aloud. "If your father learned of this . . ."

"Please don't tell him." I try—and fail—to keep the panic from my voice. "He must never know. Please."

A strange smile touches the prince's face. He places the sapphire on the table between us and gives me a curious look. "And what would you give me, in exchange for my silence?"

I pull a ruby from my purse and place it on the table beside the sapphire.

The prince's eyes stay fixed on me. "What *else*?"

His question confuses me. "I . . . I've brought nothing with me but the gems," I admit. "They're all I have to offer. But I know from my scrolls that they're worth a great deal."

Prince Maheer stands, crosses the room to pour himself more wine, and drinks deeply from his goblet. Only once he's drained it does he look at me again. There's a new glint in his eye that unsettles me.

"I won't tell your father about all this," he says, gesturing to both me and the two gems. "But I'm afraid I cannot accept your offer."

My pulse quickens. I look to the sapphire and ruby still on the table, then look up again, confused. "But I thought . . . ?"

"They're beautiful stones," Prince Maheer acquiesces, "but did you know, my homelands are rather famous for having a great deal of precious stones embedded in the natural rock? My people mine them, then sell them to the Greeks and Egyptians and anyone else who wants to pay for them. Naturally, I always take the best for myself. So, I have no real need of these."

The blood drains from my face.

"What I *do* need is a wife of respectable birth," Prince Maheer continues. "Euryale is pretty enough and the daughter of two formidable sea gods. I think she will do nicely."

My head begins to pound as his words sink in. *Foolish,* some voice in my head says. *This was a foolish idea.*

Prince Maheer takes a step closer to me and cocks his head. "Remind me, what is your name?"

"Meddy, my prince."

"Meddy . . ." he repeats. "That's an odd name."

"It's what my sisters call me," I say quietly. "My real name is Medusa."

He takes a second goblet from a nearby table, pours wine to its brim, then offers it to me.

"*Drink,* Medusa."

It is not a request, I am smart enough to understand that. I cross the chamber, take the goblet from him, and raise it to my lips, careful to allow only a swallow's worth to pass through them. When I lower it, he's moved closer to me, too close. Gently, he pinches one of my locs and examines it. Again, he looks at me that same way he did in the garden just yesterday.

"How old are you, Medusa?" His eyes are still trained on my loc.

"Seventeen." I inch back just slightly, but he mirrors the movement.

"Seventeen." The prince nods. "And have you begun to bleed monthly yet?"

I fidget. I have only ever talked about my monthly blood with my sisters. "Yes," I admit. "I started three years ago."

Prince Maheer lets go of the loc and meets my gaze. "So, you're a woman," he murmurs. "Though I see your body isn't fully developed yet."

I take another step back.

"You misunderstand." A smile touches his lips as he mirrors the move a second time. "It isn't a bad thing. In fact, I prefer a woman's body before it changes."

"You're to marry my sister." I can't keep the trembling from my voice now. I take a third step back, well aware that I am coming close to meeting the wall. Maheer seems to understand that, too, because when he takes another step closer to me, it is unhurried.

"It is not uncommon for men in my kingdom to take multiple wives." He drinks deeply from his goblet. "Euryale is beautiful and immortal. She'll make a fine queen for me. But *you* . . ." There is a new huskiness to his voice. "You're just the age I like them."

I reach back with my free hand, and my fingertips graze the wall. The hairs on the back of my neck stand on end as the prince grabs at his own groin, and I notice that there is a new bulge there.

"Take off your clothes." His charm is suddenly gone. His eyes are deadened, void of any emotion. *"Now."*

"I—" Any words I might have said in answer lodge themselves in my throat.

Foolish. This was a foolish idea.

I did not come to the prince's chamber unarmed. After what Euryale had told me that morning, I made sure to stow one of Theo's small carving knives in my sack along with the gems. But now that knife is across the room, useless to me. It occurs to me too late that I should have kept it on my person. I know that what I should feel in this moment is fear. Fear because I'm alone in a room with a man who's looking at me the way predators look at prey; fear because I don't know what Prince Maheer intends to do next. But the fear doesn't come. Instead, a familiar anger flints against my skin.

Helpless. I'm always helpless.

All my life I have been a victim in some form or fashion. Never in my life have I had the ability to protect myself. Never have I known how to fight, only flee.

My eyes shoot to the door, and Prince Maheer follows my gaze. It happens too fast. He closes the gap between us, placing his hands on either side of my head so that I am pinned between him and the wall. The smell of wine and spiced perfume assaults my senses, and all reason abandons me. I strike my still-full goblet of wine against the side of the prince's head, and he cries out in pain, stumbling back. As soon as there's space, I slip away from him, grasping at the wall as I try to think of the best way to get around him without putting myself within his reach again. Maheer blinks several times, then looks at me, teeth bared. Red wine drips from his soaked hair.

"You *bitch!*" he seethes. "You stupid, ugly little—" He stops. "My eyes!" His voice rises with new panic as his eyes screw shut. "What have you done to my eyes?"

I stand, frozen in confusion, as he begins crushing his fists into his eye sockets. He groans and doubles over. The wine has gotten into his eyes. He begins shaking his head over and over, like a wet dog.

"They're burning!" he screams. "My eyes are burning—*help me!*"

My gaze cuts to the pitcher of water on another nearby side table, but I don't move. I do not immediately recognize the feeling rising within me. It is surprisingly warm, calming even. For once, I realize, I am not helpless.

"Stupid bitch!" Maheer's eyes are screwed shut again. He is fumbling around, his arms flailing and reaching aimlessly. I edge farther along the wall, farther away from him. I know I could slip past him and get to the door; I just have to time it right.

"I'll kill you for this!" he bellows. "I'll have you flogged. I'll—"

Maheer steps back, tripping over one of the animal pelts on the floor. It sends him tumbling backward, and I see what is going to happen a second before it does. The prince falls, and the base of his skull collides with the corner of the table. I hear a terrible crack, hear the sickening splinter of wood and bone, then I see the brief surprise in Maheer's eyes as they fly open. His body slumps to the floor, and I draw in a breath as dark red blood pools under his head. Seconds pass, but I don't dare even breathe.

". . . Maheer?"

The bastard prince doesn't move. His eyes are still open, but now they are unmoving, staring blankly up at the ceiling. I move closer, nudging his bare foot with my sandaled one.

"Prince Maheer?"

There is no answer, only silence.

I do not know how long I stand there, staring at Maheer's body as it grows stiff and loses color. He is dead, I know that, but the relief I expect to feel does not come. Maheer was evil, of that I have no doubt, but his death cuts closer than expected. It reminds me that—in some small, unsettling way—he and I are threads pulled from the same cloth. He was the son of a god—an Olympian—and it didn't matter at all. Death still found him easily. It would be just as easy for death to find me. I close my eyes and imagine my sisters finding *me* dead, finding *my* body in a pool of blood like this. My mouth grows sticky, and at that moment, I begin to truly panic. If someone heard Maheer's screaming, or heard him fall . . .

I need to leave.

Something tickles the back of my mind, but I take little notice of it as I retreat. I edge along the chamber's walls, my gaze trained on Maheer's body, until I feel for the door's handle.

Then I flee into the dark.

VI

THE SLAVES FIND Maheer's body the following morning.

I am in bed, pretending to be asleep, but I know the moment it happens. There is a series of screams, a rush of running feet. The strange tickle at the back of my mind, the one that's making me feel as though I've forgotten something important, stayed with me all through the night while I tossed and turned, but I still can't place its source. Not that that is the only thing that held sleep at bay. For hours, I replayed what had happened in Maheer's bedchamber; for hours, the echoes of his words skittered across my skin like centipedes.

You're just the age I like them.

Even now, the memory of the prince's smell makes me want to vomit. He briefly pinned me against the wall, but the worst moment was when he touched my hair. I washed it thoroughly after I went back to my room, but his phantom scent still lingers in my nose. More than once, I thought of going to Sthcno, thc way I had whcn I was small, aftcr a nightmare. I wanted to crawl into her bed and curl against her while she held me close and told me everything would be all right. In the end, though, I understood that telling my sister would only make everything worse. I stayed in my own bed.

In the distance, someone raises their voice. That someone, I suspect, is my father. I hear pottery shattering, then another roar of fury. Finally, when I can stand it no longer, I dress and make my way to the great hall.

. . .

A small crowd of slaves is already gathered in the middle of the room, as are my parents and both sisters. Immediately, I note the first casualty of the morning: A large clay vase depicting a beautiful tangle of black and white flowers now lies scattered in tiny shards on the floor. My father is standing beside it, palpable rage rolling off his entire body. My unease coils tighter around me, and I take care to stand as far from him as possible. For several seconds, no one speaks.

"Phorcys." My mother sounds agitated. She's massaging her temple vigorously and appears to be only half dressed. Judging by the slightly slurred quality of her words, I suspect she's still nursing the consequences of the previous night. "What's going on?" she asks. "What's happened?"

All eyes in the room fall to my father.

He still seems angry, but when he takes a deep breath, there is resignation in the gesture. He frowns as he addresses my mother. "There has been an incident involving Prince Maheer," he says grudgingly. "He's dead."

Some of the household's slaves—the ones who found Maheer's body—already know; the great majority who don't, gasp. Members of Prince Maheer's envoy drop to their knees at once. They cry out, shoulders trembling as they wail and cover their faces. Only I am standing close enough to notice that most of them don't shed a single tear. My mother's mouth falls open in a perfect O, Stheno tenses, but I look to Euryale.

My second-oldest sister's eyes have gone wide. "Dead?" she repeats softly. "But how?"

"I'm not sure," my father admits. "He was found on the floor of his bedchamber this morning. I believe it was an accident. He may have fallen."

I recall the sound of Maheer's screams, the terrible sound his skull made as it met unforgiving carved wood. A clamminess spreads over my skin, and I shiver. Thankfully, no one seems to notice.

"How terrible." My mother clasps her hands together. "He was so young, so handsome."

Stheno turns to our sister. "Eury, are you all right?"

At the sound of her name, Euryale starts, then shudders. She hugs herself tight as one fat tear slides down her cheek, then another. Her chin quivers. "Dead," she repeats. "He's . . . dead?" She seems to teeter in place a moment, then she falls to her knees, sobbing.

I wince, feeling as though someone has driven a dagger into my chest and twisted it. I understand that Euryale is not grieving the death of Maheer. She's grieving the life her marriage to him would have promised. Yesterday, she fantasized about queenship, about a new life beyond this island and my parents' reach. For one day, she had hope for something better. Now she has lost both her betrothed and that hope in one blow. I know *I* am responsible for that loss. *I* am responsible for her pain.

Better than the pain she would have been in if she'd married him, an internal voice argues fiercely. *It was for her own good.* I cling to that justification with a strangling grip.

"Take Euryale back to her bedchamber and give her a calming drink," my mother orders her attendants. "I will be there shortly." Once they have helped Euryale out of the room, she addresses my father. "What does this mean?" she asks quietly. "For us?"

My father shakes his head. "I don't know."

I watch, still numb, as he and my mother leave the hall with their heads bent together. The slaves leave shortly after. Only when Stheno and I are alone does she finally turn to me.

"*You* had something to do with this," she murmurs.

I whirl around to face her. "What? What do you—?"

"Don't lie." Stheno waves me off with an impatient hand. "I saw the look on your face when Father said Maheer was dead. You weren't surprised at all. You've been fidgeting from the moment you entered the hall." I can't decide if she looks more annoyed or concerned. "And you're my little sister. I *know* you, and I know when you're hiding something."

I hang my head in defeat, recognizing a battle lost. Stheno crosses her arms.

"Speak."

"I-it was an accident," I stammer. "I didn't mean to kill him. I only intended to bribe him."

One of Stheno's brows arches. "I'm afraid you've missed that mark rather spectacularly."

"You were right." The words tumble from me. "He was cruel, Stheno. He hurt Euryale. He would have hurt her again, so I went to his chamber late last night—"

"You did *what*?" Stheno's eyes flash.

"I tried to pay him to rescind his offer of marriage," I continue quickly. "He refused, and then . . ."

"And then?" Stheno presses.

I recount the rest quickly. By the time I finish, Stheno is scowling.

"Did he hurt you?" she asks quietly. "Tell me the truth."

I pause. Maheer did not physically harm me—I stopped him before he could—but I think of the moment I was pressed between him and the wall. The stink of him, the words he said, and the way he looked at me are still burned fresh into my memory. I didn't know exactly what Prince Maheer wanted to do with me, but whatever it was, he didn't manage it. I hold on to that.

He didn't actually hurt you, I remind myself. *You're all right. No need to make her worry any more than she already is.*

"No." I hold my sister's gaze. "He didn't hurt me. I escaped before he could."

Stheno studies me for a long moment, then nods. "I'm glad he's dead," she says simply. "By all accounts, he was a drunken, lecherous brute." She points at me. "But this was sloppily done. You should have come to me."

"Stheno." I can't keep the trembling from my voice. "I didn't mean for this to happen, truly. I never intended—"

"Whatever you intended doesn't matter now," she says gravely. "A demigod is dead. You must repeat what you've just told me to no one, do you understand? Gods have been incited to violence and retribution for far less."

The knot of fear in my stomach tightens. Tears well in my eyes. "Stheno, what do we do now?"

"We do the only thing we can," my sister says solemnly. "We wait."

FOLLOWING PRINCE MAHEER'S death, a gloom like I have never known falls over our island. The summer storm that threatened before finally breaks, and with it come iron-gray skies and air thick with humidity. Every time a bolt of lightning knifes across the sky, I find myself thinking of Zeus.

I wake the following morning to find that my usual white tunics have all been replaced with black ones, and I learn that we are all now expected to join Euryale in a period of mourning for her would-be husband.

Prince Maheer's envoy takes his body and boards their ship to return home a few days later, despite the inauspicious weather. I'm not surprised when I hear one of the island's slaves whisper that they did not take the lion with them, emphatically insisting that it had been a gift. Admittedly, I'm glad to see the envoy go—the image of Maheer's bloodied corpse has haunted more than one of my dreams—but the general atmosphere does not return to normal after their departure. The torrential rains worsen, and if anything, the island's tension seems only to heighten. No one will say it aloud, but everyone is waiting for something—a different kind of storm we cannot see on the horizon, but one whose approach we sense in the very air we breathe. The days slow to a crawl as I wait. More than once, I think to find Theo, but for the second time in recent memory, I'm hesitant to confide in my best friend. Stheno's warning has stayed fresh in my mind, and I know it's an apt one. I cannot risk telling my friend anything that could implicate him in what's happened. I ultimately make the painful decision to avoid him.

In the seven days after Maheer's death, anxiety runs rampant across the island. Our halls grow quiet as wariness is replaced by short tempers and agitation. My father shatters more pottery and rips tapestries from the wall in random fits of rage. My mother snaps at the slaves, who in turn snap at each other. It is as though we all sense that whatever doom is pending, it is drawing perilously close. Perhaps that is why no one is truly surprised when, on the eighth day, a male slave comes crashing into the great hall wide-eyed and panting while we are eating breakfast.

"My lord!" he says breathlessly. "Forgive me!"

My father looks up, alarmed. "What's this? What's happened?"

The slave's chest is rising and falling; he struggles to speak. "We had no warning," he says. "We received no word that she was coming. She just—"

"Good morning, Phorcys."

My eyes snap to the great hall's entrance, along with the rest of my family's. In it stands a fair-skinned woman I've never seen before. She is notably tall, and her thick red hair, braided down her back, reminds me of a fire's dying embers. Her ankle-length tunic is crisp, white, and perfectly pressed. She is beautiful, but that's not what holds my attention. It's the spear in her grasp. Both its shaft and blade are golden; it's easily the length of her body, but she wields it like it weighs nothing. I now understand why the slave was so frightened. Only gods and goddesses carry this kind of natural confidence, and there is something undeniably formidable about this one. She doesn't feign extreme youth, like so many of the goddesses I've grown up around; she could be in her forties, even fifties. She inclines her head toward my father, and I see a challenge in the gesture. I also think I know who this goddess is. My father stands so quickly that the legs of his chair scrape the floor.

"Athena." His voice is uncharacteristically hushed. "This is unexpected."

Athena enters the hall in self-assured strides, a light smile upon her face. She stops before our table. "Forgive me," she says. "But the matter I have come to speak with you about is urgent. There was no time to send a message."

Across the hall, I look to Theo, who has been helping serve our breakfast. We both have read about Athena in scrolls, and suddenly everything I know about her is rushing to the forefront of my mind. She is not just an Olympian, she is among the highest ranking of them, the goddess of wisdom, war, and craft. I have even heard other gods of the Sea Court whisper that she is the favorite daughter of Zeus, a sort of Olympian princess in her own right. She is known to be powerful, intelligent, and, beyond all things, shrewd.

If she did not inform my father of her intent to visit, I know it was no accident.

"I am here on behalf of my father," Athena continues. "It has come to his attention that a mortal bastard of my brother Ares died here recently, while in your care."

My father is still standing, eyeing Athena the way a mouse might eye a snake. "Prince Maheer was to marry my daughter." He gestures toward Euryale. "He died in a tragic accident. We have been in mourning ever since."

"Be that as it may"—Athena's voice is still light and offhand— "Maheer's envoy brought a different account back to his mother. That account was relayed to Ares, and then to Zeus. Of course, normally the death of a mere mortal would be inconsequential, but Ares is angry."

"Ares is *always* angry," my mother mutters.

Athena pretends not to hear her. Her silver eyes are bright. "The circumstances surrounding Prince Maheer's death seem . . . peculiar."

"Peculiar?" my father repeats.

Athena nods. "Evidently, Prince Maheer was found on the floor of his bedchamber soaked in wine and blood."

"Yes," my father says, "it seems he had been drinking."

"It seems he was," Athena continues, "but apparently there were two cups of wine found in his chamber. There was also *this.*" She reaches into the fold of her tunic and withdraws a sapphire and a ruby. The breath leaves my body, and now the cause for that tickling sensation in the back of my mind becomes plain entirely too late.

"Precious gems," Athena explains. "These are notably larger than most, and Maheer's envoy had no recollection of them. Do they mean anything to you?"

"They're mine," my mother snaps, "but I have no idea how they came to be in Maheer's bedchamber."

"You understand how this looks, Phorcys." I notice again that Athena has pointedly ignored my mother. "We Olympians may be young by your standards, but we still adhere to xenia, and the old laws." She gives him a significant look. "In particular, we honor the law of hospitality."

My mouth goes dry. The law of hospitality is an ancient principle of decorum dictating that a host must offer certain courtesies to those who visit their home, including assured safety under their roof. My gaze flies from my mother to my father. They exchange a look, and I don't miss the new shared unease in their eyes.

"Maheer died while he was a guest in your home." Athena clasps her hands together. "In Zeus's view, this violates the law of hospitality. He is displeased."

The temperature in our hall seems to plummet. Euryale, who I have seen only glimpses of in the last week, begins to weep softly into her hands. From her place at the table, Stheno's lips grow drawn and thin.

"Perhaps we should speak with more candor," my mother says sharply, and this time I know there is no way for Athena to ignore her. "What is your business here, Athena?"

The goddess juts her chin. "To appease Ares, Zeus wants Maheer's death investigated," she says, "to determine that it was, as you say, an accident."

"What exactly are you implying?" my mother asks. Her eyes turn to slits, and my father shoots her a warning look.

"Ceto—"

My mother rises. "There is an accord. You are not to come to our domain without invitation. Now you do so with slanderous accusations on your lips—"

"They are only *slanderous* if proven untrue." Athena's voice has hardened. "But if you refuse to comply with my father's command, I'll be glad to tell him myself."

My mother and Athena stare at each other for a long minute, and though they do not exchange any more words, I can feel a silent battle of wills raging between them. I don't understand their animosity, just as I don't know what "accord" my mother is referring to. While it's true that she has never cared much for any Olympian, excluding Poseidon, her dislike of Athena seems to come from a deeper place. Even my father seems unsettled. Despite my unease, a part of me is curious about the origins of their mutual enmity. A few more seconds pass before my mother takes her seat, though she now looks as if she has swallowed a lemon slice. I know why she has yielded. My parents are ancient, powerful deities, but even their combined might is inconsequential compared to the power of Zeus, the king of the gods old and new. The stories of his might are nearly as infamous as the stories of what he does to those who've drawn his ire.

"You may conduct your investigation, Athena." My father's voice is courteous but clipped. "I grant you free rein of this island and its inhabitants. Utilize whatever resources you require to discern the truth and see this matter resolved."

Athena eyes my father, then tightens her grip on her spear. "Believe me," she says, "I intend to."

I SPEND THE rest of the morning and early afternoon in my bedchamber, pacing.

I began by counting my steps, tracing a path between my door and the foot of my bed, but as the minutes slipped into hours, my anxiety burrowed deep within me, then bloomed into something monstrous.

The gemstones. How could I have forgotten the gemstones?

It's a question I've posed to myself a hundred times. I cover my face, groan, then once again look to my bedchamber door. I desperately want to go to Stheno's room, but I dare not risk running into Athena. Every time I think of the red-haired goddess and her cool silver eyes, I find it difficult to breathe. The truth is, she terrifies me.

At the sound of a knock at my door, I jump. The door cracks open, and Theo sticks his head into the room. I'm so relieved to see him that I don't notice at first his drawn expression.

"Theo!" I close the gap between us and wrap my arms around him. "I'm glad to see you. I've been so worried."

When he doesn't answer me, I pull back, and then my friend's strain is more obvious. He is tensed, as though every muscle in his body has been pulled taut like a bowstring. His mouth is set in a short, severe line.

"What's wrong?" I ask. "What's happened?"

Theo looks over his shoulder, steps fully into my bedchamber, then closes the door behind him. I realize that he doesn't just seem tense; he's frightened. "I was forbidden from coming to see you," he whispers, "but I had to tell you."

"Tell me what?"

Theo begins picking at his nails. "Athena's summoning the slaves for interrogation."

I draw in a sharp breath, remembering what the goddess said earlier. Two goblets were found in Maheer's room alongside the gemstones. She must now suspect one of the slaves. I refocus on Theo. "Has she summoned you yet?"

"No," he says. "But I have heard she intends to question everyone." He swallows. "Meddy, I'm scared."

"Why?" I ask. "You've done nothing wrong."

Theo looks up at me, solemn. "No," he says in a strangled voice. "But I *was* in the prince's bedchamber just before he died."

I go still. "What?"

"I wasn't supposed to be attending to him," Theo says quickly. "But I was walking past his door when he saw me. He ordered me to fetch him wine . . ."

My heart hammers so hard in my chest, I can barely hear the rest of his words. I think of the full pitcher of wine, recently replenished, that I saw in Prince Maheer's bedchamber when I arrived there.

"I wasn't there long, but I believe I was the last person in the prince's room," Theo continues, oblivious to the change in my demeanor. "Which means, I'm the last person who saw him alive."

You weren't, I think bitterly. *I was.*

I do my best to sound neutral as I address him again. "Athena wouldn't blame you just because you were the last person to see Maheer alive," I say, forcing a levity into my voice that I don't really feel. "That wouldn't make sense."

Theo is still frowning. "There's more," he says quietly. "I can't be sure, but some of the slaves are saying something else was found in the prince's bedchamber: a sack with a knife in it." He gives me a meaningful look. "The kind of knife *I* use when I carve."

I feel as though I've been plunged into a winter sea. Goosebumps stipple my skin, and my mouth goes dry. I brought more than the two gemstones with me when I went to Maheer's bedchamber; I also brought a knife for protection. Theo had given it to me ages ago. In the chaotic aftermath of what had happened, I left it behind, too.

"The other slaves know what my carving knives look like," Theo goes on. "Athena will learn that I was the last one to see Prince Maheer alive, and then she'll learn that one of my knives was found where he died." He swallows hard, and tears prick his eyes. "I'm sure that'll be more than enough for her."

New anger rises within me like a bright flame, but just as quickly, it's extinguished. I realize I have no one to blame for this but myself.

"Athena is a goddess of wisdom and logic," I say, trying to sound calm. "Logic says you didn't do this. You had no reason to."

Theo's smile doesn't reach his eyes. "Whenever something in a household goes wrong, it's the slaves who are held responsible. Missing jewelry, spoiled food, bad weather—slaves are always easiest to blame."

"But—"

Theo speaks over me: "Athena and your parents will all want this matter resolved quickly. Everyone would like to name a culprit so that this can all be over. It's just how these things go, Meddy. Believe me, I've seen it before. *Logic* won't count for much."

I open my mouth to tell him he's wrong, but the words stick in my throat. An uncomfortable silence hangs between us, and it's not the first time I've felt it. Theo is my dearest friend, and Theo is a slave. I'm keenly aware that, in the eyes of the world, we are not equals, no matter how much I wish it were different.

Now I watch as Theo stares at the floor. He's the same age as me, seventeen, but in that moment he looks younger, somehow smaller despite his tall frame. It takes me a moment to realize what's changed in him, and with a terrible clarity, I understand that it's Theo's light that's now missing from him. I have seen any number of emotions in my friend, but for the first time, I see true resignation.

"It was my father who taught me how to carve," Theo murmurs, still staring at his feet. "I don't remember what he looks like anymore, but I do remember his hands. I remember him teaching me."

New pain tears through me. We don't speak of it often, but I know well how Theo came to be on this island. Like most of those who serve my parents, he was found marooned on the beach, the lone survivor of a shipwreck off the coast. My father gave Theo the same wretched ultimatum he gave any mortals who washed up on our shores: *Serve or die.* Theo was so young when he made that impossible choice. Now I am the closest thing to a family he has left.

And *my* actions have put him in danger.

"I'm sorry," I whisper, taking his hands in mine.

Theo swallows hard. "It's all right."

"It's not." I shake my head. "And I'm not letting you take the blame for this. You didn't do anything wrong."

Theo looks up at me. His eyes are wet with tears. "You believe me."

I regret not having told him the truth earlier, and for one impulsive moment, I consider doing it now. I want to tell him every horrid detail of what really happened, not just to absolve him but so I won't have to carry the weight of it anymore. Almost as quickly, I hear the echo of Stheno's voice in my mind.

Gods have been incited to violence and retribution for far less.

I open my mouth, then close it. The less Theo knows, the safer he'll be.

I take a deep breath and offer a tight smile. "Everything's going to be all right," I say with a confidence I don't feel. "I'll always protect you, Theo, I swear it." I glance over his shoulder. "For now, just find somewhere to stay hidden, if you can."

Theo looks equal parts curious and confused, but I can already see some of the muscles in his jaw relaxing.

"All right."

He stays with me a few minutes longer, making idle conversation.

When he finally slips out the door and I am alone again, I breathe a sigh of relief and lean against the wall.

I've sworn to protect Theo because he's my friend, but as I begin pacing back and forth around my chamber again, I realize it is more than that.

I have felt helpless all my life. Helpless because I am not strong or beautiful or immortal; helpless because I have never had the power to protect myself, let alone those I care about. My steps slow. I realize that, for the first time, I *do* have power. It isn't much, but it's still something. I know the truth about what happened to Maheer, and I have the power to protect Theo from taking the blame.

That knowledge hums through me as I turn and make my way out the door.

VII

THE WALK FROM my bedchamber to the drawing room Athena has commandeered for her interrogations seems to take centuries. When at last I reach its double oak doors, I come to a stop.

There's no turning back. The voice in my head sounds a lot like Stheno's. *Once you go in there, there's no turning back.*

I'm cold despite the summer afternoon's sultry heat. The relentless rain that's plagued our island for the better part of a week has at last abated, but in the rainfall's absence, there is an eerie, unnatural quiet. I take a steadying breath and rub my arms. Never in my life have I been so afraid, and a part of me thinks to return to my room. Then Theo's face fills my mind. I'm doing this for him; I have to. I remember this as I turn one of the doors' golden handles and step inside.

The drawing room is small and simple. Today its windows have been thrown open to combat the mugginess, so that a light breeze carries in the sweet scent of flowers from the gardens. In the middle of the room, I find Athena seated on a satin settee I've grown accustomed to seeing my mother sprawled across after a night of drinking. One sandaled foot is tucked beneath her, and her head is bent over a scroll in her lap, so that a lock of her dark red hair brushes her cheek. Even amid my fear, I cannot help but think there is something otherworldly about her, something so lovely it almost hurts. I stand by the door, perfectly still, unsure of what to do. Several seconds pass before she looks up and notices me.

I flinch. Her eyes are an unnatural light gray that reminds me of lightning. She studies me for a moment, her brow slightly furrowed.

"I recognize you," the goddess says without preamble. "You're one of Ceto's daughters, aren't you? You look like her."

I start. Of the three of us, Euryale is the one most often likened to our mother. In all my years, no one has ever said that *I* look like her. I stare back at Athena a moment, eyes wide, before sense finds me and I remember to bow.

"Y-yes, Your Grace." Though I can't be sure, I think I catch the barest quirk in the corner of Athena's lips as she tilts her head.

"What are you doing here, child? Did your parents send you?"

"N-no." I realize that this is my very last chance to run, to save myself. I can hear the Stheno-like voice in the back of my mind again, urging me to do just that. Instead, I force myself to say the words I practiced on my walk here. "I've come to speak with you about Prince Maheer."

Athena sets aside the scroll she's been reading. This time there's no mistaking it. A small smile touches the goddess's lips. "You're curious about it all," she says. There's warmth in her voice. "I suppose that's only natural."

"I heard that you were questioning slaves," I say, wishing my voice weren't so small and tinny compared to hers.

Athena gestures to the scroll. "This is a list of every slave who served Prince Maheer during his stay here. I can't be sure that one of them was responsible, but there are indicators it's possible. I plan to ask each of them to provide a timeline of their whereabouts on the night of Maheer's death. Then I'll cross-reference those timelines to find inconsistencies. There, I'll find the culprit."

"It wasn't a slave who killed Maheer."

Athena sits up straighter. For the first time since I've entered the room, I sense that I have her undivided attention.

"Killed," she repeats. "How would you know that Maheer was killed?"

"Because I'm the one who killed him."

Several emotions cross Athena's face as my words register. Her red brows knit, and a frown pulls at her mouth.

"You?" she says quietly. "Why would *you* kill him?"

I take a deep breath, and then I speak. I tell the goddess about Maheer's lion first. I tell her about the slaves with their gruesome wounds and then about Euryale. As I go on, Athena sits back on the settee. By the time I'm finished, her face is a perfect mask.

"How did he die?" she asks. Her voice betrays nothing.

I tell her quickly about my visit to Maheer's bedchamber and my offer. But when I reach the end, I stumble. I don't want to sound small and afraid, but my voice shakes as I repeat what Maheer said about my body and what he asked me to do. Suddenly, I cannot look the goddess in the eye. I don't believe I did anything wrong, but I find that I'm still embarrassed. I stare at the rug.

"The wine blinded him," I finish quietly. "He couldn't see, so he tripped, fell, and hit his head. *That* is how he died."

The silence between Athena and me stretches for so long that I'm eventually compelled to look up at her. I'm surprised to see that she does not look angry but, rather, intrigued.

"And how did it feel?"

I start. "Feel, Your Grace?"

Athena leans in, a strange new look in her gray eyes. "When you hit Maheer with the goblet, how did it feel?"

I close my eyes and remember the white-hot rage that overcame me as I slammed the goblet into the side of Maheer's head as hard as I could. I didn't want to admit it to myself at the time, but I know I felt satisfied, too. For once, I wasn't helpless.

"Good." The word leaves me before I can stop it. "It felt . . . good."

Athena blinks, and I cannot help but wonder if I've answered her question wrong or failed some test I didn't know I was taking.

She raises her chin slightly, as though in challenge. "I didn't suspect you in the slightest," she says. "Had you not come forward, it's very likely that you would have gotten away with this entirely. I'm left to wonder . . . why did you?"

My gaze drops to the floor again. "I didn't want a slave to take the blame."

Several seconds pass before Athena speaks again. "You knew that you'd likely be punished," she murmurs. "You knew that you risked the wrath of Ares and, by extension, my father? And you came forward anyway?"

"I did." I'm still staring at my feet.

"I find that rather admirable."

My head snaps up.

"My nephew was handsome." She wrinkles her nose as though she's smelled something sour. "He was also spoiled and boorish, like his father."

I gape. Never before have I heard one Olympian openly speak ill of another.

Athena goes on. "If what you say is true, Maheer's death truly was an accident. You are not guilty of murder."

I remain silent.

Athena leans forward again, and this time I get the sense she's appraising me in some way. "How old are you, girl?"

"Seventeen."

She purses her lips. "There is something about you." She cocks her head, her gray eyes narrowed. "You are different in some way, but I cannot say how."

I am grateful for my dark brown skin just then. It hides the blood rushing to my cheeks. Now, more than any other time in my life perhaps, I want to hide the truth. I know there is no point. "I am mortal, Your Grace. That is what you see."

There is a long pause.

"Your father did not tell me he had mortal children." Athena's tone has softened.

"My two older sisters are immortal." I force the words, though each one costs me something. "I am the only one of us three who is not. No one knows why."

"And the other children?"

I frown, confused. I have no idea what she's talking about. Something seems to register in Athena's eyes, because she waves a dismissive hand and goes on.

"Your father would punish you, if he learned what you did," she says. "Yet you risked his ire in defense of your sister. You risked *my* ire by confessing what you did, yet you confessed anyway." Athena's expression turns curious. "What do you do in your spare time, child?"

I know my mother would expect me to answer with a list of suitable womanly pastimes—music, dance, and so on—but intuition tells me there is no point in lying, not to Athena. I stammer a moment before the words come to me: "I read."

There's no mistaking it. Athena looks amused now. "What do you read?"

"Whatever I can, but I enjoy history and philosophy most, also epics."

She squints. "You live on an island. Your parents aren't permitted to leave. How could you possibly possess scrolls?"

"Sometimes, ships wreck," I explain. "Things wash up on our shores—maps, trinkets, trunks full of scrolls. I've collected whatever I could for as long as I can remember." I pause, then add, "I don't get scrolls as often as I'd like, and sometimes they're too wet to be any good, but I still have a few."

"How fascinating," Athena says. "And how many languages can you read in?"

"Four."

This garners the goddess's attention. Her brows rise. "What did you say?"

"We speak Greek on the island, sometimes Meroitic, but I can read in Latin and Arabic, too," I reply. "I've learned bits and pieces of a few others, but I'm less than proficient."

"Were you taught by a tutor?"

"My sisters and some of the slaves helped a little, at first." I fidget. "But mostly I have had to teach myself so that I could read my scrolls. They are not all written in the same languages, you see. There are some I still can't read at all."

Yet another silence hangs heavy between the goddess and me, a silence long enough to make me nervous again.

Finally, she speaks. "I'd like to discuss something with you, girl," she says. "Something serious."

I brace myself. I've known since I decided to come to her that even if

Athena was impressed with me, there would have to be a punishment for
what I'd done. I begin to think of the very worst punishments I've heard
of Olympians doling out. For stealing fire from Mount Olympus and
gifting it to mortals, Zeus infamously condemned the Titan Prometheus
to be chained to a mountain and disemboweled by an eagle for all eternity. I clutch at my own abdomen as Athena opens her mouth.

"Each year, new priestesses are inducted into my temple at Athens,"
she says. "To become priestesses, they must undergo rigorous training as
acolytes, as well as pass a series of prerequisite tests to prove their suit-
ability. Only young women of high intelligence and ethical standards are
invited to participate." She inclines her head. "Young women, I believe,
like you."

These are not the words I expected. "Me?"

"You are young, educated, and your valor impresses me." Something
flashes in the goddess's eyes. "As I see it, these attributes would be ideal
for a priestess of my temple."

For a moment, I forget how to breathe. I can barely believe the words
I've just heard.

"You mean . . ." My voice trembles. "You mean for me to go to Athens?"

"I appreciate that it is not close," Athena says. "I will arrange transportation, and speak to my high priestess."

Athens is a city I know of from my readings, one I've heard my parents talk about, but it is not one I ever believed I would see in person.
My mind starts to race. All my life, for as long as I can remember, I have
wished for only one thing: to see the world beyond my island. Now
Athena has handed me that wish on a golden platter.

"What is your answer, child?" Athena asks. "Will you come to Athens?"

"Yes." It takes great effort to maintain a façade of calm. "I would be
honored."

"I will speak with your father," she says. "Provided he grants his con-
sent, you will report to Athens in a fortnight."

I can do nothing more than nod.

"My final question." Athena cocks her head. "What are you called, girl?"

"Medusa."

"Medusa." She repeats my name, and I stand taller. "Spend these next two weeks preparing, and be sure to find time for rest." The goddess smiles. "I will see you in Athens."

VIII

ATHENA LEAVES OUR island a few hours after we speak. I do not hear directly from my father about what she said to him, but instead rely on the whispers of slaves to fill in the gaps. From their accounts, I learn that Athena simply told my father she'd heard from enough witnesses to believe that Maheer's death truly was an accident. My involvement, it seems, never came up. I hear no mention of her invitation for me to serve at her temple, but I have to believe she discussed that with him, too. Even now, I find myself unable to entirely believe that that invitation was real.

Dinner that night begins without incident. The slaves, I notice, move with new levity, and I imagine they are as relieved as the rest of us that Athena's investigation of Maheer's death is complete. I make a mental note to find Theo later and tell him all that's happened. So far, I've shared the news of my invitation with no one, not even my sisters. I will eventually, but for now it feels like something precious, something that belongs only to me and Athena. I think of the words she said to me earlier.

You are young, educated, and your valor impresses me.

I impressed Athena. *I* impressed one of the most powerful goddesses in all the pantheon. Involuntarily, a smile pulls at my lips.

It is at that exact moment that my mother's eyes cut to my father.

"When?" Her voice is low and lethal, and the smile drops from my

face at once. Everyone in the hall, my sisters and the slaves alike, look up at her in surprise. My mother's gaze stays fixed on my father.

"When what, Ceto?" My father's feigned nonchalance fools no one. He is eyeing my mother warily.

"When were you going to tell me that you sold our daughter off to that pale, gray-eyed bitch?"

If our hall was quiet before, that was nothing compared to the silence that fills it now. The attendants who have been serving us stiffen. My sisters exchange confused looks, then turn to me. For his part, my father looks more fatigued than angry.

"I did not *sell* any of our daughters," he says patiently, massaging the bridge of his nose. "Medusa has been invited to undergo the tests to serve as a priestess in Athena's temple."

Stheno and Euryale don't speak, but I see them both start in surprise, then stare at me. Guilt stabs my chest. As an unspoken rule, we've never kept secrets from one another, until now. I wanted them to hear about it from me.

"It is not unprecedented," my father continues. "Other Olympians have chosen mortals and demigods to serve them. It is an honor. Athena has also given me her word that Medusa will be permitted to return home intermittently. I have discussed the details of this arrangement with her at length."

"She did not discuss them with *me!*" My mother bangs her fist against the table so hard the plates on it rattle. It has been quite some time since I saw her this irritated, and I can't understand why this specifically has rankled her so. I think back to the way she and Athena eyed each other when Athena first arrived, and again I have the feeling that I am missing something deeper.

"Ceto," my father warns, "compose yourself. I do not need to confer with you on matters of this household. *I* am lord and master here."

"And yet, where the Olympians are concerned, you behave like a groveling boy," my mother jeers. "Tell me, did Athena even ask your permission, or did she demand our child's servitude to make further fools of us?" She laughs humorlessly. "Ah, I can see it now: the granddaughter of the once-revered Pontus and Gaia, the daughter of the once-great Phorcys and Ceto, no more than a common *cupbearer.*"

I want so badly to interrupt my mother. I want to tell her that Athena did not demand my servitude at all, that I'm happy to go. As if she can read my thoughts, Stheno casts me a sharp look that warns me to stay silent.

"Athena has no quarrel with us, nor with any gods of the Sea Court." My father's voice grows louder. "I will not risk inciting one by offending her."

"You actually think this politicking with Olympians will raise your status and win you their favor." My mother scoffs. "All you'll win is their mockery when your back is turned. You will never be one of them."

My father's eyes flash. "What would you have me do, Ceto?" He rises, coming around the table to stand before her. "Would you have me spite Zeus's favorite daughter? We would be decimated within a day, banished to the depths of Tartarus on sheer principle."

My mother raises her chin imperiously. "I would rather spend an eternity in Tartarus's darkness than a single day without my honor." She stands, too, so that their faces are nearly level. "You forget we are primordial, Phorcys. *We* are the progeny of gods who came long before the Olympians." Her eyes grow wet. "*We* were once the ones with power. Now look at what we have been reduced to, appeasing the demands of that tyrant's daughter."

"Zeus has been more than fair to the gods of the Sea Court," my father says in an impatient voice.

"*Fair?*" My mother spits the word as though it's poison. "Is that what you called it, when he stripped us of our true power, when he commanded us to stay on this forsaken island? Was that *fair?*"

I go cold at the same time Stheno and Euryale tense. My parents rarely speak of their origins, of the lives they had before our births. I detect something unfamiliar in my mother's voice, a pain so old and raw it feels wrong to hear.

My mother changes tack, placing one hand on my father's cheek. "There are whispers among some in the Sea Court," she says in a softer voice, pressing her body against his. "Eurybia keeps an ear to the ground;

she says Oceanus is plotting. There may soon be an opportunity for us to take back our—"

"Quiet yourself!" My father jerks away from my mother. "Do you mean to see our halls laid to waste? What you speak of is treason."

"I will make no apology for standing with our kind." My mother rises to her full height. "I am a loyalist."

"You are a drunk," my father says irritably, "and stuck in the past."

The vulnerability I saw in my mother disappears. "And *you* are a coward," she bites back.

My father's eyes close, and I feel his anger shift to something my mother does not see: rage.

"You are no more than a spineless sycophant," my mother goes on. "You might as well cut off your own cock and present it to—"

My father strikes, slapping my mother across the face so hard she stumbles to the ground. When she looks up, her eyes are wide.

"Phorcys."

Already, she's scuttling away from him like a crab. Already, I know it is too late.

My father stalks toward her, his face stony.

"Phorcys, I'm sorry. Please. Please, I didn't mean—" She tries to stand, but the rest of her words are cut off as his fingers wrap around her throat and squeeze.

Stheno closes her eyes, Euryale bows her head and stares determinedly at her hands in her lap. Only I watch as my father lifts my mother by her neck. Her sandaled feet kick helplessly in the air. Her wheezes grow more desperate as she claws at his hands, eyes bulging and turning golden, but my father remains impassive. His ancient gaze is cool. White-hot anger sears my insides, and not for the first time, I imagine what it would be like if I had a fraction of my father's power, if I could hurt him the way he has hurt my mother so many times. Not for the first time, I remember that here I am still helpless.

"Medusa will go to Athena's temple," my father says quietly. "Not because she has ordered it, but because *I* order it." He brings their faces close. "You will not question me again. Do I make myself clear?"

"I understand," my mother rasps. "Please, forgive me, my love."

My father gives her one more contemptuous look before dropping her. She collapses in an inelegant heap on the ground, and he storms out of the hall, not looking back once.

My sisters and I stay seated at the dinner table, waiting for our mother to rise. She does not. She only pulls her knees to her chest and stares off into the distance. I do not know how long it is before she begins to cry, but when she does, it is an ugly, broken sound. It nails me to my chair, renders me immobile. Someone touches my arm, and I look up to find both my sisters standing over me. Their expressions are solemn, guarded.

"Come, Meddy." Stheno's voice is uncharacteristically gentle as she puts a hand on my shoulder. She is careful to avoid looking at our mother. "It's time for bed."

I do not think to argue. Without a word, I stand, and the three of us leave the dining hall together, our mother's sobs fading into the night.

PERHAPS, IN MY heart of hearts, I already know my mother will come to my bedchamber that night.

In bed, I lie on my side, eyes open and waiting. I do not move when I hear the soft creak of my door opening or the pad of her footsteps. My bed gives slightly as she settles onto its edge, and for a few seconds, neither of us speaks. I take in the scent of her—the scent of grapeseed oil, wine, and myrrh. Beneath those, I detect others. My mother smells of damp earth after rain, of fresh hyacinth. I imagine her barefoot in her gardens with her curly hair unbraided, her face turned moonward so that her dark brown skin is bathed in silver light.

My thoughts are interrupted when she speaks.

"You were my most difficult pregnancy," she says softly. "All the time I carried you, I was so sick, I could barely eat. When it was, at last, time for your birth, my midwives told me you were trapped inside me. They suggested cutting you out of my womb, but I wouldn't let them. I told them you'd come in your own time, when you were ready.

"When you did come out, you looked healthy, but I knew at once that you were . . . different from Euryale and Stheno. Your body was smaller, your cries thinner. I knew, even before I discovered that you were mortal, later on, that you would always be more fragile. I knew I'd have to protect you, especially from the Olympians." She looks down at me. "I hope you always remember that. I did my best to protect you from them."

The words seem strange, incongruous. I've always known my mother disliked the Olympians, but I see no reason for her wanting to protect me from them. I'm not used to this kind of vulnerability from her unless it's aided by wine, and even then it's only brief. I stare up at my mother and realize she is completely sober. Somehow, that makes it harder to answer.

"I'll be all right, Mama." I do my best to sound brave. "I met Athena earlier today and . . . she was kind. She wouldn't hurt me, I know it."

My mother's laugh is harsh. "You know nothing, child," she whispers, "and you do not know Athena as I do."

"What do you mean?"

My mother stares into the dark. Though she's still sitting beside me, I sense she's somewhere else.

"I could tell you a story," she murmurs. "The tale of a young, ambitious god called Zeus. He was born of Titans, and when he became strong enough, he rallied his brothers and sisters in revolt, overthrew his father, and declared himself king of the gods." Her smile is mirthless. "He abolished the ancient laws of the Titans and implemented new ones more to his taste. He gathered the many sovereign sea gods and banded them under one Sea Court, to be ruled by his own brother Poseidon. Accords were made among the men, and the Olympians vowed never to enter our domains without invitation. Above all else, Zeus promised the sea gods that they would retain their individual strength and power, that the 'court' was only a formality." My mother shakes her head. "It was all a lie. Within a few centuries, we became shadows of what we once were."

I have known, all my life, that my parents were once greater beings. What I didn't understand, until now, was *how* their power was diminished, who was responsible for it.

"I realized then that the Olympians were slippery creatures," my mother goes on. "They were not like the old gods; they were hungry for power in a way we had never been. Then came the Gigantomachy."

". . . Gigantomachy?" I repeat. I've never heard that word before. It feels awkward and ungainly on my tongue.

"Sometimes it's called the War of the Giants," my mother says. She has lowered her voice now, and I have to strain to hear her. "The Giants were an ancient race of creatures, children of Gaia herself. In a way, they were my own brothers. They were stronger than the rest of us old gods, but not quite as strong as the Titans. Zeus abided them, for a time, but of course peace did not last. No one remembers the exact catalyst, the moment disagreement turned to war. But everyone remembers the end. Zeus gathered his Olympians for one final battle with the Giants, and then he ordered the Giants to be executed. We gods of the sea elected among ourselves not to participate in that war, but we knew when it had ended. We heard the screaming as the Giants met their end. It was . . . gruesome."

Terrible images fill my imagination. I can see it all as though I were there, the Giants of old being felled by the more powerful Olympians, one by one.

"It was Zeus who led the fighting during the Gigantomachy," my mother says, "but make no mistake: Athena was right there alongside him. I still remember what she was like in those days. She killed gleefully, brutally, without mercy. And when she was done, she made sure to hunt down any other perceived threats to her father's throne."

I find I can't reconcile the version of Athena that my mother is describing with the one who said just hours before that she admired my valor. There's something else I can't reconcile.

"If the Gigantomachy was fought between the Giants and the Olympians, why do *you* hate Athena so much?"

My mother's expression turns stony. "That is not for you to know."

We sit in silence for a minute before I speak again. "I don't know what

Athena did to you, Mama, but I believe she's changed. She's not the goddess you remember. She's not a monster."

My mother says nothing in answer, and without thinking, I reach for
her. It's a small, imperceptible gesture, but she notices. My mother stares
at my hand as though she's never seen anything like it in all her eons. Her
eyes flit from my hand to me, uncertain, and suddenly all I want is for
her to take my hand and squeeze it. I want her to tell me everything will
be all right, even if she has no way of knowing whether that's true.
Maybe that's what I've always wanted from her. Instead, my mother stares
at my hand a second longer before standing. Her expression shifts, and I
know that she is not my mother anymore. She is just an ancient sea goddess again. A humorless chuckle leaves her.

"That's the curious thing about monsters," she whispers. "The worst
ones don't bother hiding in the dark."

She says nothing else as she pads out of my room, leaving me alone
again.

IX

I SLEEP LITTLE over the next two weeks.

At the first hint of sunlight on the day of my departure, I am out of bed and on my feet, barely able to contain the excitement coursing through me. Already, the midsummer sun warms the air, and I do not wait for the slaves to bring clothes for me, as they usually do. Instead, I head straight to Euryale's bedchamber. She is already awake and seated at her vanity. She meets my eye and smiles knowingly.

"I *thought* I might see you this morning," she teases.

"I don't know what to wear," I say in a small voice.

Euryale offers a half smile, then gestures. Together, we kneel before her wooden chest and she throws the top open with a flourish. A sigh of admiration escapes me. The chest is filled with tunics in every color, each more finely made than the last. I let my fingers graze the fabric of a particularly pretty yellow tunic embroidered at the hem with white flowers.

"What about this one?" I ask hopefully.

Euryale regards the tunic, then shakes her head. "It's not quite right." She continues rifling through the trunk until she finds another and holds it up. "Here, this one is better."

I can't disagree with her. The tunic my sister is holding is silver gray and embroidered with green thread. In the morning light, it shimmers as though it has been woven from strands of the wind itself.

"I'll help you dress," Euryale offers, and I don't object as she helps me remove my old tunic and step into the new one. Once she's pinned it, she steps back, a hand on her chin. She looks thoughtful.

"Good . . ." she says slowly. "But it's still too plain. You're missing something." A wicked grin touches her face. "You know, you *could* borrow some of mother's jewelry. She still keeps it in a box under her bed."

Without thinking, I shake my head. "Not anymore," I say. "That was the first place I looked when—" I stop short, realizing too late that I've said too much.

Euryale frowns, confused. "When . . . what, Meddy?"

I hold my sister's gaze for as long as I can before I look away. In that moment, I *want* to lie to her, I want to avoid the pain I know I'm about to inflict. It would be easier. But I have already taken so much from Euryale. I know I can't take away her right to the truth.

"Eury . . ." My voice cracks. "It . . . it was me. I'm the one who visited Maheer's bedchamber the night he died." I watch understanding splinter across my sister's face as I tell her the rest. I see the moment shock turns to hurt, then to anger. By the time I'm finished, her eyes are wet with tears.

"I told you I wanted to marry him." She doesn't yell, but I wish she would. Her soft words are far worse. "I told you I wanted to marry him so that I could *leave* this island."

"You deserved better."

Between the three of us, Euryale has always been the sweetest, the gentlest. There's none of that in her countenance now. Instead, I find something in my sister's face I've never before seen: resentment.

"You had no right to make that decision for me." Her voice trembles. "You had *no right* to interfere with my life."

When I told Athena what I'd done, she praised me for my valor. Now I understand how easily valor can be disfigured.

"I thought I was doing the right thing," I whisper. "I thought I was protecting you."

Euryale laughs, but it's a harsh sound. "You're my *baby sister*, Meddy," she snaps. "I don't need *you* to protect *me*."

The words sting, but I don't flinch from them. I know I deserve this.

With a single act, I've managed to steal my sister's chance to leave this island while inadvertently securing my own. Guilt pricks at me like a stubborn thorn, then burrows deep beneath my skin.

"I'm sorry." Even as I apologize, I know it's not enough. Euryale doesn't answer; she only continues to stare at me in horrible silence, as though seeing me anew. I'm grateful when there's a knock at the bedchamber door. Seconds later, Stheno enters.

"I like your tunic," she says matter-of-factly, glancing at me. "But your locs need to be moisturized and retwisted before you go." She turns to my sister. "Eury? You'll help me?"

For a moment, I consider the possibility that my second-eldest sister will refuse; I even half expect her to leave the room entirely. I'm surprised when, instead, she grabs several clay jars of pomade and a bottle of rose oil from her vanity. Her expression is distant but resolved as she nods to Stheno.

"Let's get to work."

I should feel tension as Stheno directs me to a chair for her and Euryale to begin oiling my scalp and retwisting my locs, but the truth is that from the moment their fingers touch my head, a familiar ease settles over me that steadies my breathing. My sisters stand on either side of me, each taking a section of my hair to work on as they slip tiny golden cuffs into different locs. Though I can't see what they're doing with my own eyes, I can picture it perfectly because I've learned to do the same for them over the years. I realize something with a sharp pang: This will be the last time for the foreseeable future that my sisters do my hair.

As they work, I think of my mother, too. The memory of her visit to my bedchamber two weeks earlier now has the haze of a dream around its edges, but I still recall the look on her face, what she said about Athena.

She killed gleefully, brutally, without mercy.

I've tried to push those words out of my mind, but they've remained snared in my consciousness. I am grateful to be pulled from my thoughts as Euryale circles me and tips my chin upward to look at her. Somehow, she manages to look at me without meeting my eyes.

Forgive me, I silently pray. *Please forgive me, one day.*

"You're ready." She holds up a bronze-rimmed looking glass, and I peer into it.

The girl staring back at me looks like me, but older and more mature. I let my fingers comb through my locs and relish their feel, their sweet aroma. For perhaps the first time in my life, I feel truly beautiful, and it's all because of my sisters. My throat tightens, and I find I can't speak.

"One more thing." Stheno withdraws something from her own tunic's pocket and offers it to me. It is a necklace made of a single white seashell looped through a plain leather cord.

"For you," she says, "so that you don't forget home."

I recognize the gift as a parting one, and suddenly I'm struck by the great and terrible irony of this moment. All my life, my greatest fear has been that my sisters would leave me behind. Now I'm the one leaving them.

"Thank you." The words are choked.

"Oh, don't make a fuss." Stheno rolls her eyes half-heartedly. She blinks quickly, but I don't miss the tear she hastily wipes away.

"We'll miss you," Euryale says. As always, she is gentler. I meet my sister's gaze and see a storm of emotions there. I know she is still angry with me—perhaps a part of her always will be—but I also see tenderness. I remember the story she told me, about when I almost drowned at the beach when we were small. I realize she likely sees me the same way I see her: as someone to be cherished and protected. She pulls me into a hug, and I am surprised to feel Stheno's arms wrap around us, too. I stand there for a few seconds, trying to memorize this moment. As quickly as it started, it's over, and then my sisters are stepping back from me.

It's time.

I FIND THEO in the gardens.

I'd known that I would—the gardens have always been our place—but I'm still relieved to see him sitting on the lawn, whittling away at a piece of wood with a small blade. He's focused as he works, still as a statue except for his hands, and with a pang, I realize it's going to be a long while before I get to see him again. He looks up when he hears my footsteps, and when his eyes land on me, they light up.

"Is it too much?" At once, I'm embarrassed. "Eury picked out the tunic, and I told Stheno not to make my hair too—"

"You look beautiful, Meddy."

They're simple, earnest words, but at once, I'm calm again. Theo has always had that effect on me. He stands and crosses the lawn, so that we're face-to-face.

"How do you feel?" he asks.

"I'm nervous."

"Don't be," he says. His words are kind but firm. "You're going to do well in Athens. I'm sure of it."

"I hope so."

Saying goodbye to my sisters was hard; somehow, saying goodbye to Theo is even harder. I feel the same knife-sharp pain, but in a different place. All our lives, Theo and I have nurtured the same dream. We have spent hours fantasizing about what it might be like to leave this island. We always promised each other that when we did, we'd go together. I'm breaking that promise now. Theo is yet another person I'm leaving behind.

"I wish you could come," I whisper. "You deserve to."

"I'll be all right." His smile never wavers. "Just bring me back some new maps and scrolls, if you see any."

I pull him into a fierce hug, and his arms tighten around me. I try to memorize everything about this moment: the tickle of Theo's curly hair, the way he smells like my mother's gardens.

"I'll miss you, Meddy," he whispers.

"I'll miss you, too."

"Medusa."

We break apart, and I find my father standing a few feet away. He gives Theo only a cursory glance before his gaze locks on me.

"Come," he orders.

Theo gives me one last wave as I walk toward my father. I look over my shoulder, trying to preserve that picture of him standing among the flowers, until I'm forced to look away. Then he's gone, too.

I follow my father away from our palace and down to the island's shoreline. I've been given no information about how I'll be traveling to Athens, and if my father knows, he offers nothing as we amble carefully along the line where the shore yields to the sea.

"Athena is among the most powerful of the Olympians," he says finally, without preamble. "To have garnered her attention and favor is no small feat."

I realize detachedly that that praise should mean something to me, but it doesn't. There was a time, years ago, when I desperately wanted my father's approval. There was a time when this morsel of it would have elated me. But I now know my father better. I understand that it is not me who brings him joy, but the new opportunity I have presented him. I am, I understand, nothing more than another avenue by which he can politick for power and clout among the Olympians.

"You have done well," he says.

"Thank you, Father."

"When you arrive in Athens, you must always remember that you represent more than yourself," he continues. "You represent our family, our kin, and our court."

I know he means himself, my mother, and all the gods and goddesses of the Sea Court. He means my blue-haired aunt Eurybia and my quiet but kind uncle Thaumas. He means harpoon-eyed Amphitrite and her Nereid sisters. I'm old enough to understand that we are all part of a court that is considered lesser by other gods and that my small elevation is, in some ways, an elevation of us all.

Under that weight, I stand straighter.

"I understand, Father. I will represent the Sea Court well." I want to sound confident and strong, but all I can manage is a whisper. "I promise."

His eyes crinkle, and I see the hint of a rare smile, a real smile. Its warmth disarms me, and I try to turn away from it. I want to categorically hate my father. I want to hate him for the way he treats my mother, not just that night two weeks ago, but so many nights before. I want to hate him for the way he uses my sisters and me, like disposable game pieces on his board of ambition. I want to hate him, but I can't quite manage it.

"Mortals are strange creatures." My father adds the point as an after-thought, and I find myself wondering with some humor if he remembers that *I* am mortal. "They are fickle beings, easily frightened." He gives me a serious look. "You are not to tell anyone in Athens that you are the child of gods. Nor are you to tell them where you are from."

I nod. In truth, I've already expected this. "Yes, Father."

"I'll leave you now," he says brusquely, eyes cast toward the sky. "He will be here soon to retrieve you."

"He?"

In answer, my father squeezes my shoulder, then turns on his heel and heads back up the beach. Suddenly, I am alone. My eyes fall to the sea. It is still, for the most part, but I think I see an undercurrent brewing be-neath the surface. Perhaps that is my mother's doing, a kind of quiet send-off of her own. In the end, she didn't come to say goodbye. I look over my shoulder, hoping against hope that she might still appear at the last moment. Something in me wilts a little with disappointment when she does not.

I don't know exactly when I feel it, the press of eyes on my back, but the longer I stand on the beach alone, the more keenly I'm aware of it. I turn slowly, squinting into the thick tangle of vines and trees that make up the island's small jungle. A pair of large golden eyes meets mine.

Ah, so that's where you went.

I keep my eyes on the lion, but the fear I felt the first time I saw it doesn't come. I'm respectfully wary of the creature, but it's far enough away for me to feel safe.

You should be able to have your fill of food now, I think. *As long as you don't mind gulls and fish.*

The lion stares at me for a few moments longer before disappearing deeper into the bush. I turn my gaze to the sky. My father said that a *he* would take me to Athens, but as I pan the surrounding sea, I see no ship anywhere on the horizon. I study the clouds, cotton-thick and still, and wonder if my escort has been delayed, or if he is playing some sort of cruel game.

That's when I see them.

At first, it is only two tiny winks of golden light, brief enough for me to dismiss them as gulls. When they appear a second time, though, brighter, my eyes narrow until I make out something peculiar. It looks like a man striding toward me in midair. He is indistinct at first, but as he draws closer, his silhouette sharpens. The god approaching me is undoubtedly an Olympian. His skin is pale, but still beautifully illuminated with the subtlest glow in the sunlight. He grins, revealing a set of gleaming white teeth.

"Daughter of Phorcys."

I retreat as the god descends from the sky with all the ease of a person walking down a flight of invisible stairs. Now I know where the winks of gold came from. Tiny iridescent wings attached to his ankles flutter like two frantic hummingbirds. He comes to a stop on the sand, and I give him a quick once-over. The god standing before me has wavy, golden-brown hair and a constellation of brown freckles dusting his face and wiry body. He regards me with a decidedly haughty expression.

"They did say you were plain-looking," he notes. "I see they weren't wrong."

I do not know what disarms me more: the comment or its brashness. *I see they weren't wrong.* Who are *they*?

"You know me." I take a step forward. "But I do not know *you*."

The unnamed god grins again, and it strikes me how deceitfully young he looks, almost boyish.

"I have many names," he says genially. "I have been called the Luckbringer, the Traveler . . ."

My mind connects the pieces. "You're Hermes, the messenger god."

Hermes tuts. "That is both my most apt and least imaginative name." He inclines his head. "My sister has asked me to escort you to Athens this morning."

I blink, remembering. "Athena is your sister."

"A *half* sister," Hermes corrects, "and arguably one of the more well-tempered ones."

Confused, I look from him to the clouds he has come down from. "You have no chariot?"

Hermes pouts, feigning hurt. "You wound me. My brother Apollo drives a chariot," he says. "I am afraid my preferred method of travel is less conventional." He extends a hand, and suddenly I understand his intentions.

"You mean for us to *fly* to Athens?"

"I do," says Hermes. He is bouncing on his heels, and there is no mistaking it now: I see a streak of pure mischief in the god's pea-green eyes. "Do you trust me?"

I know at once that I do not. My knowledge of Hermes, like every other Olympian I have read or heard about, is mostly informed by Sea Court gossip. I know he has a reputation for deceit, that his other monikers—the Prince of Thieves and the Trickster God—are well earned. Trusting him would be foolish.

Hermes's hand is still extended, and I see the silent question in that look.

How badly do you want this?

All my life, I have dreamed of leaving my island. I always thought that, if given the chance to see the greater world, I would not walk so much as *run* to it. Now the moment has come, but my feet feel as though they have been rooted to the ground. Some part of me understands that whatever I do next will change my life forever. I take a deep breath in, steadying myself.

"Very well." I square my shoulders. "To Athens, then." *To adventure. To freedom. To a new start.* Those are the hopes I cling to as Hermes clasps my hand, as, together, we soar up and into the clouds.

PART II

MAIDEN

X

I AM NOT sure what I expect to feel as Hermes ascends, holding me by the arm with all the ease of a child carrying a straw doll, so that we are side-by-side. In a matter of seconds, though, I become absolutely certain of one thing.

I am not a creature made for flying.

Below, I watch an expanse of blue-green waves—thousands of nautical miles—fly past us with nauseating speed. Only once do I look over my shoulder in time to see the tiny white speck that is my island getting smaller and smaller in our wake. The air grows chill and damp as we rise past the first stratus of clouds, despite the golden sunlight on our backs. We are moving at such a speed that breathing is difficult; my eyes burn as the wind tears past, but I cannot bear to close them. At first, I think to ask the messenger god to slow down, or at least to lower us to warmer air. In the end, I decide it's better to keep my mouth firmly shut, lest I swallow a bug.

From his slightly raised vantage point, Hermes smirks, as though he can hear my thoughts.

"We are almost there, Daughter of Phorcys." His voice should be difficult to hear over the roar of the wind, and yet I hear him clearly, as though he were whispering directly into my ear. "Athens is up ahead."

Meddy, I want to say, *my name is Meddy*. I never get the chance to correct him. I look ahead, and my breath catches.

The crashing tides below have suddenly given way to an expanse of golden grass peppered by viridescent olive trees. Beyond them lies a sprawling walled city. My vision blurs as I take in a thousand red-clay rooftops, a twining maze of brown dirt roads, and then . . . *people.*

There are people packed in everywhere, appearing in all manner of shapes, sizes, colors, and garb. I have never seen so many people at once, people moving about like ants emerging from a hill. Hermes's pace doesn't slow, but as we soar across the city, I catch snatches of life— a marketplace packed with stalls and vendors, a pair of well-dressed, clean-shaven men walking side by side in stern conversation. As quickly as I spot them, they're gone, but I find myself craving more of all of it, more of Athens. My stomach swoops as we suddenly plunge, and I hold on to Hermes tighter. The god, for his part, seems unfazed as the ground rises to meet us. I am grateful when my feet find solid land again, and Hermes chuckles when I let go of him and stumble. Once I've regained my footing, I take in my new surroundings.

We are standing at the base of a stony gray hill. At its peak, I make out a collection of white marble buildings set high above the rest of the city. I feel an innate power emanating from them, a foreboding that makes my heart thump wildly in my chest.

"The Acropolis," Hermes explains. "Up there, you'll find my sister's temple, and her priestesses. This is where I leave you, Daughter of Phorcys." He offers me a small smile that I find is not unkind. Then, without another word, he leaps into the air and disappears in the clouds again.

By the time I reach the Acropolis, I am trembling in earnest. It turns out summer in Athens is just as hot as summer on my island, but the city seems to draw out an even stickier kind of humidity. Already the front of my tunic is dampened; the muscles in my calves are throbbing. But my steps still slow as I behold the buildings before me. Against a deep blue sky, the Acropolis complex stands gleaming high on a flat grassy lawn. My eyes take in its white Pentelic marble, the intricate frieze that runs the length of one building's perimeter. A carved stone pediment has been neatly fitted into another building's triangular roof.

I have only ever seen buildings like these in my scrolls, and even then they were rough, lifeless sketches. With each step closer, I find myself reminded of the power I felt practically radiating from Athena's person when she visited my island.

Farther down the lawn, I see a line of girls standing shoulder to shoulder with their backs to me. A quick head count tells me there are nine of them. Before the girls stands a stern-faced woman who looks to be in her sixties. She is olive-skinned and wears her dark, gray-streaked hair in a severe-looking bun low on her neck.

"Excuse me," I say in Greek, stepping forward. "I'm here for—"

"You're late!" the older woman says curtly. "See that it doesn't happen again."

I quickly join the line of girls, choosing to stand at the end. The woman's eyes stay on me a beat longer before she speaks again.

"I am called Eupraxia," she says. "I serve our Goddess as her high priestess." Her eyes move among us. "If you are here, you've been chosen to serve as an acolyte to this temple, which means you will be given the opportunity to undergo the prerequisite tests required of those who wish to serve the Goddess as priestesses. It is a great honor to be chosen, and my job while you are here is to ensure that each of you conducts herself in a way that befits that honor, starting with your appearance. The first thing you'll need to do is change into clothes appropriate for your station. All acolytes are expected to wear a plain white chiton." She holds up what looks to be a large square of folded linen. "You will be issued only two each, and you will be responsible for keeping them clean. Additionally, you are expected to remain modest." She eyes my locs, then nods at the golden cuffs in them. "*Those* will need to be removed."

Several of the girls in line lean forward slightly to eye me as the skin on the back of my neck prickles with embarrassment. My sisters spent the better part of an hour just this morning meticulously placing each one of those cuffs onto my locs. I'm now grateful that the shell necklace Stheno gave me is tucked behind my tunic's neckline and out of sight.

"Yes."

She arches a brow.

"Yes, *what?*"

I stare at her a moment before I realize what she's waiting for me to say. "Yes, High Priestess."

"You will change in the acolytes' quarters and then report back here for further assignment," Eupraxia says. "Be quick."

The acolytes' quarters, as it turns out, are on the eastern side of the Acropolis complex. They consist of a bare room that is mostly unfurnished save for ten rolled-up sleeping pallets and a few wooden benches along the walls, where some of the girls sit as we shed our old clothes in favor of the uniform white chitons we've all been issued. I sit at one of the benches alone and begin the work of gently pulling each of the golden cuffs from my locs. It takes far less time to remove them than it took to put them into my hair, which makes parting with them feel all the worse. When I'm finished, I stare at the small pile of cuffs beside me and feel as though I am saying goodbye to my sisters all over again. Eventually, I force myself to look away from them.

This morning, I woke in my own bed, back on my island, my home. It's hard to believe so much has changed in the course of mere hours. In truth, the change is jarring. I survey the room, taking subtle note of each acolyte. Most of them are fair- or olive-skinned, and I feel some of their eyes on me when they think I'm not looking their way. I stand to lift my gray tunic over my head, and I immediately hear giggles. When I slip on my chiton and turn back around, several of the other acolytes are now staring at me. One in particular steps forward, looking intrigued. She is fair-skinned and short, with springy blond hair, a pert nose, and rosy cheeks. Objectively, she's pretty, but there's something in the way she's looking me over—*examining* me—that puts me on edge. She draws closer, then tilts her head.

"What's your name?" she asks.

I answer automatically. "Meddy."

"'Meddy,'" she repeats. "That's an interesting name."

I'm not sure what to say in answer to that.

"We were wondering . . ." She gestures to the other acolytes as though she speaks for all of them. "Is your hair real, or is it a wig?"

I pause, confused. I've never been asked a question like that before. It seems so ludicrous that at first I wonder if she's asked it in jest. I self-consciously roll one of my locs between my forefinger and thumb. "It's mine," I say quietly. "It's my hair." I make a point of tugging on the loc just slightly, so that she can see it's attached to my scalp.

"Oh." The blond girl now appears fascinated. There's nothing particularly malicious in her expression, but the way she's looking at me reminds me of the way one might inspect an exotic species of bird. She stares at me a moment longer before she speaks again.

". . . Could I touch it?"

I start. "Excuse me?"

She doesn't wait, and I jump again when she closes the gap between us, plucks a single loc of my hair, and holds it up. "It's so *fuzzy,*" she says, delighted. "Not nearly as heavy as it looks!"

I feel as though I'm being pulled in two opposing directions. I know this girl is an acolyte like me. We may very well end up serving as priestesses together in this temple, and I don't want to start things off with her on the wrong foot. Beneath my chiton, I feel against my skin the light press of the shell necklace Stheno gave me. I think of what she would say if she were here.

You are not a pet, her imaginary voice reminds me. *Do not allow her to treat you like one.*

The blond girl grabs another one of my locs, but this time she tugs it, so I'm forced to step even closer to her. There's a brief pain in my scalp, and it takes a moment for me to realize what all this reminds me of. At once, I'm back in that bedchamber with Maheer. I remember the way he grabbed my locs without asking, the way he'd looked at me like I was something to be devoured.

Like I was a thing, not a person.

I knock the blond girl's hand away and step back.

"Please don't touch my hair." My voice is soft, but the room is small enough that the words carry. Several of the watching acolytes shift, visibly uncomfortable, but I keep my eyes trained on the blond girl. She's now looking at me with both surprise and confusion, as though she can't quite believe what's happened. I have the vague notion that she is not often refused, if ever. For a second, her hand remains half raised from where I knocked it away. Then the surprise gives way, and her features twist. She suddenly looks as though she's tasted something sour.

"It's just as well." Her voice is still syrupy sweet, but there's a new undertone. "I wouldn't want to touch a metic's hair anyway."

I rack my brain, trying to place that word. *Metic.* I know it is shorthand for the Greek word "metoikos," another word for a foreigner. It isn't an inherently bad word, but the way the girl spat it makes me bristle. She steps toward me, sniffs the air, then makes a show of holding her nose. Some of the other acolytes laugh.

"You *smell,*" she declares. "Do they even bathe where you come from?"

Tears prick my eyes. This morning, Stheno and Euryale had lathered my skin with shea butter and oiled my locs with rose oil. I had thought I smelled good.

"First, they come into our city and take our homes and food," the blond girl continues, turning to the other girls. "Now even our holiest places aren't safe from foreigners. Next they'll want to be citizens."

There is muttering among the other acolytes, and I note that some of them are eyeing me with new hostility. It is as though some invisible partition were forming, separating me from the rest of them. I swallow, trying to find words to stop it, but the blond girl goes on.

"I don't know what the high priestess was thinking, inviting *you* to be an acolyte," she says, inspecting me. "Were it me, I'd never let you so much as set foot in the—"

"I'd choose my next words carefully, if I were you."

Several heads—including mine—turn to the back of the room. I'm surprised to find that the voice belongs to one of the acolytes. She is tall, with dark curly hair and the slightly golden-brown skin of someone who's spent ample time under sunshine. Her eyes are light, though I can't quite discern their color in the room's dim. I notice something else about her. It's the way she stands, with her shoulders back and her chin slightly raised. I realize, with a start, that her confidence reminds me a little of Athena.

The blond girl seems less impressed. "*You* agree with this, Apollonia?" She sounds offended. "You think foreigners should be allowed to serve in the temple?"

The brunette—the one the blond had called Apollonia—shrugs. "*I* heard that the high priestess selected her because she received a divine vision, from the Goddess herself."

The room's atmosphere changes almost instantly. Several of the acolytes who've just been frowning now regard me with renewed interest, while the blond girl's eyes widen. I remember what Athena told me on the island. She said she would organize my transportation to Athens and speak to her high priestess about my arrival. Perhaps this vision is what she meant.

"The high priestess wouldn't have had a vision about *her*," the blond says dismissively. "She's just a—"

"The high priestess has had other visions," Apollonia interjects. I notice she's speaking slightly louder. "She has never been wrong. To openly question a vision's validity . . ." She pauses. "One might consider that blasphemy; others might even consider it grounds for an acolyte to be *dismissed*."

The acolytes who've been standing near the blond girl move away, as though she's been contaminated.

"No." The blond girl pales. "No, that's not what I said. That's not—"

"I won't tell the high priestess." Apollonia's tone remains light, though I detect a slight teasing in it. "But only if you go, now."

The blond girl says nothing else as she quickly changes into her chiton and leaves the room. The rest of the acolytes follow suit, all careful not to make eye contact with me. When only Apollonia and I remain, I turn to her.

"Thank you. You didn't have to do that."

Apollonia waves a hand. "Kallisto is a bully. Everyone knows it."

"You know her?"

"Sure," says Apollonia. "Most of us know each other. Acolytes are usually selected from the city's aristocratic families. We've all grown up together."

"Oh." I think again of that imagined partition I felt before, the one that had made it seem like I was somehow inherently separate from the rest of the acolytes.

As if she can read my thoughts, Apollonia changes the subject. "Your Greek is quite good," she notes.

"Thank you."

"But you're not Greek?" The question isn't unkind, and I hear earnest curiosity in it. Up close, I now see that her eyes are an indeterminable color that falls between green and hazel. There's an intensity to her gaze, one that makes me feel I have her full and undivided attention, and would have it for as long as I spoke. That stare reminds me of Athena, too. It takes me a moment to find my words.

"N-no," I answer. "I'm not Greek."

"Where are you from?" she asks.

I consider, uncertain. I've never given any thought to my island's name, I've never had to before. In the back of my mind, my father's instructions echo.

You are not to tell anyone in Athens that you are the child of gods. Nor are you to tell them where you are from.

Apollonia is still looking at me expectantly.

"I'm from an island," I begin. "It's . . . far from here. You would not have heard of it." That, at least, is a partial truth.

For a second, I think Apollonia is going to press me for more. I'm relieved when she merely nods. "I thought you might be Egyptian, or Aithiopian." She looks thoughtful for a moment. "The truth is I overheard Eupraxia talking about you with the other priestesses before the rest of the girls arrived earlier." She looks at me with real intrigue. "Is it really true you received an invitation from the Goddess herself?"

"Yes." I swallow, nervous. "Athena . . . came to my island."

"You've *seen* her." Apollonia's eyes widen. "What was she like?"

As soon as I've spoken, I realize I've made a mistake. I have spent my entire life around gods; seeing Athena was surprising, but it was not the ethereal experience I know Apollonia is probably imagining. I have to remind myself that mortals like her—like all the acolytes, probably—don't think of gods as the flawed beings I know they are, but as truly divine beings, worthy of worship and reverence.

I choose my next words more carefully. "She was . . . like nothing and no one else I've ever known," I say in a small voice.

Apollonia nods sagely. "Your parents must be so proud of you."

I think of my father's severe face and nod.

"Don't listen to anything Kallisto says," Apollonia continues. "If the high priestess had a vision that says you should be here, then you deserve to be here just as much as anyone else, Greek or not."

The words are simple but kind. I feel myself warming again. "Thank you." Something suddenly crosses my mind. "You said that most of the other acolytes already knew each other," I note, "but how were you selected? Did the high priestess come to your home?"

To my surprise, Apollonia looks distinctly embarrassed. "That might have been the case for the others," she says carefully. "But the women of my family have served terms at the Temple of Athena for the last two hundred years. It's a bit of a tradition for us. When I came of age, my father simply informed the high priestess."

I blink as her words sink in. I'd learned about Athena's temple only two weeks prior. In contrast, Apollonia's family has served it for two centuries.

My face must betray my anxiety, because Apollonia's brow furrows with concern. "What's wrong?"

I hesitate, unsure of how to say what I'm thinking. "The other acolytes didn't give you any trouble because it's obvious you belong here." I gesture in the direction they went. "But what Kallisto said, the way she and the others looked at me . . . I don't know that I'll be treated that way or ever feel like I belong."

Apollonia's face takes on an expression of calm determination that reminds me of Stheno. She puts a hand on my shoulder. "If the Goddess invited you to be here, you belong here," she says. "Never mind what people like Kallisto say. They try to make you feel like you don't belong because you intimidate them."

I frown. "I do?"

Apollonia nods.

"But . . . why?"

"You're not Greek like the rest of us," she says. "You're different, which sets you apart." She holds my gaze. "Here, that's an advantage. *Use it.*"

I let her words sink in. If these tests are truly a competition, perhaps sticking out *could* be useful. When I look to her again, I find myself smiling.

"Thank you."

Apollonia smiles back, then nods. "We should go. They're probably waiting for us."

My first day at the Acropolis is spent shadowing its various priestesses. Among other things, I learn quickly that no one in the temple is *merely* a priestess—alongside the expected religious duties, everyone here contributes to the maintenance and welfare of not only the Acropolis, but also the people of Athens. Some of the priestesses work as weavers; others clean and cook. There are even priestesses whose work is so secretive that it is shared only among a select few. It is all a great deal to absorb alongside the newness of Athens itself, and by the time the sun sets, my mind feels like a goblet filled to the brim.

Our dinner that night is modest, an assortment of fresh vegetables, plates of cheese, and bowls of porridge. I have enough time to register a small pang when I think of the lavish meals I'm used to at home, but just as quickly, I'm distracted. Eupraxia has entered the room, and at once, all the acolytes rise. It's impossible to be certain, but the look in the high priestess's dark eyes seems almost conspiratorial.

"Come with me," she orders.

Several of the acolytes exchange looks, but we all obey. Eupraxia leads us out of the courtyard and to the very edge of the Acropolis.

Though the sun has already dipped below the horizon, a few of its lingering rays still cast the city in rose-gold light. There's a slight rustle to my right, and when I turn, I find that all the temple's priestesses have gathered. Acolytes wear plain white chitons, but the ones the priestesses don are sleeved, and dyed a blue that reminds me of an ocean's depths. Each one of them is holding a lit candle, and though no one has instructed us, not a single one of the acolytes says a word as we are shepherded into a tight line shoulder to shoulder while the priestesses form a circle around us. For several seconds, there is only the sound of distant cicadas and brushing leaves.

Then Eupraxia begins to hum.

I'm at once taken by the low, dulcet timbre, by the way her hums reverberate through my entire body. One by one, the other priestesses join her in unison, adding to and harmonizing with that melody. Several of them bow their heads, and many close their eyes. A part of me wonders if I should do the same, but the new, tangible current of energy in the air stops me. It makes the hair on my arms and neck stand on end. I sneak a glance at Apollonia, standing to my left in our small half circle. Her head is bowed, but she looks back at me, and I know from her expression that she feels it, too. This sensation is entirely new to me. I want to dance, or sing, or cry out in jubilation, but I am compelled by some invisible force to remain still. Eventually, the priestesses stop humming. In my peripheral vision, I detect new movement.

A small figure has broken away from the priestesses' circle. I'm surprised to see that it's not an older woman but a little girl, no older than six or seven. Her fair face is still pudgy and soft, but the solemnity in her expression belongs to a woman ten times her age. Earlier in the day, I heard brief mention of the arrephoroi—the youngest priestesses of the temple, who serve only two years—but actually seeing one, this child, is more intimidating than I imagined. On her thin arm she wears a leather gauntlet, and perched on that gauntlet is a large white owl. The other priestesses bow their heads lower in reverence as the arrephoros passes them. Then, as if on silent cue, they all raise their candles and begin to hum again, louder this time. The owl on the little priestess's arm soars into the air, and at once, each of the candles' flames turns blue. I hear gasps from the other acolytes as the flames burn brighter than should be possible, vivid like glowing sapphires. Then, as quickly as it starts, it's over. The candles extinguish themselves in unison, and we are left in the dark. The owl swoops down to land on the arrephoros's covered arm again, and each of the priestesses bows to it before leaving the Acropolis's lawn. Once the last priestess is gone, Eupraxia gestures for us to follow her. She does not speak until we are all back inside the acolytes' quarters.

"You have just witnessed a mere glimpse of our Goddess's power," she says. "As you begin your service to this temple, remember it, cherish it. There are many girls in this city and beyond who would take your place. As acolytes, you are to hold yourselves to an unimpeachable moral standard. You are to be rigorous, humble, chaste, and disciplined—anything less will result in your immediate dismissal. You are also instructed to stay within the bounds of the Acropolis at all times, unless you are given explicit permission to leave." She juts her chin, as though daring someone to challenge her. No one does, and she goes on. "As you all know by now, to become a priestess of this temple, you must undergo tests. Only those who pass all of them will enter priestesshood."

"When will we find out what the tests are?" asks Kallisto.

"I'm not at liberty to tell you," says Eupraxia. "But I would advise you all to get a good night's sleep and be prepared to rise early on the morrow." Her eyes flash. "At sunrise, we will see exactly what you are made of."

She leaves us after that, but her words echo in my mind long after she's gone. One by one, the acolytes turn in to their bed pallets, and eventually the sole oil lamp illuminating the room is extinguished.

I know I should be trying to fall asleep, but even in the dark, my mind is racing. For the first time in all my life, I am not ending the day on my island or in my bed. A quiet thrill arrows through me, and it's all I can do not to kick my legs like a child under my blanket. I think now of all the scrolls I've read, the maps Theo and I have spent hours poring over. For years, we only guessed and dreamed about the world beyond our island, but in a single day, every one of those guesses has been supplanted by a far greater reality. I can still hear the echo of the priestesses' hummed song; the remnants of the sensation that came with it still tingle on my skin. It all felt so different from the dullness of home. I realize, for the first time, that I feel truly alive.

I cling to that feeling as my eyes close and I fall into a peaceful, dreamless sleep.

I wake at dawn the next morning, my heart pounding like a drum.

For several seconds, I have no grasp of where I am or how I've gotten here. Then the pieces fall into place.

I am in the sleeping quarters allotted for the acolytes of Athena's temple.

Acolyte. That's what I am now.

A horn's brassy blare tears through the quiet, jolting me upright. My eyes adjust, and through the pale gray light of a small window, I make out Apollonia's silhouette beside me. She's already risen from a modest pallet identical to my own and is slipping into her chiton. I follow suit.

Around us, the other eight acolytes are waking, too, blinking and yawning in the dark. Once we're all dressed, we make our way to the temple's main atrium. Eupraxia is there waiting for us.

On her right stands another middle-aged priestess; on her left, there is a table with several inkpots, styli, and what appear to be neat stacks of parchment paper on display. I note that there is also a small black urn on the table.

"Good morning, Acolytes." Eupraxia's tone is light and oddly friendlier than it was yesterday, which puts me on edge. "The time has come for you to begin the first test. It will evaluate your intellect, your wit, and most chiefly your wisdom." Eupraxia's gaze sweeps over us. "You'll be solving a riddle today, predetermined by our Goddess." From the folds of her chiton, she produces a golden hourglass filled with white sand. "Once I turn this over, you will have until the last grain of sand falls to submit your answer. Anyone who fails to submit an answer or who submits the incorrect answer will not proceed to the next test."

A nervous ripple moves through the acolytes.

"You'll each be given one of these styli, one inkpot, and one small piece of parchment on which to write your answer to the riddle along with your name," Eupraxia continues. "Once it is written, you will place your answer in this urn. You may not share or discuss your answer, and to ensure this, one final precaution will be taken before you begin." She regards the other priestess, who reaches behind the table and produces a clay pitcher and a brass-colored goblet. As she pours from the pitcher, I see a silvery liquid stream out of it.

"What is that?" asks one of the acolytes.

"Tacetaqua," says Eupraxia. "A potion crafted by the god Apollo himself. Once consumed, it will render you completely silent until we provide you with its antidote."

At the mention of Apollo's name, the air itself seems to crackle. Next to me, Apollonia shudders involuntarily, and goosebumps stipple the bare skin on my arms. The drink is a reminder that we are consorting with very real and very powerful gods. The nameless temple priestess standing next to Eupraxia finishes pouring the tacetaqua into the goblet, then holds it up like an offering to us. No one moves.

"Who will be the first to drink?" asks Eupraxia.

I look around and find that every acolyte is eyeing the goblet with uncertainty. Apollonia had said just a day before that I had the advantage of standing apart in this group. For the first time since arriving in Athens, I decide to stand apart on purpose.

My feet are moving before I've truly registered my decision. I feel the other girls' eyes on me as I approach the second priestess. I take the goblet from her and peer into the cup. I've never seen tacetaqua before. It's silvery and slick. I bring the goblet to my lips and sip. The moment the drink touches my tongue, the inner walls of my mouth numb and my throat prickles. I try to clear it, but there is no sound. My voice is entirely gone.

"Next," says the priestess.

I hand the goblet to Apollonia—who has followed me—then watch as, one by one, the other eight acolytes take the tacetaqua. When we're finished, we face Eupraxia again.

The light of sunrise is beginning to creep in through the atrium's windows, and a single ray of sunlight winks against the hourglass she holds aloft. Our unnatural silence thickens the air.

"The riddle is as follows," she says. "'Men may give and take me, yet I consume them all. Who am I?'" She turns the hourglass over and places it on the table. Then she and the other priestess leave the atrium, their footsteps echoing on the stone. A door shuts in the distance, and my eyes shoot back to the hourglass.

The first test has begun.

XI

SEVERAL OF THE acolytes remain frozen, staring at the place where the priestesses have gone as though half expecting them to return. I move away from the group to settle in a corner of the atrium where I can collect my thoughts without distraction. There, I turn the riddle's words over in my mind.

Men may give and take me, yet I consume them all. Who am I?

I've solved riddles before; it was a pastime I enjoyed with Theo on many afternoons back home. I think of what he would say if he were here. *Riddles are one of two things,* he once told me. *Words to be untangled or puzzles to be solved.* I calm a little. I don't know the answer to this riddle yet, but that doesn't mean I can't solve it.

I pick apart the riddle's words in my mind, rearranging their order. I am barely conscious of the other acolytes around me anymore. My eyes bore into the stone floor before me as brighter and brighter morning light continues to filter in through the windows.

Men may give and take me.

There are plenty of things that men give and take all the time—food, money, land—but those all seem too practical, too literal, too easy. I change tack and think more metaphorically.

Men may give and take me.

There are other things, less tangible things, that men can give and take. I go over some of the possibilities quickly. Joy. Sorrow. Love. Hate. All of those answers are plausible, but none of them feels right. It takes me a moment to understand why. Athena is not a goddess of joy, sorrow, love, or hate—she is a goddess of wisdom, intellect, and knowledge. A chord within me hums. *Knowledge.* That feels closer to the right answer. Men can give knowledge, and they can take it away, too. Then I remember the second part of the riddle: *Yet I consume them all.* Could knowledge truly consume?

I dip my stylus into its inkpot, my hand hovering over the bit of parchment I've been given to write my answer on. Knowledge is the best answer I've come up with. It feels credible, yet . . . something stops me from writing it down. I can't entirely quiet the tiny voice in the back of my mind, the one that worries I am wrong. Anxiety pulses through me, and my hand trembles so violently that a fat drop of ink falls from the stylus and blots the parchment.

The sudden sharp chirp of a nearby bird breaks my focus, and for the first time, my gaze cuts across the atrium to the hourglass Eupraxia placed on the table. It is far away, but not so far that I can't see that half of its sand is already in its lower chamber, with more and more slipping through by the second.

A movement in my peripheral vision catches my attention, and I'm surprised to see Kallisto making her way to the urn. I'm not the only one who watches as she drops her parchment into it with a look of intermingled triumph and relief. Disappointment twists in my side like a blade. *I* wanted to be the first to answer the riddle. My morale dips again when a second acolyte drops her parchment into the urn, followed by a third, fourth, and fifth girl. Half the acolytes have now submitted their answers. I stare at my parchment again, willing it to reveal a clue, anything that can help me.

Men may give and take me, yet I consume them all. Who am I?

Joy.

Sorrow.

Love.

Hate.

Knowledge.

Hubris.

Life.

Death.

Every one of these answers is plausible; every one of them feels off to me. I swallow, fighting the urge to vomit, then look at the hourglass yet again. More sand has poured into the bottom chamber, impossibly fast, too fast. I begin to sweat. If I submit the wrong answer, I'll fail the test, but if I don't submit *any* answer, being wrong or right won't matter. I clench my jaw. I need to be sure, and to be sure, I need one more clue, a hint, I need—

I suck in a sharp breath. It is as though I've been struck by lightning, so suddenly does the revelation come to me. I have the answer to the riddle; now I'm sure of it. *Of course.* It's so simple that I'm almost angry at myself for not having seen it immediately. I scrawl a single word onto my scrap of parchment, then add my name and stand, striding confidently toward the urn. I can see Kallisto watching me, but when I drop my parchment into the urn, I do so without regret or doubt. The hourglass's sand still trickles from its top chamber to its bottom one, but I am no longer afraid of it. Relief crashes over me in waves. I turn from the table and, for the first time, really look around the atrium.

The five acolytes who've already submitted their answers are sitting together in a cluster, unable to speak to one another but clearly reveling in their success. Three more are scattered throughout the room, and I realize that one of them is Apollonia. She's drawn her knees up to her chest, and tears slick her face. She is staring at her parchment with a wild, hopeless expression. Suddenly, she looks up at me. There is pleading in her eyes. I open my mouth to say something comforting, but of course there's no sound.

A loud scrape of wood against stone interrupts the silence. I turn and see a door on the other side of the atrium opening. Eupraxia and the other priestess have returned. Neither of them speaks, but I know why they are here. The sand in the hourglass is almost gone. If Apollonia doesn't submit an answer—the *right* answer—in the next few minutes, she won't advance. I imagine what Stheno would say if she were here: Apollonia is my competitor in this space, not my friend. I shouldn't feel bad for her. But then I remember yesterday, when she stood up for me even though she didn't know me. She protected me even though she'd had no real reason to.

I make up my mind.

I'm still standing in the middle of the atrium, but I turn around, praying that my idea—harebrained though it is—works. By now, Eupraxia and the other priestess are standing at the table again. I stop before them and point at the urn.

"Have you submitted your answer, girl?" Eupraxia asks.

I nod, then point to the urn again urgently.

Eupraxia shakes her head. "Once you've submitted your answer, you cannot change it." Her tone is surprisingly gentle.

I know that, of course. I just hope Apollonia is still watching me. I turn from the table and pretend to slip, knocking my body into it. The hourglass wobbles precariously, and I reach out, careful to let my fingers brush against it as I use the table to steady myself. In an instant, Eupraxia has come around the table and grabbed my forearm. The gentleness in her expression is gone, replaced with irritation.

"Mind your feet, girl!"

I offer a low bow of apology and make a show of walking away from the table quickly. My back is to Eupraxia now, so she doesn't see the glance I sneak at Apollonia.

Apollonia, for her part, has watched the whole exchange. She frowns at me, and I deliberately look from the hourglass to her. I see the moment understanding dawns on her face; her mouth falls open in a silent O. She is tactful enough to wait several seconds before she scrawls something onto her own parchment, then runs to the urn to submit her answer.

She's barely turned from it when Eupraxia raises a hand. "The first test has now ended," she announces. Her hawklike gaze sweeps over us. "'Men may give and take me, yet I consume them all. Who am I?' I am *time*."

I still can't speak, but I exhale. The temple's hall felt stifling before; now I feel the lightest brush of a morning breeze on the back of my neck, cooling me.

"The following acolytes submitted the correct answer: Kallisto,

Amersa, Medusa, Galene, Xanthe, and . . . Apollonia. To those of you who guessed correctly: Congratulations," says Eupraxia. "You will advance to the next test. To those who did not submit an answer or who guessed incorrectly: You will not proceed. Once you have taken the tacetaqua's antidote, you may gather your things and leave the temple."

Four of the acolytes bury their faces in their hands, and I feel a pang. Then I find Apollonia's eyes. We still can't speak, but the bright smile on her face matches mine. I breathe relief. We've both made it.

The second priestess—the one who gave us the tacetaqua before— now comes to each of us with a new goblet. When she reaches me, I notice that the antidote looks just like water. I drink eagerly, relieved when I clear my throat and hear my own voice again. The atrium begins to fill with the sounds of other acolytes finding their voices; there are hums, breathy gasps of laughter, and occasional sobs from the four who have not been successful in solving the riddle. It occurs to me that, in a mere hour's time, our number has already dwindled down to six. Eupraxia claps her hands, and we fall silent again.

"Those of you who were successful may now eat breakfast in your quarters," she says.

No one needs to be told twice. The anxiety that racked me during the first test is gone, and hunger replaced it almost instantly. My stomach growls, and mine isn't the only one. I almost weep when we return to the acolytes' sleeping quarters and find a generous spread of food at its center—plates of fruit, cheese, and flatbread piled high. No sooner have I filled my bowl and sat down than Apollonia joins me.

"You helped me." She speaks so that no one but I can hear. "You helped me, even though you didn't have to."

I'm about to bite into an apple, but I stop. "And you helped me yesterday," I whisper. "So we're even."

Apollonia shakes her head. "That's not the same, not even close." She cocks her head. "Why did you do it?"

I consider the question for a moment. Part of the reason I wanted to help Apollonia was because she had defended me the day before, but I know there is more to it than that. I think of my mother, of the way she is always in constant competition with the other goddesses of the Sea

Court. I realize I don't want to be like her, threatened by other powerful women. "I want to become a priestess," I say, "but I want *you* to become one, too. I see no reason we can't both pass these tests, together."

Apollonia meets my gaze and holds it. "Together, then," she says. "We'll do this together." She squeezes my hand. It is brief, but I feel its warmth and cherish it. We eat the rest of our breakfast in silence, together.

XII

I EXPECT US to have our second test the following day. The high priestess, however, has other plans.

For the next several days, the other acolytes and I are delegated a series of menial chores around the temple. We are sent to a nearby grove to harvest produce from the olive trees, tasked with laundering the tunics of the older priestesses, and expected to ensure the temple's oil lamps remain filled throughout the day. At times, it is admittedly rather dull work.

"We shouldn't be doing this," Kallisto mutters one day while we're all scrubbing the floors of one of the temple's courtyards. "This is *slave* work, unbefitting of a priestess acolyte."

Though I'd never admit it aloud, the truth is I secretly agree with Kallisto, at least in part. When Athena invited me to serve as an acolyte at her temple, she seemed impressed by my intelligence, by my self-taught education. I hoped—even expected—that I would get to apply some of that education here at the temple. This kind of menial labor requires no education at all. I still want to be in Athens, I still want to be here at the Acropolis, but I realize with some sadness that the initial spark of excitement I had upon my arrival doesn't burn quite as strongly as it did before. Not for the first time, I find myself wondering about the goddess and whether I'll see her at all while I'm in Athens.

. . .

Almost a week after we arrive, Eupraxia assigns me and Apollonia to
clean the Acropolis's small barn. It is by far the least beautiful building
in the complex—hot, loud, and thick with the stink of livestock and
refuse—but I find the work tolerable alongside Apollonia. Our shared
work gives us more time to get to know each other.

"Do you have any siblings?" I ask as we muck hay side by side.

Apollonia nods. "Three older brothers—Lycus, Agathocles, and Menan-
dros. They'll all be senators someday, like my father."

I chuckle. "How convenient, that they all want to be the same thing."

Apollonia smiles, but it doesn't quite reach her eyes. "It's not so much
about what they want, it's what my father wants." She pauses. "He always
gets what he wants."

It's my turn to offer a sad smile. I remember all too well what my own
father said to me before I left home. *When you arrive in Athens, you must
always remember that you represent more than yourself. You represent our family,
our kin, and our court.*

I understand what Apollonia feels, more acutely than she realizes,
and it frustrates me that I can't tell her about my parents, about the
world I come from. I think of my mother and the scheming gods of
the Sea Court, of the Olympians and the complicated games so many
gods play to curry favor with them. In truth, I have no idea what Apollonia would make of it all. I pause, considering what I want to say to
her.

"The Goddess invited me to come here," I start. "I wanted to, but
even if I hadn't, I think my father would have forced me. He'd be . . .
disappointed if I didn't pass my tests."

Apollonia keeps mucking. "I think mine would cast me out," she says
lightly. "No woman from our family has ever failed them."

"What about your mother? Did she want you to do it?"

Apollonia's shrug is forced. "I wouldn't know," she says. "She died when
I was small. By all accounts, though, she was a much-beloved priestess,
too, before she met my father and married." Her expression briefly takes

on a faraway quality. "She went on to have three sons, then me before illness took her. She was a good, honorable Athenian woman."

When she first told me of her family's extensive legacy of service to the Temple of Athena, I was not only in awe of Apollonia; a part of me was even a little jealous. Now, though, I see the other side of the coin. As much as my father wants me to bring esteem to our family, I know that I am always allowed to go home. I wonder what it feels like for Apollonia, knowing that that isn't an option.

We continue our work in silence after that, both of us lost in our own thoughts. Eventually, I move to the back of the barn. At first, I think the last stall is empty, but then there's a flutter of wings, and I jump back. When my vision adjusts, two bright yellow eyes meet mine in the darkness. I realize it's the white owl from the ritual on the first night.

"His name is Glaukopis," Apollonia volunteers as she joins me. "The Goddess's emblem is an owl, so it is the tradition of the Acropolis's priestesses to always house one here, in her honor."

Apollonia returns to her work one stall over while I continue to study Glaukopis. He's a regal creature, notably larger than most common owls, and something in his piercing yellow gaze is curiously intelligent, almost human in its sharpness. I realize, in a strange way, that his gaze reminds me of Athena's. He's still watching me warily, so when I approach, I do it slowly, carefully.

"I'm not going to hurt you," I whisper. My eyes fly to the owl's black talons. They're curved, each as long as my index finger.

I'm not going to hurt you, but you could certainly hurt me if you wanted to.

I note the hay beneath the owl. It's littered with bird dung and what look like the tiny skeletons of some ill-fortuned vermin. I make a face, then look up at the owl.

"I won't be able to clean your area with you perched there," I tell him. I notice a gauntlet hanging on the wall and slide it over my left arm. Glaukopis is very alert now. I smile.

"Ah, now I have your attention." I have no experience with animals, but I trust my instinct as I hold up my covered arm and wait. To my delight, Glaukopis instantly swoops down to perch on it.

"That's not so bad," I croon. My shoulder has already begun to ache from the angle at which I'm holding my arm up, but I dare not lower it. Vaguely, I remember the slaves back on my island, the ones who once called my large eyes "owlish." Now I can't help but think it's a compliment. Glaukopis's golden eyes are luminescent in the barn's dim, impossible to look away from. There's a strange power in them that reminds me of the ritual on our first night at the temple, the way I felt as the priestesses held their candles aloft in unison.

"I can't say I've met many owls," I tell him softly. "But you, my friend, might be the most handsome yet."

"Talking to a *bird,* metic?"

I jump. I didn't hear Kallisto enter the barn. Since our first encounter, I've been careful to avoid her unless absolutely necessary. A few feet away, Apollonia turns as she notices Kallisto, too, then tenses as she stops before me. The triumphant smile on her face promises nothing good. I decide not to answer her, but Kallisto goes on.

"It doesn't matter how many chitons you wear, you know," she says to me snidely. "You'll *never* be an Athenian, and you'll never belong here."

Her words sting, but I remind myself of what Apollonia said that first day. *Never mind what people like Kallisto say. They try to make you feel like you don't belong because you intimidate them.*

I stand straighter. "You're right," I say gently. "I'll never be an Athenian. But at least I earned my spot here on my own."

Kallisto's eyes narrow to slits. "*What* did you say?"

I jut my chin, doing my best to mimic Stheno's haughtiness. "*I* was invited to serve at this temple because of my merit, not because my father made a generous donation."

Kallisto turns crimson, and I know I've hit my mark. Among other things Apollonia has explained to me in my first days at the temple, I've learned that there are some aristocratic Athenian families who politick to have their daughters serve as temple priestesses. Some of them pay a fortune for the privilege; others do any number of unsavory things to secure a spot.

"Meddy *does* belong here." Apollonia has stepped forward. "She passed the first test, same as you." She nods to Glaukopis. "Even the Goddess's sacred bird has taken to her."

Kallisto's eyes slide to the owl, and she frowns. "That doesn't mean anything," she says. She grabs another gauntlet hanging off one of the barn doors and slips it on, then holds her arm out.

"Glaukopis, here," she orders imperiously.

The bird looks at her and only blinks.

"Here!" she commands, holding her arm higher. "Come to me!"

Seconds pass, then a whole minute.

Apollonia smirks. "I don't think he likes you," she remarks, barely containing the amusement in her voice. "Maybe he's a good judge of character."

Kallisto gives me a withering look before she pulls the gauntlet off and throws it to the ground. "It doesn't matter," she spits, "he's just a stupid bird."

I know immediately that she's made a mistake. Glaukopis's head snaps in her direction, his yellow eyes flashing. Through the gauntlet, I feel his talons' grip on my arm tighten, and I know what's about to happen.

"Kallisto," I warn. "Look—"

Glaukopis launches himself from my arm in a flurry of white feathers and charges directly at Kallisto. The girl's eyes go wide, and she shrieks as the owl swoops above her, his talons inches from her face. She begins to run around the barn, screaming, while Apollonia and I watch in horror as Glaukopis flies up to the barn's highest rafters. Kallisto's howls grow louder.

"Kallisto!" Apollonia hisses. "Stop making all that noise—you're frightening him!"

But then Glaukopis swoops down again, and Kallisto's screams only grow more frantic. It should be funny, watching her run around the barn with the owl chasing her, but it's not. I have the feeling that something bad is about to happen.

"Glaukopis!" Apollonia seems to be trying to regain control. She's put on the gauntlet Kallisto abandoned and is holding her own arm up. "Glaukopis, here!"

Glaukopis stops chasing Kallisto for a moment and lands on a perch near Apollonia. Then Kallisto takes her chance and dashes out the barn door. Glaukopis's eyes whip back to her. My heart plummets.

Don't do it. Please don't do it.

The owl takes one more look at us, then launches itself from the perch and out of the barn.

"No!" I feel something in my chest plummet. Apollonia and I run out the open door, but it's to no avail. Already, I can see Glaukopis's white body growing smaller as he soars down and into the city of Athens. I turn around quickly, worried that someone else has seen, but to my immense relief, the surrounding lawns are empty.

"Where did Kallisto go?" Apollonia asks.

"Probably somewhere to hide," I say bitterly. There's a small consolation in knowing that she won't be in a hurry to tell anyone what's happened. I turn to Apollonia. "What do we do?"

"We tell Eupraxia," says Apollonia firmly. "We'll tell her what Kallisto did. She'll be punished instead of us."

I shake my head. "If what you said about Kallisto's family making a generous donation to the temple is true, I don't know that she'll be punished at all." *And that still won't bring Glaukopis back,* I think privately. That seems a far bigger problem. I think of the ritual from our first night at the temple, of the young priestess who brought Glaukopis forward. I'm not sure what the temple will do without its emblem. I'm not sure I want to find out.

Now Apollonia looks to be on the verge of tears. "I don't know what else we can do."

We both still have gauntlets on our arms. An idea comes to me.

"We could get him back," I say quickly. "If we go down into the city with food for him, we could try to lure him to us. Owls are nocturnal, he'll be disoriented in the daytime. He can't have wandered far, and he's bound to land somewhere down there."

Apollonia looks uncertain. "I'm not sure that's a good idea, Meddy."

I stare at her. "Why?"

"It's . . ." She seems to be struggling with something. "We're not supposed to leave the Acropolis. Eupraxia said so, remember?"

"Surely if we're acting within our duties as acolytes—"

"It's not just that," she goes on. "Women aren't supposed to be in the city unattended. It's . . . frowned upon. We may get in trouble."

I look in the direction I last saw Glaukopis fly. I remember the way the priestesses of the temple gazed at him during the ritual, and what Apollonia said before. The bird is more than just a temple pet; he is the living symbol of the goddess we are all meant to serve.

I make up my mind. "We'll get in more trouble if something happens to him," I reason. "Come on, let's go."

I'D THOUGHT THAT I understood the scope of Athens when Hermes and I first flew over it days before. As Apollonia and I make our way through its streets, I realize just how wrong I've been.

I peek out from under the transparent white veil I've donned. Beside me, Apollonia is wearing one, too, both of us hoping to obscure our faces. My heart pounds as we trek farther into the city's bustling crowds. The people I saw from the sky are suddenly very real, close enough to touch. Some of them do touch me as they pass, knocking into me and jostling me left and right, but it doesn't upset me; I relish it. We pass fishermen, butchers, potters, and other artisans. Eventually, we reach a grass courtyard teeming with even more people.

"This is the Agora," Apollonia explains. "It's the city's main marketplace."

I stare in wonder. The Agora is crammed with stalls arranged side by side. I try, and fail, to take everything in. All my life, my knowledge of the world beyond my island came in fragments—from trinkets washed up on its shores without context, or from half-remembered stories from those forced to serve my parents. Through them, I thought I had gleaned an understanding of mortal practices. Now I see there is so much I don't know. The stalls I pass are crammed with ripe fruits and vegetables I've never seen before and desperately want to taste; people shout across the courtyard in tongues I've never heard, pointing and gesturing to the goods they want. There's something else I also notice: The people of Athens don't all look the same. In fact, they come in a wide variety of shapes, sizes, and colors. We pass a group of tall, muscular men with skin far darker than mine and thick woolly hair that reminds me of Theo's; seconds later, I see a woman with milk-pale skin and a sheet of straight, glossy blond hair that stops at her knees. The gods who visited our island may have had different skin tones, too, but I've never seen so much variation in one place all at once.

"Stay close," Apollonia warns. "It's easy to get lost here."

I do my best to keep in step with her as we move with the flow of the foot traffic, but my eyes continue to wander. One heavyset man sitting on a stool is holding up beaded leather sandals and shouting; another skinnier one farther down is surrounded by carved statuettes of the Olympians. I read the tiny inscriptions carved into each one and laugh to myself as I identify Hermes, Dionysus, and Hera before thinking of how much Theo would enjoy all this. I'm so distracted that I don't notice the oxcart barreling our way until it's almost upon us.

"Meddy!" Apollonia reaches out to grab my hand, but it's too late. The crowd parts as the cart cuts right through it. Apollonia is pulled left, while the crowd carries me to the right. Once the cart has passed, I look for Apollonia, but she's gone.

No. I try to stem my panic. I don't know the first thing about navigating Athens on my own. Everything around me seems to be in constant motion, making it impossible for me even to get my bearings. I lift my veil and rotate in place once, then a second time. The third time, tears well in my eyes. I think, with dread, of what might happen if I don't return to the Acropolis by nightfall . . .

I crane my neck, searching desperately, but someone knocks into me and sends me flying back. Instinctively, I reach out, looking for anything that might break my fall, and grasp the edge of a stall filled with figs. In seconds, I've steadied myself, but the same can't be said for several of the figs. I watch with dread as at least three on the edge roll right off the stall and disappear under the crowd's pounding feet. When I look up, the stall's owner, a sun-browned, dark-haired woman, is glaring at me.

"You'll pay for every one of them!" She's already coming around the stall. "That was good produce!"

"I-I'm sorry," I say in my best Greek.

"Two drachmae!" She holds her hand out, expectant.

New anxiety courses through me. I've forgotten about this particular mortal practice. Here, people pay for goods with whatever currency is used in their own land. I think of my small collection of foreign coins back home and suddenly wish I'd had the foresight to bring them. The older woman's eyes turn to slits as she examines me. It's clear I'm carrying nothing on my person but the owl gauntlet. I start to back away, but she snatches my bare upper arm and holds tight. My veil slips, exposing my face.

"You little rat," she seethes. "You give me my money!"

I struggle against her. "I'm sorry, I don't have any—"

"I'll send for the magistrate!" The woman's voice grows shriller. Around us, people are beginning to stare. "Don't think I won't! You know the punishment for theft in this city? *The whip.*"

My mouth goes dry. I am afraid of being flogged, but I am more afraid of what will happen if I am jailed and fail to return to the temple. Will I be dismissed from service? My heart begins to pound, blood roars in my ears.

"Magistrate!" the old woman shouts, shaking me. "Someone call the magistrate! This girl's a thief, she—"

"Excuse me," says a new voice. "But that won't be necessary."

The old woman and I both look up in surprise. A boy has materialized out of the bustling crowd. He looks to be my age, tall, lanky, and tanned. He also looks entirely unruffled by the disturbance we've caused. Before the peddler woman can speak, he holds up a small leather coin purse.

"This should cover the price of the figs," he says in a low voice, dropping it into her hand. "Plus a little more for your trouble."

The woman's free hand closes around the purse instantly. I don't know much about Athenian currency, but I suspect the amount inside it is far more than two drachmae. She stares from the purse to the young man, speechless.

"I . . . ?"

The young man pries her fingers from my arm. "Have a good day," he says, tactfully pulling me out of her reach. The woman mutters something unintelligible before turning back to her remaining figs. Gradually, the surrounding vendors return to selling their wares, too. The young man jerks his head left, and I follow him down the road. Once we've reached a slightly less busy area, we both slow.

"Thank you," I say.

The boy waves me off. "It was nothing."

"It *wasn't* nothing," I press. "You helped me, and you don't even know me."

"I know you're wearing a veil." He nods to my head. "My guess is you work at the temple. Are you a priestess?"

"Acolyte," I correct, looking away. "I'm in training, though probably not for much longer."

The boy's brow furrows. "Why?"

"I've lost something, something important." Even as I say the words aloud, a little more hope leaves me. "I came into the city to try to find it."

"Perhaps I can help," he says. "What have you lost?"

"An owl."

The boy blinks. "An *owl*?"

"It belongs to the temple," I add quickly. "It's a special bird."

The boy is still staring at me, though now he looks as though I'm a puzzle he's trying to solve. "You came down from the Acropolis . . . to find a single owl?" There's no missing the incredulity in his expression. "Do you have any idea how large this city is?"

"I had to try," I say defensively. "I had to do *something*."

That seems to have an effect on him, because his face softens. "A girl who won't be thwarted," he says. "That's very admirable."

My cheeks warm. It's impossible not to notice that the boy is handsome. He has traces of stubble on his chin, but his tousled dark hair gives him a youthfulness. His lean build and deeply tanned skin suggest a life spent in the sun, likely doing some sort of physical labor. I have enough time to wonder if he might be a shepherd or a fisherman before he asks his next question.

"This owl . . ." he says slowly. "What does it look like?"

"It's large and white," I reply. "Hard to miss."

For a moment, he looks distant, as though searching his mind for something. He blinks, then seems to remember I'm there. "There's a small thicket not far from here. If your owl flew down from the Acropolis, I imagine it might go there. The city would be noisy for a nocturnal bird."

This revives my hope. "Would you tell me where to find it?"

A smile returns to the boy's face. "I can do better; I'll take you to it."

I start to thank him again, then stop. "You'd do that for me? Why?"

The boy gives me a mock-serious look. "You're a servant of the gods," he says. "Helping you can only improve my fortune."

I'm not sure if he's right about that, but his answer makes me laugh.

"Come on." He gestures, heading up a new path, away from the city. "Let's find your owl."

The boy leads me from the bustling streets of the Agora to a quieter, more residential part of Athens. I know I should be solely focused on getting Glaukopis back, but my eyes wander as I try to take in everything I'm seeing. On the stoops of some homes, old men crouch together with boards and dice, and I gather that they are playing some sort of game. It's a simple enough thing, but I'm still fascinated. We pass a curious-looking structure: What looks like a large mud-brick bowl is affixed to the ground and set between two pillars. I watch as a young woman plunges a bucket attached to a rope into the bowl and slowly pulls it back up. When she does, I'm surprised to find it now filled with water. My mouth parts, and a chuckle escapes the boy.

"You look as though you've never seen a well before," he teases.

"I . . ."

"Come on," he says, "the thicket's not much farther."

It is one thing to fly over a city as large as Athens; it is another entirely to walk it. By the time we reach the cluster of trees the boy indicated, my feet have begun to ache slightly. My gaze lifts. The cypresses here are far larger than the ones in my mother's gardens; they seem wilder, too. I search them a moment, holding my breath, then cry out with joy when I notice a small white tuft high up among the dark leaves.

"Glaukopis!" I slip on the gauntlet I've brought and hold it up. The owl is far beyond my reach, in the boughs of a tree, and I hold my arm out, praying he notices. A second passes in which I feel his piercing yellow gaze on me, assessing. Then, to my relief, he swoops right down and lands gracefully on my arm. I think to pat his head, then reconsider when he clicks his sharp beak.

"You gave me a fright," I say softly, slightly lifting my arm. Glaukopis looks past me, and I realize he's looking at the boy, who has moved a few steps back.

"Curious," he says, eyeing the bird. If I'm not mistaken, I detect a slight wryness in his tone. "I've never seen a domesticated owl."

"He's special," I say with new fondness. Glaukopis preens. "You know, you can come closer, if you'd like."

"That's all right." There's no mistaking it. The boy is definitely eyeing the owl with wariness. A laugh escapes me, unbidden, and I turn to face him.

"Thank you for helping me find him. I'm sorry I don't have any way to repay you."

"Say a prayer for me." The boy grins and tips his head. "That is repayment enough."

"I can do that."

He offers a wave before heading down a different street. I wave back until he's out of sight.

Only when he's gone do I realize I never learned his name.

I'M RELIEVED TO find Apollonia just before I reach the Acropolis. Her brow is sweaty from the afternoon sun, and her normally neat hair is slightly mussed beneath her veil; she spent our time apart searching closer to the Agora. More than anything, she seems impressed that I managed to find Glaukopis safe and sound. For some reason, I stop short of telling her about the boy who helped me.

By the time we've deposited Glaukopis safely back into his stall in the barn, my shoulder and biceps ache from the effort of holding him, but I can't bring myself to be unhappy about it. Apollonia returns to the acolytes' quarters to wash her spare chiton before supper. I decide, instead, to visit the Acropolis's small garden. I've been to it only once, and in truth, it pales in comparison to my mother's gardens back on our island, but there's still a calm here I appreciate after the day I've had. I find a bench and settle onto it, breathing deep.

"I hope you enjoyed your time in my city, Acolyte."

I turn and find myself staring directly into the gray eyes of Athena.

XIII

FOR A FEW seconds, I don't move.

It has been several weeks since I last saw the goddess, on my island, but no amount of elapsed time could have prepared me for how glorious she is standing in the afternoon light. Today, she wears a deep green peplos; her red hair falls loose around her shoulders.

I rise, elated. "Athena!" I exclaim. "I'm so glad to see you. I've been—"

"You were told not to leave the Acropolis without permission." The goddess's tone is cool. "Yet you did it anyway."

I stiffen. Athena isn't smiling at me, and there's no trace of the warmth I saw back on my island, when she first invited me to be an acolyte. I have the uncomfortable sensation of missing a step on the stairs.

"Athena, I—"

"Here in my temple, your role is a deferential one." Her tone cools even more. "*You* are to address me as Goddess."

The words smart, but I know she is right. My most basic job as an acolyte—and hopefully, someday, as a priestess—is to represent and serve the interests of Athena. She is not just another Olympian to me anymore; here, I am in service to her, and to Athens.

"Apologies, Goddess." I bow low, an act of respect Eupraxia has taught us to give to more senior priestesses when they enter a room within the Acropolis. When I straighten, Athena is still watching me.

"As I said, you left the Acropolis without permission."

"I went into the city to get Glaukopis back," I say quickly. "He was accidentally let out of the barn and—"

"A good excuse is still an excuse." Athena doesn't raise her voice, but she doesn't have to. The severity in her words hangs in the air between us. "You've been at this temple for barely a week, and already you defy its authorities and flout its rules." She arches a brow. "Perhaps you think that because you are the daughter of two gods, those rules are beneath you?"

"No, Goddess." My voice is small as I drop my gaze. "I don't think that at all."

She stays silent for so long that I look up to find her still studying me.

"If you're curious," she says, "I'm currently debating whether I should share with my high priestess what you've done."

"No, please!" I fall to my knees, unable to keep the crack from my voice. "Please, don't make me go back home. I . . . I offer my humblest and most sincere apologies."

Athena's frown deepens. "You truly do not wish to return to your island."

"No, Goddess. I like it here."

She nods. "Then take heed when I say this, Medusa: Your presence here in my temple is a privilege, not a right. Don't ever forget that."

"No, Goddess." I bow my head again for good measure. "I will not."

"Good," she says, and at once her tone is much lighter. "Now you may rise."

I get to my feet unsure. Just moments ago, Athena sounded so cold and distant; now a smile touches her face. I feel as though I've just passed some test I didn't know I was taking.

Athena settles on the very bench I've just been sitting on while gazing out into greater Athens.

"Sit with me," she commands.

I obey at once, taking care to leave enough space on the bench for us not to touch, in case that is perceived as another slight. Athena lets the silence between us stretch a while longer before she gives me a wry look.

"Now that you've gotten a firsthand look at Athens," she says, "how do you find it?"

"I love everything about it." My answer is immediate. "Athens is nothing like my island. It's big and noisy and full of people doing things all the time . . ." I search for words. "My favorite thing is the movement."

"The movement?" Athena repeats.

"Something's always moving in Athens; it's never still," I explain. "Back home, nothing ever changed—the views, the smells, the food. Everything was always the same, but *here* . . . the opposite is true. I'm convinced you could go down one Athenian street in the morning and see it one way, then by afternoon it would be completely different."

"The other acolytes are Athenian-born," she says. "This city is all they know, so they cannot appreciate what makes it special." She smiles at me. "I suspect that you *can*."

I nod.

"You've had some time to adjust to your role as an acolyte," Athena goes on. "How do you find the work?"

I'm slower to answer this time, and the goddess notices.

"If I was mistaken and you are unhappy . . . ?"

"It isn't that," I say quickly. "It's just . . . if I may speak freely?"

"You may."

"I am honored to serve." I stare at my hands. "It's just that, I don't feel particularly useful here. The work I've done so far has been . . ." I struggle to find a word that isn't offensive.

Athena throws her head back and laughs. It's a warm, melodious sound. I find myself thinking that I could listen to it forever. "Your work is dull," she finally says, and I'm relieved the words don't come from me. "That is by design. It is meant to teach you discipline, patience, and above all else humility. Those are traits I deeply value in my priestesses."

At once, I feel foolish. This makes sense. I duck my head, ashamed. "My apologies, Goddess."

"Hold your head up, Medusa."

I look up and find that Athena's expression has hardened, but not with anger. "I did not invite you to be an acolyte because you are meek of spirit," she says. "I invited you because I saw a girl with unrealized potential—intelligence, selflessness, and a natural instinct toward justice. In short, I saw part of myself in you."

The compliment floors me, and for a moment I don't know what to say. "Thank you, Goddess," I manage.

"Have you ever given thought to what your life's purpose might be, Medusa?"

I frown. "I wish to serve as a priestess, if I pass my tests."

Athena shakes her head. "That is your occupation. What I want to know is what drives you, what is it that brings you a sense of fulfillment?"

I pause. For as long as I can remember, I have been told my purpose was to marry and have children, just as my mother did. The only thing I have ever truly wanted—to leave my island and see the world beyond it—has now happened. I've never had to think about a bigger purpose to my life. The idea daunts me.

"I'm afraid I don't know what my purpose is, Goddess." Even as I say that, I feel like I've failed a different test. "I wouldn't even know where to start."

I'd expected Athena to be disappointed by my answer. Instead, she smiles. "I am quite sure we will find purpose for you soon enough," she says warmly. "Provided you continue to do your work well and pass your remaining two tests, I am sure of that."

The words give me something else I've felt only a few times in my life: hope.

"Thank you again, Goddess."

She stands, and I instinctively rise, too.

"That will be all," she says.

I recognize the dismissal, but don't mind. I offer Athena a final deep bow before leaving the garden.

I feel her eyes on my back well after I have left her sight.

THAT NIGHT AT dinner, I discover I have made new friends.

Though Eupraxia and the temple's other priestesses remain thankfully oblivious, it seems word of my adventure with Glaukopis has spread among the acolytes. I have a strong suspicion that Apollonia is responsible for this, though when I ask, she feigns ignorance. As the other girls ask me questions—how I got Glaukopis back and how I managed to carry him all the way to the Acropolis—I gradually realize that my status as a foreigner has been forgotten. I may not ever be Athenian, but these girls now count me as one of them.

"You're braver than me," says a sandy-blond girl called Amersa. "Glaukopis scares me. I'd never be able to carry him on my arm like that."

"I don't know why you all are making such a fuss," a voice grumbles. "It's just a bird."

I turn to find Kallisto sitting in a corner of our quarters looking very much like a wet cat. I smile at her, smug. Kallisto can say nothing about the fact that she was in the barn, too, without outing herself as having run away from the bird. Apollonia told me that, apparently, Kallisto hid in a bush for nearly an hour until she was sure Glaukopis was gone.

I open my mouth, tempted to say as much, but we are interrupted as Eupraxia enters the room. She gives us all a severe look.

"We will walk to the Acropolis for our nightly meditation," she says. "Come."

We file along the edge of the Acropolis in silence.

Our meditations are a ritual of the temple that I am still learning. In this hour just after nightfall, we acolytes and priestesses are to spend time in silent reflection, considering our piety and how we might be of better service to Athena. I know that I should be thinking about all I have to learn, but the truth is I am utterly captivated by Athens at night. Loud and bustling during the day, it is a different city after sundown. A thousand glittering stars dust a deep blue sky; only a few flickering torches below give life to the city itself. I take a deep breath in, relishing the distant smell of cypresses. My island home is beautiful, but it's not like this. I think about what Athena said. *This* could be my home for the rest of my life. I feel a pang of sadness when I think of Theo. I wish he could be here to see these stars, too.

Eupraxia, who's leading our procession, nods. We are free to break from our line and find a place to settle for a few minutes before we go back in for the night. Some of the younger and more fervent priestesses fall to their knees and pray under their breath; the older, more seasoned priestesses, the ones who've been doing this for many decades, simply find a bench to sit down on, groaning as they relax tired joints and old knees. I sit on the grassy knoll and reflect on the day's events. I think of Glaukopis, with his piercing yellow stare; of the wood-carver in the Agora and how much Theo would have enjoyed the statuettes. I even find myself thinking of the boy who helped me find Glaukopis and of how kind he was.

Something small strikes me in the arm, and I lurch, startled. Next to me is a small, sharp rock that wasn't there before. I lift my gaze, searching the lawn, and trace an invisible line back to Kallisto. She's not looking at me, but she's studying her fingernails with slightly too much focus. I know, instinctively, that she's the one who threw it, just as I know she's taken care to make sure no one else saw. My eyes dance between her and the rock, and I clench my teeth.

In the end, I enjoyed my time in Athens, but that doesn't take away from the fact that it was Kallisto's actions that sent me into the city in the first place. I think back to Athena's stern words with me earlier. I nearly lost my opportunity to be an acolyte—to stay in Athens—because of Kallisto. I'm still staring when she looks up and meets my gaze. There's a taunting smile on her face. Her gaze drops briefly to the rock before she shrugs, then turns back around. I curl my hands into fists.

An old anger flints against my skin for the first time since my arrival in Athens. I haven't felt it since the night my father wrapped his hands around my mother's neck, but it's there now, hot and tingling, just beneath my skin. I stare at the back of Kallisto's blond head and imagine everything I *wish* I could do: hurl the rock back at her, or march right up to her and pull her hair the way she pulled mine the morning I arrived. Instead, I take a deep breath and force myself to calm.

Something rustles near my hand, pulling me from my thoughts. I start, then relax. It's only a harmless black garter snake with a yellow stripe running down its spine. I keep still as it slithers closer to me, then settles. I find that I'm not afraid of it at all. I've come across plenty of snakes in my mother's gardens. A thought occurs to me, sudden and vicious.

"Our time for meditation has concluded," Eupraxia announces. "Acolytes, you'll now return to your quarters."

There's only a half second to consider the potential consequences. I bat those thoughts away as I turn to make sure no one is looking, then nudge the garter snake into the pocket of my chiton before standing to join the other acolytes.

Our preparations for bed are uneventful.

We have now finished our fifth full day at the Acropolis, enough time for us to begin to fall into a kind of rhythm and routine. Our daily work is intensive enough that there's little chatter as we wash our faces and prepare for bed, and after Eupraxia comes into the quarters to do a final check and extinguish the oil lamps, it doesn't take long for the room to fill with the sound of soft snores. I lie in the dark staring up at the ceiling, waiting. Moments later, I hear a slight rustling in the bed pallet a few places over from me, a confused groan, then a shrill scream. In an instant other acolytes are yelling, running around the room in a panic. I rise slowly and move to stand against the wall. It takes only a second for Eupraxia to return to our room, eyes wide. She holds the oil lamp she is carrying high, and I see that the room is now in disarray. Several pallets have been trampled, and the acolytes are clustered together in the opposite corner. In the middle of the mess stands Kallisto. Her usually tidy blond hair is disheveled, and she's shaking.

"What is the meaning of this?" There is no tenderness from Eupraxia as she looks around at all of us. "What happened?"

At first no one speaks, but then Kallisto points. Her words are barely audible, but I hear "In my bed."

Eupraxia's nostrils flare. "Stop mumbling and speak plainly, child."

"There's a snake in my bed pallet!" Tears fill Kallisto's eyes. She begins to redden. "It tried to bite me."

Eupraxia gives Kallisto a wary look, then crosses the room to the place where the girl has pointed. She picks up a blanket, jumps, then groans. The high priestess glances over her shoulder, looking annoyed.

"Foolish girl," she snaps. "It's just a garter snake." She stomps down hard. There's a single hiss that's cut off abruptly, and I flinch. It was not my intention for the snake to be killed. Eupraxia picks the dead snake up by its tail, then eyes the room.

"To bed," she orders. "All of you."

Slowly, the acolytes shuffle back to their respective pallets. Only when we are all beneath blankets again does Eupraxia leave a second time, casting us back into dark. In the quiet, I hear someone sniffling. I'm almost sure it's Kallisto. I lie on my back and stare up at the ceiling as I listen to her toss and turn on her pallet. My stomach twists.

I expected to feel vindicated when I slipped the snake into Kallisto's bed pallet, like some score between us had been settled.

The truth is, the emotion I feel as my eyes close is very much like guilt.

WHEN I OPEN my eyes, my mother's gardens are cast in a strange, silver light.

It is the first indication that I have left the waking world and entered a different one. The sky above has darkened to a deep violet and is devoid of its usual stars.

I inhale unseasonably crisp night air and let my eyes wander. I am standing before an aged olive tree I've never seen before—it's thick, knotted, and ripe with fruit. My gaze traces along its boughs, then stops. A white owl is nestled within its dark green leaves, large and unassuming. Glaukopis. His round eyes wink in the night like golden coins, but what holds my attention is what is clutched in one of his talons. A garter snake hangs limp from it, dead.

"Why?" The word escapes me before I can stop it, and in my dream I do not question that I am speaking to an owl as though it can under-stand me. "Why did you kill it?"

Silence stretches between us as Glaukopis stares back at me, as I wait for an answer. Without warning, he opens his beak. A woman's voice, low and sonorous, fills the air. It's Athena's voice.

You are my greatest disappointment.

"What?" I frown at the owl. "What do you mean?"

Glaukopis does not answer my second question. Instead, he launches himself from his perch, dropping the dead snake at my feet before soaring up and into the night. I wait until he's gone before looking down.

The garter snake's mouth is slightly ajar in death; moonlight gleams off one of its white fangs. A profound, inexplicable grief fills me as I study it. I know the snake tried to bite Kallisto only because it was threatened, because that was the only way it could protect itself. My eyes travel to the lacerations near its neck. The creature has been nearly decapitated. In that moment, I cannot think of a worse way to die. I drop to my knees, letting my fingers hover just above the snake's bright black scales.

"I'm sorry," I murmur. "I'm so sorry."

I sit there, alone in the garden, for what feels like a century. I do not know when the uneasiness begins, when the sense that something is wrong skitters across my skin like a spider. I glance down at the ground, and the hairs on my arms stand on end.

The snake is alive, and it is not.

Its once-bright eyes are empty caverns as it raises its wounded head. It hisses, and dark blood spurts from its neck. I crawl backward on my hands and knees, but it is faster than me. The creature coils, then strikes at my arms, my face—

I shoot up in my bed pallet, a scream in my throat. For several seconds, in the dark, I don't know where I am. I hear the sound of the other aco-lytes' soft breathing and run my hand over my arms. The skin is smooth and unbitten.

It was just a dream, I tell myself. *It wasn't real.*

I tell myself that over and over until sleep finds me again.

XIV

WE HAVE BEEN at the temple for a full week when Eupraxia calls us into the main courtyard after lunch.

I have spent most of the morning watching some of the priestesses work on the sacred peplos to be presented at the upcoming festival of Panathenaia. As an acolyte, I am not allowed to touch the peplos, and watching the older women work is a dull pastime. My mind is foggy with fatigue as we make our way toward the courtyard, but I stop when I see what's within it.

The normally empty space now has several baskets in its center filled to the brim with reams of fabric, beads, and balls of yarn. A few of the acolytes murmur their appreciation, but a sense of dread begins to creep up my neck.

"The time has come for your second test," Eupraxia announces. "Our Goddess is one of superior intellect, but she is also a patron of craftwork. Her temples serve as sanctuaries for those gifted in such arts." She smiles. "For your second test, your own abilities in craftwork will be tested."

There it is, the source of my dread. The courtyard's temperature seems to plummet, despite its abundance of sunlight. I feel distinctly as though I've swallowed a sea urchin.

"You will have three hours to create some work of craft to honor our Goddess," Eupraxia goes on. "You may use any items found in this courtyard, but you must create and complete your work *entirely on your own* before the time is up. Your crafts will then be judged and voted upon. Those who receive a favorable vote will advance. Are there any questions?" When no one answers, Eupraxia nods. "You may begin."

We haven't been given tacetaqua this time, so the other acolytes begin to talk among themselves as soon as Eupraxia is gone. I barely register their voices as I stand in the middle of the courtyard, frozen. Several seconds pass before Apollonia glances over at me.

"Meddy, are you all right?"

I meet her gaze, but I can't actually make myself say the words in front of the others. Apollonia seems to understand and guides me to a far corner.

"What's wrong?" she whispers.

"I can't do it."

"Can't do what?"

The confusion on her face makes it so much worse. I have to force every syllable out through gritted teeth. "I can't *make* anything. I have no skill in craftwork."

Apollonia's expression turns sympathetic. "Did your mother never teach you embroidery, or weaving?"

"No." In truth, I doubt my mother even knew a craft to teach. "I don't know how to do anything—embroidery, weaving, pottery—nothing."

"There has to be something you can make with the supplies here," Apollonia argues. I note that she doesn't say what both of us are likely thinking: that it won't be enough to simply *make* something. If this is a test, I'll need to make something good, something to impress the temple's priestesses. Apollonia purses her lips thoughtfully.

"I was going to weave a basket," she says. "I could teach you, and we could—"

"*No.*" The word comes out more forcefully than I intend, but I don't care. "You heard what Eupraxia said. We have to do this entirely on our own." I glance at Kallisto across the courtyard. "I don't want to give anyone here a reason to think we've cheated."

Apollonia seems to be at war with herself. She gnaws at her bottom lip, and I see her hesitation, her pity. I also see a desire in her eyes that I recognize. I know in that moment that she wants to be a priestess just as badly as I do.

"It's all right," I insist. "Really."

Apollonia sighs. "Keep thinking. An idea will come to you."

I'm doubtful, but I settle by her side while she gathers her materials and begins to weave her basket. The terrace is bathed in brilliant gold; early afternoon sunlight casts a silhouette around Apollonia's frame. I note that she's pretty in that light, with her thick lashes downcast and her lips parted just slightly while she works. I watch her in awe.

"Where did you learn to basket-weave?" I ask before I can stop myself.

A wistful, faraway look passes over Apollonia's face. "One of our servants taught me, when I was seven or so. It's funny." She looks down at her work. "I don't really remember learning how to do it. It feels like something I've always known how to do, like an instinct."

I nod, understanding that. Of course, neither Stheno nor Euryale ever taught me something like basket weaving, but they taught me other things. I don't remember, for example, learning how to read and write, but I know it was Euryale who patiently went over my letters with me until I understood them. The memory is hazy, but I can just barely recall the first time Stheno took my hand in hers and placed it into my own locs, guiding my fingers and showing me how to wash them.

Be gentle and start at the roots, she explained. *Then work your way down. Moisturize them with castor oil and shea butter, to keep them healthy.*

Absently, I tug on one of my locs. I'm still rolling it between my forefinger and thumb when a thought renders me perfectly still. It comes crackling through my mind with an urgency so sudden, I draw in a sharp, involuntary breath.

Apollonia looks up. "Meddy?"

I don't answer her, I can't. An idea has taken root, and now it's sprouting so fast, I fear I will lose it if I don't move.

"Meddy!" Apollonia's voice is sharper. "Meddy, what's wrong?"

"I have an idea," I say, standing, "but I don't have much time."

I run to the supplies at the center of the courtyard. They've already been picked through, so my choices are limited, but I snatch as many beads as I can from the bottom of one of the baskets. My gaze pans the room quickly, searching, and I'm relieved to find a single oil lamp in the courtyard's corner. I snatch it. Eupraxia has said we can use any item in this room . . .

Some of the other acolytes watch me as I settle on the floor; Apollonia shoots me a concerned look. I ignore them all as I grab several of my locs, begin at my temple, and start to braid. I have no mirror, no idea what I look like, but I trust my instinct as I plunge my fingers into the lamp oil and keep working. Within minutes, my biceps are trembling with the fatigue of having to keep my arms raised; my fingertips ache as I twist and coil my locs. I try to ignore that, too. There is no hourglass to mark my time here, but I can still feel time slipping away from me. Every second counts. I can't stop.

I will do this, I tell myself through the pain. *I won't just pass this test. I will win it.*

When Eupraxia returns, there are four other senior priestesses with her. They give us all one sweeping look before they settle together on the ground. I look around. At least two of the acolytes—Galene and Xanthe—are holding crafts I know will not be acceptable. Galene's reed basket is half finished, while Xanthe's tunic might have been nice if not for its clumsy stitches. Kallisto is brandishing a small but undeniably beautiful piece of embroidery, and it looks like Amersa has made some type of beaded necklace. I don't miss the curious way Eupraxia glances at me.

"Your time is up," she announces. "If your craft is incomplete, you are dismissed."

Galene leaves the room at once, weeping.

Eupraxia looks at me expectantly, but I stay put.

"One by one, the remaining five of you will come forward and present your crafts," she continues. "You must receive a majority vote of favor from the five of us to advance."

Kallisto approaches the priestesses first, her head held high. In a matter of seconds, she receives a favorable vote and moves to sit in a spot on the floor Eupraxia indicates. Xanthe, the girl who sewed the clumsy tunic, goes next; almost as quickly as Kallisto, she receives an unfavorable vote and is dismissed. Amersa is luckier, and after a moment's deliberation, she is directed to sit next to Kallisto. When it is Apollonia's turn, I hold my breath, but the moment the priestesses see her basket, they collectively sigh in appreciation. It takes mere seconds for her to receive the third favorable vote. Eupraxia indicates a place on the floor for her to sit, too, then turns her attention to me.

"Come here, girl."

My entire body trembles as I step forward. Several of the priestesses look to my empty hands and frown. Eupraxia clears her throat.

"You were asked to create a work of craft," she says. "What do you offer?"

I steel myself, then say: "I offer myself."

If the priestesses looked confused before, they look absolutely bewildered now. Eupraxia's brows rise. *"Yourself?"*

Slowly, I turn so that my back is to her and the other priestesses. There is a gasp—from whom, I'm not sure—then a silence, sudden and total.

"You . . ."

I look over my shoulder, enough to see the expression on Eupraxia's face. Of course, I can't see exactly what she can, but I have an idea of it.

I've braided my locs down my scalp so that they form a crosshatched design that much resembles the interlocked pattern of a woven basket. Some of the inspiration came from Stheno's and Euryale's teachings, but most of it was informed by years of inadvertent practice. All the times I had to take down my own locs to wash them, all the times I helped my sisters braid their own, proved useful.

After a moment, I turn and reface Eupraxia. *"This* is my craft," I say to her and the rest of the room. "Hair braiding."

The high priestess's mouth opens and closes. For the first time since our initial encounter, she seems speechless.

"That can't be allowed!" Kallisto interjects. *"Hair braiding* isn't a real craft!"

Fear pulses through my body, but I'm careful not to show it. Instead, I stand tall and meet Eupraxia's gaze squarely. "I was tasked with creating something with my own hands. I have done that."

Eupraxia crosses her arms. "So you have." She cocks her head. "You did this just now, in the time allotted?"

"Yes, High Priestess."

Eupraxia frowns. "Do you not know any other craft, child?"

I shake my head.

"We will have to rectify that." She turns and addresses the room. "In all my years of conducting these tests, I've yet to see an acolyte choose hair braiding as their craft." She purses her lips. "It is an unusual choice, but impressive."

"But, High Priestess"—Kallisto is turning red—"surely it can't count as a *true* craft?"

Eupraxia arches her brows. "Quite the contrary," she says flatly. "Hair braiding is one of the oldest crafts, and not one easily learned or mastered. I would expect an acolyte to know as much, Kallisto."

Kallisto flushes even more deeply, but Eupraxia has already turned back to me.

"What you did was clever," she says matter-of-factly. "And well executed."

"Thank you, High Priestess."

Eupraxia nods. "That will be all, Acolytes. The four of you may return to your normal duties."

I stammer, unsure of what to say, but it doesn't matter. Without another word Eupraxia and the other senior priestesses rise and leave the courtyard. It's only when they're gone that I realize I'm grinning from ear to ear.

I have passed my second test.

XV

IT DOESN'T TAKE long for me to learn that, though the Acropolis is not an especially big place, there are endless jobs to attend to as an acolyte. The labor is long, often tedious, but as the days pass, I mind less and less. Back home, on my island, I'd never done physical work, or held any responsibility. Sometimes, I imagine what my mother and sisters would think if they saw me scrubbing floors or mucking out the barn. In time, I stop caring. The priestesses of the temple are, I discover, a sort of family. Eupraxia walks the temple's halls checking to make sure we are doing our work, but it's not uncommon for one of the older priestesses to sneak us a piece of honeyed bread when she isn't looking, or help us finish the last of our chores for the day so we can enjoy our supper together.

By the end of the second week, Eupraxia has decided we are ready for slightly more responsibility. She informs us that we will be venturing into the city to hand food out to those in need.

"I appreciate that while some of you are from Athens, others have never been permitted to go into Athens proper before," she says, nodding to a few of the acolytes, including me. "Be assured that, as servants of the temple, you have a different status from that of most of this city's women. Our roles here are recognized throughout the city, and well respected."

I do not tell Eupraxia that, in fact, I've already been to Athens proper. As we make our way down from the Acropolis and into the throngs of people, however, it all feels as new as it did on my first visit. Somehow, it seems even more vendors are out today. There's a frenzied energy in the streets that makes my heart pound faster and faster. By the time we reach our designated spot, there is already a queue of people waiting. Their eyes light up as they see us coming laden with baskets of bread, fruit, and grain.

"Form orderly lines," one of the older priestesses leading us instructs. She is calm, clearly well practiced in this. "Everyone will be fed."

While the people do as she commands, she arranges us acolytes so that each of us is in charge of one line of people. As we sort the food, my eyes flit to those waiting. Some are in rags, others have matted hair and unwashed skin. The other priestesses and acolytes seem unfazed. I think uncomfortably of how little of the world I experienced from my island home. What other things am I ignorant of? I'm torn from my thoughts as the first person in my line approaches. It's a little girl, no older than ten.

"Here you go." I hand her a sack filled with grain, and she hugs it to her chest.

"Thank you!" she squeaks. I've never had anyone look at me the way she is now. There is naked admiration on her face. She flashes a wide smile at me before dashing away. The next person in my line is an old man. He walks with a slight limp, and judging by the permanent grimace on his face, the effort is a painful one.

"For you," I say graciously, handing him a sack. "Be well, and may the Goddess watch over you."

The man takes the sack and offers a clumsy bow. There are tears in his eyes. "Bless you," he whispers. "Blessed are those who serve the Goddess. For she is as great as she is merciful."

I do not know why the words move me so, but I feel a pressure behind my eyes, a tightness in my throat. I've never felt like this before, this swell of new emotion. I realize that this is the first time I have truly felt fulfilled, purposeful.

"Be well," I whisper back.

. . .

The rest of the afternoon passes in a hot blur. Athens is a rich city, but I learn quickly that there are many in this city who don't see even a fraction of that wealth. By the end of our allotted two hours, we have nothing left.

"We'll come back next week," the lead priestess says, waving away a few stragglers.

The afternoon sun has drained even the strongest of us, and the lead priestess allows us to stop at a well for water before we make our way to the Acropolis in groups. Apollonia and I take our time walking back. In the late afternoon, the bustle of the streets has calmed a bit. I find myself still reflecting on the people we served.

"They really love her," I say as we amble along.

Apollonia looks up. "Who?"

"Ath—" I correct myself. "The Goddess. I knew she was admired in Athens, but . . ." I try to find the words. "It's more than that. She is truly revered."

Apollonia gives me a curious look. "Well, of course she is," she says. "This is her city."

"How did that happen?"

Apollonia stops walking and looks out to sea. "The legend holds that, many years ago, Athena and the sea god Poseidon both wanted to patronize this city, to claim it for their own. They could find no fair way to decide, so the king of the gods"—she lowers her voice—"Zeus, decided that it would be settled with a contest. Each god was to put on a display of sorts, and the people themselves would decide. According to the story, Poseidon struck his trident into the ground at the Acropolis, and a large fountain of water sprang up. The people of Athens were impressed, but when they tried to drink the water, it was too salty. Then Athena knelt and planted a seed into the ground. From it, a single olive tree grew. The people saw that the tree could provide lasting food and shelter, so they named her the victor." Apollonia smiles. "They even changed the city's name and built the temple on the Acropolis in her honor."

I am floored. I've heard many stories about Athena—some good and some not—but never this one. I look down at the city of Athens, trying to imagine what that kind of adoration must feel like. My mind turns to Poseidon, too. On my island, among the other members of the Sea Court, the sea king is painted only with reverence. It's strange to hear him in this context, as the loser.

"I wonder what it must be like to have that kind of love," I say aloud. "That kind of power, over so many."

Apollonia shrugs. "I've never cared much for power," she says. "It's enough for me to help people."

By now, the sun is setting in Athens. Street dogs pad along, looking for scraps.

"We should probably head back," Apollonia says.

We turn a corner, and I freeze.

I recognize the little girl I gave a sack of food to earlier in the day. She is hopping up and down, desperate, trying to get that very sack out of the hands of an older boy who's taken it. By my guess, he's around twelve, but tall for his age. He openly sneers at the little girl as she cries.

"Give it back!" she says. "It's mine!"

"Not anymore." The boy sneers. "Little *rats* don't get food."

Apollonia takes me by the elbow as though to steer me away, but I shrug her off. The anger comes suddenly. I feel it building within me like a storm, enormous and consuming. Images flit through my mind in rapid succession. I remember my mother throwing her goblet at Euryale; Maheer pinning me against a wall simply because he could. I imagine my father's cool indifference as he wrapped his hand around my mother's throat, and I envision the smug look on Kallisto's face when she threw a rock at me. I feel the anger I've tempered time after time bubble to the surface, hot and reckless. All my life, I have been unable to protect myself or anyone I cared about. I look at the little girl now and I remember every moment I was made to feel the way she does—helpless, unprotected.

Something in me snaps.

I see a brief fear touch the boy's face as I close the space between us and slap him as hard as I can. The force of the blow sends him reeling back, and my palm smarts in the place where it connected with his cheek. Beneath that pain, I feel the prickle of something else. It takes a beat for it to register that I feel satisfied, *vindicated*.

"Meddy, stop!"

Apollonia is tugging at my arm, pulling me away from the children. The boy is now glaring at me, holding one of his hands against the side of his face, but it's the girl's look that renders me still. She is staring at me with a mixture of horror and . . . fear. It jars me. So many times, *I* have been made to feel afraid, but no one has ever looked at *me* with fear. The prickling triumph I felt moments ago gives way to something stickier, less pleasant.

"Go," Apollonia orders the boy and girl. "Now."

The children, it seems, need no further prompting. At Apollonia's words, the boy shoves the sack at the girl, and then they both pelt down the street. She waits until they're out of sight before turning back to me. Her hazel eyes are devoid of any warmth.

"What were you thinking?" There's a sharpness to Apollonia's voice that I've never heard before, and I start. "He was a child!"

"So was the girl he stole from!" I fire back, not entirely able to keep the defensiveness from my voice.

Something in Apollonia's expression gives, and in place of anger, I see disappointment. "We are acolytes," she says. "Our job is to *serve* the people of this city, to help them." She shakes her head. "What you just did . . . that wasn't your place. It was out of line."

The words are soft, but I feel as though I've been slapped, too. A part of me knows, deep down, that Apollonia is right, but the remnants of the anger I felt before spark to life again.

I glare back at her. "So, as acolytes, we're expected to just stand by and watch while the weakest of this city are harmed?" I ask. "Do you have any idea how that feels?"

Apollonia raises a brow. "I do," she says coolly. "Because I'm *from* here."

I stiffen.

"You have lived in Athens for a little over a fortnight, Meddy," she continues. "I have lived here my whole life. I've seen good things happen to bad people in this city, and I've also seen bad things happen to good people. You can't right every wrong, but you can make a difference." She lowers her voice. "That's what we are called to do, as servants to the Goddess."

The storm that raged inside me earlier is gone, and in its place I feel the cool, undeniable press of shame. She's not here, but I feel Athena's disapproving gray gaze. Silence falls between Apollonia and me.

"I'm going to head back to the Acropolis," she says. "Are you coming?"

I know I should go with her, but I can't make my feet move. I realize I'm not ready to return to the temple and face a thousand tiny reminders of the goddess whose expectations I've just failed to live up to.

"You go ahead," I say quietly. "I'll catch up."

Apollonia hesitates a moment, then nods. I watch as she makes her way up the road, keeping my gaze fixed on her until she turns a corner and is out of sight. I'm struck by how alone I feel in her absence.

I cast my eyes skyward, noting the darkening sky and the clouds rolling in. It will be nightfall soon, but I opt to double back the way Apollonia and I originally came, choosing a longer route to return to the Acropolis. The walk will give me time to think.

Apollonia's words nip at my heels as I trek along the winding street. When I'm honest with myself, I know she is right: What I did to that boy *was* out of line. The problem is, I can't reconcile that with the fact that a part of me still isn't entirely sorry. I let my anger get the better of me when I slapped the boy, but I also stood up for someone who wasn't able to stand up for herself. I helped, didn't I?

Then why did that little girl look at me like I was the monster?

I can't identify a satisfactory answer to that question, so I bury it and continue walking.

I don't know the exact moment I realize I've entered an unfamiliar part of Athens. Above, the sky has darkened to a mauve, and the setting sun casts long shadows across most of the buildings. Deep in my thoughts, it seems I have made a wrong turn. I can't quite discern if it's my imagination, but this part of the city seems filthier than the others I've seen. There are no women chasing small children or old men playing board games together on stoops. In fact, it doesn't seem that anyone lives here; there's a stillness that leaves me slightly unsettled. The streets are littered with rubbish, and every so often, I lift the hem of my chiton to avoid trailing it through a foul-smelling puddle. The farther down the street I walk, the uneasier I feel. I'm increasingly aware of how out of place I must look in my crisp white acolyte's chiton. Suddenly, a warning bell sounds in my head.

This is not safe. You need to leave.

I turn on my heel, making my way back up the street, but just before I reach its end, I stop short.

I didn't notice the small alley the first time I passed it, and I certainly didn't notice the young woman sitting near a small door within it. I look at her now: She is older than me, but not by much. My guess is that she's closer to Stheno's age, perhaps in her early twenties. Her skin is already fair, but she wears white powder on her face and neck, a pale canvas only interrupted by the bright red of her painted lips and the thick black cosmetic drawn around her eyes. That isn't what renders me still, though.

The woman is all but naked.

Technically, I suppose the sheer, shapeless white garment draped over her form could constitute clothes, but it leaves nothing to the imagination. I have certainly seen unclothed bodies before—every day as acolytes, we change in front of one another without a second thought—but this feels different. The woman is standing with a well-dressed man who looks to be much older—in his forties, if I had to guess. His tunic is white, unblemished, and perfectly pressed. He's clean-shaven, and his dark hair, shot through with gray at the temples, is neat. He is clearly someone important, wealthy.

I step back so that I'm out of sight while I watch the two of them speak in low voices. She murmurs something I cannot hear before holding out her hand, and the man drops a fat purse into it. I watch, now even more confused. The woman does not seem to mind that this man is seeing her without clothes, and it appears that some sort of transaction has been made, though I didn't see the woman give the man anything. She says something else I can't hear before taking his hand and leading him inside the building behind her. He goes willingly.

I stand at the opening of the alley for several minutes, still. It's impossible to say what prompts me, but I find myself moving closer to the door the woman and the man went into. It's closed now, but as I approach, I hear sounds. From the other side of the door, there's shouting, laughter, and then . . . moans. I hear what sounds like a chorus, men and women. I can't tell if they're in some sort of pain or if it's . . . something else. I can't see what's going on inside, but I find myself remembering what Theo and I saw the sea king and the nymph doing in my mother's garden. The sounds from the other side of that door are very much like the sounds I heard then. I'm startled by the sudden swoop in my lower stomach, the new hard lump in my throat that makes it hard to swallow. These sensations are new, strange, and so total that I'm not sure what to do with them. I back away from the door and leave the alley as quickly as I came, taking care not to look back until I'm farther up the main road.

By now, only a few lingering rays of sunlight are left in the sky, and I swallow a slight panic. I need to get back to the Acropolis, quickly. In the dark, I can now see it, rising on the hill in the distance, but not nearly as far away as I imagined. I could still return before supper without my tardiness being noticed.

I've just started in that direction when a voice interrupts the quiet. "Don't tell me you're looking for another owl?"

I turn. I'm surprised to see the boy I met on the street in Athens, the one who helped me find Glaukopis. He's walking toward me now, and I note that he's carrying a fishing net.

He stops before me and cocks his head. There's a playfulness in his smile that at once puts me at ease. He is even more handsome than I remember.

"No owls today," I reply, keeping my tone light. "The priestesses did some work in the city earlier this afternoon. I was just taking a short walk before returning to the Acropolis."

The boy's smile fades just slightly. "You should be careful in Athens at night," he says, his tone serious. "Certain parts of the city aren't as safe as others."

I look around the empty street and remember the unsettled feeling I had before. I believe him.

"I'll walk you back to the Acropolis," the boy offers.

"That's generous."

"It's friendly."

I raise a brow. "Are we friends?"

The boy grins, and I feel a jolt like I've been struck by lightning. "I'd certainly like us to be."

"I don't even know your name."

The boy waves a dismissive hand. "That's because it's common and boring. You'd forget it tomorrow." His voice softens. "Tell me yours."

"My name is Meddy."

"'Meddy.'" He says my name like it's something precious, rare. "Please allow me to escort you back to the Acropolis."

There's a warmth to his voice that puts me at ease after the tension of the afternoon.

"All right."

He nods chivalrously, then falls in step with me as we walk up the road. It's dark, but the streets feel less sinister now that I'm not alone.

"So, you're a fisherman." I point to the net in his hand.

"Something like that." The boy's lip quirks, as though he's thought of something funny. "I've always loved being near the sea. There's something about it . . ."

"It can be powerful and destructive," I note. "But it can also be gentle and healing."

The boy lights up. "That's exactly it."

"I'm not from here, but I grew up near the sea." I'm not sure what compels me to say the words, but they come freely. "I love it, too. It's another thing I love about Athens."

"This is the greatest city in all the world," the boy says. He's looking up at the sky now, and I see real adoration on his face.

"You're lucky to call it home, then."

He looks to me again. "It's your home, too, now, isn't it? As an aco-lyte?"

At once, everything that's happened today is brought back to the fore-front. Some of my levity fades.

"It's my home for now," I agree. "But I'm not sure it will be for much longer."

"Why?" he asks. "What happened?"

I barely know this boy; a part of me realizes that the ease I feel around him is unwarranted. But when I look into his eyes, I see real concern in them, sincere interest. All I've held in breaks like a dam, and then I'm telling him everything. I tell him about the people I helped today, about the little boy and girl. I expect him to look disapproving when I tell him what I did to the boy, but to my surprise, he only nods with under-standing.

"You know, I'm no priestess," he says. "But, from my view . . . I actu-ally think you did the right thing."

I look up at him. "You do?"

"I do," he says. "Athena isn't just a goddess of craft and wisdom. She's a goddess of *war*. I'm sure even she understands that sometimes violence is necessary to maintain order."

I blink. That didn't occur to me before, and now I wish I'd said as much to Apollonia. I'd started to think maybe she was right, but now I feel vindicated again. Perhaps I *did* do the right thing.

Before I realize it, we reach the entrance to the Acropolis. I'm relieved to see that there are no priestesses near it and that I'll still be able to slip in, hopefully unnoticed. The boy stops just short of the torchlight and tips his head.

"As promised," he says. "Safely delivered to the Acropolis."

"Thank you."

There's a long pause in which neither of us speaks. I find myself at a loss for words, unsure of what's supposed to happen next.

Eventually, the boy smiles. "I hope to see you again, Meddy, gods willing."

I have no idea how that would even happen, but I still nod. "As do I. Good night."

He offers a final wave before he turns on his heel and walks back the way he came. My eyes stay trained on him until he's out of sight.

THOUGHTS OF THE boy stay with me as I walk across the Acropolis's lawn.

In the quiet, I find myself recalling the words he said, remembering the attentive way he looked at me as I spoke. Back on my island, Theo always listened to me, my sisters tried to make me feel that the things I had to say were important, but this . . . this feels different. Every time I remember the way the boy grinned, there's a fluttering in my chest, and I catch myself wanting to smile or laugh. I find myself hoping that I do see him again, somewhere, somehow. I'm still thinking of him when I enter the acolytes' quarters and discover that they're not empty. Apollonia is sitting on her pallet, brushing her hair. She looks up as though she's been waiting for me.

"I'm glad you made it back," she says. "I worried." The words are kind but too formal. The fluttering in my chest vanishes, replaced by the same heaviness I felt when Apollonia walked away before. For a moment, I think of repeating what the boy said, pointing out that my actions had actually been valid ones. Something stops me. It dawns on me that Apollonia is my only true friend in the Acropolis. Even if she and I disagree, I don't want to lose that. Different words leave my mouth.

"I'm sorry." I don't bother with any sort of preamble. "I'm sorry for upsetting you."

Apollonia shakes her head. "You didn't upset me, Meddy," she says. "You . . . surprised me. I've never seen you like that before."

The truth is, I surprised myself, too. My anger always sat coiled within me like a snake, waiting. The only other time I acted on it, a prince ended up dead.

I swallow, then force myself to speak. "I've never told you about my family," I say quietly. "My father . . . he doesn't treat my mother well. He never has. Sometimes, he hurts her."

Apollonia pales.

"The things I've seen him do to her make me want to . . ." I choke on the words. I can't say them. "I hate people who hurt others, Apollonia."

Apollonia looks up at me. "Is that why you put the snake in Kallisto's bed?"

I jolt. I didn't realize she knew.

"I hate people like that, too, Meddy." Apollonia's voice is soft. She sounds tired. "But going after them, trying to avenge every wrong . . . that kind of hate can consume a person, you know. That kind of hate doesn't avenge; it just destroys."

I don't know what to say to that. Apollonia squeezes my shoulder, then leaves me in the quarters alone.

XVI

TWO WEEKS LATER, we rise at dawn for the festival of Panathenaia.

Excitement crackles in the air as I don my freshly washed chiton alongside the rest of the acolytes, taking special care to braid my locs in an elaborate crown atop my head in honor of the celebration. When we are ready, we meet Eupraxia and the other priestesses in the courtyard; then, together, we head into Athens.

The sun has not risen over most of the city yet; the sky is still a leached pale blue. I did not expect many Athenians to be awake at this hour, so I'm pleasantly surprised to find that when Eupraxia finally stops us in a small neighborhood in the eastern part of the city, there is already a crowd of people waiting. There are old men dressed in fine white tunics, women with weather-beaten faces, and children who've obviously just been scrubbed clean by their mothers. Eupraxia regards them all with a gracious nod, then begins to walk. There is no one to direct the crowd, no one to give instruction, but everyone seems to know where and when to move. As the high priestess, Eupraxia continues to lead the procession; the senior priestesses and acolytes follow, and I'm surprised to see people of the city now joining us, too. Others bow their heads as we pass; some fall to their knees or touch their fingers to crude pendants of owls. Athena may not be physically present, but as we walk, I feel the people's love and veneration for her, directed toward us as her chosen representatives. Yet again, I find myself wondering what that kind of love, power, and influence must feel like.

Another senior priestess is waiting for us when we reach the monumental gateway of the Acropolis. Beside her is an old white bull whose hide gleams in the morning light. We gather around in silence as Eupraxia steps forward, holding a beautiful peplos of yellow, blue, and purple. Embroidered flowers line its hems, and though I'm not close enough to examine their detail, I know the craftwork is precise. When I sat with the priestesses of the temple responsible for making that peplos, they explained to me that their work took nine months, sometimes longer. Now Eupraxia carries the sacred peplos and stops right before the bull. She regards the creature solemnly.

"To our Goddess, holy Athena." Her voice is sonorous as she lifts the peplos high in the air. "Goddess of wisdom, warfare, and craft, on this sacred day, all of Athens sings your praises and lifts your name. In a show of our gratitude, we offer you this gift, and this sacrifice."

Eupraxia nods to the priestess standing beside the bull. When she cuts the beast's throat, it dies quietly—a good omen. As its dark blood seeps across the ground, the crowd begins to cheer; some break out in song. Pride swells within me until I'm certain I will burst. Tears fill my eyes.

"Meddy?" Apollonia has stayed beside me all morning. I'm not sure we've totally recovered from what happened in the city two weeks earlier, but we've repaired things enough for her to look at me now with sincere concern. "Are you all right?"

At first, I don't have the strength to speak. For so many years, I've dreamed of leaving my island and seeing more. It occurs to me that now I have realized that dream.

I turn to Apollonia, beaming. "I'm glad to be here," I say earnestly. "I'm really glad to be here."

My friend smiles back. "I'm glad you're here, too."

When the crowd stops singing and cheers again, we both join them.

The rest of Panathenaia is marked by a series of various events across the city, but the one I'm most looking forward to is the chariot racing. I've never seen a race before, and Apollonia does her best to explain its rules as we head to the Panathenaic Stadium. Still, nothing prepares me for the sight that greets me as we reach the top of the hill.

The Panathenaic Stadium is the largest site I've ever seen, larger than even the Acropolis. It consists of a long, narrow dirt track in an oval, with rising hills surrounding it on all sides for spectators. Already hundreds of people are sprawled on the grass, and a race is about to start. I can make out two teams of chariots parading toward the starting line. Both teams' horses are black, but one charioteer wears a blue tunic, while the other wears green. I decide at random to cheer for the latter. The men orient their horses as an official raises his hands, indicating that they should wait. There is a moment of stillness, a beat in which a thick tension builds.

Then a horn blares, and the chariots surge forward.

I'm now sitting on a soft knoll with the other priestesses, a safe distance from the track, but my heart still thunders wildly in my chest as the two chariots fly past us and head for the first bend. Both manage it without error, and the crowd roars its approval as they pick up speed. They pass the second bend as easily, but when they reach the third, the driver in blue rams his chariot into the green's. The latter flies off his chariot and lands in the dirt with a sickening crunch. The crowd collectively groans, and the green driver doesn't get up again.

"Chariot racing is one of the most exciting sports," Apollonia says in my ear. "It's also one of the bloodiest."

I find myself staring at the green driver, still unmoving, as the crowd cheers on for the blue. Mere minutes ago, the green driver was alive; now he's likely dead. For a second, I remember Maheer's body on the floor of his bedchamber, and a chill stipples my skin. It is a reminder of how easy it is to die. The suddenness of it is oddly sobering amid so much festivity and cheer, but I seem to be the only person who notices.

After the first race, while a crew of men work to retrieve the green charioteer's body and corral his abandoned horses, Apollonia and I venture slightly closer to the track. As we draw near, new smells fill my nose—the stink of sweat, old wine, and horse dung—but I find I don't mind it. I've seen illustrations of horses in my scrolls, but we did not have them back home on my island. I find myself awed by the creatures, lithe and glossy, but still so full of power.

Already, the drivers for the next race are on the track and readying themselves. One of them has attracted a crowd of women. He's tall, pale, and skinny, with shorn blond hair that gives him a slightly hard edge but doesn't hide the fact that he's young. His opponent, who is sitting beside his own team of horses alone, is almost the exact opposite. He looks to be in his late thirties, with fair freckled skin and light brown hair. Scars and cuts mark his bare arms, and I find myself wondering how many of these races he's completed. When he notices I'm looking at him, he smiles and stands.

"Would you like to see the horses?" he calls out. "They're friendly, I promise."

I look to Eupraxia, who nods from her spot on the hill, then approach the charioteer cautiously. Up close, I can appreciate his horses. All four are a glossy chestnut brown and share the same dark, intelligent eyes.

"Your horses are beautiful," I remark. "What are their names?"

The charioteer nods to each of them. "Boreas, Zephyrus, Notus, and Eurus."

I grin. "You've named your horses after the wind gods," I note, then point to one of them. "Is he truly as fast as the southern wind?"

The charioteer nods again. "*She* is, as are her sisters."

"Then I'm sure you'll win with them."

The chariot driver's smile turns rueful, and he shakes his head. "I'm afraid you might be the only one who thinks so," he says.

"What do you mean?"

"I'm not favored to win this race," he says. "You see that other driver? He's younger, faster. The better odds are on him."

"Well, *I* still believe in you and your four winds."

"Thank you." He smiles in earnest now. "My name is Kallinikos," he says. "Yours?"

"I'm Meddy."

"You're a priestess?" he asks.

"I'm an acolyte, training to become a priestess."

His eyes crinkle at their corners. "That's close enough. I wonder if you might be willing to do me a small favor?"

The question surprises me, but I nod. "Of course."

"I wonder if I might ask you to pray to Athena for my victory. The Goddess listens to her priestesses." He winks at me. "And her acolytes."

"I will." The words sound more solemn than I intend.

He inclines his head and, before I can say anything else, climbs aboard his chariot and takes off. His blond opponent is already at the starting line, and I scramble back up the hill to my spot with the other priestesses as the official from the first race returns and raises his hands. I close my eyes quickly, unsure of how best to shape my prayer, and let instinct lead me.

Athena, please watch over Kallinikos. Please let him be victorious.

The horn blares a second time, and my eyes open again. The two chariot teams are off.

I thought I'd been attentive during the first round of chariot racing. But that was nothing compared to how I feel now as I watch Kallinikos and the blond driver reach the first bend in the track. The blond, perhaps inspired by the former race, tries to ram his chariot into Kallinikos's, but the latter deftly shifts out of the way just in time. When they reach the second bend, the blond tries again, but this time Kallinikos is ready. He rams back, nearly sending the blond driver out of his seat. The crowd roars its approval. They pass the third bend without issue, then begin the second lap, but now it's obvious the blond's horses are faster. His crop flies through the air as he goads them on, leaning forward so he's nearly parallel to their backs. Slowly, he inches ahead. Kallinikos pushes his four winds to follow suit, but the horses can't keep up. The harder he pushes, the more quickly they seem to fall behind. The gap between the chariots widens.

He's not going to win. I come to the realization slowly. *He's going to lose.*

I watch the blond round the final bend. Already, he's grinning in celebration. He releases the reins to wave a hand at the cheering crowd: a mistake. Something swoops into the stadium, too small for me to see, and flies right in front of the blond charioteer's horses. I can't be sure, but it looks suspiciously like an owl. The blond's front horses come up short, frightening the others in the process so that they do the same. It's a momentary lapse, but it's all Kallinikos needs. He soars past the blond and crosses the finish line. The crowd erupts, and I jump to my feet. I have never felt such sheer elation before. I feel triumphant as the blond charioteer's screams of frustration are drowned out by the crowd's praise. Kallinikos takes his four winds around the track for another whole lap as Athenians clap their hands and stomp their feet for him. When he reaches the starting line again, Eupraxia is waiting for him with a prize amphora. He takes it from her and raises it high; the applause from the stadium is so total that I feel it in my rib cage. A crowd of well-wishers is waiting to congratulate him once he's dismounted his chariot, but he searches until he finds me and waves.

"It was you!" he says, pointing. "It was your blessing!"

I'm more inclined to think that it was Kallinikos's skill and experience, coupled with a bit of chance, that won him the race, but I still wave back and smile.

Apollonia joins me. "Here's to your first Panathenaia," she says, grinning from ear to ear. "And to many more!"

"What happens now?" I ask. Already, people are clearing from the stadium, and many seem to be heading back toward the city.

"There will be festivities, parties in the streets," she says. "I expect they'll go well into the night."

I look toward the city, wistful. "That sounds fun."

Apollonia's expression changes. Suddenly, she looks decidedly mischievous. "We could go."

I eye her, surprised. "We aren't supposed to."

Apollonia waves a hand. "This is Panathenaia. The entire city will be celebrating, even the priestesses." She looks into the distance, as though remembering something fond. "When I was younger, my brothers would take me with them into the city. We'd eat and dance until the sun came up. We had so much fun." There's a wistfulness in her voice now, a longing. Something in my stomach knots.

After what happened on our last trip into the city, I've worried that my friendship with Apollonia might change. In the days after the incident with the little boy, we seemed to fall back into our normal routine, but the worry has remained, stuck in me like a stubborn thorn. She is my only true friend in this city, the one who has made me feel welcomed from the very start. In the end, that's what makes me say the words.

"All right," I say. "Tonight, we'll go."

XVII

HOWEVER LONG OR short they may be, our lives can usually be pared down to a collection of choices made on a few fateful nights. Rarely do we know for sure which of these nights will be the ones that will alter everything to come. But if you pay close attention, there is a sensation, a light tingle beneath the surface of your skin, that hints at destiny.

The night Apollonia and I leave the Acropolis to venture into the city proper is one of those life-altering nights, for both of us.

Leaving the temple itself wasn't difficult. Apollonia was right: In the midst of so much preparation and planning for Panathenaia, most of the Acropolis's priestesses had either already gone to sleep, exhausted, or headed to one of the courtyards to nurse generous cups of wine.

My nervousness eases as the temple disappears behind us, and Apollonia leads the way down one of the dirt roads, between old buildings made of mud brick and timber. Around us, children are running up and down the streets despite the late hour; more than a few women cluster together on the stoops of their homes to gossip while their husbands share flasks of wine. I try not to stare as we pass them, but every so often, curiosity wins. I've spent just over a month in Athens now, but so much of it still feels new. All my life, I've wondered about the outside world. Now I am *in* it and not entirely certain this isn't all some fever dream I'll wake up from.

Apollonia has grown up in Athens, so I let her take the lead as we travel closer to the city center. The festivities here seem to be in full swing. I hear the lively pluck of lutes, the jingle of hand drums with bells attached to them. Around us, people are half singing, half shouting different songs in a discordant harmony, but I find I relish the sound. My stomach rumbles as the air fills with new scents, and I note a street vendor selling barley cakes drizzled in honey. My mouth waters.

"For most people here, meat is a delicacy," Apollonia explains as we walk. "But during festivals, everyone's more generous." She guides me toward a market stall and hands the bearded man standing behind it several drachmae. In exchange, he hands us both sticks of roasted lamb. A groan escapes me as I bite into it, savoring the sharp tastes of thyme and basil. Back home, the meals I was served were certainly grand, but in Athens, everything feels more *vivid*. My parents' feasts were attended by immortal gods who dined and feasted as a pastime; the Athenians in these streets dance and sing and feast with an enthusiasm I've never seen before.

They live as though tomorrow isn't promised, I realize.

A small crowd has gathered in the middle of one of the streets, and I nudge Apollonia toward it until we are close enough to see what's going on. Over the heads of the onlookers, I make out a trio of girls. They look my age and are all dressed in modest but prettily dyed chitons. They are performing a dance I vaguely recognize. I realize it's a slightly varied version of one of the many dances my mother forced my sisters and me to learn. I suppose that it should surprise me, seeing that same dance here in Athens, but somehow it doesn't. If languages can traverse land and sea, it stands to reason that so can anything else, including a dance.

Apollonia notices the look on my face. "Do you dance?" she asks.

I hesitate. "Yes, but—"

She doesn't give me time to say anything else: She grabs my hand and pulls me with her into the middle of the ring. She begins to twirl, kick, and stomp her feet in time with the music. Then my own instinct takes over. Suddenly, I am back on my island. I begin to move my arms and clap, trying my best to look graceful. An encouraging cheer goes up from the crowd, and it takes me a moment to realize that sound of approval is for *me*. More people have begun to clap in time with the music, and my heartbeat synchronizes to it. My blood pumps through my veins faster and faster, and my steps come lighter. I throw my head back, letting my locs fly out around me, and someone in the crowd whoops. A cry of joy escapes me. I have danced at my mother's behest, as a performance to appease others. I realize I've never danced just for myself. I turn and find that Apollonia is beside me again. She takes my hand, and our steps fall into sync. We spin faster and faster, until her cheeks are flushed and my heart is beating so fast it feels as though it might burst through my chest. When we stop, we're both breathing hard.

"You didn't tell me you could dance so well," she says, her chest rising and falling.

I smile. "You didn't, either." I look down and realize we're still holding hands. Apollonia seems to notice, too, because the color in her cheeks deepens, and she pulls away. My heart is still thundering, but now I'm less sure if that's a consequence of our dancing or of the way Apollonia's palm felt pressed against mine. I open my mouth, unsure of what to say, but a voice behind me interrupts.

"Excuse me."

Apollonia and I look up and find three young men standing before us. They are all tall, suntanned, and have the long, gangly frames of boys who've grown up fast without much in the way of nourishment. The one in front is carrying a large pitcher and walking with a slow, lazy swagger. His eyes wander leisurely over Apollonia and me in turn as he stops before us. He smiles.

"The two of you danced well," he says. "What are your names?"

"I'm Kallisto," Apollonia answers for both of us. "She's Amersa."

The boy nods. "My name's Christos." He gestures to the other two boys. "This is Haris, and Platon. We're shepherds." He holds up a pitcher. "We thought you might want something to drink."

I am grateful when Apollonia takes the pitcher first. She sniffs at it, then brings the rim to her lips and sips.

"It's . . . sweet," she says slowly, handing the pitcher to me.

I feel everyone's eyes on me as I mirror her sip. The moment the liquid touches my tongue, there is a rush of flavor and then, beneath it, the familiar aftertaste of alcohol. I've only ever drunk wine on my island, with my sisters or Theo. These boys don't seem to mean any harm, but I still look to Apollonia, unsure. Her expression is neutral, but I know her well enough to translate that look. If I asked, she would return to the Acropolis with me, without question. We'd go back to our quarters and never speak about this night. In the back of my mind, I think about our last time in the city, when I slapped that little boy. I disappointed Apollonia in that moment.

I never want to see that look on her face again.

I drink from the pitcher a second time, more deeply, then smile. "It's delicious."

The boys cheer, and Apollonia's shoulders relax. We stand, and the boys throw their arms over our shoulders.

"Stay with us," says Christos. "We'll show you a good time."

IT QUICKLY BECOMES clear that wherever Christos and his friends procured their wine, it is of a *very* fermented variety. As is often the case, the realization that I'm drunk is not immediate; rather, I wade into intoxication slowly. Christos, Platon, and Haris lead us through Athens's streets for hours, pulling us into card games, dances, and peddlers' street shows. They are kind, easygoing, and quick to laugh. Gradually, I feel myself relax with them. Apollonia does, too. Every so often, we're pulled into another group of dancers, but Apollonia and I never get to dance the way we did the first time. Some small part of me is sorry for that. By the fourth hour, the world has taken on a blurred quality, and I find walking harder than it should be. I stop, but everything around me keeps tilting.

"Amersa?" Apollonia's words are slurred and overloud, but I still see the concern in her eyes when she turns to look at me. "Are you . . . you all right?"

I've almost forgotten the fake names we gave the boys. I nod, but only because I don't quite trust myself to speak. Technically, I have been this drunk before—once, when Theo and I stole a pitcher of wine from one of my parents' feasts—and I know that I am balancing precariously on the line between pleasant inebriation and real nausea.

"I need . . . I need to . . ." I pause. I'm not so intoxicated that admitting I need to relieve myself in front of three boys isn't embarrassing.

Fortunately, one of them—maybe the one called Haris—seems to understand my predicament without my having to say it aloud. He nods over my shoulder. "There are public latrines just up the road," he says. "Go to the end of the market, then turn left. You'll see them."

"I'll go with you," says Apollonia. She takes a step, then stumbles violently. Haris catches her before she can fall on her face.

"No, no." I wave her off. "I'm fine, I'll come right back."

Apollonia looks as though she might argue, then seems to think better of it. "All right," she says, "we'll be here waiting."

The directions Haris has given me are accurate but misleading. The city's public latrines aren't "just up the road"; rather, they are several blocks away. At this hour of the night—I've long since abandoned trying to discern exactly what time it is—they are empty, and I realize I've left the main area designated for the festivities. I duck inside, grateful to sit somewhere cool and dark for a spell. When I am finished, I carefully trundle down the building's steps and lean against one of the massive stone columns at its front. I tell myself that I will return to Apollonia and the boys soon. I just need a moment's rest. I ease down to sit on the steps.

My eyes wander lazily, taking in my surroundings. I discern that I am in a more residential part of Athens; the sounds of the city are subdued enough for me to hear trilling cicadas, the light trickling of a well somewhere in the distance. I can tell that someone in one of the nearby buildings has lit a lamp; the smell of burning olive oil suffuses the night air. That smell reminds me of the Acropolis and my waiting bed pallet. I sigh, closing my eyes just for a moment.

"Hello there."

I sit bolt upright at once, uneasy as I look around for the owner of the new voice that has interrupted the quiet. The fair-skinned man who emerges from the dark is older, with salt-and-pepper stubble dusting his cheeks. His clothes are ragged, and he offers me a toothy grin as he approaches. I get to my feet and step back.

"Got any coin?" he asks in a low, raspy voice.

"N-no. Sorry." I try to keep my tone calm as I inch away. The man matches me step for step.

"Come now," he presses, "I don't need much, just a drachma or two?"

"I'm sorry. I don't have anything." I steal a glance left, tense. "I really need to get back, actually. My friends are waiting for me."

The man leers. "They won't miss you." He moves faster than I anticipate, snatching my upper arm and pulling me toward him.

"Take your hands off her."

I feel my assailant's grip loosen as both of us look in the direction of the third voice that's filled the street. The first thing I see doesn't make sense: a pair of eyes, blue-green, searing impossibly through the darkness. Then I make out the shape of a young man. I realize, with a start, that he is familiar.

It is the young man from the market.

Without hesitating, he charges forward, his gaze locked on the older man. "Release her," he bellows. "Now!"

The older man seems just as startled as I am, but he doesn't comply. With a slightly less confident voice, he says: "Mind your business, boy. She's none of your concern."

"I won't say it again," says the boy. "Let her go."

"And if I don't?"

It happens suddenly. There is a great flash of light, a whooshing sound, and then the boy from the market is gone. In his place stands a man who isn't a man at all. He has long black hair that falls to his shoulders and those same vivid blue-green eyes. In his right hand, he holds a golden trident.

He is a god.

"Great Poseidon." My assailant whispers the name at the same time it blazes through my mind. "How—?"

"I offered clemency." Poseidon's new voice—his *real* voice—is both great and terrible. He sounds like a living, breathing storm. "Instead, you challenged a god."

"Please!" My assailant releases me as he drops to his knees, sputtering. The air is fouled by a new stench, and I realize with some revulsion that he's urinated on himself. I step away from him. "P-p-please, O mighty lord. Have mercy."

"Leave my sight," Poseidon commands.

The man doesn't need to be told twice. His legs tremble so badly that the first time he rises, he nearly falls again, but once he's found his feet, he is gone in seconds, running down the road. Poseidon stares after him, eyes narrowed, then looks to me.

"Medusa," he says in a quieter voice.

A jolt of shock runs through me. I'd met the king of the sea—in this form, at least—only once. I offer a deep bow. "Y-yes. Yes, my king." I stare at the ground, waiting for him to speak, and am surprised to feel a finger tap my chin and direct my eyes up. Poseidon has come closer. He is staring down at me with a much softer expression.

"What are you doing here?" His tone is chiding but gentle. "I've told you parts of this city are not safe at night."

Shame fills me. At once I know he's right, I shouldn't be here. I am standing upright now, but again I look away. "Apologies, my king. I—"

"Poseidon."

I look up. "Sorry—?"

"I would have you use my name: Poseidon." The words are kind but imperative. "I prefer it."

It takes me a moment to find my words. "Very well . . . Poseidon."

He cocks his head. "You were telling me why you'd come to this place."

I bite my lip. "I wanted to see Athens. Well, more of it."

He gives me a sympathetic look. "I can understand that," he says. "There's no city like it."

I think of the story Apollonia told me once, about the contest Poseidon and Athena waged to lay claim to this city. Though I'm not certain of it, I think I see a quiet grief in Poseidon's eyes. It's only there for a moment. Then he blinks, and his smile returns.

"Come," he says kindly. "I will take you back to the temple."

XVIII

THE WALK BACK to the Acropolis feels far longer than the one into the city. In part, it's because I'm walking uphill instead of down, and the alcohol still in my blood makes my steps clumsy. But I know there is another reason.

Poseidon.

He has stayed in his true form, but has subdued the golden aura about his skin. His trident has disappeared. Someone watching us would see a young man and young woman strolling side by side.

"Did you know?" I ask as we walk. "Did you know who I was when you saw me in the market? Is that why you helped me?"

"I did," Poseidon admits. "I've been watching you for a while now, from afar."

"You have?" I'm not immediately sure what to make of that. I am mortified, but . . . a small part of me is also honored.

Poseidon nods. "Your father is quite proud of you. He told nearly every god in the Sea Court that his daughter was going to be an acolyte for Athena."

My cheeks warm. I've always known that my father is prone to self-aggrandizing, and the idea that Poseidon has heard about me that way embarrasses me.

Poseidon's expression softens, as though he can read my thoughts.

"You mustn't be hard on your father," he says. "He has every right to be proud of you."

"I suppose." My answer is noncommittal. "Did he ask you to watch over me, then?"

"No." A new light touches Poseidon's eyes. "I chose to do that myself."

"Why?"

"You are of the Sea Court, the daughter of one of my subjects," he says. "That makes you my responsibility."

"Oh." I'm not sure why, but that answer disappoints me.

Poseidon offers a sidelong glance. "You're still wearing the uniform of an acolyte," he notes. "I take it that means you've successfully passed your challenges so far?"

"Tests," I correct. When the god raises a brow, I duck my head. "Apologies, my king."

Poseidon smiles. "From what I've heard, these *tests* are quite difficult. Passing them is no easy feat." He inclines his head at me. "You must be impressive."

I am so surprised I stop walking. Until a short while ago, I hadn't even thought that the king of the sea remembered my name. Now I've learned that he not only remembers me, but he has been watching me, protecting me. He thinks *I'm* impressive. I feel a familiar fluttering in my chest. I shift, suddenly uncomfortable, and Poseidon stops to look at me.

The skin between his dark brows pinches. "Did I . . . offend you?"

"No!" My voice rises several octaves. "No, not at all. It's just . . . you're the king of the sea. I didn't think someone like you would find someone like me interesting."

Poseidon smiles again. "I find you *very* interesting, Medusa."

My breath catches. "You do?"

"Of course." He nods. "You're the mortal daughter of two sea gods. There are very few beings like you."

If my elation were a candle, those words snuff it out in an instant. I look away but still feel Poseidon's gaze on me.

"I take your silence to mean you dislike being mortal."

"I certainly wouldn't have chosen it." Even I can hear the bitterness in my voice. "All being mortal has done is made life harder."

Several seconds pass before Poseidon speaks again. "Mortals are like flowers," he murmurs, "fragile and fleeting, yes, but . . ." He stops walking to look at me. "When a flower blooms, there is nothing more beautiful because it is *real*. We gods, we pretend to revel in our immortality, but the truth is most of us spend our eternities searching for just a glimpse of what a mortal feels: vitality, real and precious life. Never take that for granted, Medusa."

I have no words to answer Poseidon's. Never in my life has anyone—even Theo—made my mortality seem like something beautiful, something to be treasured and coveted. Poseidon offers me a wan smile.

"Forgive me," he says. "We should continue home."

Before I know it, the gates of the Acropolis are in sight. Its torches cast a pool of golden light onto the street, but we're far enough away to still be hidden in the shadows.

Poseidon stops. "This is where I leave you, Medusa," he says. "I'm sure you know your way from here?"

There is a slight teasing in his voice, but it isn't unkind. I gather what little remains of my dignity and offer him an unsteady bow. "Thank you again for all your help, my king."

We're still staring at each other, neither of us speaking. I know this is the moment when we are supposed to say goodbye, but I struggle to summon the words. Poseidon's expression has changed, too. He's studying me now, like I'm a riddle he's trying to solve.

"My king—"

He closes the gap between us, and his lips meet mine.

Heat arrows from the place our lips touch, warming my blood and coursing through my veins as his hands find my waist. My hands tangle in his hair as he pulls me closer, turns and presses me gently against one of the buildings' walls. When his tongue slips between my lips, a gasp escapes me, and I hear a growl, low in his throat. His kisses come faster. He moves from my lips to leave a trail of them down my cheek, my jaw, my neck. My heart beats wild and frantic in my chest, and some part of me wonders if it's possible to forget how to breathe.

But when Poseidon pulls away, we're both breathing hard.

"You should go," he whispers. "Good night, Medusa." Without another word, he turns, leaving me alone in the dark.

With every step I take, I am sure one of the priestesses will catch me, but I make it back to my sleeping quarters without being spotted. By now most of the heady rush from the wine is gone, but a drowsiness hangs over me as I pull my chiton over my head and crawl into my bed pallet. In the back of my mind, some nagging thought tugs, and I think vaguely of Apollonia still in the city.

She'll be fine, some sleepy voice assures me, and the rest of my thoughts quiet as I lay my head on my pillow. So much has happened in one night; I can barely believe that it has all been real and not some fever dream. The thought that is most vivid in my mind is that of Poseidon. I think of how he looked on that road, the way the starlight traced silver into his black hair. I think of the way he smiled at me.

I find you very *interesting, Medusa.*

The king of the sea thinks *I* am interesting. The king of the sea kissed me. I've never been kissed before.

I turn to lie on my back as a warm buzz moves through my body that has nothing to do with the wine I've drunk. I remember the way Poseidon's lips felt, the way his hair grazed my cheek. I find myself wondering how *other* things might feel. I imagine his lips in other places, my neck, my shoulder. I'm barely conscious of my hand moving, tracing the skin along my lower stomach, then drifting to the place between my legs. I jolt at that touch, unsure at first as my fingers begin to move. A strange new sensation runs through my body like a current, tensing and releasing as my fingers move faster—clumsy but determined. I've never felt whatever this is before; I have no way to describe it. I only know that I don't want it to stop. Instinct tells me that I am careening toward something, a great crescendo. It is similar to how I felt when I was dancing with Apollonia earlier, but better. My knees part on their own as a soft sigh escapes me. I think of Poseidon's face, of the way he'd called me beautiful, and my breath hitches. There is a pause, and then that crescendo comes, frightening and wondrous, until I am utterly lost in its oblivion.

PART III

MISTRESS

XIX

AS SOON AS I wake up the next morning, I know something is wrong. I feel it in the pit of my stomach, foul and rotten.

The acolytes' quarters are too bright, and that is in part due to the modest curtain, which usually covers the window, having been pulled back to let the morning sunlight in. It takes me a moment to appreciate the significance of that.

Sunlight.

The sun is up, which means . . .

I jump up from my bed pallet, horrified. I am supposed to already be awake; my chores begin at dawn. I glance at Apollonia's pallet, directly beside mine. It is empty, too, but made. That seems odd, as does the idea of Apollonia making up her pallet while leaving me to sleep in. Did she get in later in the night, or never come at all? No one else is in the quarters; I am alone here. Quickly, I douse my face with water and change into a fresh chiton. My head throbs violently, but I blink the pain away as I leave the sleeping quarters.

Blessedly, the temple is still quiet. It seems Apollonia and I weren't the only ones who indulged in celebration of the last day of Panathenaia. The priestesses who are awake are moving slowly, and several of them seem to be trying to avoid any direct sunlight. It should be a peaceful morning, but the stillness only worsens my anxiety.

Where is Apollonia?

I step out onto the Acropolis's lawns and at once regret it. It's too bright here as well. I fall to my knees and retch, upheaving the contents of last night's meal across the grass. The taste makes me want to vomit all over again. I wipe my mouth and stand unsteadily. I have to find Apollonia, before someone else does.

"Meddy!"

The sound is faint, but I know it's real. I squint. There, at the front gates of the Acropolis, is a lone figure. I half run, half walk. When I'm close enough to properly see Apollonia, I stop short. Her chiton is ripped in several places, and one of her shoulder pins is gone so that she has to hold up the front of the chiton to prevent her breasts from being exposed. There's a small cut near her chin, and her beautiful brown hair is riddled with leaves and bramble.

"Apollonia, what happened?"

My friend stares at the ground. "I tried to find you last night."

"What?"

She looks up at me, and her gaze is empty. "When you'd been gone awhile, I tried to find you," she says slowly. "I left those shepherds we met and headed for the public latrines."

A stone drops in my stomach.

"You weren't there," she continues, "so I started walking the streets, looking for you. There were some soldiers." Her face twists. "I told them I was an acolyte, but they didn't believe me."

"Apollonia," I whisper. "What did they do?"

She looks up at me. "I . . . they . . ." She looks down. "They hurt me."

I think of Maheer, of the way he looked at me in his bedchamber all those weeks ago. I can still hear the phantom echo of his voice.

You're just the age I like them.

I don't know exactly how the soldiers hurt Apollonia, but I don't need to know. Fresh anger blazes through me. "We'll find them," I vow. "And we'll make them *pay.*"

Apollonia shakes her head. "There's no point. I was drunk. I didn't know their names, and I wouldn't recognize their faces."

My anger turns to something else, a sense of hopelessness and helplessness that leaves me nauseated. I open my mouth to say something, anything, to make Apollonia feel better, but there's nothing.

It's your fault, says a voice in my head. *It's your fault this happened.*

"Meddy." Apollonia sounds tired, more tired than I've ever heard her. That scares me most. "I just want to wash, I just . . . I need to change out of these clothes."

"Of course." I take her arm gently and put it over mine. "Here, see if you can walk. Lean your weight on me. We'll go slow."

I wasn't there for Apollonia last night, and I know that truth is going to eat at me for a long while after today. But in this moment, I recognize that it isn't about me right now. I was not a good friend to Apollonia before, but I can be one now.

The Acropolis's bathing area isn't far off, but Apollonia flinches every time she moves, as though her whole body hurts, so we move slower than usual. Apollonia tries to shrug out of her chiton once we've reached the bath, but when she winces in pain again, I help her peel the clothes off, careful to avoid contact with her skin whenever possible. What I see once her chiton is gone is even worse than I imagined. There are bruises all over Apollonia's back and arms. I help ease her into the bathing pool and note that there is spotting on her inner thigh, as though she has started her monthly blood. Some of it is on her tunic, too.

"I'll get you a fresh chiton and some linens," I say, rising.

"No." Apollonia is up to her neck in the water now, but she turns, eyes wide. "Please don't . . . please don't leave me."

There's a desperation in her voice that shatters me. I ease to the edge of the pool and nod. "All right," I say gently. "I'll stay with you."

Apollonia tries, at first, to scrub herself clean, but soon I take over, letting her lean against the pool's edge while I dab at her bruises and ease the mud and twigs from her hair. I work in silence awhile before I speak again.

"Do you want to talk about what happened?"

Apollonia's eyes have been closed. Immediately, they open. "No." Her voice is still strained with exhaustion, but the word is firm. "I . . . I can't." I don't push her to say more, but she adds: "Meddy, no one else can know about this."

I start. "What do you mean? Shouldn't we report the soldiers? Shouldn't we at least tell Eupraxia?"

"No!" This time Apollonia is more forceful. She half rises from the pool. I note that she's trembling.

"I don't understand, Apollonia . . ." I'm trying to mind my tone, trying not to let my confusion show. "If those soldiers hurt you, that was wrong." I look away, thinking. "We'll go to their commanding officer. They'll be disciplined."

Apollonia is still holding my gaze. She shakes her head. "That's not the way things work in this city, Meddy. What those soldiers did to me . . ." She looks down and wraps her arms around herself. "Please promise me you won't tell anyone, ever."

I don't understand Apollonia's reaction, or why she doesn't want anyone else to know what's happened to her. In the end, I decide I don't need to understand.

"All right. I promise." I take her hand and squeeze it gently.

Tears fill Apollonia's eyes. "Thank you."

"You need fresh clothes," I say, rising. "You can borrow my second chiton for now, then we'll—" I pause, turning.

"What's wrong?" Apollonia sinks lower into the pool, covering herself.

I don't answer, but my eyes search the pillars around the bathhouse until I catch a slight movement behind one of them.

"Come out!" I shout. "We can see you."

A beat passes before a figure steps out from behind a pillar, and my heart sinks when I see a head of blond curls.

"Well, well." Kallisto's voice is soft, but her eyes glint like blades. She's not looking at me. "That *was* an interesting story, Apollonia. Fraternizing with Athenian soldiers in the night? I'm sure that'll be of great interest to the high priestess."

I look back to Apollonia. She's gone impossibly pale. "Kallisto," she whispers, "please."

"I won't tell her," says Kallisto lightly. "But I want something in return for my silence. *You.*" Her eyes cut to me. "Kiss my feet."

I stare for a moment, waiting to see if her words are in jest. When she raises her chin in challenge, I realize they are not.

"For that trick with the snake," she says in a low voice.

Now I understand. I have caused this. I look from her to Apollonia and detachedly think of Theo. I think of that moment in my bedchamber when he once told me he was afraid because of something I'd done. Now, yet again, my actions have implicated someone else, someone innocent.

Kallisto cocks her head, waiting. I take one more look at Apollonia and then make my decision. Every step I take toward Kallisto costs me something, but I make myself walk until she and I are standing inches apart.

Her lips quirk as she points. "Down."

I want to hit her, kick her, do something to wipe the triumphant look off her face. But I think of Apollonia, still behind me in the pool, and take a deep breath. I try not to imagine what my sisters would say right now if they saw me sinking to my knees. I glare down at Kallisto's sandaled feet, and my fists clench.

"Go on," she says sweetly.

It seems to take a century for my spine to curl into a bow. At the last second, I jerk back slightly, my mouth hovering inches from Kallisto's feet in revulsion. I take a second deep breath and force myself to bow lower, until my lips brush the top of them. As soon as it's done, I stand and back away. Kallisto is grinning in earnest now. I turn in time to see Apollonia trying to lift herself from the pool and rush to her. I have nothing but her old clothes to cover her, but I do my best, while Kallisto laughs.

"I don't know which will be better, Apollonia," she says, "the look on Meddy's face after she kissed my feet or the look on your face when I tell the high priestess you were consorting with soldiers on the night of a holy festival."

My head snaps back to her at the same time Apollonia gasps. "You *said* you wouldn't tell—"

"What?" Kallisto's brows rise in mock confusion. "I don't recall that."

"Kallisto." There's a tremor in Apollonia's voice. She sounds like she's on the verge of tears, and I find I can't look at her. "We've known each other since we were little girls," she says. "Please, don't do this."

I think I see a momentary waver in Kallisto's armor. She eyes Apollonia, and I think there's a chance the words might have gotten to her. Then she looks to me and her expression hardens.

"You should have thought about that before you chose to be friends with a filthy metic," she says snidely. Without another word, she turns from us and heads quickly and purposefully toward the temple.

MY MOUTH IS dry as I stand among the other priestesses, waiting.

Each of their faces a mask of austerity. It's late morning, and nearly everyone in the Acropolis is here, but three people are missing.

Kallisto. Apollonia. The high priestess.

By the time two priestesses came to the acolytes' quarters for Apollonia, we'd managed to get dressed at least. They didn't answer her questions about where she was being taken, only insisted that the high priestess had summoned her. They held up their hands when I tried to go with her, emphasizing that the high priestess had asked for Apollonia and Apollonia alone. That was several hours ago.

I picked at my breakfast alongside Amersa and the other priestesses, all of them blissfully unaware of what had happened. We were called to the Acropolis's central courtyard a short time after and instructed to wait.

After what feels like a century, a set of doors to our left opens and, finally, Apollonia is led out.

She has been crying; I can tell that much from her tear-streaked cheeks and bloodshot eyes. My pulse quickens. The two senior priestesses walk at her flanks, while Eupraxia trails behind her. The high priestess's expression is inscrutable, which somehow makes me feel even worse. I watch as the older woman crosses the courtyard to stand at the base of the stairs, so that she is slightly elevated. She waits until all eyes are on her before she speaks.

"This morning, I received a report of serious misconduct regarding Acolyte Apollonia." There is a heaviness in her voice. "After speaking to her separately, I now believe that I have a full and truthful account, directly from Acolyte Apollonia, of what transpired. Before I share my verdict, I would ask Apollonia to address you all."

Everyone in the courtyard looks to Apollonia, whose head is now bowed.

"Last night, my actions did not reflect the moral code befitting an acolyte or priestess of the Goddess." Her voice is flat. "For that, I offer my sincere and humble apologies to the women of this temple."

I frown. This doesn't make sense. Apollonia told me that the soldiers went after her, hurt her. I don't understand why *she* would be apologizing.

"Do you have anything else to add?" Eupraxia asks.

Apollonia shakes her head.

The priestesses begin to murmur among themselves, but Eupraxia raises a hand, and at once, everyone is silent again. She takes a deep breath.

"Then know that I did not come to my choice easily. Apollonia, you are hereby dismissed from service as an acolyte and banned from serving again in future."

There are several sharp gasps, a collective sound of astonishment from the other priestesses. A great roaring fills my head, and I find it hard to make sense of anything as Apollonia's mouth opens in horror.

"*Banned?*" she repeats softly. "But my . . . my family has served this temple for centuries."

Eupraxia bows her head. "Which makes this all the sadder."

"But . . . but you can't." Apollonia looks around the courtyard. No one will meet her eye now. "I'll have nowhere to go. My father won't take me back if I've been expelled from priestesshood. I'll end up on the street!"

Eupraxia says nothing else.

"You can't do this." Apollonia seems to be past the point of reason. Her voice rises in pitch. "High Priestess, please, I beg you to reconsider!"

Two priestesses, the same ones who escorted Apollonia in, break away from the crowd. There is a new steel in their eyes. Each of them takes Apollonia by the arm; at their touch, she becomes hysterical, trying to wriggle free from their grip. They hold her firm and begin to lead her from the courtyard.

"Please!" Apollonia is screaming now, her words nearly unintelligible as she wails. "High Priestess, please! Sisters, please!"

The screams bring me to my senses. I step forward. "She didn't do anything wrong!" I shout. "She was attacked by two soldiers!"

"Acolyte Medusa." Eupraxia's voice is suddenly sharp. "Be silent."

"No!" I run to Apollonia, and she grabs my hands, holding on with a viselike grip. "This isn't right!" My eyes search the room. "She's done nothing wrong!"

Apollonia is still wailing, still holding on to me. I feel two sets of hands grab me by my arms and pull until we've broken apart. When I look up, I see that the priestesses who pulled me away have tears in their own eyes. They hold me back while Apollonia is dragged from the courtyard, though her screams can be heard for several minutes as she's escorted off the Acropolis's grounds. Eventually, the priestesses release me. I whirl around to face Eupraxia. She hasn't spoken again, but a new fatigue has settled on her face. She looks as though she's aged an entire decade.

"Our oath is a sacred one." She stares at her folded hands as she speaks. "And our service to this temple is an honor and privilege, not a right. You would all do well to remember that."

No one says a word as she turns and leaves the courtyard. After a few minutes, the priestesses of the temple follow, walking with their heads bowed and whispering low. Eventually, only Amersa and I are left.

"She was always really nice," says Amersa. She looks to be on the verge of tears herself. "I don't understand this."

My heart constricts like it's being crushed in an iron fist. My last sight of Apollonia is seared into my mind—the desperation in her voice, the fear in her eyes.

"She didn't do anything wrong," I say in a quieter voice. "I talked to her this morning. She was the one attacked by two soldiers. She didn't—"

"Oh, please."

I look up. I don't know when Kallisto slipped into the courtyard. She's standing where Eupraxia was, smirking.

"Is that what she told you happened?" Kallisto goes on before I can answer. She looks between Amersa and me. She scoffs. "Apollonia wasn't expelled because she was roughed up by some soldiers. She was expelled because she *slept* with them."

"What are you talking about?" It takes everything I have not to scream. "She didn't go to sleep."

Kallisto frowns, confused, and then something seems to dawn on her. Her laugh is cruel. "Gods on high," she says. "You don't even know what I'm talking about." She cocks her head. "Do they really not teach girls what sex is where you come from?"

Amersa looks away, and my cheeks burn. I don't know what Kallisto is talking about, and I don't want to admit that, either.

"I shouldn't be surprised," she says. "You always were just an ignorant little—"

I lunge.

It's satisfying to see a brief look of fear in the moment before my body collides with Kallisto's. My shoulder explodes in pain as we slam against the stone floor, but in my rage, I ignore it. My focus is singular and defined. The first time my fist comes down on Kallisto's pretty face, a strange thrill pulses through me. Kallisto cries out the second time I strike her, and I relish it. I want to *hurt* her, because if I can hurt Kallisto, if I can make her scream the way Apollonia screamed as the priestesses dragged her away, then I won't have to think about the fact that all this happened because of me. *I* left Apollonia in the city alone. Somewhere behind me, Amersa is shouting.

"Meddy! Meddy you mustn't—"

"Enough."

I freeze with my fist still raised in the air. Kallisto groans as her head rolls to the side, and when I look up, Amersa is staring at something behind me, frightened.

"Medusa." The high priestess's voice is low, yet the sound of my name reverberates around the whole room. "Rise, and do not strike Acolyte Kallisto again."

My body seems to act of its own accord as I obey. Kallisto mutters something incoherent and spits blood, but no one pays her any notice. The high priestess is studying me, and I can discern nothing from her expression. The thrill I felt a moment before is entirely gone, replaced by a dull dread that begins to build in my stomach. This is it; it's over. I understand that with a sort of detached resignation. Attacking a fellow acolyte, within the Temple of Athena no less, is unacceptable; I'm going to be dismissed from service, too.

The high priestess beckons. "Come with me," she says. "Now."

I expect her to admonish me as soon as we are away from the other acolytes, but Eupraxia walks in silence, her hands reverently folded. I realize as we continue that she's taking me to a part of the temple I've never been permitted in, down a corridor that's dark and cold. New fear stipples my skin. Am I going to be punished in some other way for what I've done, locked in some sort of cell?

Eupraxia reaches a small door, turns the handle, and enters. She does not look back to see if I've followed, but I stay on her heels. At once, I encounter a wave of warmth and a flickering light. Eupraxia steps aside, and I see who it is sitting on a stool beside the hearth.

Athena turns from the flames and meets my gaze.

WITHOUT ANOTHER WORD, Eupraxia ducks out of the room, leaving me and the goddess alone. For several seconds, we only stare at each other. Then Athena speaks.

"You're angry."

I start. These are not the words I was expecting. When I look up at Athena, she is serene as a draft ruffles her red-gold hair. I'm not sure what to say in response, so I remain silent. She looks up at me.

"I think we should speak frankly."

No matter how many times I am in her presence, I always feel small next to Athena. Under her cool gray gaze, the anger dissipates further.

"Eupraxia has relayed to me what happened," the goddess says. "She tells me that you and Acolyte Apollonia were close. She warned me that you would be upset."

I flinch. Even hearing Apollonia's name hurts. I can't get the sound of her screams or the look on her face out of my head. I still feel the places where she clung to me. When I don't answer her, Athena arches a red brow.

"If you do not agree with my high priestess's judgment, your anger should be directed toward me," she goes on. "*I* was the one who instructed her to dismiss the girl."

The revelation makes everything worse. I feel a stinging betrayal.

Beneath that sting, there's something else, a return to anger that terrifies me. I clench my hands into fists, bite down until my jaw hurts.

"You're full of rage. Speak plainly."

I want to sound angry, but the words that leave me are full of anguish. "She was loyal to you, she loved you. She . . . she would have been a devout servant to you, I'm sure of it, and you dismissed her because . . ." I stop myself. Kallisto's words crouch in the back of my mind. I didn't understand some of what she said.

"Did Apollonia tell you exactly what the soldiers did to her, Medusa?"

I shake my head.

"They violated her, took her honor."

"I don't understand."

Athena looks slightly impatient now. "The priestesses who serve in this temple serve at different parts of their natural life cycle. Apollonia is young, unmarried. Women of her status are to maintain their chastity while in my service. She did not, and so she can no longer serve."

Something she's said stops me. "Chastity, Goddess?"

Athena's expression sharpens. "Dear child," she says, "did your parents never explain to you how babies are made? How women become pregnant?"

"No." My cheeks warm. "They didn't."

Athena is staring at me with a new assessment. "You speak four languages, but you've never been taught about procreation." She shakes her head. "There are many names for the process in which babies are made. 'Intercourse' is one of them. Others call it 'sex.'"

That was the word Kallisto used earlier.

Do they really not teach girls what sex is where you come from?

"Procreation requires a man and a woman," Athena goes on. "The man must empty his seed into a woman." She fidgets. "To do that, a certain . . . closeness is required."

"Forgive me, Goddess." My voice is small. "Closeness?"

Athena takes a deep breath, leans in, then whispers a few quick words in my ear. When she's finished, I pull back, uncomfortable. At once, vivid images flash before me. I think all the way back to that moment Theo and I stumbled upon Poseidon and the sea nymph in my mother's garden. That was what they were doing, I'm now almost sure of it, but something doesn't make sense.

"Goddess." I consider how to ask my next question. "Do men and women always practice intercourse just to have babies?"

Athena wrinkles her nose. "No," she says curtly. "There are some who do it as a lewd and indecent pastime to appease their more carnal and base desires." She sniffs. "There are some who allow others to pay for it."

I think about the man and woman I saw on Athens's streets, of the building they disappeared into together. I heard moaning, but I didn't know what they were doing . . .

"Your parents should have explained this to you much sooner," says Athena. "Seventeen is far too old to be ignorant of these things."

I flinch. I never expected my parents to teach me about anything like this, but the truth is my feelings are hurt that Stheno and Euryale never bothered to talk to me about this. It makes me wonder what else they might not have told me, what else I might have remained ignorant of had I not come to Athens.

"Thank you for answering my questions, Goddess." I bow my head. "If you'll allow me, though, I have one more."

She nods, signaling for me to go on.

"Apollonia told me what happened to her," I start. "She told me that those soldiers found her and hurt her. She didn't seek them out. If they practiced any kind of . . . intercourse, I don't believe that that was her choice. I believe she might have been forced to do it." I pause. "Isn't that wrong?"

Athena studies me a moment before answering. "It is wrong," she says. "And certainly, I will speak to Eupraxia to ensure the soldiers of this city are reminded about the sanctity of my acolytes and priestesses, but Apollonia has to accept a level of responsibility for what happened to her last night. She voluntarily confessed to Eupraxia that she'd been drinking heavily, that she was in the city alone at night at the time the soldiers found her." Athena shakes her head. "She was all but asking for something to happen to her; she put herself in a compromising position. Does that make sense, Meddy?"

The truth is, it *doesn't* make sense. I know almost nothing about intercourse, but I remember the way Apollonia looked when I first found her. I remember the bruises on her body and the fragility in her voice and the hurt in her eyes. She and I were friends, and she wasn't even able to tell me in detail what had happened.

I open my mouth to say as much, but Athena continues to speak.

"I've no doubt that she would have been a devout and hardworking priestess of this temple," she says. "But I simply cannot have girls who lack sound judgment in my service. It is a poor reflection on me." She looks off for a moment and then returns my gaze. "But I don't wish to speak about Apollonia anymore. Now, Medusa, I wish to speak about *you*."

"Me?" I start.

Athena nods. "I have been receiving reports from Eupraxia, updates on your progress here at the temple. I'm told you passed your second test rather memorably, and that you have shown a natural affinity for service to the people of the city."

I smile, then feel guilty for it. A part of me isn't ready to move on from Apollonia yet; I want to plead her case and try to convince Athena to reverse her decision. But there's another, smaller part of me that relishes Athena's praise, wants it to continue. The last time we saw each other, she expressed disappointment in me. The difference between that exchange and this one is night and day. Today, there's no disappointment in the goddess's eyes, only fondness.

A part of me just wants her to keep looking at me that way.

"There's another matter we need to discuss," says Athena. "Your father."

I stare at her. "My . . . father?"

"He has asked that you return home for a visit," she says. "I have told him you may have a week."

I'm not sure what to make of her words. My father has never expressed much of an interest in me; it seems strange that he would miss me enough to ask for me to come home.

He's never had to be without you, an inner voice reminds me. *Perhaps the time apart has done some good.*

"I will speak to Eupraxia," says Athena. "You will not have your third test until you return."

"Thank you, Goddess."

At my slightly deflated tone, Athena's brows rise. "You still don't wish to return home." It's not a question.

"It isn't that," I say, staring at my hands. The truth is, I do miss my sisters. I miss Theo. But in the month I have been in Athens, I have found a new kind of home, a sense of purpose I never thought possible. The idea of giving that up, even for a little while, saddens me. I don't know how to say any of this to Athena, so I simply say, "I've come to really enjoy Athens. I suppose I'll miss it."

The goddess smiles. "It will be here." She stands, prompting me to as well. I know our conversation is over. "Go home, Medusa." Her voice is warm. "Enjoy the time with your family. I expect you to maintain your standard of excellence upon your return."

"Yes, Goddess." I offer her a bow as she stands and leaves the room. Only once I'm alone do I feel I can breathe again. Absently, I lift a hand to rub at my neck.

That's when I realize, for the first time, that my seashell necklace is gone.

XXI

ATHENA KEEPS HER WORD.

For the rest of the day, I set to work performing my standard tasks as an acolyte alongside Kallisto and Amersa. If either of them questions where Eupraxia took me after my altercation with Kallisto, they've been instructed not to ask or are too afraid to. Kallisto, for her part, shoots dirty looks at me every chance she gets, but their effect is slightly muted by the swollen lip she now sports because of me. It should feel vindicating, but the truth is, everywhere I look in the temple, I see reminders of Apollonia.

By the time I reach the acolytes' quarters, her bed pallet has been rolled up and taken away, but that only leaves a conspicuous space where it used to be. I keep imagining her face, remembering how she cried as the priestesses took her away. It bothers me that I don't have any idea where she is now. I wouldn't even know where to start looking for her.

The next morning, when Eupraxia tells me I'm going home, a part of me is less sorry for it.

Just as he took me to Athens, it's Hermes whom I find at the base of the Acropolis's hill waiting to take me home. Our journey back to my island is just as smooth as the one before—which is to say, not at all smooth for me—but all that's forgotten as we fly across ocean waves and the island comes into view. Tears well in my eyes as I glimpse the first hints of its golden shore, the familiar trees that make up its tiny jungle.

I've missed home more than I thought.

Hermes bids me farewell with a quick wave before he departs again, and I make my way up the crooked stone path that leads to the palace. It has been just over a month since I left home, but already I feel as though it has changed. The sand is hotter and grittier on the soles of my feet than I remember, the gulls overhead are louder. I'm struck by the realization that maybe it isn't this place that has changed, but me.

Once I'm inside, I walk the palace hoping to find Stheno or Euryale; my heart plummets when I enter the great hall and find my father instead. Today, he's sitting on one of the carved driftwood thrones he has ordered his slaves to make for him. I wonder if he is pretending he is still a powerful god, still a foreboding high lord of the sea. His dark eyes land on me as I enter the room. I can read nothing in his face, and it occurs to me that I've forgotten how stoic he can be.

"Athena kept her word." His voice is neutral, and I'm relieved not to hear any anger in it as he looks me over. "You've returned."

"Yes, Father." I start to bow just as I would at the temple when speaking to a senior priestess, then realize what I'm doing and stop.

My father appears to be waiting for me to do something or . . . *say* something. "Well?" he urges, crossing his arms. "What news have you to report?"

Of course. If I believed, even for a second, that my father had asked Athena to send me home because he missed me, this is a timely reminder of how foolish that assumption was. My father cares nothing for me or for my actual well-being. His sole interest in me is as it has always been: directly tied to what I can *do* for him. My personal achievements are to his political benefit. I remember that as I give my report.

"I am progressing well at the temple." I keep my head bowed, my voice low. "Already, I've passed two of the three prerequisite tests to become a priestess. I do honorable work as an acolyte, serving the people of Athens—"

"I don't care about that nonsense." My father waves a dismissive hand. "What of Athena? Have you spoken with her?"

"Yes," I say quickly. "She has taken an interest in my progress and checked on my welfare several times."

My father nods. "That's good, you have her ear. And what do you tell her of the Sea Court?"

I falter. "I . . . I haven't talked with Athena about the Sea Court."

At once, my father's expression turns stormy. "Do you mean to tell me that you have spent your entire time in Athens playing foolish mortal games? You did not think even once to use your proximity to Athena to the Sea Court's advantage?"

My reply comes out in a small voice. "You . . . you never asked me to."

My father's lip curls. "You're more useless than I thought," he says in a low voice. "I knew you'd be no good for marriage alliances, but I believed you could be of some use to me if you had the attention of one of the more powerful Olympians." He looks at me now the way one might look at a beetle underfoot. "I see I was mistaken."

My legs start to tremble, and I resent that I can't hide how much he frightens me. For the last few weeks in Athens, I have felt smart, strong, capable.

In a matter of seconds, my father has made me small again.

"If you are not clever enough to use this opportunity," he says, "I see no reason why you should continue to stay in Athens." He twists a golden ring on his finger. "Perhaps it would be better for you to remain here."

"No! Please, Father!" I fall to my knees, hating how small my voice sounds. "Please, I will work harder. I will speak to Athena about the Sea Court. I have not yet, but . . ." I scramble for words and then think of something. "But I have spoken to the sea king."

"The sea king?" My father's expression changes instantly. "*You* have had an audience with Poseidon?"

I nod, standing. "More than once. He knows I'm your daughter, and he knows I'm in Athens. He has watched over me, too. He . . . he says you impress him a great deal." At best, this is an egregious stretch of the truth; at worst, it's a naked lie.

My father doesn't seem to notice, though. He's stroking his beard and now looks thoughtful. "Good." He sounds more like he's talking to himself than to me. "That is . . . good."

"I know I could curry more favor with the sea king, if I had more time in Athens," I add quickly. "Please, Father."

It's almost as though he's forgotten I'm there. A faraway look has entered my father's eyes, and I wonder if he's imagining himself on Mount Olympus now, finally accepted by the Olympians. I wait patiently for him to look my way again.

"Very well." He sounds like a god, rich tones and a rich timbre to his voice. "You may continue to stay in Athens, for now."

"Thank you, Father."

"Go."

I nod in thanks, then leave the hall before he can change his mind.

I DON'T FIND my sisters inside, so I make my way out to the island's shoreline.

Like the rest of the island, nothing is markedly different here as I walk along the beach, and yet it feels different, less peaceful. The waves still crash against the breakers farther out, but for the first time, something strikes me as violent about them. That violence makes me think of my father. When I stood in his presence, I was frightened; now, safely away from him, I realize that the feeling that remains is anger. Anger because I've worked so hard in Athens to prove myself and he didn't even acknowledge it; anger because I've managed to do more to elevate our family's so-called status in seventeen measly years than he ever has, and he can't even thank me for it.

Anger because I'll never know what I did to deserve a father like him.

I say none of this aloud as I continue my walk along the coast, past clusters of palm trees and several shallow tide pools. I'm heading toward a small grouping of rocks I sometimes like to climb atop to get a better view of the island. I'm surprised at what I find when I reach it.

Someone is already there, perfectly still atop one of the rocks. At first, I think of Stheno or Euryale, then I realize with a start that I'm wrong. It's someone else.

"Mama?"

My mother is sitting with her knees pulled to her chest. Waves spray her face, soaking her dark, kinky hair, but she doesn't so much as turn when I call for her. Her lips are moving, but I can't hear any words. A sinking feeling settles in my chest as I draw closer.

"Mama!" I call to her again as I stumble across the dunes. "Mama, I'm back. I'm home. What's going—?"

I freeze, because now I see what has captured my mother's attention so entirely.

The creature at the base of the rocks is enormous, the size of a small whale. Most of its body is below the water's surface, but I can still discern a long pink head, tentacles, and one yellow eye larger than my whole body. As I draw near, a wet sucking sound emits from it, followed by a series of sharp, eerie clicks. The sound makes my skin crawl, and only one word comes to my mind as I stop to stand beside my mother.

Monster.

"Mama," I say more quietly. "What is that?"

My mother still doesn't look up at me. "One of my pets," she says quietly. "She visits sometimes, but our time together is always limited. Always brief."

As though the creature understands my mother, it blinks, then sinks below the ocean depths and out of sight. I'm further unnerved by the fact that the water had barely rippled with the monster's departure. For several seconds, I stare at the place where it disappeared. "What is . . . she called?"

My mother shrugs. "Men have given her any number of names in their native tongues. I've never thought to ask which ones she prefers."

"Mama." I don't like the way this feels, as if our roles were reversed and I am the parent. I crouch beside her. "You should go inside. Your clothes are soaked."

"It doesn't matter," my mother murmurs. "I cannot leave this island. I can never see my children."

"*I'm* back, for a little while," I point out, trying to inject a cheer into my voice that I certainly don't feel. "And Stheno and Euryale are still here. I know they—"

"Not you three." My mother is staring out into the waves. "I'm talking about my *other* children."

The hairs on the back of my neck stand on end. The sun is still shining, but I feel none of its warmth as I stare at my mother. I have a bad feeling, a sense that I am teetering on the edge of some terrible revelation. My mother's words echo.

My other *children.*

"What are you talking about?" My voice is barely a whisper. "What other children?"

My mother remains silent for so long that I wonder if she's even heard me.

"I gave the first three their names," she finally says, still not looking at me. "I called them Deino, Enyo, and Pemphredo. They were born strange, with only one shared eye between them, and hair like spiders' silk. I cared for all three of them myself; I wouldn't let anyone else nurse them. I thought that they would stay with me." She shivers. "Until *she* came and took them away."

"Who, Mama?"

"Echidna was next," my mother goes on, ignoring me. "And *she* was a real beauty. The top half of her body was like yours, human, but instead of legs, she had a beautiful blue-green tail. She was marvelous, really." A smile touches her lips, then fades. "Then she was taken, too."

I don't ask my mother questions anymore. I remain silent as she continues.

"The hardest was Ladon." My mother lowers her voice, and now I hear a tremble in it. "My sweet boy, my hideous, wonderful, fierce boy-child. Your foolish father thought the Olympians would be merciful with us that time. He thought surely they wouldn't take our only son." She shakes her head. "He didn't understand what I did: that taking is what the Olympians do best. It's how they came to power, it's all they know."

"Who took them away, Mama?" I steady my voice as I brace myself. "*Who?*"

A cold smile touches my mother's lips. "I did try to tell you, in a way. I told you that after the Gigantomachy, Zeus tasked Athena with removing any perceived threats. He never saw your sisters and brother as children, only as dangerous, and so she took them far from me." She turns and, for the first time, really looks at me. "Now she's taken *you*, too."

I want to tell her she's wrong. I think of how Athena looked at me only yesterday, with such fondness. With her offer for me to serve as an acolyte, she gave me an irreplaceable gift, a chance to leave this island. But I think about Apollonia again. I think of the way Athena cut her away so easily, despite her loyalty. I remember a conversation Athena and I had, back on the very first day we met.

My two older sisters are immortal. I am the only one of us three who is not. No one knows why.

And the other children?

Athena's question confused me at the time because I didn't understand what she meant. Now I see that she knew about my other siblings all along. I think of the way Athena and my mother looked at each other, the mutual enmity I saw in their eyes. I understand it now, and I can't reconcile the version of Athena who would take children from their mother with the one the people of Athens adore with such loyalty and fervor.

A single tear slides down my mother's ancient face.

"I'm sorry, Mama."

My words seem to break something within my mother. A second tear falls and then a third. Soon, she's crying uncontrollably. I can do nothing as her wails grow louder, keener, more desperate. I know that I am hearing the sound of true grief.

"D-don't go back to h-her," my mother says between sobs. "The O-Olympians are not to be t-t-trusted. They'll ruin you."

More than anything, I wish Stheno or Euryale were here to tell me what to do. When my mother stops crying, I put an arm around her. "You should rest," I say to her gently. "Come on. I'll help you to your bedchamber. We'll get you something to drink."

My mother looks up at me. When our gazes meet, I find that hers is dull, lost.

"Wine?" she murmurs. "Will you get me some wine?"

"Yes, Mama. I'll get you some wine."

She nods. Together, we make our way up the dunes and back into the palace.

BY THE TIME I've put my mother to bed, I'm exhausted.

It isn't the first time I've had to do it, but something about this time has been particularly draining. I watched as my mother's eyes slowly closed, watched as she tossed fitfully for a few minutes before going still. In her bedchamber's silence, the things she told me echoed over and over in my mind, like some terrible refrain.

I had more siblings. Other sisters. A brother.

If Athena wasn't who she purported to be, did that mean everything I'd built in Athens was a lie, too?

That possibility is so terrible, I bury it at once.

I'm still mulling over my mother's words when a voice I recognize pulls me from my thoughts.

"Meddy?"

I look up, and a surge of relief fills me when I find two familiar faces. Euryale and Stheno are both standing at the other end of the hall. Within seconds, they are upon me, wrapping their arms around me.

"Meddy!" Even Stheno has forsaken her usual reserve. "We didn't know you were back!"

"Athena let me come home to visit," I say, still holding on to her. Her locs tickle my cheek, and I blink hard as I realize how long it's been since I felt that particular sensation. She pulls back so that she and Euryale can look at me.

"We're so glad you're home," Euryale says, beaming.

"Come." At once, Stheno has gone back to her usual self. "We're going to deal with your hair, *immediately*."

By "deal" with my hair, I learn that Stheno means wash it. I start to object when she and Euryale guide me to a basin, but when they lean me over it and pour the cool water on my head, whatever words I intended to say vanish. I close my eyes, relishing the feel of their nails scratching all the hard-to-reach places on my scalp. I love so much about the temple, but this kind of care is something I *have* missed about home. Once they've finished washing it, Stheno directs me to a stool where she and Euryale begin the task of separating my locs into sections. She pinches one between her fingers and sighs.

"Honestly, Meddy, do Athenians even *use* rose oil for their hair?"

I give Stheno a noncommittal sort of reply. She grumbles, then continues her work.

"Tell us more about Athens, Meddy," Euryale says as she massages my scalp. "What's it like?"

I want to tell my sisters about everything—Hermes, the acolyte tests, the chariot races during Panathenaia. There's so much, I don't even know where to start. At the same time, something else rises to the forefront of my mind.

"Stheno, Eury, I need to talk to you about something, something I learned about while I was in Athens. It's called . . . intercourse."

The effect is instant. Stheno nearly drops the bottle of rose oil she's been holding, while Euryale's hands go still on my scalp. When neither of them says anything, I rise from the chair to look at both of them.

"Well?"

Stheno looks to Euryale, lips pursed. "I *did* tell you this would happen."

"You knew?" I can't pretend to hide my hurt. "You knew about it, and you didn't tell me?"

"We tried, Meddy!" Euryale's voice has gone up in pitch, the way it always does when she's nervous. "We really did, we just . . . never could find the right time."

"What about when I started my monthly blood?" I accuse. "Why not then?"

"You still seemed so young," Euryale says. She looks to be on the verge of tears. "We didn't think you were ready, and there really was no need yet—"

"We were trying to protect you," Stheno adds. "We thought it was the right thing to do."

I bite back a laugh. Those words are only a slight deviation from the very words I said to Euryale when justifying why I'd tried to stop her marriage to Maheer.

"Meddy." Euryale's voice is softer. "I'm sorry."

"*We're* sorry," Stheno amends. "We should have told you about it sooner. We shouldn't have let you go to Athens without that kind of knowledge. You were bound to find out, but it should have been from us."

A part of me wants to stay mad at my sisters, but the truth is I've already forgiven them. We stand in silence for a few more seconds before Stheno speaks.

"If you have any questions for us, anything you don't already know," she says, "you can ask us now."

There's already one question on the tip of my tongue, though I don't know if I should ask it. In the end, curiosity gets the better of me, and I do.

"Have either of you . . . well, done it?"

"Meddy!" Euryale's eyes go wide. "That's a personal question!"

I note that she did not say no.

"I haven't," says Stheno calmly. "It's not something I've ever had much interest in, to be honest with you." We both turn to Euryale, who's gone uncharacteristically quiet. After a moment, Stheno rolls her eyes.

"If you don't tell her, I'll—"

"Once!" Euryale says quickly. When Stheno's eyes narrow, she shifts her weight. "Twice. Four or five times at most. She was a very pretty forest nymph who came to several of Mother and Father's feasts." Euryale looks peeved. "In my defense, this island can be incredibly dull."

I blink. Athena had only spoken of intercourse as something that happens between a man and a woman, but the idea of it being something that could happen between two women is equally intriguing. I nod, then sit back in my chair to let them continue. I don't say it, but a part of me is relieved. I didn't realize how much I'd missed the easiness of being with my sisters. I knew, when I left for Athens, that I would miss seeing them, but it's the small things, too—the sound of Euryale's voice when she's exasperated, the way she and Stheno bicker. Euryale begins to twist my locs, and I feel a pleasant, familiar drowsiness. I close my eyes.

"Now that we've satisfied your curiosity." I detect a hint of amusement in Stheno's voice. "Do tell us more about Athens, before Euryale drowns in a puddle of embarrassment."

"Please," Euryale adds.

I sit up straight, alert again. *This* is something I can talk about with ease.

"Athens is glorious," I say honestly. "It's so big, and there are *so* many people. I think you could spend days there and still not see all of it."

"It sounds lovely," says Euryale softly.

"The citizens really love to celebrate," I go on. "I got to participate in a festival called Panathenaia, and my friend Apollonia—" I falter.

"What's wrong?" Stheno asks.

I think of the last time I saw Apollonia's face, the anguish in her cries. "One of my friends, another acolyte, was dismissed from service for something she didn't do. I haven't seen her since."

"Oh, how sad!" says Euryale. "Stheno, will you pass me a bit of that rose oil?"

"She was one of the best acolytes," I add as my sisters continue to do my hair. "And the way she was dismissed . . . It was awful."

"I'm sure it was," Stheno says distractedly. "Meddy, did you moisturize your hair *at all* while you were gone?"

I feel a brief hint of annoyance as my sisters continue to fuss over my locs, clearly unmoved about what I'm telling them. Slowly, I realize that I can't fault them for it. My sisters don't understand the significance of what I'm telling them because they *can't* understand. They have never

left this island; everything I'm telling them must feel distant, abstract, ir-
relevant. It's a strange and sad revelation. All my life, my sisters and I have
shared most of the same experiences, walked along the same path.

For the first time ever, I wonder if our paths have begun to diverge.

BY THE TIME my hair meets Stheno's approval, it's nearly noon. My
stomach growls as I think of lunch, but a better idea comes to mind,
and I head to the gardens. They're as beautiful as I remember, and I
take in the collective scent of so many flowers in bloom, the birdsong
high above. I can't say exactly how I find Theo—my compass to him
has always felt more like an instinct—but when I do, he's sitting beneath the boughs of an old olive tree, carving away at a piece of wood.
Sunlight dapples his brown skin, and he's wearing that look of focus
I've so dearly missed. I wait a minute or two before I speak.

"I'm afraid I've forgotten to bring a new map for you. Could you
forgive me?"

Theo looks up, and his eyes go wide. "Meddy!" He casts the carving
knife and block of wood aside as he stands and closes the gap between
us in a few strides. I'm expecting a hug, but Theo takes it a step further,
wrapping his arms around my middle and spinning me around until
we're both dizzy and laughing. Even once we've stopped and the world
isn't blurred anymore, he's still grinning.

"You're back!" he says. "How long do you get to stay?"

"A week."

"That means you've passed your tests so far." He claps. "I knew you
would!"

"You knew more than me, then." More seriously, I add: "I've really
missed you, Theo."

"I've missed you," he says with equal sincerity. His eyes fly up to my
freshly retwisted locs. "I see your sisters have already found you."

"They have." I roll my eyes, though the gesture's half-hearted.

"Good," says Theo. "That means they won't be waiting on you." He settles back on the grass and pats a spot beside him. "Tell me everything."

Talking with Theo about my time in Athens is much easier than it was to talk to my sisters. In the month I've been gone, I almost forgot what an attentive audience my friend is. Theo listens, laughs, and asks questions at all the right moments, never taking his eyes off me as I regale him with stories. I try to describe what the Acropolis looks like, what the myrrh the priestesses burn smells like. When I try and fail to explain the exact taste of the olives in the temple's grove, my shoulders slump.

"I'm not doing a very good job of painting a picture for you," I note. "I wish you could come see it all for yourself."

Theo waves me off. "I can see it all in my head," he insists. "Go on."

I tell Theo about the first and second acolyte tests, and about Panathenaia. His face begins to fall when I tell him about Apollonia's expulsion, and as I go on, a frown pulls the corners of his lips down.

"Wait," he says, interjecting for the first time. "Are you telling me that Athena did that to one of her own acolytes?"

"Yes," I say quickly. "But it was Kallisto who told—"

"That's so cruel." Theo looks horrified. "And did she really blame Apollonia for her own attack? If so, that's awful."

"The Goddess cannot have servants who lack sound judgment." The parroted words surprise me as they leave my lips, but I don't take them back.

"But—"

"It reflects poorly on her, Theo. You wouldn't understand."

Theo opens his mouth, as if to argue, then seems to think better of it. "No," he says thoughtfully. "I suppose I wouldn't." A strange silence hangs between us a moment before a smaller smile returns to his face. "Please tell me more, Meddy."

I want to, but suddenly I don't know what to say. I can't discern exactly what's changed, but now I'm less keen to talk about Athena with Theo. His critique of her, the horrified way he looked, make me feel defensive. For the second time since my return home, there's a sense of disconnect I can't shake. I realize that, like my sisters, Theo's never going to truly understand the things I'm telling him because he's never been to Athens.

"I'm a bit hungry, actually," I say as I stand. "I'm going to go get some lunch, but I'll find you later on, all right?"

Theo's eyes are full of sadness. "All right, Meddy."

I turn from him and leave the gardens without looking back.

XXII

THAT NIGHT, MY parents order our cooks to prepare a special meal to celebrate my temporary homecoming.

It is no great feast—certainly, there is less on our table tonight than there was for the spring feast earlier in the year—but I still find myself quietly awed by how much food has been prepared for five people, four of whom don't even need to eat. My eyes take in the roasted meats, the assortments of sliced fruit, the flatbreads and cheeses, and I think about the Athenians to whom I and the other acolytes distributed sacks of grain. This meal alone could feed at least twenty of those people well. It all feels so excessive—though if anyone else notices or shares my sentiments, they don't say so. My parents still argue from their end of the table, while my sisters talk about mindless things at the other. Slowly, I realize I'm a stranger in my home; Athens is becoming the place where I feel more like myself. It is an unmooring sensation.

We're still dining when I feel a subtle but undeniable shift in the air. I know I'm not the only one who notices it, because at once, my father looks up, frowning, and my mother tenses.

"What is it?" she asks no one in particular.

My father turns to stare at the main doors to the hall, his sea-foam-white brows furrowed. Stheno, Euryale, and I exchange a look as a salty breeze blows into the room, tickling my skin and brushing my locs over my shoulder. Then I hear it: the unmistakable echo of footsteps in the corridor just beyond the doors my father is staring at. No one speaks as the footsteps come to a stop on the other side of the doors.

Then they swing open with a bang, and I have a sense of déjà vu as another Olympian enters our great hall. This time it isn't Athena, though.

Poseidon himself stands before us.

"My king!" My father stands as though he's been struck by lightning. He comes around the table at once and bows as Poseidon strides into the room. "This is a wonderful surprise!"

"Phorcys, Ceto."

A pleasant shiver runs the length of me as Poseidon's warm voice fills the room. I watch as he embraces my father like an old friend and then offers my mother a courteous nod. "Please forgive my intrusion, but I found myself in close proximity to your island tonight. I hope I'm not imposing."

"Not at all, my king." My mother's voice is nearly a purr. "For the second time this year, you honor us." I can practically hear the smugness dripping from her voice. No doubt, she'll boast of this impromptu visit to the other goddesses of the Sea Court as soon as she has the chance. "Please, join us for dinner. Our table is yours."

Poseidon nods. "Thank you for your hospitality."

My father snaps his fingers, and a flurry of slaves run toward the table, moving plates and goblets around to make space for the sea king. I hope he might pick a seat next to mine, and I fight off a wave of disappointment when, instead, he sits beside Stheno. My heart starts to pound. I last saw Poseidon the night before last, when he escorted me back to the Acropolis. Suddenly, my mind is overrun with memories of the way his lips felt on mine, the way his hands seemed to burn pleasantly in all the places he touched me. I say nothing as he settles into his seat and then turns to address us all.

"I enjoyed the feast your family hosted earlier this spring," he says. "It was entertaining."

"Thank you, Your Grace," says my mother. "We were just thinking of hosting another in the autumn."

This is news to me. It feels strange, no longer being totally apprised of the happenings of this household. I look to my sisters. Was this planned feast another attempt to find suitors for them? I make a note to ask them about it later.

"That would be splendid," says Poseidon. "If you did host such a feast, perhaps I could extend the invitation to some of my siblings."

Silence falls.

"Forgive me, my king," my mother says cautiously. "But you do have so many siblings. Which . . . ?"

"Zeus, Hera, perhaps Demeter." He pauses thoughtfully. "Hades so rarely leaves the Underworld these days, but it's always worth trying."

My mother's eyes go wide, and I can only imagine what she's thinking. I know now why she hates the Olympians, Athena specifically. But if she and my father managed to host several highly ranked Olympians, the king of the gods among them . . .

My parents exchange a look.

"It's settled, then," my father announces. He is maintaining a façade of calm, but only just. "We'll begin the planning at once."

"I'm sure I will enjoy it immensely," says Poseidon. His eyes land on me for the briefest second, but I still jolt in my seat. He smiles, then turns back to my parents.

My father dominates the rest of the dinner conversation with syco-phantic questions for the sea king—how relations fare between the estranged Demeter and Hades, whether it's true that Zeus has sired yet another mortal bastard. I wait for a break in their talking, hoping I might find an opportunity to add something of my own to their con-versation, but when the hour grows late, my sisters and I are dismissed before such a moment presents itself. I am loath to go, and I lie in bed for hours listening to the distant sounds of Poseidon and my father talk-ing well into the small hours between night and morning.

Eventually, the conversation ends, or perhaps I simply fall asleep. When I wake up next, all is quiet, and one of the slaves has dimmed the hall's candles, so that only a tiny golden flickering is visible beneath the crack in my door. It is that quiet that allows me to hear the soft pad of approaching footsteps, and at once, I sit up. I rise from my bed, gently pry my door open, then peek outside. At first, I think no one is there; then something shifts in the shadows.

"Who's there?" I ask. "Eury? Theo?"

"Forgive me, little priestess."

My heart stutters as Poseidon emerges from the dark. His smile is careworn. Tonight, he is wearing a white tunic, but everything else about him is exactly as it was that night in Athens. A sea breeze abruptly blows through the hall, ruffling his blue-black hair.

"I've woken you," he says. "I apologize."

I don't know what prompts me to step out into the hall, only that I do so without thinking. I'm aware than I'm wearing only a thin silk night slip—not a garment that would usually be considered appropriate for an audience with someone like Poseidon—but I find I don't care as our eyes meet.

"You didn't wake me, my king." At his raised eyebrow, I remember what he once asked me to call him. "Poseidon."

The sea king's smile grows. "It's good to see you, Medusa. I have thought of you."

He's thought of me. I suck in a sharp breath. I so want to ask him *what* he's been thinking, but I'm not brave enough. We stare at each other for several seconds before he goes on.

"There's something I need to speak to you about." His gaze drops, and he looks abashed. "The other night, after I escorted you back to the Acropolis, we . . ."

"I remember." My face warms.

"I shouldn't have kissed you," he said.

Something in my heart plummets.

"It was impulsive on my part, irresponsible," he goes on. "But now there's a more serious problem." Suddenly, he looks directly at me. "I haven't been able to stop thinking about it."

If what he said just before stopped my heart's beating, this sends it in a frantic new cadence. I almost can't believe the words I've just heard.

"You've . . . you've thought about it?"

Poseidon nods, looking pained. "The way I felt with you . . ." He shakes his head and laughs, but it's a humorless sound. "I don't understand what you've done to me."

Poseidon is the king of the sea; I am just the mortal daughter of two lowly sea gods. The idea that I might have any power or effect on someone like him thrills me, terrifies me, intrigues me.

"I have to confess something else," he says. "But I would ask you to keep it a secret, something between only us."

He trusts me with a secret. Me. I'm nodding before I've even processed his words. "Of course."

Poseidon's smile turns wry. "I was not entirely honest when I told your parents why I've come here."

"You weren't?"

"No."

A familiar current of energy races through my body as Poseidon takes another step forward, closing the gap between us.

"The truth is, when Athena mentioned in passing that you'd gone home, I came to your island to see you, to give you this."

My breath hitches as he reaches into the pocket of his tunic and withdraws my seashell necklace.

"You found it."

"It was on the streets of Athens," he says. "I thought you might want it back."

"Thank you."

"I'll put it on you." Before I can speak, he's moved behind me and gently shifted my locs from my neck. I shiver as his knuckles graze my skin, warm to the touch as he carefully ties the cord of the necklace so that its shell falls to the middle of my chest. When he is done, his fingers trace down my neck, stopping at my shoulder. He pinches one of my locs, and when I turn my head slightly, he's winding it gently around his finger.

"You favor your mother and sisters," he whispers. "But you're prettiest."

Warmth floods me, starting in my core and working its way to all my extremities. Slowly, I turn to fully face Poseidon. He is still holding one of my locs.

"Thank you. You're kind."

Poseidon's eyes drop to my lips. "How old are you, Medusa?"

I think of the way he leaned in and kissed me in Athens, how I want him to do that again. "Seventeen."

I don't exactly understand the look that flashes across his eyes, the brief, strange hunger. The god takes the loc he's been holding and brings it to his lips. His eyes never leave mine as he lets his mouth linger there. I start when his hand moves to my side to trace along my rib cage, and when he pulls me to him so that my back is against his chest, I gasp.

"You're so *young*," he says. The words buzz in my ear. "So beautiful."

I am an acolyte of the Temple of Athena. Deep down, I know I am not supposed to want. But the truth is, in this moment, I *do* want. I want Poseidon to kiss me again. I want him to press me against the wall the way he did before, and I want to feel the brush of his stubbled mouth scraping gently against my skin.

I want to know what comes after that.

"Medusa, I—" Suddenly, Poseidon looks up, then steps away from me. I blink, as though I've been awoken from a trance, but then I hear it, too. Footsteps farther up the hall, faint but growing unmistakably louder.

"I must go," Poseidon says. At once, his tone is more formal. "I do hope we see each other again, Medusa, in Athens. If you ever wish to see me, come to the city's shoreline and say my name. I'll find you."

"I—" He's gone before I can form a reply. I watch him walk in the opposite direction of the noise, disappearing into the dark with that easy rolling gait that reminds me of the ocean's waves.

The approaching footsteps grow louder, then:

"Meddy?"

I whirl around and find Theo standing at the opposite end of the hall. His arms are crossed, and he's frowning.

"Theo!" My voice is a fraction too high. "What are you doing here?"

He nods. "I could ask you the same. It's late."

"I couldn't sleep," I say, which is a half-truth.

Theo's eyes narrow. "I saw someone walking away just before. Who was it?"

"Poseidon." I say the name more carefully, but I'm still unable to to-tally temper the quiet thrill that comes from saying his name.

"Poseidon," Theo repeats. "I didn't know you were so familiar with the sea king."

I shift my weight, uncomfortable. "I'm not. He's just . . . kind."

Theo cocks his head. "What were you two talking about at this hour of the night?"

"We barely talked at all." At Theo's arched brow, I add: "He just gave me back a necklace I'd lost in Athens."

Theo frowns. "Why did he have it?"

"He found it!" I say, trying to keep the exasperation from my voice. "It was just good fortune that he recognized it."

Theo says nothing for a beat. "And that's all? He said nothing else to you?"

I shrug. "He complimented me," I add. "He said I looked like my mother."

Theo's face twists. "Your mother is an ancient goddess, thousands of years old."

"So?"

"So, you're seventeen and nothing like her."

I know what he's trying to say; I can even acknowledge that it's mostly true. I don't revel in the politics of the Sea Court the way she does. I don't spend my days in a red wine haze. I'm not like my mother, and in some ways I'm glad for it. That doesn't mean hearing it aloud doesn't hurt. Normally, I'd want to tell Theo everything, but this doesn't feel like something I can share.

"You've made your point," I say coolly. "What quarrel do you have with Poseidon?"

Theo gives me a significant look. "I've heard things about him, Meddy."

I roll my eyes. "Don't tell me, gossip?"

"It's not gossip." He bends his head and lowers his voice. "Slaves hear things, the things people say when they forget we're there."

I don't want to be curious, but I can't help myself. "Things like what?"

Theo looks around us. "There are palace slaves who have worked here longer than you or I have been alive," he says. "Poseidon doesn't have a good reputation, even among gods."

"What do they say?"

"That his charm is all for show; that in reality, he has a foul temper," says Theo. "I've heard he's cruel to those who serve him and crueler still to mortals. He destroys entire towns with his earthquakes and floods, just for the sport of it." Theo looks down, embarrassed. "He's married to the sea queen, but he takes countless mistresses and has sired hundreds of bastards. Few of them are acknowledged, but it's an open secret. His wife despises him."

I think of Amphitrite then, of the way the sea queen's beautiful mouth twisted into a scowl as she looked around our great hall.

"You saw him," Theo says in a quieter voice. "You saw him with that sea nymph, in the gardens, same as me."

It's the first time he's ever acknowledged that night, and a part of me is angry that he's chosen this moment to do it.

I shake my head. "I'm sure there's an explanation."

"Unbelievable." Theo shakes his head. "You're actually defending him."

I can't say what exactly it is that ignites my anger, only that it comes suddenly, warming my blood. "You don't know him!" I shout. "He has been kind to me in Athens. He has protected me when you and my sisters couldn't."

Theo flinches as though he's been slapped. I know the words are hideously unfair, but I can't take them back. I wait for him to say something, anything, but he only stares at me a moment longer, then turns and walks away.

XXIII

I AM GLAD when it's time to return to Athens a week later.

The truth is, though I've only spent a short amount of time here, Athena's temple has, in some ways, come to feel more like home than my island ever did. Most of the priestesses are glad to see me when I return—I learn later that they were told I was visiting a gravely sick relative—and I find surprising comfort in throwing myself back into the rhythmic routine of temple life. Kallisto, Amersa, and I are the only three acolytes left, and it's hard to believe that just a few weeks ago, there were ten of us. Though my conversations with them are always brief, I know that all of us think constantly about what the third test will be. At night, when we go to bed, I instinctively still look at the place next to me where Apollonia's pallet used to be. The priestesses have gone into the city several times to distribute food since her expulsion, but no one has heard or seen any sign of her. It's that ambiguity about her fate that keeps me awake most nights. I have now lost two friends in the course of a month. Theo did not speak to me again after our fight back on the is-land, and I didn't say goodbye to him when I left. There are twin holes in my heart in their absence, and though I'm glad to be back in Athens, everything does seem slightly less bright without them.

A fortnight after my return to Athens, Eupraxia tasks me, Kallisto, and Amersa with cleaning the Acropolis's entryway.

"It is the first thing guests see when they arrive," she says. "We want to ensure that it remains pristine."

I don't complain aloud, but the truth is, more cleaning is the very last thing I feel like doing. Late summer has somehow summoned even more heat into Athens, and my whole body is layered in dirt and dried sweat that I badly want to scrape off with a pumice stone. Amersa and Kallisto seem to feel the same way, because as soon as Eupraxia is gone, Kallisto begins her grumbling.

"It's a waste of time," she says bitterly as she wipes a column with a rag. "All that old woman does is give us busywork under the pretext of it being something noble and sacred. If you ask me, she's just using us for the free labor."

I continue focusing on the broom in my hand, on the whisk of it across the marble floors. When neither Amersa nor I respond, Kallisto goes on.

"But maybe you don't mind the labor because you're used to it," she says, goading. "Maybe where you come from, that's the only kind of work you can get."

I don't tell Kallisto that, in fact, I come from immense wealth or that until coming to Athens as an acolyte, I never so much as touched a broom. Sometimes, I fantasize about the face she'd make if she learned the truth about where I "come from." Instead, I shake my head and keep working. Amersa kneels down to hold a dustpan for me while I sweep dirt into it.

But Kallisto isn't finished yet. A new, malicious look crosses her face. "You know you say her name in your sleep," she says. "I've heard it."

I stiffen at the same time Amersa looks between us, nervous.

"*Apollonia!*" Kallisto mimics. "*Apollonia, no!*" She snorts. "It's pathetic. You barely knew her."

I haven't felt true rage since my altercation with Kallisto in the court-yard, but it comes to life instantly at her words. My grip on the broom handle tightens, and I open my mouth—

Then there's a scream.

It's long, shrill, and sets my teeth on edge. Amersa jolts, while Kallisto's head whips around, trying to find the sound's origin point. There's a second scream, and I realize that the first came from *outside* the Acropolis, not within. The three of us step onto the sloping path that leads down into the city.

"What was that?" Amersa whispers.

I have no answer for her. In the city's rapidly fading light, it's difficult to see anything at first. Then, suddenly, I discern movement. A figure is running toward the Acropolis at full sprint. She draws closer, and I make out a middle-aged woman. She is slight, with olive skin and a clear sheen of sweat on her brow. Ribbons of dark hair fly out behind her, and I can see even from here that her eyes are wide with terror. A beat later, I understand why. Two uniformed soldiers are running after the woman. Their steps are heavy, slowed down by their matching armored uniforms, but they're still moving fast, closing the gap between themselves and the woman. She looks over her shoulder, then to the temple. When she sees us, she screams a third time.

"Help me!" she shouts. "Please, help me!"

I'm moving before I've registered the choice, racing down to the bottom of the Acropolis's main path so that the woman and I meet halfway. As soon as she reaches me, she latches onto me, nearly knocking me over. A sour smell fills the air around her, and up close I see she has several sores around her mouth. There is something decidedly unsettling about her, but I barely have time to take that in before the two soldiers are upon us.

"Stand aside, girl," one of them orders. The other makes to grab at the woman, but she dances out of the way.

"Wait." I step between them. "What's going on?" By now, Kallisto and Amersa have joined me at the end of the path. The woman tactfully places herself behind them.

"I did nothing!" the woman shrieks.

"She's under arrest." The soldier has not so much as looked at me once. His eyes stay trained on the woman. "For theft."

"I was hungry!" the woman protests. "Do you know how it feels to go hungry for *three days*? It was one apple; I told the farmer I would repay him—"

"It isn't her first offense," the second soldier adds.

"They're going to hurt me," the woman whines. "Please don't let them hurt me."

I look between the woman and the soldiers. "What happens to her, after she's arrested?"

"She'll stand trial," says the first soldier. He's short, blond, with severe dark eyes. "The farmer she stole from in the Agora will give testimony, and when she is found guilty, she'll be fined. If she can't pay it . . ." His expression hardens. "She'll lose a hand."

The woman whimpers.

"I'm going to find help," says Amersa. She turns and runs back up the hill toward the Acropolis, leaving Kallisto and me alone with the woman and the two guards. Kallisto looks at me, then scowls.

"Take her, for all I care," says Kallisto. "She's none of our concern."

The woman backs away as though she's been burned.

"Kallisto!"

"What?"

"We're acolytes," I say through my teeth. "We're supposed to help people."

"And we do," Kallisto snaps back. "Every week, we distribute food to those who need it. Everyone knows that. It's not our fault if this woman didn't take advantage of the temple's generosity and chose to steal instead."

"Enough." The second soldier, a taller, darker-haired man, advances. "Step aside."

I feel a rush of white-hot anger. It takes me a moment to find its root, to understand why the sight of these two men makes me especially angry. Then I have it. These aren't just two men, they're two *soldiers,* like the ones who harmed Apollonia. I look at the callousness in their eyes as they start toward the woman who now looks too tired to run any farther. Kallisto moves aside, but I go to stand in front of the woman.

"No," I say firmly. "You're not taking her."

"Meddy." Kallisto sounds annoyed, but when I meet her gaze, I see a touch of real fear in it. "Stop it. Don't get in the way—"

"*Move,* girl." The blond soldier has a new menace in his voice. "We won't ask again."

"Leave her alone."

The dark-haired soldier scowls, then reaches around me to try to grab the woman by the arm. She begins to scream again, this time so loud I'm amazed the whole city can't hear it. Without thinking, I raise the broom still in my hand and swing it at the dark-haired soldier's head as hard as I can. The force of the blow sends him to his knees, groaning. When he sits up, there's a bright red gash just below his eye. He glares at me, and now the blond soldier steps forward.

"Assaulting a soldier who's acting in duty to the city is a crime," he says. "Punishable by flogging or death." He starts toward me with new purpose. I tighten the grip on my broom, trembling.

"STOP THIS!"

Everyone—me, Kallisto, the woman, and the two soldiers—looks up at the sound of a new voice. I turn and, to my relief, see Eupraxia making her way down the Acropolis's hill, her priestess chiton billowing behind her. Amersa is at her heels. When Eupraxia stops before us, her face is white. She does not look at me or Kallisto, but she glares openly at the guards. Never before have I seen her so angry.

"What is the meaning of this?" Her voice is cold; even the soldiers flinch. They look at each other before the dark-haired one I hit stands to address her.

"*That* woman"—he points—"is guilty of theft. She ran toward the Acropolis to avoid punishment. And *that* girl"—he points to me—"obstructed her arrest. She—"

"Am I to understand correctly," says Eupraxia, "that you entered the sacred grounds of a temple with violent intent, then proceeded to threaten three of its chosen acolytes? Young, defenseless girls, no less?"

The soldiers both shift uncomfortably.

"We have duties, too," one of them mutters, but it's only a half-hearted response.

"Leave," Eupraxia orders. "And pray to the gods that I don't find your commanding officer and report you."

The soldiers hesitate a moment, but when Eupraxia juts her chin, they turn and go.

I expected to feel relieved once they were gone, but the tension in the air remains thick as the high priestess turns to look at me, Kallisto, and Amersa.

"The three of you, come with me." It's impossible to interpret the tone in her voice, but something about it isn't right. She gestures, and we wordlessly follow her back up the hill. I wonder momentarily about the woman, but my thoughts return to Eupraxia as we reach the Acropolis's lawns. Under starlight, she turns and faces us again.

"The temple is a sacred place for all, but especially women in need," she begins. "Each of you has been told as much."

The three of us nod.

"Tonight, a woman came to this temple seeking refuge." She points to Amersa. "You went to find someone else to help." Amersa opens her mouth, but Eupraxia continues. She points to Kallisto. "You did not even offer to help," she says. "I saw you step aside. You would have let those soldiers take that woman away."

To my surprise, Kallisto looks ashamed.

Finally, Eupraxia turns to me. "While your methods were . . . un-orthodox, *you* were the only one who tried to personally help that woman. You were willing to endanger yourself to protect her."

I don't have an answer for that.

"The three of you were brought here with seven others," says Eupraxia. "You have been tested on your logic, your talent in craft, and now a test of courage has revealed to me that only one of you is worthy of priesthood." She looks up. "Would you agree, Goddess?"

"In fact," says a familiar voice, "I would."

I turn sharply, confused. The woman from before has crept into the courtyard quietly, unnoticed. No longer does she look timid or weak; there is now a surety about her that I recognize. Slowly, her features begin to change before my eyes. The sores around her mouth fade, re-placed with smooth, pale skin. Her dark hair grows lighter, *redder*. I blink, and suddenly it's no longer a plainly dressed common woman standing before us.

It's Athena.

"Goddess!" Amersa cries out, falling to her knees, and Kallisto follows suit. It takes me a moment to remember that neither of them has ever seen Athena in the flesh.

"We . . . we are humbled," Kallisto says, her voice trembling.

I'm suddenly aware that we are not alone. In the dark, other priestesses seem to have materialized. Athena crosses the lawns so that she's standing before us.

"Rise," she says to Kallisto and Amersa.

They both scramble to their feet.

"My high priestess is correct," says Athena. "Your final test was one of courage, and only one of you succeeded. The two of you are dismissed."

It happens so fast, Amersa and Kallisto seem not to process the words. Kallisto looks around. "But—"

Already, two priestesses have broken from the circle around us to escort the two acolytes away. I watch for a moment, as they disappear into the darkness, before my gaze returns to Athena. Another priestess approaches me with a white candle and prompts me to take it. The rest of the priestesses close in, so that there is a tight circle around only me and Athena. The goddess waits a moment before speaking.

"Acolyte Medusa," she says solemnly. "You have passed each of the prerequisite tests used to determine your worthiness for priestesshood in this temple. The time has come for you to make certain vows before your sisters. If it is not your wish to continue, you may leave now."

I don't move.

"Very well." She nods. "Do you vow to uphold the moral code of this temple and all who serve it?"

The words leave me easily. "I do."

"Do you swear to be allegiant to me? Loyal, steadfast in your faith, and obedient?"

"I do."

"And lastly." My candle's light flickers in Athena's silver eyes. "Do you swear to remain chaste, pure of mind, body, and spirit?"

Poseidon's face crosses my mind, and I think briefly of the want I left in the halls of my palace just a few weeks ago. That want was real, powerful, but it paled in comparison to the want I have for this. When I speak, my voice is resolute.

"I do. I swear it." *I swear it always.*

There is no warning for what comes next. My candle trembles violently in my hand, then the flames turn a deep, vivid blue. Its light is unnatural: It bathes the whole of the Acropolis and every one of the surrounding priestesses in azure, as though we have all been pitched below the surface of the ocean. In a matter of seconds, it is over, and the candle extinguishes of its own accord. For several beats, there is no sound, then a cry of joy from one of the priestesses. It is followed by another, then another, until they are all shouting and cheering.

Athena smiles. "Well done, Medusa."

I am lost in the chaos of hugs, kisses on my cheeks, and congratulations. It takes me a moment to understand that it is real, that it isn't all some wonderful, cruel dream.

I have done it.

I have become an anointed priestess of the goddess Athena.

XXIV

IN THE DAYS following my initiation into priestesshood, little about my life in Athens changes.

Some of that is by design. Though the other priestesses tell me I'm not required to do the labor of an acolyte anymore, I find comfort in the routine of rising early and beginning my day by cleaning. I'm told that, technically, I may now share quarters with the priestesses—I don't have to stay in the now-empty acolytes' quarters—but the truth is the idea of sleeping anywhere else in the Acropolis feels stranger than sleeping in that room alone.

For the next several days, I work to find a new rhythm. I resume some of my old duties—sweeping the temple's floors, making sure the oil lamps stay filled—but I also investigate new interests. I learn that some priestesses assist with the temple's recordkeeping, a task that involves dealing with copious numbers of scrolls. It is a job most of the priestesses actively avoid, but I can think of no better one. In the mornings, I still clean and do simple chores, but in the afternoons I find quiet places to pore over centuries of old temple records. Sometimes, with a pang, I still think of Theo and wish he were here to see all this.

Six days after my initiation, Eupraxia asks me to go with a group of priest-esses into Athens to deliver more food to those in need. Admittedly, the prospect makes me nervous—I haven't been back in Athens proper since the night of Panathenaia—but I also relish the opportunity to prove that I am a fully fledged and capable priestess. As before, there is a crowd of people already waiting when the other priestesses and I arrive, but I school my face to look calm and assured as they crowd in and become rowdy.

"Please form an orderly line," I instruct. "Everyone *will* be served."

Once the other priestesses and I have set up our stations, we begin distributing food. The first person to approach me is a haggard young woman who looks only a few years older than me. She has a small girl in tow who has to be a relative of hers—they share the same fair, freckly skin and dirty-blond hair. I also notice that they're both hazardously thin and that the girl is paler than she should be for late summer.

"Excuse me," says the woman. "Are you Medusa?"

I start, surprised she knows my name. "Yes," I say cautiously. "That's me."

"You're an acolyte?" she asks.

I stand a bit taller. "I'm a priestess now." The words still thrill me.

The woman stands up straighter. "I've heard about you," she says. "The charioteer from the Panathenaia games, Kallinikos, says that *you* were the one who blessed him before he won his race."

I shake my head. "He's kind, but that wasn't—"

The woman nudges the little girl with her forward. At once, the child begins to cough. It's a dry, harsh sound. I flinch.

"My daughter has been sick for two weeks. Now she coughs up blood," the woman says quickly.

I feel a sharp pang of pity. "I'm sorry," I say slowly, "but I'm no healer. I can't—"

"I can't afford a healer," the woman goes on. There's a new edge of desperation in her voice. "What I ask is for your blessing."

I start. "My . . . blessing?"

The woman nods. "Pray to the Goddess on my behalf. Tell her that my girl is devout, and ask that she restore my daughter to good health. You are her favored priestess. She will listen to your prayer."

The little girl coughs again, this time so hard her eyes water. I make a decision in that moment. I may not be able to save this child's life, but it costs me little to offer her mother hope. I kneel before the girl and take one of her small hands in mine. I place my other hand on her chest.

"Do you pray to the gods before you sleep each night?" I ask softly.

The little girl nods, then is racked by another bout of coughs.

"Pray with me now," I instruct. "Bow your head."

She obeys, and her mother does, too. A few people are watching us, but I ignore them as I also bow my head and close my eyes. I have no idea if Athena is listening, if this will work, but I still try.

If you can hear me, Athena, save this child, I ask. *Protect her, heal her, and put food in her and her mother's bellies. Relieve their suffering, if only for a little while.*

When I open my eyes, more people are watching us, including some of the priestesses. I stand and put my hand on the woman's shoulder. "I've prayed to the Goddess, but there's something else you can also try," I add in a lower voice. "Find a laurel plant and take some leaves from it. Steep them in hot water, then have your daughter drink it three times a day. It may help." It's a remedy I learned from Theo, many years ago. I'm unsure of its efficacy, but it's something.

"Thank you." The woman falls to her knees. When she looks up at me, tears streak her face. She brings the hem of my dress to her face and kisses it. I'm rendered momentarily speechless, equal parts humbled and intimidated. "Thank you, Priestess Medusa."

"Be well." It's all I can manage.

The woman accepts a sack of food, stands, and steps away with her daughter. I move on to the next in line, but their faces stay with me for the rest of the afternoon.

The priestesses and I return to the Acropolis a short while later.

I notice the shift on our walk back from Athens and ignore it at first, but it becomes more pronounced once we've returned to the temple. I can't explain it, but the other priestesses have changed somehow. Before, they looked at me fondly—I had been getting to know them better little by little, hoping to find a friend like Apollonia among them; now they seem to regard me with an unmistakable wariness in their gazes. I can only assume it has to do with what happened in the city, though I don't understand why. Normally, after supper, I might sit with them in the gardens, but when night falls and I still feel their coolness, I take advantage of the freedom my new priesthood allows and decide to go for a walk on the beach instead. The walk takes me close to an hour, but as soon as I've reached Athens's shoreline, I feel better.

By this hour, the sun has dipped below the horizon, and the city is hushed save for a few soldiers patrolling the streets. I find a spot on the beach and settle there, not minding the tide lapping at my toes. I sigh. Being here reminds me of being on my island, and suddenly homesickness overtakes me in a rush. I miss Stheno and Euryale, but I especially miss Theo. I'm haunted by the last time we spoke, by the look I saw on his face afterward. When I can't take the ache of it any longer, I bury my toes in the beach's sand and force myself not to think of him.

I'm so lost in my thoughts that I don't realize I'm no longer alone until a familiar voice interrupts the quiet.

"It's good to see you, Medusa."

I look up, and my gaze locks with that of the king of the sea. For several seconds, I can only stare at him, and he laughs. There is something utterly consuming about his presence that I find I can't resist.

"You're pretty when you're startled." His smile lingers.

"I'm sorry, I . . ." I search for the right words. "I just didn't expect to see you."

Poseidon laughs softly. "I did say that you could always find me by the city's shores."

I remember that he did, and now some part of me wonders if that was the thing that brought me here, subconsciously. Poseidon settles beside me, and I find it hard to keep still. Power seems to emanate from his very being, and once again, I am struck by the fact that he could be in so many places, with so many more important people, yet he has chosen to be here, with me.

"It seems Athena shared the news of your priesthood with your father," says Poseidon, staring out to sea.

I sigh. "Which can only mean every god in the Sea Court now knows about it."

Poseidon laughs. "In the Sea Court and beyond, I'm afraid. He's very proud of you."

"He's proud of the accomplishment," I clarify.

Poseidon turns to me. "*I'm* proud of you," he says more gently. "Congratulations. To be selected as an acolyte of the Acropolis is no small feat. Being chosen as a priestess is greater still."

The compliment warms me. "Thank you."

For several minutes, he and I sit there side by side, listening to the ocean's waves. I want to enjoy this moment. I want to be flattered that the sea king himself has come to congratulate me, is *proud* of me, but other thoughts still swirl in my mind.

"You seem troubled," Poseidon says.

"Is it obvious?"

"Only because I've spent a lot of time with mortals." Poseidon nods. "What troubles you?"

"I'm not sure you'd understand."

"Tell me anyway," he encourages. "You might be surprised."

I hesitate, then the words spill from me. "It's the other priestesses. I think . . . they're upset with me."

"Upset?" Poseidon raises a brow. "But you're one of them now. You were only recently initiated."

"Yes, but . . ." In a rush, I tell him what happened earlier in the day. I tell him about the woman and her daughter, the blessing, and the way the priestesses treated me after.

When I finish, Poseidon shakes his head. "You should never feel bad for helping those with less than you," he says. "And if that's why the other priestesses are upset, then they are fools."

"Thank you, my king."

"*Poseidon,*" he insists.

"Thank you, Poseidon."

The sea god smiles again, and this time the corners of his eyes crinkle. "You look truly beautiful tonight."

My heart skips. The truth is, I've thought—more than once—about the kiss he and I shared on the night of Panathenaia, and then about our encounter in my family home. More than once, I've wondered what might have happened if we hadn't been interrupted.

"Tell me what you're thinking," says Poseidon.

"I'm thinking . . ." I try and fail to find the right words. The truth is, I'm still thinking about the way that kiss felt. I'm thinking about his hands, the press of them on my hips. I'm thinking about the want, how intense that want was that night back on the island. But . . . I'm also thinking about my vows, about Athena.

"When I lived on the island, the only thing I wanted was to leave," I say slowly. "I thought I would never want something as badly as that ever again. But now . . ." I stare at my hands. "Now I think I was wrong. It turns out you can want lots of things, and you can want them equally. Sometimes I wish that I didn't have to choose."

In the dark, Poseidon's green eyes seem brighter than usual. He leans in, and I know I should pull away from him, but I don't. He presses his forehead against mine, and my breath stops.

"*I* think," he murmurs, "you should have whatever you want."

I don't know who moves first, but our lips meet, and I find that his are just as I remembered. His hands find my knee, and I relish the way his calloused palms feel against my skin. He kisses me more deeply, and a thrum vibrates through my body. I want him. I realize this with vivid clarity. I want Poseidon, I want *this*.

He seems to feel the same, because he gently pulls me to the sand, so that we're lying side by side. Detached, I think about the sand in my locs, but I can't bring myself to care much. Pulling back for a moment, Poseidon grazes his knuckles gently against my cheek and gazes into my eyes.

"I've never felt like this," he whispers. "No one has ever made me feel like this."

Kissing Poseidon was wonderful, but nothing rivals the feeling coursing through me now. He is an Olympian, the sea king, one of the most powerful gods on earth, but I have some effect on him that no one else ever has. He looks at me, and I'm convinced that nothing in all the world has ever been more beautiful than he. I could lie here beside him for an eternity, I realize, and not even notice the passing time.

"It's late," Poseidon says. "I should walk you back to the temple."

I can't deny the fleeting disappointment his words summon, but I know he's right. He rises first, then helps me up and brushes the sand from my back.

"You're going to change the world, Medusa," the sea king says, offering his hand. "Of that I'm absolutely certain."

I don't agree with him in the slightest, but I still take his hand. Together, we walk up the dunes and into the night.

XXV

I WORK DILIGENTLY in the temple for the next few days.

We don't return to Athens proper to serve the people, and I use my time at the Acropolis to win back the favor of some of the priestesses. Though I'm not required to do it, I take up even more of the old duties usually reserved exclusively for acolytes—like mucking out the barn. At mealtimes, I offer to clean up after, so that everyone else can go to bed. It doesn't take long for my efforts to be noticed, and slowly, the priestesses who'd been cooler to me warm again. I count it as a triumph.

"You'll be good for this temple," one of the older ones says to me one morning. "The Goddess has picked well."

I relish the compliment, but behind it, I feel the tiniest bit of guilt. Though I haven't seen Poseidon again since our impromptu meeting on the beach, I find myself thinking more and more about the second kiss we shared. I knew, when it happened, that it was probably wrong, but I wasn't able to help myself. I still remember the way Poseidon looked at me, like I was some rare treasure to be cherished. No one had ever looked at me like that before, and the truth is I crave more of it.

You made vows, I remind myself. *You made vows to Athena, not Poseidon.*

I bury the thought of his face and continue in my work.

. . .

Days after these musings, I'm standing in the temple's small olive tree grove harvesting when it happens.

At first, I don't understand what's going on. I hear a commotion, and when I turn, I see Eupraxia racing toward me. She looks unusually harried.

"Medusa." There's an edge to her voice that I've never heard before. "You need to come with me. At once."

Something is wrong. I sense it immediately. "What? What's happened?"

"There are people outside the Acropolis's main entrance," she says. "They're . . . asking for you."

I stare at her, not understanding her meaning. "For me?"

"Yes," she says in a strained voice. *"Come."* Already, she's turned on her heel and started to walk—run, really—out of the grove and toward the front of the Acropolis. I follow, trying to keep calm. By the time we've crossed the entry, we're nearly sprinting, our peploses fluttering in the wind like banners. We reach the front gates, and I stop short.

A crowd has gathered just outside the Acropolis. I can't possibly count them, but I estimate there to be at least fifty people. I see men and women, children and elders, finely dressed senators and slaves wearing only rags. None of them seem angry, but there is a frenetic energy about them that somehow feels off. I see a desperation in their eyes that puts me on edge. Some of them are shifting their weight anxiously from foot to foot; others are craning their necks as though searching for something.

One of the men toward the front of the crowd spots me and points. "There she is!" he shouts. "It's her, Priestess Medusa!"

At once, the crowd becomes more raucous. My steps falter, and Eupraxia gives me a sidelong glance before raising both hands to quiet the crowd. *"I* am the high priestess of this temple." Her voice rings with authority. "And I demand to know why you all have gathered here."

There's a pause. No one in the crowd seems willing to be the first to speak. Then a woman emerges from the throng. It takes me a moment to pinpoint why she looks familiar, but then I recognize her. It's the woman from the market, the one whose sick daughter I prayed for nearly a week ago. She looks different, though. Her body has become fuller; her cheeks have a fresh color that makes her look younger. She looks at me and smiles.

"We are here for Priestess Medusa." There's an undeniable reverence in her voice. "We are here to receive her blessings and to ask for her to pray to the Goddess on our behalf."

Eupraxia frowns. "Every priestess of the Acropolis is empowered to give blessings and pray to the Goddess," she explains. "You don't need Medusa to—"

"We want *her*!" a man shouts. He has swarthy skin, a burly frame, and numerous burns across his bare arms. My guess is that he's a blacksmith. He lowers his eyes before me in deference and, in a lower voice, adds, "The Goddess listens to *her* prayers. She is favored."

Several people in the crowd murmur their assent.

"Favored?" Eupraxia now looks confused. "What do you mean, 'favored'?"

"She prayed for Kallinikos, the charioteer who won the Panathenaic games even though he was predicted to lose," says the first woman. "Then, when I brought my sick child to her in the market, she prayed to the Goddess and asked for her health to return to her. She was nearly dead." She holds up her child for the crowd to see. To my surprise, the girl is much plumper, rosy-cheeked.

"Now look!" the woman exclaims. "My daughter is healthy, entirely healed!"

The people around her grow more excited as I grow more nervous. What the woman *hasn't* mentioned is that I also told her to give her daughter water steeped with laurel leaves, which probably contributed to the child's improvement. Before I can say so, another man steps out from the crowd.

"I came to Priestess Medusa a few days ago, too," he says. "My barley crops were suffering, and I asked her to pray for me. That night, when I got home, we had a rain shower. You all remember it?"

Several in the crowd nod.

"My crops immediately began to come to life again," he says. "It was a real miracle." He points at me. "And it was because of her."

Now real fear arrows through me. The truth is, I barely remember this man or his prayer for crops. I tell myself that his claims are only a coincidence. I am just a mortal girl. I am not a god. This doesn't make sense. People are beginning to shout at me, fighting and clamoring for my attention. One woman breaks from the crowd and grabs at the hem of my peplos, prompting others to do the same. I'm being pulled into the throng.

Eupraxia grabs my arm just in time. "Stop this!" she orders. "Stop at once!"

The crowd is no longer listening to her. There's a feverishness among them now. I'm suddenly very aware that the two of us are badly outnumbered.

"Eupraxia," I say in a small voice. "They're not going to leave."

For as long as I have known the high priestess, she has exuded surety, confidence. Now, for the first time, I see that confidence falter. "Then what can we do?" she mutters.

"Trust me."

She says nothing, but I take that as an assent. I step forward and raise my hands. At once, the crowd goes silent.

"People of Athens!" My voice rings with new authority I didn't know I possessed. "I will hear every one of your prayers," I promise. "But in order to do that, we must have order. We must respect the sanctity of this temple."

Some of the more boisterous members of the crowd look down, appropriately shamed. While I still have their attention, I continue.

"Form one orderly line," I instruct. "Anyone who shoves or becomes unruly will be asked to leave."

At once, the crowd begins to file into a neat queue. Perhaps on another day, I might find their obedience impressive, but now I find it unnerving. Eupraxia looks on for a few more minutes with an expression I can't read before turning and going back into the Acropolis. That worries me, but I redirect my attention to the first person in line, a stout woman with curly dark hair shot through with gray. She's holding a basket. When I lift the cover, I see it's filled with olives.

"The trees in our orchard have not bloomed well in four years," she says. "Please, Priestess Medusa. Ask the Goddess to restore them."

I take her hand in mine and smile. "Let us pray."

For the next three hours, I pray with the people of Athens.

I keep my word, listening to every prayer request. Some men ask for their investments to prove fruitful; some women ask for good marriages. Children come into my line asking for silly things like sweet bread. Every so often, an elderly person asks for relief from their suffering. By the end of it, I am exhausted.

I expect to find Eupraxia once I return to the Acropolis, but the high priestess is nowhere in sight. In fact, most of the priestesses seem to be elsewhere, and those I do see quickly make themselves scarce when they see me. I head to the acolytes' quarters, thinking a short nap might do me some good, but when I reach the door, I realize the room isn't empty.

Athena is standing in its center, her face drawn. "*What,*" she says through clenched teeth, "do you think you're doing?"

The iciness in her voice seeps into my skin. Any pride I felt as I offered blessings dissipates as we stare at each other.

"What do you mean?"

"Do not play coy with me, girl." Her hand slices through the air, and I'm glad I'm not standing close to her. "The people who came to the Acropolis's front gates today, what were they doing?"

"Th-they asked for blessings," I stammer. "They asked for me to pray to you, on their behalf. I didn't see any harm in it."

"They credited *you* with the acts of a god!" Athena thunders. "And you did not contradict them."

"I am your priestess, Goddess." I am fighting to keep the tremor from my voice. "They know that anything I do is in service to you."

Athena looks away from me, scowling. "They were all but worshiping you today," she says bitterly. "You, a common mortal."

The words smart like a slap to the face. Tears prick my eyes, but I don't let them fall. "They revere *you*, Goddess," I say in a small voice. "They look at me only as a vessel. *You* are the one the people of Athens love. They have always loved you. I saw it at Panathenaia, I see it every time we go into the city to give out food. It is *you* they thank, not me." I pause, then add: "They know who loves them most, who protects them."

Athena eyes me for a moment and several emotions pass over her face, too quickly for me to assess. When she speaks again, her voice has softened.

"I am . . . sorry."

I start. In all her years, I'm not sure Athena has ever apologized to anyone, for anything. She crosses the room so that she's standing before me. Suddenly she looks very tired.

"Mortals are capricious," she says. "When you do answer their prayers, they love and revere you. When you do not, they hate you and curse your name. It is, at times, exhausting."

I have no reply for that.

"Do you know how we gods—Olympians and the like—maintain our power?" she asks. "Have your parents ever explained it?"

I shake my head.

"Our power comes from *faith*," she says softly. "The more people who believe in us, and the more fervently they believe, the stronger we become. When fewer people believe in us, we grow weaker. We perform miracles and great deeds to ensure they do not forget us, to ensure our survival."

I've always pictured Athena as indomitable, too strong to ever fall. Now, for the first time, I see a weakness in her armor, in the armor of all gods and Olympians. They may live forever, but their immortality has limitations.

"That seems like a high price to pay," I whisper.

Athena's smile is wry, but I detect a sorrow behind her gray eyes. "It is," she says quietly. "I'm not sure I've ever told anyone that before."

I don't know what to say, and Athena turns to me.

"You are a promising young woman, Medusa," she says warmly. "I have no doubt that you will do great things, but you must remember your *place*. It doesn't do well for women to be too ambitious. Do you understand what I mean?"

I don't. For the second time, Athena has said something I don't understand at all, but I don't admit that. I only bow my head.

"Yes, Goddess."

That earns a small smile, a real one. Without another word, Athena pats my cheek, then leaves me alone in the acolytes' quarters.

THAT NIGHT, I go to the beach again.

I don't know exactly when I decide to do it; my feet seem to carry me there of my own accord. The closer I get to the rolling tides, the more salt air fills my lungs, the more at ease I feel. I walk until the tips of my toes skim the water, and then I breathe the name.

"Poseidon."

Nothing happens.

Disappointment floods me. Of course, it was silly of me to expect Poseidon to come at my mere summons.

He's still the king of the sea, I remind myself. *I'm sure he has other things—*
"Medusa."

I pivot sharply, and my pulse quickens. To my right, where seconds before there was no one, Poseidon now stands before me. He looks regal tonight, dressed in a dyed tunic of deep purple. A golden pendant necklace rests near his chest, and there's more than one thick golden band on his fingers. He looks like a true king. For a moment, all I can do is stare.

"Did you call for me?" he asks.

"I . . ." Suddenly I feel foolish. What if I've pulled him away from something more important? "I'm sorry," I say. "I just . . . I suppose I wanted . . . but you're busy . . ."

Poseidon's expression softens. "I'm never too busy to speak with you, Medusa. Is something wrong?"

"No, not exactly . . ." I don't know how to tell him about the people who came to the Acropolis earlier, so I say something else. "Can I ask you a question?"

"Of course. Anything."

"Why do you like me?"

I expect him to laugh or roll his eyes—it's a silly question, really—but he does neither. Instead, his expression grows more intent.

"Do you not think you should be liked?" he whispers. "Do you not know what I think of you?"

I don't answer.

He shakes his head. "You're beautiful, to be sure, Medusa. But there's more that draws me to you. You're smart, determined. The Fates dealt you a cruel hand, making you the only mortal member of your family. You should have lived out the rest of your days stuck on that island." His eyes light up. "But you didn't. You took the destiny handed to you and made it your own. If that's not admirable, I'm not sure what is."

The words are sweet. I instantly crave more of them, but something stops me.

"Can I ask you a second question?"

Poseidon smiles. "And a third."

This one is harder for me. I find I can't look at him when I ask it. "Several months ago, when you came to our island for the spring feast, I saw you . . . with someone else."

Poseidon's brows rise. "Someone else?"

"A sea nymph." I force the words out. "She had blue hair."

Recognition dawns on Poseidon's face. His answer comes slowly. "I won't deny it," he says. "But that nymph . . . there is nothing between us anymore."

I stay silent, wanting him to go on.

"I meant what I said to you." His voice lowers. "No one has made me feel the way you have. Ever."

"Not even the queen?" I ask.

For a second, I think I've made a terrible mistake. Poseidon frowns at the mention of his wife. "No," he says more coolly. "I have never felt that way for Amphitrite because she has never felt that way for me. Our marriage was arranged centuries ago by her father and my brother, to ally our families." He gives me a significant look. "I imagine that's something you can understand?"

I nod. I understand all too well.

"I did try, in the early days, to make my wife happy," says Poseidon. "But I soon learned it was to no avail. Our marriage is in name only. There is no love in it."

In that moment, I cannot think of anything more tragic.

Poseidon stares out to sea, then looks to me. "I don't want to talk about Amphitrite anymore."

"I'm sorry." And genuinely, I am.

"I want to talk about you," he says. "You've had some time to acclimate to your new station. How do you find it?"

The question immediately takes me back to earlier in the day. "Truthfully," I say, "it's been overwhelming. The people seem to believe that I can perform real miracles, like a god."

"In fairness," says Poseidon, "healing a sick child and summoning a rainstorm is impressive."

"It is," I say, "but—" I stop short. "How did you know about that? About the child and the rainstorm?"

I see a look I haven't seen before on Poseidon's face. One of guilt. "I wanted the people of this city to treasure you as I do," he says.

"It was *you*," I realize. "You were the one who made all those strange things happen."

"With some help," Poseidon amends. "I cannot make crops grow, but Demeter owed me a favor. I cannot heal children, but . . . well, my nephew Apollo is fond of me." In a more serious tone, he adds: "I didn't intend any harm. Forgive me."

Some voice in the back of my mind notes that this is the second time Poseidon has kept something from me. He appeared to me in disguise, without revealing who he was. Now he has directly interfered with my role in Athena's temple. I can imagine what my sisters might say to that, what Theo would say if we were still speaking. But a different voice in my head drowns them out.

He was only trying to help. He cares for you. Don't ruin it.

"There's nothing to forgive," I answer. "Thank you, for all you've done for me."

Poseidon grins. "Come here."

It doesn't occur to me to do anything other than obey him. As soon as I close the gap between us, he takes my face in his hands and kisses me. This kiss isn't like the first two. There is a hunger to it, an urgency that makes my knees tremble as though they might give out beneath me. Poseidon seems to know that, because he eases us onto the sand. He kisses my mouth again, then bites my lower lip, hard. There's a bright spark of pain, but then . . . I'm surprised to feel a new tightness, an ache in the lower parts of my body.

A deep rumbling sound rises from his throat. "This is what you do to me," he says. "You drive me mad."

I'm lost in too many different sensations to answer.

Poseidon kisses me again, using one hand to suspend himself over me. I feel the other hand slide down my leg, to my thigh, then—

"Wait." It takes everything I have to grab his wrist.

"What's wrong?" Poseidon's pupils are blown wide, so that only slivers of his green irises are visible.

"I . . . I can't do this." I gently push him away from me and sit up. "I made a vow to remain chaste. I can't do this."

For several seconds, there's only the crashing of the waves.

"I see," Poseidon finally says. He stands, adjusting his golden pendant. "I'm sorry."

"There's nothing to apologize for." The words are formal. "I'd thought maybe you felt the way I did, but perhaps . . ."

"No!" I scramble to my feet. "No, that's not it! I do care for you, Poseidon, a great deal, it's just—"

"I need to visit with my brother." He cuts me off. "I should go. Will you be all right, walking back to the Acropolis on your own?"

Something in the pit of my stomach drops. "I . . . Of course."

"Good." Poseidon nods. "Then I bid you good night."

He doesn't give me a chance to say anything else before he turns away and strides down the beach until he's out of sight.

XXVI

THE NEXT TIME I visit the beach and call for Poseidon, he does not come. Nor does he come the time after that.

At first, I tell myself that it doesn't bother me. Poseidon is lord of the Sea Court, after all. He has many demands, and though he promised he would never be too busy for me, I know that may not be a promise he can keep. I tell myself that his absence is a result of his duties, and not because of what happened the last time we saw each other, but as the days grow shorter and autumn draws nearer, I lie on my pallet fighting off crueler imaginary voices in my head.

It's your fault, one of those voices says. *You've wounded him.*

He cared for you, another says, *and in return you made him think you don't feel the same way.*

A part of me wishes I could speak to Stheno and Euryale about all this, but another part of me knows that even if I were back on our island, I'm not sure I would. The last time I talked to my sisters about my life in Athens, they didn't understand it, and I ended up feeling more alone than ever.

As the days turn to weeks, I decide to bury all my feelings about Poseidon and focus on my work. Athenians still come to the Acropolis's entrance sometimes, asking me for prayers, but with Poseidon no longer interfering, the stories of the miraculous foreigner priestess begin to fade. I can't say I'm sorry for it. I've done my best to try to win the priestesses over again, taking up extra chores around the temple, but they treat me with a wariness I fear is permanent. I spend what recreational time I have alone.

The second time my parents send a summons that I return home, Athena does not deliver it. Instead, I receive a simple missive with information about the autumn feast my parents are hosting, with a note that I am expected to attend. I'm not surprised that my presence is requested. Now that I am in a position to further my father's political agenda, I am his pride.

The last time I had to leave Athens, I was sad to do it. This time, a part of me relishes the chance to go home.

On the night of the feast, my mother sends an entire fleet of slaves to my bedchamber, and I find myself being pulled in every direction. One set of hands scrubs my skin raw while several others lather me with lotions and oils. My lips are painted deep red; lines of kohl are drawn around my eyes. But the real surprise comes when Euryale arrives with a tunic for me to wear. I recognize it immediately. It is the yellow one I saw in her trunk months before, on the morning I first left for Athens. She slips it over me, and I relish the feeling of the fabric. She and Stheno arrange half my locs into an elaborate style atop my head, then Euryale holds a looking glass for me to examine myself.

I draw in a sharp breath.

The girl staring back at me is nearly unrecognizable because she isn't a girl at all. She is a young woman. Sometime in the months since I first left for Athens, the last of the baby fat left my cheeks. My lips seem fuller, my neck longer. I realize with a start that I do resemble my mother and my sisters.

"Lovely," Euryale says, grinning at me. "You look lovely, Medusa."

I lift my gaze to meet hers. "So do you, Eury. Always."

She puts the looking glass down and pulls me into a hug.

Stheno rolls her eyes. "Come on," she says, gesturing. "We should make our way to the great hall."

. . .

I thought my parents had been extravagant for the spring feast, but their autumn one proves me wrong.

Banners of gold, red, and orange festoon the room; enormous arrangements of yellow roses from the garden decorate every free surface. Even the slaves have been outfitted in new white tunics with brown cords. I know at once that the extra effort is for the imminent arrival of the Olympians. Not long after the feast begins, they arrive.

I have heard of the gods of Mount Olympus many times, but seeing them in the flesh is different. First, I note Zeus, a powerfully built olive-skinned man with a shock of long dark hair shot through with gray. On his arm, as he enters, is his wife, Hera, queen of the gods.

"They favor each other," Euryale notes.

Stheno snorts. "That's because they're not just husband and wife," she points out. "They're brother and sister."

Hermes is next, looking as boyish as ever, but he's traded his plain white tunic for a light green one that matches his eyes. When he winks in my direction, I can't help but smile.

More gods come in—from Mount Olympus and the Sea Court alike. I see a young, waifish-looking goddess with fair skin and a mane of wild brown hair and learn that she is none other than Artemis, yet another of Zeus's children. A heavyset god with darker skin and curly black hair saunters right up to my mother and kisses her cheeks with great fervor.

"Dionysus," says Euryale before I can ask. "As you can imagine, he and Mother get along well."

Eventually, my uncle Nereus joins the fray, and just as before, he brings the Nereids with him. Amphitrite walks a few paces behind him, looking much more tranquil than the last time I saw her, but I find I cannot meet her gaze. Soon, there are only two noticeable absentees from the festivities.

"Did Mother and Father say anything about Poseidon or Athena coming?" I try to make the question sound casual and offhand as I pose it to Stheno.

"No word from Poseidon," says Stheno. "But according to Mama, Athena declined. She said she didn't have time for such frivolities."

In truth, that sounds exactly like something Athena would say, but I'm still disappointed. I'm pulled from my thoughts as my father stands, and the hall quiets.

"Gods of Olympus, gods of the Sea Court!" He holds up a wooden goblet. "Tonight we celebrate the onset of the harvest season. As we honor Demeter, I encourage you to drink, feast, and enjoy this night of festivity!"

Many goblets rise in the air, clinking against one another. I feel a nudge against my shoulder, and when I look up, Stheno's eyes are bright. She shoves a different wooden goblet into my hand. It's filled with a curious golden liquid.

"Here, drink *this*."

I give her a dubious look before bringing the cup to my lips and trying a sip of its contents. To my surprise, the golden liquid is sweet to the taste. I take a second longer sip. On my other side, Euryale laughs, and I feel a warm sensation flood my entire body.

"Is this wine?"

Euryale beams. "Not just any wine." She leans in, and I smell the sweetness of it on her own breath. "It's *Olympian* wine, made by Dionysus himself."

I've had red and white wines before, but never wine from the Olympians' home. At once, I can tell it is different, more potent than any wine I've ever had. I take a third sip from the goblet, then, to Euryale's delight and Stheno's amusement, down the rest. Everything around me begins to take on a vividness—the colors seem brighter, and the hall's noise fades into one pleasant buzz. Euryale takes one of my hands and Stheno takes my other as they lead me to the center of the festivities and begin to dance. At first, I worry that I might trip, that my brain won't be able to keep up with my feet, but the opposite happens. I've never felt this graceful before. As a child, I always wished I could move like my sisters, that I could imitate their grace. Now I find I can. I sashay, holding the hem of my tunic as I twirl, and let my locs fly out behind me with each move.

Euryale and Stheno dance with me, clapping in time with the beat. Stheno grabs my arm and leans in. "They're watching," she whispers.

I lift my gaze, glancing over her shoulder to see whom she means. The Olympian wine has blurred the edges of my vision, but between smears of color, I see them. Everyone *is* staring at us with undeniable admiration. There are the usual gods from the Sea Court, but also new ones— the ethereal, white-haired moon goddess Selene, and a bleary-eyed, blue-skinned god I think might be called Morpheus. I even think I catch a glimpse of Queen Amphitrite, standing among her sisters. Only when the soles of my feet begin to ache do I step off the dance floor for a rest, though my sisters have more stamina and keep going.

I've just stopped to lean against a wall when I feel a tap on my shoulder. "Meddy?"

I turn and find myself face-to-face with Theo. Like the other slaves of my parents' household, he is wearing a newer tunic, one that properly fits him, but he still looks painfully underdressed among the lavish gods and goddesses filling the room. His eyes are intent as they meet mine.

"I wondered if . . . if I could speak to you," he says in a low voice. "Alone?"

My sisters are still dancing and no longer paying attention to me. The Olympian wine coursing through my blood draws a smile to my lips, and I offer Theo my hand.

"Of course," I say lazily. "Lead the way."

Theo takes my hand and leads me from the dance floor. We weave together through the crowd and out of the room, and it is only once we are down the hall and well obscured in its shadows that he drops my hand and turns to face me. His expression has grown softer.

"You look beautiful, as always," he says.

Another pleasant wave of warmth rises in my cheeks. "Thank you." I know there is nothing romantic in the gesture. Theo is as he's always been, honest to a fault.

He fidgets for several seconds, as if searching for his words, then says: "Meddy, I want you to know that I'm really sorry for what I said to you last time you were home."

"Theo." In my head, my voice sounds too playful and light, but I can't stop it as I step forward and place a hand on his shoulder. "That's all okay now, really. You don't have to apologize for—"

"No, Meddy." Theo's tone is gentle but firm. Carefully, he moves my hand from his shoulder, but holds on to it. "Let me finish, please. I apologize for what I said. You're my friend, and I never want you to feel that you can't come to me, that you can't talk to me."

Even under the influence of the wine, I hear the sincerity in his voice. I blink hard and make myself focus. "I'm sorry, too," I say, hoping the words aren't too slurred. "What I said, that wasn't fair. You're my friend. You're my *best friend* . . ."

Suddenly, the corridor begins to spin violently. I lean against the wall again and close my eyes, pressing my forehead against the cool stone.

"Meddy?" Theo's voice sounds worried. "Are you all right?"

I force myself to crack one of my eyes. "I'm fine," I say, feeling anything but. "I just . . . I think I need some fresh air and maybe some water."

"Come on." I feel more than see Theo slip one of my arms around his waist. "I'll take you outside."

We make our way slowly to the end of the hallway, out a set of double doors, then onto the veranda. Carefully, Theo eases me down onto the stairs leading to the gardens. I can still hear the sounds of the feast inside, but they're all blissfully muted now. I delight in the brisk night air as it fills my lungs.

"I'm going to find water for you," Theo says, crouching beside me. "Stay here and *don't move,* all right?"

"Trust me," I say, holding my head in my hands. "I don't think you'll have to worry about that."

"All right, then," he says. "I'll be back." His lips graze my forehead before he stands again. I listen to the fading sound of his footsteps a moment, then close my eyes. I take a deep breath, relishing the cool and wishing the world around me would stop spinning. I wonder how long the effects of Olympian wine last, compared to those of normal wine. I look over my shoulder as I hear a footfall again, hoping Theo has come back. But when I turn, it isn't Theo standing before me.

"Medusa."

A set of blue-green eyes flecked with gold shine in the darkness, unnaturally bright.

"My king."

I rise and try to bow, but nearly stumble down the stairs. Poseidon catches my upper arm at the last moment and rights me. An amused smile tugs at the corners of his lips.

"I've been looking for you," he says in a low voice. "I was hoping you'd look for me."

My cheeks warm, and I can't tell if that is the effect of the Olympian wine or of his words.

"Forgive me, my king," I murmur, "I was with my sisters. I didn't see you."

Poseidon chuckles. "I must be very unremarkable."

"Not at all, my king."

"My king?" One of Poseidon's brows rises. "I thought you and I were beyond that kind of formality."

"Apologies, my—" I stop myself. "Apologies, Poseidon."

The sea king smiles, and my stomach swoops. "It's been some time since I've seen your father's palace at night. I'd forgotten how splendid it is." He looks around, thoughtful. "I wonder . . . if you would be so kind as to show me the grounds?"

I know what my parents would say if they were here. Poseidon isn't just an Olympian; he is the sea king. In the Sea Court, he is the most powerful god. My parents would want me to honor him, to be a good host.

"Of course, my king." The world tilts as I try again to bow.

"Poseidon," he murmurs. "I wish for you to call me Poseidon."

"Very well." I nod. "This way, Poseidon." I take his hand in mine and lead him into the garden.

XXVII

I DON'T FIND it strange that, even though Poseidon has asked me for a tour of my mother's gardens, he's the one who leads the way as we walk among their towering hedges and walls of hanging vines.

The evening air is cool, an early sign of the harvest season's approach. I listen as the last of the cicadas trill, as slivers of moonlight guide me through rows of hyacinths and crocuses. With each step, I become more and more keenly aware of the sea king walking beside me. When we reach a grassy lawn among the flower beds, he gestures.

"Let us rest here a moment."

I settle on the ground, and he joins me, placing his hand on my knee.

"Are you all right?" he asks gently.

"I'm fine." I swallow hard once, then a second time. "I'm just a bit dizzy." Around me, the flowers are blurring, indistinct.

Poseidon nods. "You should drink some water." He produces a silver flask, and I drink eagerly, relishing the cool relief of the water in my throat.

"Thank you."

"Of course," he says. When I look up at him, there is a hint of a smile in his green eyes. "I remember all too well the first time I drank Olympian wine. I fared far worse than you."

A question occurs to me then, and in my drunken haze, nothing stops me from asking it. "Were you ever young? Truly young?"

"Once," says Poseidon, "though, it's been so long now . . . I'm not sure if my memories of youth are real or merely something I've conjured in my mind because I find that version preferable."

I sit back, silent. It is a more honest answer than I expected. I find it difficult to imagine Poseidon as a boy, or as a tiny helpless infant. There is nothing at all helpless about him; he exudes nothing but limitless power, even while he is at rest. There is something about that power that draws me in, like a bee to a flower, or a moth to moonlight.

A cool breeze grazes my bare arms, and when I shiver, Poseidon wraps his arm around my shoulders. He is wonderfully warm. I lean against him and inhale. If all the good smells of the ocean could be blended into one, *that* is what he smells like—crisp morning air, salt water, and sun-warmed sand.

"I've missed you, Medusa," he says into my hair.

I savor those words. "I've missed you, too. I . . . I thought you were angry with me. When I came back to the beach and called for you, when you didn't come . . ."

"That was nothing personal," he says quickly. "My brothers needed me. I feel a great responsibility to be there for them." He nods. "You have two sisters. I figured you'd understand."

I do understand, and suddenly I feel silly for ever thinking Poseidon was angry with me.

"You were speaking with a slave before." I can't see Poseidon's face, but I hear the rumble deep in his chest. His tone is mild, conversational. "Who was he?"

"Hm?" It takes me a moment to connect the words. "Oh, you mean Theo."

"He is something to you?"

I think I hear new emotion in his voice. Is it hesitation? Jealousy? A small laugh bubbles up from my throat. "He's nothing," I say. I'm drunk, but not so drunk that I don't hear the tinny voice in the back of my mind ask: *Why did you say that?* Theo isn't nothing to me. He is my friend. My mouth starts to form those words, but when I look up at Poseidon, he's smiling. As easily as that, Theo is forgotten again.

"You look beautiful tonight, Medusa."

"Thank you." I stare at my hands. "I think I owe you an apology."

"An apology?" Poseidon frowns. "What for?"

"The last time we saw each other, when we . . ." I can't make myself finish the sentence. "You said you thought maybe I didn't feel the way you do."

Poseidon doesn't say anything in answer.

"I want you to know I do," I say. "I . . . I care for you, Poseidon, in a way I've never cared for anyone else." I don't know what else to do, so I reach for his hand. For an instant, I worry that the gesture is too brazen, but he laces his fingers into mine at once and circles the pad of his thumb against my skin. My entire body hums like a plucked string at that touch.

"I'm glad to hear that," he murmurs. "I'm glad to know that what I've felt for you isn't unrequited."

"It isn't," I whisper.

He looks down at me, and in the moonlight, his silhouette is traced in silver. "In another life, I would have married you."

I can see it all in my head. King Poseidon and Queen Medusa, rulers of all the sea. Free to go wherever we want, free to *do* whatever we please. Free to be together. None of it's real; it's all in my imagination. But it *feels* real, so close I can almost touch it.

Poseidon hooks a thumb under my chin and tilts my face upward. He bends toward me, and when he kisses me, I think to myself that this is better than the most potent Olympian wine. He slips his tongue between my lips, and a moan escapes me. I wrap my arms around him, and he gently pushes my back to the grass before he rolls on top of me. The world around me spins, blurs. Poseidon bends slightly, kissing the place where my neck and shoulder meet, then lifts the hem of my dress so that it bunches at my waist. I've worn nothing underneath it; in the night air, goosebumps stipple my bare legs.

"Exquisite," he murmurs, running his hand along my inner thighs. I jolt when he touches the place between them—in all my life, no one has ever touched me there—but he doesn't seem to notice. With one of his knees, he pushes my legs apart, then hikes up his own tunic. I've never seen a real man exposed before; detachedly, I note that it is different from the illustrations in my scrolls. Poseidon lowers himself onto me so that our naked bodies are pressed together, and my eyes catch on something over one of his shoulders, two tiny pinpricks of light in the dark. They are positioned near one of my mother's olive trees, round and yellow gold. It takes me a moment to recognize them for what they are.

Eyes. An *owl's* eyes.

It isn't Glaukopis, Athena's owl—this bird is small and black and common—but the sight of the creature is enough. Athena's face and all my oaths to the temple rush back to me.

"Wait," I say as Poseidon adjusts. "Wait, I can't—"

"Shh." He bends his head to me. "It's all right."

I move slightly, testing to see if I can wriggle free. With one hand, he suddenly pins both my arms above my head, and I know then that I cannot. Poseidon is bigger than me, I've always known that, but I've never really accounted for *how* much bigger he is. My pulse leaps as there's more fumbling, a pause, and then a sudden sharp pain, low in my belly as he pushes inside me. I cry out, but he silences me with a hard kiss.

"Shh." He begins to rock back and forth against me, still holding my arms above my head. His chest grows damp and sweaty as he moves faster and faster and his face turns ruddy with the effort. Eventually, he stops looking at me altogether. His eyes glaze over, and his mouth hangs slack as the strange rhythm quickens.

"Good," he says between the grunts, "good girl."

I don't know exactly how long it lasts, only that, at some point, Poseidon lets out a long moan and collapses on top of me. The lawn's grass prickles my bare shoulders as he pants, and in the back of my mind, I think of the fact that my dress is now ruined. Something wet slicks my inner thighs, and a violent shudder of disgust rolls through my body, but Poseidon still holds me pinned there, unable to move.

I am staring blankly at the stars when I hear footsteps approaching. I stiffen, but Poseidon only raises his head and peers into the darkness. Seconds later, a smile spreads across his lips, and the next words he says chill my blood.

"Ah, Athena, this is a surprise."

"Honestly, Poseidon?"

There is audible exasperation in Athena's voice. "You may care little for your wife, but Hera is here, and you know how she gets when you—"

Athena's eyes find me in the dark, and she goes perfectly still. I expect rage, but what I see in her eyes is a more complicated array of emotions—intermingling traces of shock, grief, then betrayal. Her lower lip trembles as she speaks.

"*You.*"

Poseidon rolls off me, but I barely feel it. He doesn't seem to have heard her. He chuckles as he rises and unhurriedly pulls down his tunic. I rush to pull my own down.

"As always, your timing is impeccable," he says with a snort. "I didn't think you were planning to join us tonight—"

There is a terrible crack as Athena's fist connects with Poseidon's jaw. From the ground, I watch as Poseidon's entire head snaps to the left with the sheer force of that blow. His eyes widen in shock, momentarily stunned. He grabs his lower face with one hand, and there's a wet pop as he resets bone. Of course, the injury is nothing to him, really. He spits golden blood into the grass beside me, then turns back to face Athena. He isn't smiling anymore.

"You would dare," she says between her teeth, "you would *dare* touch one of my girls?"

My girls. I hear those words and think, for one finite moment, that there might be a fragment of hope left after all. I am a temple priestess, one of *hers.* She will understand, she will forgive me. I let myself believe that everything will still be all right.

Poseidon drags an arm across his mouth slowly, assessing Athena with an inscrutable expression. The two of them stare at each other for what feels like a century, saying nothing at all.

Then Poseidon strikes.

He takes Athena by her forearm and wrenches her down to her knees, so that she is forced to kneel before him. If she tries to resist or struggle, I can't tell; it makes no difference at all. The coils of muscle in Poseidon's arm bulge and flex as he holds her, the same way he held me. There is something deeply disturbing about it. I know that they are both immortal, centuries and centuries old, but passersby would not see that if they looked into the garden. No, what they would see is a young man holding down a woman who looks old enough to be his mother. Poseidon does not grimace as he looks down at Athena. He does not even look angry. His expression is cool and indifferent; somehow, that is the most frightening thing.

"You forget yourself, little niece," he says in a quiet voice. It is courteous, unemotional; he might be discussing something as banal as the weather. "You are a powerful goddess, perhaps the most powerful of them all. But you are no *god;* nor are you my equal. If you ever think to raise a hand to me again"—he yanks her to her feet so that their noses are mere inches apart—"I will see to it that you are a virgin goddess no longer."

Athena looks away from him, and I catch a glimpse of the tears in her eyes. They hurt to see, almost as much as the pain I felt before in my lower belly. Because there it is: another woman, brought to her knees. Athena—goddess of wisdom, craftwork, and war—is the most powerful woman I've ever known. Now even she has been brought to her knees.

Poseidon stares down at her a second longer before he releases her. He turns on his heel and makes his way inside without looking back, and in his absence, the cicadas' trill returns. The stars above flicker like candles in a gust of wind now, and it is just the two of us—Athena and me—alone in my mother's gardens. When the silence becomes unbearable, I try for words.

"Goddess," my voice shakes, "forgive me."

Athena's silver eyes cut to me like two blades as she stands. She glares at me, and I watch as the muscles in her jaw clench, as her mouth twists with disgust.

"Whore."

She doesn't snatch me by my forearm, the way Poseidon snatched her. No, Athena closes the space between us, grabs an entire fistful of my locs, and drags me back into my father's hall as I scream.

NEVER IN MY life have I been so afraid.

I scream until I'm hoarse, but it does me no good as Athena half pulls, half drags me up the stairs and back into the palace.

In one moment, everything around me is dimmed; in the next, I am cast into a harsh golden light, and I know then that we've returned to the great hall. Around us the air is tinged with the faint smells of sweat and wine. The room's din hushes as Athena marches me toward its center. When we reach the spot where I was joyfully dancing only an hour before, she lets go of my hair and throws me to the ground. I gather myself and look up; every person in the hall is staring at me.

"Father!" I hear Athena's voice echoing through the space. "I would have an audience with you."

My body begins to tremble.

Up close, Zeus is like a mountain. Unlike Poseidon, he's chosen to make himself appear slightly older, but I see raw power in the god's eyes. They are the color of an afternoon sky, a bright piercing azure. Those eyes assess me with confusion, then look to his daughter.

"What's this, Athena?" His voice rolls like approaching thunder.

"You are our king, and I would have you pass judgment," says Athena from behind me. "This girl has dishonored me."

Zeus frowns. "Who is she?"

"Medusa. Daughter of the evening's hosts: Phorcys and Ceto."

Zeus still appears confused. "And how has she dishonored you?"

"She was my priestess, sworn to an oath of chastity," says Athena. "Now she has defiled herself with your brother. I found her and Poseidon fornicating, here on the very grounds of her father's home."

There is a collective gasp, and I flinch. I thought I was out of tears, but more come as gods begin to whisper. I search wildly through the blur of unfamiliar faces to find ones I know. Eventually, I do.

Euryale's bottom lip is trembling, her own eyes wet with tears. Beside her stands Stheno. I thought she would look angry, but she does not. My eldest sister looks terrified.

That frightens me more than anything else.

"Do you have any evidence of this crime?" Zeus asks. I turn back to him. The expression on his face is inscrutable, but I don't think it is kind, either. I steal a glance at Athena and see her hands have balled into fists. She is shaking.

"I saw them myself, just now in the garden," she seethes. "There is no doubt about what was done."

I look from her to my parents. All my life they've seemed so grand and powerful; in that moment, they seem terribly small. My mother is clasping my father's arm, her fingernails digging deep into his skin. My father's face is drawn, his gaze empty and distant. My eyes continue around the room, passing over the gods of the Sea Court I've known all my life. Finally, they land on Amphitrite. Heat burns in my cheeks as I wait to see open hate on the sea queen's face. I wonder if she might join Athena in insisting on my punishment. To my surprise, the sea queen doesn't appear angry; it's worse than that. Amphitrite waits until my gaze meets hers, then she merely sighs and shakes her head. It is a strange gesture, one of resignation. I think back to the way she looked at me the very first time I saw her, the fury I saw flashing in her eyes. I begin to wonder if that anger was never for me, if it was for her husband. Had she known, all along, that he would do this? I realize it no longer matters. The sea queen stares at me a second longer, then looks away.

"Father." Athena's ringing voice commands my attention again. "I demand that Poseidon be punished for damaging my priestess."

Zeus adjusts himself in his seat, frowning. "Where is Poseidon?" I hear a hint of vexation in his voice now. He looks around the room, blue eyes blazing. "Where is my brother?"

There are murmurs among the other gods, and they look around, too. Then a door on the other side of the room opens. Every hair on my body stands on end.

Poseidon walks into the hall with a slow and easy gait, his head held high and a small smile upon his face. I don't want to look at him, but I find I can't tear my eyes away. I sit on the floor, transfixed as he approaches. He does not spare me so much as a glance as he takes the seat beside his brother, extending his long legs and sitting back as though totally oblivious to the fact that everyone in the room is staring at him. He plucks a goblet of wine from a side table, and only once he's downed its contents does he speak.

"Brother," he says silkily. "You called for me?"

"Poseidon." The irritation in Zeus's voice is plain as he regards his brother. "My daughter says you've wronged her."

"Wronged her?" Poseidon sits up and looks around. After a moment, he casts his lazy gaze toward Athena, still deliberately ignoring me. "What have I done now, niece?"

"You seduced and lay with one of my priestesses!" Athena jabs a finger at Poseidon, spittle flying from her mouth. "You fornicated with a girl who pledged her service to me, a girl who was not to be touched."

Finally, Poseidon looks at me. No longer does he appear only a few years my senior; he is ancient and cool. Revulsion shudders through me.

"I don't deny that I slept with the girl," he says lightly. "But as for 'seduction,' *she* was the one who courted me. I met her in Athens, and I knew she intended to become a priestess. My intention was only to do my duty in watching over her as a member of the Sea Court, but she grew increasingly interested in more carnal relations. Even when I cautioned her, she was . . . *persistent*." He smiles. "Tonight, I went for a stroll in the gardens, and she was there, drunk. She practically begged for me."

I feel as though I've been plunged into cold water. Chills stipple every inch of my exposed skin. It isn't true, any of it. He's taken everything that really happened between us and disfigured it beyond recognition. The whispering among the gods grows louder, and Zeus's brow furrows. For the first time, he addresses me.

"Is this true, girl?"

No. The word lodges in my throat, and a terrible whimper escapes me instead. Athena's eyes cut to me, but this time I ignore her. I rise to my feet, unsteady. "No."

Zeus leans forward. "No?"

"That's . . . that's not true." I can't breathe. It is too warm. "That's not what happened. I—"

"Listen to her." A malicious glimmer touches Poseidon's eyes. He laughs. "She's drunk right now. I doubt she even knows where she is."

". . . S'not true." The lights of the hall are too bright. Sweat is slicking the back of my neck. Saliva fills my throat. I'm going to be sick. "Please, I didn't . . . He didn't . . ."

"Enough." Zeus's voice cuts off my mumblings. "We will have the truth of this," he says calmly. "Girl. Relay your account of what happened."

The contents of my stomach still slosh around inside me so violently, I'm afraid to move, but I make myself face the king of the gods. I take several deep breaths, trying to steady myself, before I speak.

"The sea king is lying." There are gasps around the room, but I go on. "It's true, we met in Athens, and it's true we kissed, but tonight . . ." I swallow hard. "He asked me to show him the gardens."

"And you did?" Zeus presses.

"He is the sea king." I'm aware my words are growing more slurred, but I force them out. "I thought I had to."

"So, you went with him willingly," says Zeus.

"Yes, but—"

Zeus's frown deepens. "Did you fornicate with my brother tonight?"

"I . . ." *Say something.* "Yes, but I—"

"Had you had any previous physical relations with him?"

"We kissed on the night of Panathenaia," I say quickly. "And we met a few times on the beach in Athens. He came to my parents' home once, to return a necklace."

"So, this was not the first time you slept together."

"We'd never slept together." The room is beginning to tilt, and it's everything I can do to stay on two feet. "I had never done it before, with anyone."

Zeus's gaze is unwavering. "And my last question: Did you say no?"

I try to remember that moment. Already, my mind has blocked so much of it out. I remember saying "Wait" and "I can't," but when I try to recall if I actually said the word *no* . . . I realize I can't.

"Well?" Zeus prompts. "Did you?"

"I can't remember, but—"

The rest of the room titters. Tears well in my eyes until I can barely see anything at all. I still hear Zeus's next words, though.

"I've heard enough." There is a finality in his voice. "Athena, the transgression committed was made against you, therefore you may choose a punishment for the girl."

My nausea drains away. In its place comes cold fear. I blink hard, and the tears that've been held in my eyes slick down both cheeks as I stare up at Athena. Her gray eyes are flat now, expressionless. When she speaks, her voice is low, audible only to me.

"You were so promising," she whispers. "Intelligent, brave, humble. You would have been an extraordinary priestess. Instead, you've chosen to be just like the rest. Such a disappointment." In a louder voice, she addresses the entire hall. "This girl has chosen to use her beauty for blasphemy and wickedness," she declares, "so she will have beauty no longer."

She turns back to me, as if girding herself. I brace for her to strike me, rake her nails across my face, mar me. Instead, she stoops down and touches a slender finger to my scalp.

At once, the skin begins to burn.

It is like fire, searing hot as it ripples from the point of her touch and makes its way across my entire head. My knees buckle and then collapse as the pain intensifies. My head slams against the floor and stars explode in my vision, but even that isn't enough to distract me from the burning. It rips me in and out of consciousness, dappling my vision so that I see the world around me only in broken pieces. I feel something graze my shoulders, my arms. In a moment of clarity, I see my locs begin to fall around me as if they were being cut. There is so much pain, but beneath it, I still feel the utter anguish of that loss. I pray.

My hair. My hair. Please, don't take my hair.

The locs continue to fall. I screw my eyes shut, but that does nothing to block out the new sound—a hissing. My locs are gone, but something else is on my head. Beneath the pain, I feel fresh horror. Has Athena set live serpents on me? I don't see them, but I can hear them all around me. *Where are they?*

The pain stops as suddenly as it began. I didn't realize I've been rocking back and forth; my body shudders to a stop as I sit back on my heels. My head feels strangely heavy, and I stare at the floor as a new sound fills my ears alongside the hissing: frantic whispers from the gods watching all around me. My pulse leaps again. What is going on? Why do they look so afraid?

"Meddy!"

Someone in the crowd pushes through. Tears still blur my vision, but I'd know that voice anywhere. Theo. My friend is pushing through the throng of gods, struggling as one of the other slaves tries to hold him back. Theo shakes him off and runs toward me, his expression determined.

"Meddy!" There is a desperation in his voice.

"Theo." My voice breaks. "Help me, please."

"It's all right, Meddy." The words come out choked, but Theo is still coming toward me. "It's going to be all right. We—"

It happens fast.

My eyes lock with Theo's, and he falters in his steps. A look I don't understand flashes across his face as he stops moving. He is still staring at me, but there is confusion there, pain.

I stand. "Theo?"

Theo's throat bobs, as though his response were trapped there. He opens his mouth, but no words leave it. Instead, something else catches my attention. It is small, so small at first that I wonder if I'm imagining it. A tiny fleck of Theo's skin near his jaw seems to be leached of color. I watch the warm brown skin turn white, then ash gray, then harden. I go numb.

"Theo!"

My head is still throbbing, I still feel sick, but I run to him. No one stops me as I close the gap between us. Theo isn't looking at me anymore. His eyes are coin-wide and gaping at something in the distance. I grab his shoulders, vaguely aware that they are turning to stone, too. I watch as the gray spreads up to his cheeks, his ears, his curly hair.

"No." I moan. I feel myself falling, dropping down so that I'm at Theo's stone feet, clinging to his cold, hard legs. "No, please!"

The hissing returns tenfold, right against my ear, and I shudder.

There is no controlling it now: My stomach empties itself right there at Theo's feet. Someone gasps; others make sounds of disgust. I don't care. Slowly, I rise. In my periphery, I see people turning their heads away. It takes a beat for my mind to process what's happening.

They're turning away . . . because they're afraid.

I keep my head lowered until I catch a silver glint and chance a look upward. It is a mirror, a large one my father had ordered the slaves to install in the hall some time ago. I look directly into it.

That is when I understand that Athena has not set serpents on me.

Staring back at me in the reflection is a creature with brown skin, full lips, and pus-yellow eyes. Its pupils aren't round and black, but slitted like a feral cat's. Worse still is the place where its hair should be. The creature's head is covered with long black snakes. No, not covered: Its hair is *made* from snakes. They writhe against one another, tangling like so many grotesque locs. The creature in the mirror's reflection blinks back at me, and I see a single tear roll down its cheek.

My cheek.

No. I know the truth, but I still plead. *Please, no.*

He turned to stone. Theo turned to stone . . . because I looked at him.

There are no longer whispers in the hall. Somewhere distant, I hear shouts. Gods are backing away in earnest. I hear snatches of their words.

Monster.

Abomination.

Athena's words return to me.

This girl has chosen to use her beauty for blasphemy and wickedness, so she will have beauty no longer.

Monster. That word strikes me over and over. She's made me a monster.

I am still upright, but my knees are threatening to give out again. Not here: I won't fall here a second time. I can't. I taste danger in the air, and some primal instinct gives me a single directive.

Go.

I spare a final glance at Theo, at the statue of my friend. His face is still the picture of fear. That is the last way he'll ever look at me.

I turn on my heel and sprint toward the nearest door. No one stops me.

Go.

I crash through the hall's doors and run into the darkness without looking back.

PART IV

MONSTER

XXIX

I DON'T KNOW what drives me to run back to the gardens.

Perhaps it's because they have always been my favorite place on the island, the place I've felt safest. Perhaps it's because the air inside the great hall was stifling, and out here I feel I can breathe again. I run until the soles of my feet ache, until my vision is spotty and I'm gasping for breath. Then I duck into the thick, low-hanging leaves of a willow tree. I curl up at the tree's base and try to keep still. Eventually, the sun rises, but I can't bring myself to move. The adrenaline that coursed through my veins, keeping me on high alert, begins to fade, and in its place, a fatigue like I've never known sets in. I tilt my head back, easing against the trunk of the tree.

Then there's a sharp hiss and stinging pain on my neck. I touch two fingers to it, then see bright red blood. Slowly, I understand what's happened. When I leaned back, I inadvertently touched one of the snakes, so it bit me. The bite is shallow, but it riddles me with a new panic. I have not drunk water, I have not eaten, and I have not slept. I don't know how much longer I can stay upright. A sharp hunger pang twists my stomach. Some bitter part of me wonders if this is what Athena intended, if what she's really done is sentence me to a slow, painful death. I think of what Theo would do, and then another kind of pain rips through my body.

Theo is gone.

I cry for an hour, then another, but the grief eventually consumes me, so that I have nothing left to give. I remember the last look I saw on Theo's face, the way he called out my name and promised that everything would be all right. He was so sure he could fix it, he really believed himself strong enough to undo the work of gods.

He was so wrong.

A sound pulls me from my thoughts, and despite my fatigue, my senses are immediately on alert again as I hear approaching footsteps. I see shadowy figures through the willow tree's leaves, and I brace myself, closing my eyes. There's a pause.

"Meddy?"

The relief I feel at the sound of my sister's voice is at once replaced by terror.

"Don't come any closer!" I flinch at the sound of my own voice; it's grown raspy and dry from thirst and crying.

"Meddy." It's Euryale's voice. "It's all right. It's us."

My eyes are still closed, but I hear a second set of footsteps, then the sound of the willow's branches being parted. I squeeze my eyes tighter. "I don't want to hurt you."

"Meddy." Stheno sounds more like herself now—annoyed, imperious. "Open your eyes."

Perhaps it is the directness of the words, perhaps it is the utter lack of fear in my sister's voice. Slowly, I crack open one eye, then another, careful to keep my gaze trained on the ground. Both my sisters are standing before me, their brown feet bare and unadorned.

"It's all right," says Euryale. "You can look at us."

My gaze lifts slowly, from her feet to her dress. I am at her shoulders when a gasp escapes me.

Stheno and Euryale have changed.

My sisters' faces remain largely the same—youthful, lovely. But their locs are all gone; in their place, black snakes writhe and twist through the air. Our gazes meet, and I realize my sisters' eyes have changed, too. They're yellow, with slitted pupils.

"Stheno. Euryale . . ." I can only stare. "What happened?"

They lower themselves to the ground so that we are all sitting in a small circle under the cover of the willow. In spite of everything, I still envy the graceful way they move. There's a beat of silence, then Euryale speaks.

"After you left the feast, there was, as you might expect, quite a bit of commotion," she says. "No one really knew what to do next. Everyone just sort of stood around looking at each other. Then Stheno chose to address Athena using some rather colorful language—"

"I called her a hateful bitch," says Stheno flatly.

I go cold. "You didn't."

"Of course, Athena didn't take kindly to that," Euryale continues. "So she gave Stheno the same curse she gave to you. It was all deeply distressing, and I cried out, so . . . she cursed me, too." She gives me a weak smile. "It was probably for the best, really. You know I never liked being left out."

The weight of her words sinks in. Athena didn't curse just me, she cursed my sisters, too. I didn't think I had any tears left, but new ones fall as I look at them.

"What happened to Mama?" I ask. "And Father?"

"They fled," says Stheno. She speaks matter-of-factly, without any trace of emotion. "We have no idea where they are, but my best guess is that they're in hiding."

It's worse than anything I could have imagined. In a single night, the family I knew is gone. And it's my fault.

"I'm sorry," I whisper. "I'm so, *so* sorry."

"No more of that." Stheno shakes her head. "Eury and I are fine. We're just glad we found you. We've been looking everywhere for you."

"We wanted to talk to you about what happened," Euryale adds.

I avoid their gazes. "You were there," I whisper. "You saw what happened."

Stheno's finger catches the point of my chin and gently tilts my head so that I'm looking at her again. "Not what happened in the hall," she says.

"We want to know what happened before." There's no trace of teasing in Euryale's voice anymore.

My heart seizes. I've been so wrapped up in fear, in fatigue, in grief, that I haven't allowed myself to remember what happened in the garden. Now it all comes back to me in a rush. I see Poseidon's face, hear his grunts and moans, smell the sea-salt sweat of him as he ruts over me. New tears burn in my eyes, but they're angry ones now.

"When did this all start?" asks Stheno.

Slowly, I tell my sisters everything. I tell them about the boy I met in Athens who knew exactly where to find me in the market and exactly where to find the owl I was looking for. I tell them about the night Poseidon rescued me, then about the necklace he also conveniently found and used as an excuse to see me again. The more I speak, the more clearly I see it all. The more I talk, the worse I feel.

"He told me that his marriage to the queen was arranged and that she never loved him," I say. "I believed him."

"That isn't true," says Stheno. "Nereus didn't arrange Poseidon and Amphitrite's marriage, Poseidon demanded it."

"Mother told us about it, once," Euryale adds. "Poseidon found Amphitrite beautiful, but she did not feel the same way. He chased her across the sea until finally she was convinced to marry him. Of course, once she learned to love him, his attention waned. He has never been faithful to her. It's why she hates him so."

I remember what Theo once said to me, the rumors he told me he'd heard about Poseidon that I'd so easily disregarded. I shake my head, feeling sick.

"It's all so obvious now," I whisper. "There were all the signs in the world, but I didn't see them because I didn't want to." I shake my head. "I can't believe I was so stupid."

"*No,*" says Stheno. "Not stupid."

"Meddy, I need you to understand something," says Euryale. "What Poseidon did? It wasn't random. He orchestrated every encounter. He knew exactly what strings to pull, what words to say, because he is old and you are young, and because he knew he could take advantage of you. That is not your fault."

I see it all like pieces from a broken vase then, coming together with terrible satisfaction. I realize Euryale is right. Everything Poseidon did was deliberate. He methodically earned my trust, made me feel as though I was truly special to him. He lured me farther and farther away from the shore and into his depths until my toes couldn't touch the bottom.

And then he let me drown.

"We need to know," says Stheno. "Did he lie with you last night?"

A few seconds pass before I can form a single word. "Yes."

"Did you want him to?" Euryale asks. "If you did, we won't judge you. We just need to know."

Another pause. "I don't know," I say finally. "At first . . . I *thought* I wanted him to. I thought he truly cared for me, but then . . ." I remember the owl's eyes blinking at me in the darkness. "I said, 'Wait.' I told him I couldn't, because of my priestess vows, but he . . ." I can't make myself relive that part, and I fall into silence.

I wait for Stheno to say something, but she does not. Seconds pass before she takes my hands in hers.

"It doesn't matter that you might have wanted to at first," she says. "You can change your mind at any time."

"But . . ." I stare at our joined hands. "I didn't say no. I didn't—"

"You are *thousands* of years younger than him." Euryale's voice sharpens so suddenly I flinch against it. "And you'd been drinking Olympian wine. Both those things are cause enough to make what he did wrong."

It takes a moment for me to register that the emotion bubbling up within me is relief, vindication. *Someone believes me.* In a stronger voice, I say, "He was lying about everything. The way he made it sound . . . he twisted it all. I was telling the truth."

Stheno's expression hardens, while Euryale's becomes a mask.

"I'm afraid the truth doesn't matter, Meddy," says Stheno.

I frown, trying to hide my hurt. "What do you—?"

"I warned you that men with power are always the first to be believed," she says. "You should have listened. In these situations, it isn't the truth that holds weight. What matters is power and those who wield it, because they're the ones who get to decide what's true and what's a lie." She nods at me. "You are the mortal daughter of two lowly, now-disgraced sea gods. I'm sure I don't have to explain to you where you stand in the hierarchy of things."

The words don't hurt the way they might have coming from someone else. I know my sister well enough to recognize that behind their harshness, there is love.

"Your voice and your truth will never hold weight unless you also learn to hold power," says Euryale.

"But I don't know *how* to be powerful," I say in a small voice.

Stheno juts her chin, looking down her nose at me, and in that moment, she looks like a queen. "I'll tell you this: Power is not given. It is taken."

I open my mouth to ask Stheno what that means when one of the snakes atop her head suddenly begins to hiss. I watch with horror as its mouth opens, revealing a forked black tongue and thorn-sharp teeth. It weaves and spits against my sister's cheek, and I recognize the glint in its eye.

"Stheno, it's going to—"

The snake makes to strike at my sister, but Stheno is impossibly quicker. In one fell swoop, she snatches the creature by its neck and pulls it free from her head. Only her slight flinch betrays any discomfort, but in her hands, she now holds the snake aloft. I gasp softly. It is limp in her grasp, dead. Stheno regards it with a faint look of annoyance before throwing it to the ground. I notice that the other snakes coiling and writhing about her head are more subdued now. They do not hiss anymore. She meets my gaze and nods.

"Your body is yours," she says. "You control it, *all* of it, including your eyes. You don't have to turn anyone to stone unless you will it. You can learn to control it." A hint of sympathy touches her face. "I am sorry, about Theo."

The grief returns to me at once, fresh and aching.

"We moved him to a part of the gardens he liked," Euryale adds. "If you wish to see him."

My thoughts are interrupted as a now-familiar hiss sounds just behind my ear. I shudder as the snakes atop my head begin to move around one another, their scales gliding along the back of my neck uncomfortably, as if daring me to object. Stheno leans in and speaks in a low voice.

"They will not respect you unless you *make* them."

She and Euryale rise, brushing off the fronts of their tunics.

"We'll be back inside, when you're ready," says Euryale.

They leave the way they came, pushing back the rippling branches of the willow tree to leave me alone with the snakes on my head and their hissing. After a few minutes, I slowly stand, carefully, so as not to disturb them. The muscles in my legs spasm and ache from disuse, but I ignore the discomfort as I make myself walk forward, one step after the other, and then I've left the canopy of the willow tree, too. I let my feet carry me of their own volition, unsure of where I'm going until I am nearly there. Early morning sunlight dapples the small lawn, and I freeze.

In its center is Theo.

His statue is looking ahead so that, if I squint, I can almost imagine he is standing there waiting for me, like always. My throat tightens, and I choke on a sob.

"I'm sorry." He can't hear me, I know that, but I still feel the need to say the words aloud. "I'm so sorry."

My fingers creep up my neck, then latch onto the shell necklace. I don't know what drives me to do it, but I yank the thing free from my neck and kneel at Theo's feet. I don't truly realize what I'm doing until I've nearly finished digging the tiny hole in the dirt before his statue. I place the necklace into it and gently push dirt over it until it's gone. Fresh tears sting my eyes. As I cry for Theo, I realize I'm also crying for the life I had before last night. I think of all the dreams I'd collected, nurtured, then lost. I feel as though some part of me died with Theo, gone forever, like he is. I paw a lone tear from my cheek and stare up at the morning sun. A snake hisses in my ear a second time, and I do not hesitate. I grasp its head and pull. Searing pain lances through my skull as I yank it out of my head. I imagine it would feel the same as ripping a loc from my own scalp, but I ignore the pain as I stare at the snake in my hand. It is dead, but I speak so that the others will hear me.

"You are with me, or you are against me."

The snakes' hissing subsides immediately, and they come to rest at my shoulders. They aren't my old locs—they never will be—but they are still long and, I decide in that moment, beautiful, just in a different way. I rise and leave the gardens without looking back.

The snakes do not bite me ever again.

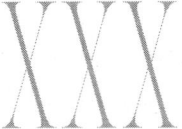

IN THE WEEKS after, I come to familiarize myself with the nuances of Athena's curse.

My sisters and I share the same affliction: snakes for hair and eyes that, when willed, turn bright yellow and transform anyone who looks at us into stone. I learn to control that power as easily as any muscle in my body. I try not to think about what could have been with Theo. Other things have changed, too. My sisters and I are stronger, faster, than we've ever been. Every one of my senses is heightened. I hear the flapping of gulls' wings far overhead; I see the dorsal fins of dolphins many miles from the coast. I am still mortal—that, I understand—but it is different. I am not helpless anymore. Some days, I walk the coastline, glaring at the water and daring Poseidon to come, daring him to step foot on this island again.

I am stronger now, I promise him. *I will never be prey again.*

I am weaving on the veranda when I see the ship in the distance.

It is small at first, a brown speck among the vast ocean waves. I soon make out sails, hear shouting.

Men are coming to our island.

We suspect it is a consequence of my parents' absence, the dissolution of whatever ancient protections previously kept mortal men from finding this island. Now there is no question. Men are coming, and they're coming fast.

"What should we do?" It's Euryale who asks the question first. She stands next to me on the veranda, looking as worried as I feel. Only Stheno, reclined beside us, maintains her composure as she rises and gives the approaching ship only a fleeting look.

"We do the only thing we can," she says calmly. "We welcome them." She turns. "Gather what food we have in baskets and take them to the beach. Act modest and say nothing. Cover your heads, and let me take the lead."

Euryale and I exchange looks, but we obey. By the time the ship has dropped anchor off the coast, the three of us are standing on the shore waiting, food baskets surrounding us. My heart pounds as ropes fly from the ship's swollen sides; men begin to teem out of the vessel like ants and climb into the waiting rowboats. I self-consciously pat my head wrap, and in answer, the snakes move among one another. The feel of them sliding across my scalp is still new—not bad but not pleasant, either. My stomach turns as the men and their boats draw nearer; the stench of ale and unwashed bodies fouls the air.

At last, the boats reach shore, and a man I assume is their leader climbs out. He has dark, oily hair and swarthy skin that speaks to a life at sea. His face is weather-beaten, and I'd guess him to be in his late forties or fifties. He has a confident gait and seems unsurprised and undaunted by our presence there. He walks up to Stheno, recognizing her as our leader, and addresses her without preamble.

"I am Linus of Argos," he says in an imperious voice. "I demand to know the name of this island and the name of the man who rules it."

As instructed, Euryale and I lower our heads slightly, performing demureness. In contrast, Stheno juts her chin so that her and Linus's eyes are level.

"This island has no natural name." She speaks softly, yet her voice still manages to carry across the beach, where the rest of the sailors wait. "Nor does it know any master."

Linus frowns. "There is a palace, up on the crags." He points. "My men saw it from the water."

Stheno nods. "It was built by our father and mother many years ago, but they have both since perished. Only my sisters and I remain."

Linus now looks truly bewildered. "Do you mean to tell me that the three of you live on this island alone? As free women, governing yourselves?"

Stheno's smile is slight; it doesn't reach her eyes. "Yes."

There is a distinct look to be found in a man who first glimpses the opportunity to exploit. Linus's smile is coy and unsubtle as his eyes roam over my sisters and me with new assessment. My stomach clenches.

"I see," he says warmly. Then, as though a decision has been made, he claps his hands and turns to his men.

"We will camp here for the night," he announces. "Return to the ship and fetch our supplies." He turns to Stheno. "Assuming this is pleasing to you?"

Stheno's expression is one of perfect calm. "Of course."

"Excellent."

While he continues directing his men, Stheno turns to us. For once, I wish I could read her impassive face. As though she hears my thoughts, she winks, and her eyes seem to flash yellow for a moment. A reminder.

"Trust me," she says in a low voice only Euryale and I can hear. "I have a plan. All will be well."

I decide quickly that I dislike having men on our island.

They are loud, smelly, and litter the sand with their waste. They grow increasingly sloppy the darker it gets, the longer they drink. All the while, Euryale and I continue to serve them, carefully avoiding their reaching hands and lecherous eyes. I try to hold on to what Stheno said: She has a plan. But the later it gets, the uneasier I feel. Finally, Linus stands, and the men quiet.

"For my three little island queens!" His words have become slurred in the hours since their landing, but his eyes are alight. "I offer you gifts!" He gestures, and three sailors approach on unsteady feet, carrying chests. They stop before us and each falls to one knee before they open the

chests. My breath catches. The chests are filled to the brim with treasure—
bars of pure gold, diamonds, and raw uncut sapphires as big as my
clenched fist. Against the firelight, they glitter so enticingly I'm tempted
to begin sorting through them at once. Stheno shoots Euryale and me
subtle but clear warning looks before she stands.

"You flatter us," she says breezily. "But what are these gifts for?"

Linus smiles. "They are tokens of celebration," he says, "gifts to com-
memorate this most momentous occasion."

Stheno's brows rise. "And what occasion is that?"

"The birth of a new nation." Linus throws his arms wide, as though
proclaiming to the stars. "The birth of my new kingdom."

"*Your* kingdom?" I don't miss the new edge in Stheno's voice. Several
sailors apparently hear it, too, because they shift their eyes to her warily.

"It will be called Linusia," says Linus, clearly oblivious to the new tension. "It will be a kingdom to rival the world's greatest. Even Athens will
not hold a candle to it."

I'm watching my sister's every move now. There's no trace of anger on
Stheno's face, but a coldness emanates from her very being. Several of the
sailors nearest to her shiver. She runs a hand carelessly along her head
wrap, and something in my own bones hums.

"I'm afraid that, regardless of your gifts, you cannot do that."

Linus laughs. "Cannot?"

She gestures. "This is *our* home. It belongs to *us*."

"Cannot." Linus shakes his head. When he looks at Stheno again, his
expression resembles that of a father managing a particularly difficult
child. "And who are you to tell me what I cannot do?" He chortles.
"You're just a woman." His paternal façade drops in an instant, and I
tense as he snatches Stheno by her upper arm, pulling her against him.
"Do you really think *you* have the power to stop me?"

"What I *think*," Stheno says quietly, "is that I have more power than
you could ever imagine." She pulls off her head wrap, then Euryale and
I follow suit. The men stare at us in naked terror, a collective scream rising from their throats.

"What? How—?" The words barely leave Linus's mouth before my sister turns to him, her eyes now vivid and yellow. He turns to stone with his mouth still open, his eyes caught between fear and confusion. It is the final straw for the sailors; at once they begin to flee, some running for their ship while others lose all sense and scatter across the beach. Stheno and Euryale stalk after them, but I remain frozen where I stand. I look to Linus's statue. He was alive seconds ago, and now he's not.

"Meddy!" Stheno calls my name over her shoulder. "Come on!"

These men, Linus's men, are not the ones who actually threatened us. Only their leader spoke, and now he is dead. From my scrolls and brief time spent among mortals, I understand vaguely that these are just lowly crewmen, no doubt paid a meager wage to manage the ship and do their captain's bidding. I understand that they are just men following orders, that it's possible not all of them are cruel.

It's even possible that some of them might be good men.

I stand there on the beach poised, split between diverging paths forward. Deep down, I know that the choice to walk one of those paths is an irrevocable one, a choice I will not be able to come back from. I watch as Stheno turns to glare at one of the ill-fortuned men. He raises his hands a second too late, and suddenly where a man was, there is now only a statue forever frozen in terror. I have seen death before, but this feels different.

I have never contemplated deliberately killing someone before.

"Meddy!"

I look up and find it's Euryale who calls to me now. Around her, men are still running, still screaming, but her gaze is fixed steadily on me. Her eyes are yellow, too, lurid against the shore's dark, rolling tides and the ink-black sky above. In them I see a new ferocity, a new hardness. I hear the words she once said to me under the haven of a willow tree.

Your voice and your truth will never hold weight unless you also learn to hold power.

I have been the youngest daughter of sea gods. I have been an acolyte, then a priestess of an Olympian. I was once the pawn and plaything of another. Never before have I held real power. Now, for the first time, I do. I once vowed that I would leave this island; now I make a new vow.

I will never be helpless again. I will never be powerless again.

I take up that new vow, armoring myself with it, as I start toward my sisters and my victims, my yellow eyes ablaze.

In the epics I pored over as a child, there were valiant tales of men who died on battlefields. In those stories, death was presented as something poetic and beautiful. I now understand that there is little that is beautiful about death—it is blunt and ugly. I run among the retreating men as they head for the water. It doesn't take much to turn them to stone, just a brief glance. Some of the men die still looking over their shoulders; others die with hands raised to cover their eyes a second too late. When it is over, the beach is eerily quiet, save for the crackling of the sailors' now-abandoned fire. I turn to Stheno and Euryale. It's strange to see them like this, standing serene amid a garden of statues.

"Are they all dead?" Euryale's voice is soft.

"No," says Stheno. She marches toward a body lying face down on the ground and kicks it over with her heel to reveal one of the sailors . . . very much alive. He coils into a ball as my sister stands over him looking supremely bored. She crouches down beside him, facing us, her eyes normal and brown once more. It is impressive how easily she once again becomes gentle and placid. The man's trembling doubles as she cups his face in her hand. His eyes are screwed shut. The snakes on my sister's head are quiet, their many heads pointed directly at him.

"*Shh.*" She must be half this man's age, but she speaks to him as though he were a frightened child. "There's no need for all of that; I'm not going to kill you. I have a job for you." She nods in the direction of the ship offshore. "You can't manage a vessel that size alone, I presume?"

The man shakes his head.

"But you *can* use one of the rowboats, yes?"

The man mouths *yes,* but no sound comes out. Stheno nods, satisfied.

"Good. Then here are your instructions. *Go.* Tell men far and wide what you saw here. Tell them that this island belongs to my sisters and me, and that we take no prisoners. Tell them not to come here if they wish to live."

The man nods fervently, then crashes toward one of the anchored rowboats. The three of us watch him until he is but a speck on the horizon and then gone entirely.

"What do we do now?" I ask softly.

Stheno turns to me and smiles. "We wait," she murmurs. "And we pray they listen."

XXXI

THEY DO NOT LISTEN.

In fact, for the next few months, many more men come to our island. It seems the sole messenger Stheno allowed to leave the first time shared more than just a warning. Men are lured to our land like ants to a bowl of honey, fueled by promises of glory or wealth. As more of them die, anger and revenge join the list of motivations.

That, I can understand.

It becomes easier for Stheno and Euryale to kill. The first time, with Linus and his crew, killing men had felt like steps to a dance the three of us did not truly know. That first time, I'd watched Euryale turn a man to stone, then flinch. Stheno had glared around the beach with yellow eyes and turned men to stone indiscriminately, without finesse. That changed as time went on. As more men arrived on our shores, as the coast became clogged with the statues of our victims, my sisters learned to make a game of it. They herded the men like cattle, sometimes letting them believe they had a chance at escape before turning them to stone at the last minute. They dragged statues to the place where the waves beat against the rocks and laughed as those statues were pummeled into tiny pieces.

I do not join them in their revelry and their games. I learn to kill with more finesse, too, but there is, for me, something sacred in the act. I tell myself that what I am doing is necessary, just, even righteous. The great majority of the men who come to our island are evil men, I know that, but every so often, I find one or two who look lost. I imagine that they did not want to come to our island, that perhaps they did not intend any harm. Sometimes, I consider asking them. My sisters turn them to stone before I ever can.

I'm seated on the shoreline alone, watching the tides roll in, when a boat appears on the horizon. Often, the boats men arrive in are large and grand, but this one is modest, small, more of a raft. As it draws closer, I see that it is occupied by a single person, a boy. His skin is dark brown, his curly hair is black as a crow's wing. He's tall, lean muscle covers his body, but there is still a trace of youth lingering in the fullness of his cheeks and in his dark, wary eyes. I say nothing as the tides pull his raft to shore. For a moment, he does not notice me among the statues. When he does, he stiffens. His hands fly to the crude dagger strapped to his hip.

"Have you traveled far?" I ask gently, rising from the sand. The snakes under my head wrap stir, but I pat them quiet. The boy looks me over, apprehensive.

"I have come to slay the Gorgons." The words are practiced, but his voice trembles as he says them. "Where can I find them?"

Gorgons. That is not a name my sisters and I have chosen for ourselves. It feels strange, like being forced into clothing that doesn't quite fit. I tilt my head.

"You look young, to be a murderer." I extend my hand. "Join me for a while?"

"I have come to slay the Gorgons," the boy says again. He will not look at me. "Where can I find them?"

I find myself wondering about the boy's mother, if she already knew, when she said goodbye to him, that she would never see him again. I sigh and pull off my head wrap. The snakes come to life, hissing and spitting with glee. The young man's eyes widen, and he takes an instinctive step back.

"Are you very sure that this is what you want?" I ask half-heartedly.

In answer, he draws his dagger.

"Very well, then."

The tide licks at our ankles as we circle each other in the sand. I can tell by his footwork that he has had some basic training, but he still moves like a novice, like a man who's never seen real battle. We circle each other for a few more seconds before he loses patience and lunges, but with my enhanced speed, I easily dodge the blow, and the next one, too. I close the gap between us, trying to make him nervous, but it seems to have the opposite effect on the young man. Something within him ignites as he grits his pearl-white teeth. With a cry, he lunges again, and this time I'm unprepared for it. A white-hot pain blazes across my skin, and when I look down I'm surprised to see a thin line of red blood trickling down my biceps. I'm momentarily mesmerized. The boy steps back, looking as stunned as I feel.

There is a discipline in the way I kill. I have rules. I save my true brutality for the older, more salacious men. The younger ones I tend to turn to stone quickly, as a kindness. I decide that this boy is worthy of at least that kindness. I start to summon the power behind my eyes as he shifts from foot to foot, reaches down the front of his tunic, and withdraws something from it.

I stop.

The pendant he wears is distinct in shape; I'd recognize the owl carving anywhere. It has been months since I last saw a token of Athena, months since I was one of her followers. The boy's eyes never leave mine as he mutters a prayer, brings the owl pendant to his lips, and kisses it with a reverence that makes my stomach turn.

Something is building behind my eyes, but it's not power. When the tears fall and slick down my cheeks, it is not anger I feel, but sorrow. I did not think, after all this time, that I'd left room in my heart for anything other than anger. Now I know that sorrow is the real monster, waiting to attack its victims when their guards are down.

I don't want to kill this boy, not really. I know that. I back away from him several steps, hands raised.

"Go home," I whisper.

He stares at me outright, astonished.

"*Go home.*" I try to keep the desperation from my voice. "Leave. Now."

Already the boy is backing away from me. He glances toward his small boat, still in the water, and I know he's calculating how quickly he could get to it.

"I won't hurt you," I say. "But you have to go quickly."

The boy starts to nod, then glances over my shoulder. I see a sudden renewed terror in his eyes, and I know without looking what must be there. He opens his mouth in a silent scream, and my heart plummets.

"No!"

It's too late: The boy is already turning to stone. I whip around and find Stheno standing perfectly still. We stare at each other.

"You were going to spare him," she says. It isn't a question.

"He was young," I protest. "He wouldn't have harmed—"

"He came here to *kill* us." There's a new bite in Stheno's voice. "He came here to kill *you.*"

My gaze drops. I have no idea if the men who come to this island know that I am mortal while my sisters are not. I stare back at the statue of the boy.

"Remember, all men are cruel, Meddy." Stheno cups my face in hers. "Some are just better at hiding it."

"But what if they're not, Stheno?" I lift my gaze to meet hers.

"That's a risk you can't take. Ever."

I don't know what to say in response to that. Some part of me understands that Stheno's viewpoint is flawed. Her universal disdain for men is no better than so many men's disdain for women, or Kallisto's disdain for all foreigners. Some part of me also understands that Stheno is what the world has made her, and that I won't change her mind.

She leaves me alone on the beach after that, and I turn to face the statue of the boy. The tide has covered his stone feet, and I can't ignore the pang in my chest when I think of how close he was to freedom.

If only you hadn't looked.

I'm walking toward his statue before I even realize it. His arms are still half raised, so it's easy to gently pick him up—even turned to stone, he is not heavy for me—and carry him out to sea. I walk until the water is up to my chest, and only then do I let go. I watch as the boy's statue sinks into the blue-black depths, and I think about his mother. I know she'll curse me and my sisters; I know that, though my arm still bleeds, to her, we will always be the villains.

I spare one more look at the sinking statue of the boy, then trek back up the beach.

THE THREE MONTHS after my skirmish with the boy pass with curious speed.

More men certainly come to our island. Some arrive in large parties, others come alone. I begin to let Stheno and Euryale take the lead in the killings, joining them only when they ask. Somewhere in that time, I turn eighteen. The occasion brings little fanfare from Euryale and Stheno, who find the idea of birthdays odd. For me, though, it is a reminder that, unlike my sisters, my time is not infinite. I find myself wondering more and more if this is to be my life's new purpose, if protecting our island alongside my sisters is my destiny.

Spring has only just begun the night I'm eating dinner and notice a new ship on the horizon. By now, the rhythm of what to do in response is like an instinct. At once, I alert Stheno and Euryale, and we head down to the beach. We have memorized the steps in our ritual as though it were one of the dances we performed in our previous lives, and now we wait in silence for the ship to moor. The men disembark with much more discipline than we're used to. They row their boats up to the sand, and they don't acknowledge us as they form a long, tight line. They are darker-skinned than is typical of our would-be hunters—

not quite my complexion, but certainly not pale. Every one of them turns as two more people disembark.

The first person, a brown-skinned man, must be their leader. He is clean-shaven, well dressed in a tunic dyed deep blue, and other than the slight rumple in his clothes, he looks well rested and clean. My gaze goes to the person trailing behind him, and I pause.

It's a young woman.

She's tall, fair-skinned, with short, dark brown hair that I remember was once long, curly, and thick. Her clothes have changed, and she walks with her hazel eyes downcast, but I would recognize my friend anywhere.

It's Apollonia.

The leader of the crew turns to Apollonia suddenly, as though just remembering she's there, and mutters something under his breath before grabbing her by the arm and marching her toward us more quickly. I don't know what to make of the two of them. When they reach us, the man smiles.

"I am Sobekemsaf," he says in a low bullfrog's croak. His Greek is clear, albeit slightly accented. "I come from the city of Alexandria, in Egypt. Perhaps you are familiar."

I *am* familiar with Alexandria. It's a wealthy city, in a distant land called Egypt. Judging by the many rings on his fingers and the many golden necklaces adorning his neck, this man has enjoyed more than his share of that wealth. I look to Apollonia again. If she were his wife, surely she'd be dressed well, too, but the clothes she wears are plain. I notice that she doesn't stand with the rest of the crew, so I still can't determine what she is to him. I try to study her face, to discern anything from it that might tell me of her condition. But her face is a perfect mask; it betrays nothing.

Suddenly, Stheno steps forward. "This island is claimed." She no longer wastes time with small talk. "Why are you here?"

If her brusqueness offends the man, he makes no show of it.

"You misunderstand," he says silkily. "I do not want violence, only business."

Stheno says nothing, but I know my sister well enough to recognize confusion in her face.

Emboldened by her silence, the man called Sobekemsaf goes on. "The three mysterious women of the lost island are infamous," he says with a new reverence in his voice. "Men whisper about the perils here. They say the island is a prize too dangerous to win." He shrugs. "But I look at your island and see something else. You are here alone."

"We have slaves," says Stheno.

Sobekemsaf arches a brow. "And food?"

"Plenty," says Stheno immediately. "The island is full of natural produce, meat, and fresh water."

"And *yet.*" Sobekemsaf raises a finger. "Your resources remain finite."

"We have sustained ourselves without issue thus far." There's a testiness in Stheno's voice.

Sobekemsaf gives her a patient look. "Perhaps you have managed it so far, but what about in a decade? Can you be sure that you will *always* have enough?"

Both my sisters glance at me, and guilt twists in my stomach. As immortals, *they* do not need to eat, but I do. If our finite resources mattered to anyone, it would be me.

Stheno turns back to Sobekemsaf. "What do you propose?"

"*I* will bring you all that you need," he says. "Food, raw materials that the island does not have, and anything else you might want. I am a merchant, and a powerful one. I will be your ally. I ask for only one thing in return."

At last, we have gotten to the heart of the conversation. Stheno juts her chin. "What is that?"

Something mirthless flashes behind Sobekemsaf's eyes. "For you to *kill* my enemies."

The beach seems to chill. Euryale shifts, visibly uncomfortable, and Stheno's eyes narrow.

"Your enemies?" she asks.

"As I said, I am a merchant," says Sobekemsaf. "There are many men in the greater world who envy me and despise me and who would seek to ensure my ruin."

Something familiar prickles my consciousness as I listen to him: In some ways, he reminds me of Prince Maheer.

"I would ask you to help me eliminate those who threaten me," he says. "I will send them to your island, with promises of great wealth and fortune, and then you must only do what you already do so well." He grins, gesturing to the many statues along our shore. "I will expand my enterprise, and you will have a great share of it. We would help each other."

I understand clearly what he wants from us. We are to be his hunting dogs, beasts to sic upon men of his choosing. There is something particularly distasteful about the proposition, worse even than the men who come to rob and kill us. My eyes go to Stheno, and the look on her face tells me her thoughts echo mine.

"We appreciate your offer of partnership," she says carefully, "but we're not interested. Go." She waves a hand. "You came to us in good faith. For that, I gift *you* with your life."

Sobekemsaf's face changes slowly. I watch his features rearrange themselves from an expression of oily kindness to one of disgust. He is shorter than my sister, but still manages to look down his nose at her.

"I might have guessed that a woman would lack proper business acumen," he says with a sniff. "Stay on this island alone, and you'll be dead in a few years."

My sister's eyes flash, and I tense. Sobekemsaf doesn't know it, but *he* will be dead by the end of the hour.

Stheno betrays nothing, only shrugs. "I'm sorry you feel that way," she says. "Please allow me to escort you back to your ship."

Apollonia has not moved or spoken since he brought her ashore. Now her eyes go wide. She looks between my sisters and me, at our calm demeanors, and somehow I know *she* knows what's about to happen. I watch her slowly move away from Sobekemsaf.

"I've no need for an escort," he says gruffly, turning his back on Stheno. He addresses his men. "Return to the ship, we're going home."

He makes it two steps before Stheno is upon him, the blade of her knife against his throat. A fat bead of blood trickles from the skin, and the man's eyes go wide.

"What's this?" he squawks as he struggles against my sister. "You can't do this!"

Stheno grins. "Can't I?"

Sobekemsaf's men, still in formation, stare between Stheno and their master, transfixed, clearly unsure of what to do.

"Let me go and I'll give you anything, anything you want!" Sobekemsaf hisses as Stheno lets her blade cut deeper into his skin.

My sister laughs. "You have nothing that I want, merchant."

"Name your price!" he says desperately. "Every man has a price."

Stheno cocks her head so that her lips barely graze Sobekemsaf's ear. She whispers the words, but I hear them.

"Unfortunately for you, *I am no man.*"

Violence has become a language Stheno speaks fluently. She cuts Sobekemsaf's throat.

Euryale and I are moving before his body hits the ground. I charge at the man standing closest to me and turn him to stone with a single look. The surrounding men scream; several try to run, but I am faster. The beach fills with the sound of men pleading, and I am no longer ashamed to admit that a part of me relishes that sound. These men aren't like the boy; they only wanted to use us. It reminds me of the way Poseidon only wanted to use me, and I feel that same well-worn rage swell within me like a storm. My vision begins to focus. I single out my victims one by one, my gaze sweeping across the beach, silencing the wails as each man turns to stone.

Then I pause.

I see a slight figure walking away quickly but carefully: Apollonia.

My feet seem to be moving of their own accord as I trace her footprints down the beach. Stheno and Euryale don't notice my departure, and soon the collective noises of Sobekemsaf's doomed men fade in favor of the churning waves and screeching gulls overhead.

"Wait!"

She doesn't stop her march across the beach, and now there is no mistaking it. There is a slight limp to her step, as though she's been recently injured.

"Wait!"

Apollonia stops walking. "I'm going to turn around," she says. "Just promise you'll get it over with quickly."

She doesn't recognize me. I shouldn't be surprised, but I still am. It's been months since we last saw each other. It occurs to me that, though we learned much about each other during our time in Athena's temple, she never knew where I was truly from. She never would have thought to find me here.

"Apollonia," I say more quietly. "It's me. Meddy."

"Meddy?" Apollonia starts, half rotating before thinking better of it.

"It's okay," I say, trying to sound as gentle as I can. "I won't turn you to stone. It's a power I can control. I won't harm you."

Apollonia hesitates, then slowly she faces me with her eyes still screwed shut. She cracks one eye, then the other. I watch as she looks at me and, for the first time, really sees me. Her eyes go wide.

"Meddy! What are you doing here?"

"I never told you where I was from because I couldn't," I answer. "Now you know."

The shock still hasn't left her face. I can practically see the questions forming in her mind, all fighting to be asked first. I determine the moment she settles on one.

"You've left Athens," she says. "So, you didn't become a priestess?"

"I did." Even now, I feel guilty admitting that. "But I was expelled when . . . I angered Athena. She cursed me and my sisters to look like this. She made us monsters."

"Why?" asks Apollonia.

"It's a long story." And in truth, I'm not sure it's one I'm ready to tell yet. I change the subject. "You're hurt." I nod to a cut on her foot, the cause of her limp. "Let me help."

Apollonia hesitates a second time before nodding, and I need no further prompt to go to her. She eyes the snakes on my head warily.

"They won't bother you, either," I say, extending an arm. "Come on, you can rest in the palace."

. . .

Our walk back up to the palace is slow. The cut on Apollonia's foot pains her more the farther she walks, and eventually, I hook her arm over my shoulders so that she can lean most of her weight on me. It is strange, having someone from my former life in Athens here on the island, but I have little time to reflect on it as I guide Apollonia to my bedchamber.

"Sit there." I gesture.

She eases down onto the edge of my bed while I search the room for supplies. I have no desire to wake one of the slaves at this hour. I'm not sure any of them would even answer my summons after hearing the commotion outside. Finally, I tear one of my own tunics, grab a pitcher of water, and kneel at Apollonia's feet. She scoots back, out of my reach.

"Please," I say, my hand hovering. "Let me."

Something in her seems to give, and she relents. Carefully, I use the strip of torn cloth to dab away the sand and crusted blood. Her skin is soft, warm, and I don't recall the last time I touched another person with this kind of gentleness. When the wound is clean and bandaged, I rise again.

"Are you hungry?" I look around the room. "I don't have much, but there's some fruit and bread."

"It's all right," says Apollonia. The hard edge I heard in her voice earlier has receded. "I'm used to eating less now."

I turn and look at her properly in the candlelight. She's thinner than I remembered. Her once-glossy chestnut hair is matted, and there's a light missing from my friend's eyes. Quickly, I gather the remaining fruit and bread and bring the plate to her. I pour her water, too. She tries to eat with the grace I know she once had, but hunger gets the better of her, and she devours the food within a minute.

"I can get more," I offer.

"It's all right," says Apollonia. "I just need rest."

"You can sleep here." The words leave my mouth before I've paused to consider them. Apollonia looks up at me.

"What happened to you?" We ask the question at the same time, but I follow up first. "What happened to you, Apollonia? After you were banned from the Acropolis?"

She takes another long sip before answering. "After I left the temple, I went to my father's house. The slaves brought me to him, but when he learned what I had done, when he learned that I'd been expelled . . ." She turns white. "It was worse than anything I'd ever imagined. He told me I'd shamed our family, that from that day on, he had no daughter. He cast me out, and told me if I returned, he'd have me flogged."

Anger flickers in my chest. "What of your older brothers? None of them would help you?"

"They wanted to." Apollonia stares down at her hands. "But my father told them that if any of them did, they'd be cast out, too. Lycus snuck me some food anyway, and I lived off that for a while. Eventually, though, I was forced to beg on the streets."

"How did you come to be in the Egyptian's service?" Even now, the thought of him sets my teeth on edge.

"He came to me, offered work," she says. "At first, I thought he meant to hire me as a scribe, since I was highborn and educated." She looks away from me. "I realized too late that he wanted me for a different kind of work."

I remember the woman I once saw on the streets of Athens, the man who paid her. It feels as though I've wrapped my hand around a rose's stem, only to find it covered in thorns.

"I'm so sorry, Apollonia."

The words are not enough, I know this from the hurt in her eyes. She holds my gaze a second longer before looking away.

"I told you what happened to me," she says. "What happened to *you*?"

It's a fair trade, I know. That makes it no easier for me when it's my turn.

"What happened to you, on the night of Panathenaia . . ." I take a deep breath. "The same thing happened to me, in a different way. When Athena found out, she thought I'd betrayed her."

"And so she punished you," says Apollonia. "Just like she punished me."

Said aloud, the words are even more gruesome. I find myself wondering how many other girls there are in the world who bear the marks, visible and otherwise, of Athena's cruelty. When I look back to Apollonia, her eyes are drooping.

"Sorry. You must be exhausted."

"I am," Apollonia agrees. "I should go to sleep." To my horror, she begins easing onto the floor.

"What are you doing?"

Apollonia looks up at me. "You've been kind, but I'm covered in sand and grime. I won't dirty the bed." She gives me a rueful look. "I may not be an acolyte anymore, but I haven't forgotten all social graces."

I shake my head. "You can't sleep on the floor, I— Here, you can borrow one of my tunics."

She considers a moment, then accepts it. "Thank you."

"I'll leave you, then," I say. "Good night."

I'm almost to the door when—"Wait." Apollonia's voice is small. "Please, don't . . . don't leave me alone."

There's desperation in those words, a vulnerability I recognize because I've felt it, too. Even with my sisters here on the island, there is an undeniable loneliness.

Still, I only nod before turning to blow out the chamber's low candle. In the dark, Apollonia is a silhouette slipping under the bed's blankets. I wrap my head, then lie beside her.

"Are you afraid of me?" I ask in the dark. "Of the snakes?"

"No." Apollonia's answer is instant. "I think they're rather fierce, actually."

Something in me warms. Athena intended my curse to be a punishment. She ensured that all who saw me would fear me, regard me only as a monster.

I realize Apollonia doesn't see me as a monster.

"Do you still go by Meddy?" she asks.

"It was always a pet name," I answer. "My real name is Medusa."

"Which do you prefer?"

"Either," I say. "But the people who love me call me Meddy."

A small smile touches her face. "Then I will keep calling you Meddy."

They're the last words she says before we both fall into sleep.

. . .

I don't know what Apollonia and I had expected, the night I told her she could stay with me. One day became a week, then several weeks, and she never did find another place to sleep, despite our palace's many rooms. In time, I introduced her to Stheno and Euryale, after a lengthy and emphatic conversation beforehand to make sure they knew she was my friend and not to be harmed. They agreed to treat Apollonia cordially, even if, I suspect, they thought the two of us a strange pair. In time, Apollonia and I developed a rhythm all our own. Each day, I showed her a new piece of the island, and each day she relaxed a little, returning bit by bit to the girl I first met in Athens. At night, we'd light fires on the beach and sometimes asked those slaves who remained on the island to play music so we could dance until we were sweaty and our feet ached.

There were difficult nights, too. On some, I woke to find Apollonia not in my bed but sitting by the window, staring out into an open sea. I knew she had nightmares about the things that happened to her in the time after her expulsion from the temple. On one of those nights, I'd taken her into the gardens and finally shown her Theo's statue. Sometimes, both of us lay in bed and simply cried. We don't tell each other to stop, or promise that it'll be all right. We let each other sit in grief for the lives we had, for the girls we could've been, if the world were kinder.

THE FIRST TIME Apollonia and I made love, I was hesitant.

She wasn't my first, but in some ways, it still felt like she was. She didn't rush me, and when her lips finally met mine, I was delighted to find them soft and sweet like nectar. She was patient as she guided my hand, showed me where to touch her and where to touch myself. Each time we went further, she'd ask, *Is this all right? Does that feel good?* Each time, I'd answer with more enthusiasm.

She crawls up the bed now, curls her body against mine, and gently kisses the place where my neck meets my shoulder. The lovemaking is good, but in truth, *this* part is just as good. In these moments, she's the one who makes me feel safe. I have never before known this kind of tenderness, this kind of care.

She walks two fingers down my side in the silence. "It's a nice morning," she murmurs. "Do you want to go for a walk?"

A part of me would like nothing more, but I sigh.

"My sisters need me," I say. "Euryale spotted a ship heading toward the island. She thinks it'll reach us soon."

Apollonia's expression changes, and I see something new in her— a weariness. "Will you ever get tired of it?"

"Tired of what?" I ask cautiously.

"Of killing men." She sits up in bed. "I've been here only a few months, and I've already lost count of how many have come to the island."

I think of the way my heart pounds in my chest when I turn a man to stone. I can't lie to Apollonia outright, so I tell her a half-truth and hope she believes it.

"I'm . . . not sure." I put a hand on her cheek, but she frowns and moves it.

"I don't think this is good for you, Meddy," she says. "Every time you kill, a little less of you comes back. One day, it's going to destroy you altogether."

The words cut. I sit up and hug my knees to my chest. "This island is my home, Apollonia," I murmur. "It's all my sisters and I have left. I have to help protect it."

Apollonia's eyes flash. "Is that what you want or what your sisters want?"

I find I can't answer that question. I realize I've never thought about it. Excluding my time in Athens, my sisters and I have always shared the same wants. The idea of having a different one from them seems strange.

"We could leave," she goes on. "We could take one of the abandoned boats, and we could go somewhere else, somewhere we could live in peace."

"We will," I tell her placatingly, still not meeting her gaze.

"When?"

"Someday."

A frown pulls at Apollonia's mouth, and I know that vague promise isn't enough. It has been months since I was last truly afraid of anything, but the look on her face now terrifies me. I don't see anger in her down-cast eyes; I see something far worse: resignation. She is beginning to give up on me. She takes my hand in hers and squeezes.

"I think I'll go on that walk anyway." She gives me a chaste kiss on my cheek before rising from the bed and wrapping herself with a fleece. She's out the door before I have time to reply, and then I'm left alone.

That night, more men come to the island.

It is only a small ship with a small crew, the kind of quick and easy work I normally don't mind, but tonight I am distracted. Every few minutes, I look from the beach back up toward the palace, at the single golden light flickering from my bedchamber window. I know Apollonia is up there, likely watching from the sill. Every time men come to our island, I tell her to stay away from the windows. I tell her it is for her safety, but that's just another half-truth. In reality, I don't want her to see this other side of me, the side that isn't gentle. Sometimes, when I'm turning a man to stone, I imagine I feel her eyes on my back. I hear the echo of her words from this morning.

Every time you kill, a little less of you comes back.

Is that what you want or what your sisters want?

The question digs into my conscience like a splinter. An uneasiness prickles inside me like a spider.

"Meddy, are you all right?"

I look up and find both Stheno and Euryale staring at me. I've always thought my sisters were magnificent, but in this moonlight, against the rippling reflection of the ocean waves, they are as breathtaking as our mother once was. In another life, they could be fierce warrior queens. I nod.

"I'm all right," I say half-heartedly. "Just thinking."

Stheno nods, satisfied, but Euryale gives her a reproachful look. Her expression is soft when she looks back at me.

"Sit with us awhile," she says, gesturing to a place in the sand.

I hesitate, then sit down. Stheno and Euryale take places on either side of me, and for a moment, the three of us are content to sit just like that, our knees pulled up to our chests, watching the tide roll in.

"Can I ask you two something?" My voice is barely audible above the crashing waves.

"Of course," says Euryale, "anything."

I consider how best to pose my question. Finally, I say, "Have you ever thought about what we might do? When this is over?"

"What do you mean?" Stheno's brow furrows, like she doesn't understand. "When what's over?"

"This." I gesture around us at the beach, the broken ship, the stone corpses strewn across the shore. "Surely we can't keep killing men forever."

Stheno scoffs. "I see no reason why not."

Euryale is gentler. "I suppose I've never thought about what we might do after." She turns to me. "Did something bring this on?"

Apollonia's name sits on the tip of my tongue, but I can't bring myself to say it aloud. It's true, her prompting is what provoked this conversation, but I know that it's deeper than that, that this is a question that has lived in the back of my mind since my first kill.

I shake my head. "I turned eighteen a few months ago," I say to both of them. "I'm getting older. I suppose, sometimes, I just wonder if there's going to be any bigger purpose to my life, or if this is it." I look between them. "Does that make any sense?"

Euryale's smile doesn't reach her eyes. "Stheno and I are immortal, Medusa. We've never had to give much thought to things like time, or our life's purpose. We'll likely stay here on this island for the rest of time, and we'll be none the sadder for it."

The words drop like a stone in my chest.

"So, you'd never want to leave?" I ask slowly. "You'd never want to see anything else?"

Stheno tips her head back. "I have all that I need on this island," she says, stretching her legs out in the sand. "I have my sisters, and I have my freedom. That is enough for me."

It's not enough for me. But I don't say that aloud.

I make sure to scrape the sand from my body and lather myself in rose water before I step into my bedchamber. I pad across the room softly to avoid waking Apollonia, but she stirs as soon as I burrow into bed, and she takes my hand in hers.

"Tomorrow, I want you to start packing your things," I murmur into her ear.

She turns to me, eyes still closed, voice slurred with sleep. "Why?"

I lie on my back and stare at the ceiling. "Because we are leaving."

XXXIII

WE RISE FIRST thing the next morning.

It isn't difficult to gather the supplies we need. The palace's kitchens have remained well stocked thanks to many years of preserving fresh water and food. We gather some apples and oranges from the gardens, too. The shoreline is littered with the abandoned boats of men who've come to the island; we pick the largest, sturdiest one and load the rest of our things into it. I am stronger, so I'm the one who pushes us off the shoreline, wading deeper and deeper into open water. When the tides are up to my middle, Apollonia meets my gaze.

"Are you sure you don't want to say goodbye to them?" she asks.

I know she means my sisters, just as I know instantly that I'm sure I don't. I glance over my shoulder, then shake my head.

"If I try to say goodbye to them, we'll never leave," I say. "They'll understand." Deep down, I know it will hurt Stheno and Euryale when they learn that I've left them again, this time without saying goodbye, but I know Apollonia is right. I have to leave this place, and I pray that one day they'll understand why.

Apollonia doesn't press the matter, and when the tide finally rises, she helps me into the boat. There's a moment when the waves carry it over a break, and I wait for some resistance, as though I'm expecting the island not to let me go. But nothing happens as we drift farther out, and I watch my island getting small again.

I turn the other way and begin to row.

. . .

It takes several days before we find land again.

When new shorelines come into sight—sooner for me than for Apollonia, thanks to my enhanced vision—I am relieved, but we quickly learn that the land at which we have arrived is not Athens or even Greece. We trail along the coast for a few days more before finally deciding to beach our boat, and then we learn where we are. There are several names for this new land, but the Greeks who have immigrated here call it Cyrene. A traveling merchant shows me a map, and I see that it is not far from Egypt. The land is hotter and more arid than both Athens and my island, but in time, Apollonia and I carve out something of a new life.

Cyrene is a city, but a slightly quieter one than Athens. Plenty of Greeks live here, but more of the city's women wear various wraps to cover their heads, so my own hardly sticks out. We live on the city's streets for a few days, and here Apollonia's experience on Athens's streets proves useful, but when an old widow learns we are both strong and able to clean with notable thoroughness, she hires us to manage her tavern in exchange for lodging. The days soon become long. The physical labor under the scorch of Cyrene's sun reminds me in some loose way of my summer as an acolyte in Athens. But, in time, I grow to relish the new start this city has given me. Apollonia learns to cook, and on the days the tavern isn't too busy, we steal an hour to sit outside and drink wine while we watch the sun set. For the first time ever, my life is calm, pleasantly mundane. Every so often, some part of me thinks about home and my sisters, but I try to forget.

Your life is here now, an internal voice reminds me. *You have Apollonia, and you have peace. That should be enough.*

I tell myself that's true until I believe it.

My days in Cyrene begin the same way most mornings.

I start by taking a vase down to the wells. It is a job I can easily do alone, but Apollonia often joins me. I enjoy her company. Sometimes we walk in silence, other times we talk about the weather or the things that make us smile. It is a tradition as mundane as everything else here, but in time, I grow to like it. I memorize the steps in the rocky path, and learn to hop over the ones that are loose. I look for familiar faces as we amble along. There's a woman who always has fresh fish, a man whose olive oil is unrivaled. I've begun to learn the cadence of this place, the way it breathes.

It's why, on this particular day, I can tell something is wrong well before I see it. By the time we reach the market, my suspicions are confirmed.

Several women are gathered together by the well, their heads bent low. One of them, a middle-aged woman whose name I can't remember, has tears in her eyes. I frown as we join their circle.

"What's going on?" asks Apollonia. "What's happened?"

The women avert their gazes.

"It's all right," I press gently. "You can tell us. We won't repeat it."

The women exchange looks, then seem to come to some sort of agreement. The oldest of the women takes a deep breath.

"It's Ephemia." She gestures to the crying woman before taking a deep breath. "Her daughter is pregnant."

Apollonia's brows rise. "Is that such unhappy news?"

The woman frowns. "It is when she's unmarried and only fifteen years old."

A shiver of utter revulsion crawls up my skin. "How did it happen?"

"Ephemia's daughter is a chaste girl," says the woman. "But there is a man who takes advantage. He looks for girls like her."

"Who?" Apollonia asks. "We could report him."

The woman shakes her head. "There are some men justice never reaches." She lowers her voice. "He is a priest."

I start. "Of the Temple of Apollo?" I'm aware the god has a rather large following in Cyrene.

The woman shakes her head. "It is a smaller temple, built for the goddess Athena."

The very mention of Athena's name is enough to make Apollonia and me stiffen.

"Each night, he makes himself available to those who would offer prayer," the woman continues. "Men pass without incident, but . . . the girls."

My jaw clenches. "He takes advantage."

Ephemia finally looks up. Her eyes are blazing. "My daughter went to him to ask for prayers to the Goddess. But she forgot to bring offering money. He told her there were *other* ways, other things she could do to make an offering."

I thought I had left the rage behind when I left my island. Now, as it rises to the surface again, I realize it's been there all along. Fury blazes through my bones as I think of the little girl, of all the little girls that this man likely exploited in his time. A roaring fills my ears, even as Ephemia continues to cry and the older woman goes on with her tale.

"He is wealthy, and popular with the king," she says. "He will not be punished. Meanwhile, the girls here are prey."

All men are cruel. I imagine what Stheno would say if she were here. *Some are just better at hiding it.* I don't trust myself to speak anymore, but Apollonia steps forward.

"I may be able to help your daughter," she says. "There are . . . medicines, herbs that can stop a woman who doesn't want to be pregnant from carrying to term."

Ephemia lowers her voice. "You know of such things?"

A shadow passes over Apollonia's face. "I once had to. If we act quickly, we may still have time to help your daughter."

Ephemia thanks Apollonia, and she agrees to visit her later. I remain too angry to speak. After we part ways with the women, she turns to me.

"Meddy."

"What?"

"Tell me what you're thinking."

The problem is, I don't know how to put what I'm *feeling* into words. My insides are a maelstrom of grief and nausea and, above all, righteous fury. Apollonia takes my hand.

"I can see the anger in your eyes," she says gently. "I can see it there, hurting you. Don't let it consume you, my love. Don't let it hold that kind of power over you."

Her voice is a raft; I cling to it so I don't drown. I screw my eyes shut and force myself to take one deep breath, in and out, then another. When I open my eyes, Apollonia meets my gaze.

"What happened to Ephemia's daughter really affected you."

"Of course it did." I stare at her, bewildered. "Didn't it affect *you*?"

"After I was dismissed from the temple, I saw many terrible things," she says sadly. "I saw horrific things happen to people who didn't have the power or the means to protect themselves." She briefly lays a hand on my cheek. "I've seen you angry before, Meddy, but *this* . . ." She gestures to me. "This is different. This is bothering you for a specific reason."

I flinch. The truth is, the priest reminds me of Poseidon. He is yet another man in a position of power, yet another man who has never been held accountable for the harm he's caused. I've talked with Apollonia about almost everything that happened in our time apart, but the rage I feel—the anguish I still feel—when I think about what the sea god did isn't something I've found the language for. It feels like a door I don't want to open, a door I'm not even sure I *can* open. Apollonia looks at me, expectant, but I shake my head.

"There's no special reason," I say brusquely. "I just think he's vile and disgusting."

Apollonia nods. "It's terrible. I wish we could do more for Ephemia's daughter, for the other girls, too."

Something ignites in my mind. "Maybe there is," I say darkly.

Apollonia pauses, uneasy. "What do you mean?"

When I don't answer, her eyes widen.

"Meddy, *no*." She takes my wrist and squeezes. When she speaks, her voice is low enough for only me to hear. "You cannot *kill* him. Cyrene is not like your island. People know each other here; you wouldn't be able to cover it up."

My eyes flash. "And if I don't want to cover it up?"

"The city's king will have you executed," says Apollonia, desperately. "He'll drag you through the streets, and then he'll take your head. Don't make me watch that. It would kill me."

Her words twist inside me like a blade. It's been so long since I felt helpless, unable to do anything at all. "So, you would ask me to stand by?" I ask, pained. "You would ask me to do nothing?"

Apollonia takes my face in both hands. There are tears in her eyes. "I would ask you *not* to throw away everything we've built," she says. "Our love, our life here, it's *good*. We are happy, finally. I want to keep being happy, with you."

There's an earnestness in the way she looks at me that threatens to undo me. In that moment, I want nothing more than to sweep Apollonia up in my arms and hide her from the world, from its evil, from every real monster that would hurt her.

Words my mother said to me come back in an echo. *That's the curious thing about monsters. The worst ones don't bother hiding in the dark.*

The priest is a monster, of that I am certain. And if there's a chance— even a sliver of a chance—he could ever hurt Apollonia, I already know what I must do. I school my features and kiss my love's forehead.

"You're right," I say calmly. "Our life together here *is* beautiful."

Every muscle in Apollonia's body seems to unclench all at once. She's still holding my face in her hands. She smiles at me and we resume our walk together through the market's streets.

Apollonia gathers the herbs she needs for Ephemia's daughter, while I begin to plot.

XXXIV

THAT NIGHT, APOLLONIA prepares dinner early.

The smell of it—fish on a bed of boiled legumes and rice—is enough to make my mouth water. As a child, I grew up with cooks who prepared luxuriant feasts for us every night. When I moved to the temple, my meals were leaner, more practical. But only with Apollonia can I taste the love cooked into the meals we share. It's just one more way she takes care of me, one more easy percussion in the rhythm we've found together.

It makes what I'm about to do even harder.

"I'll have to go into the market again tomorrow," she says cheerfully. "I've used the last of the eggs."

From my place at our little table, I make a noncommittal sound and continue whittling away at the tiny creature I've been carving. I haven't decided what it is yet.

"I'll check on Ephemia while I'm there, ask how her daughter's doing," Apollonia goes on. "When I went to them earlier, she told me the girl's going to be married."

"That's nice."

Apollonia stops what she's doing and looks at me properly. "My love, are you all right?"

"Hm?" I glance up from the wood carving. "Why wouldn't I be?"

Apollonia's brows furrow, but her words are soft. "Because I *know* you," she says gently. "I know that you've tried so hard to adjust since we came here, and I know that what the women in the market said today about that priest profoundly bothered you."

. At the mere mention of the priest, I tense, but she crosses the room and places her hands over my fist, gently prying apart each finger until my palm is open again.

"I want you to know that I'm *proud* of you," she says. "You've worked so hard and come so far. I always knew this was within you. I never doubted it."

Her words are sharp like an arrow's tip. I work to keep still as the guilt inside me twists. All my life, I've wanted someone to see the good in me. Now Apollonia does, and I don't deserve it.

She looks up, as though remembering something, and returns to the stove. My pulse quickens as she turns her back. This is my chance. I slip my hand into the folds of my peplos until I find the tiny sack of powder. The herbalist I spoke to earlier promised me that concentrated Melissa leaf powder was a powerful but natural sedative, capable only of causing its consumers to fall into a deep slumber. That doesn't make what I'm about to do any easier.

Apollonia's back is still turned, and I eye the goblet of wine a few inches from my hand. I move quickly, tossing the powder into the cup just before Apollonia turns around again.

She stops, then beams. "Dinner's ready."

She presents the cooked fish and legumes, and I do my best to mirror her smile, but I can no longer focus on the meal, eager as I am for Apollonia to drink her wine. When we near the end of the meal and she still hasn't taken a sip, I grow desperate.

"We should have a toast," I declare.

Apollonia's brows rise in surprise. "A toast?"

"To our new life here," I say quickly. "To Cyrene."

Apollonia throws me a strange look. "Meddy, are you sure you're all right?"

I try to project contentedness as I take her hand. "I'm all right," I say confidently. "I've never been better."

Apollonia still doesn't seem convinced. "And you're sure there's nothing on your mind?" she asks. "Nothing you want to tell me?"

I look directly into her eyes. "No," I say lightly. "Nothing."

She returns my gaze before picking up the goblet, and for a moment, I think I catch something like disappointment in her face. Then she raises the goblet to me and downs its contents in one gulp.

The muscles in my body relax as she drags an arm across her mouth. "Will you come to bed?" she asks softly.

I take her hand and squeeze it. "Of course."

We do not make love that night.

The Melissa leaf is effective: Within a few minutes of getting into bed, Apollonia is asleep, her breaths long and deep. According to the herbalist, she will enjoy a long night of peaceful, dreamless slumber, and in the morning, she will feel nothing. I know she will not wake up anytime soon once she's taken it, but I still lie beside her for several minutes before easing myself carefully out of bed. I tuck the snakes into my head wrap and prepare the rest of my supplies.

This will be the last one, I promise myself.

I take one more look at Apollonia. She would not approve of what I'm about to do, but I pray that, one day, she'll be able to understand.

I pray that, one day, she'll be able to forgive me.

THE SUN HAS long set by the time I reach the beach leading to the Temple of Athena.

A part of me knows I should feel guilty for deceiving Apollonia, and indeed, I think of her briefly as I walk along. But the truth is that with each step, I also feel more like myself, like I'm slipping back into my natural skin.

Cyrene's Temple of Athena is paltry in comparison to Athens's, but its basic structure is the same. I've prepared for the possibility of other priests and priestesses as I pad through the small building's rooms, but I find they are all empty. *Good.* This will make my work easier.

When the women at the well told me about the priest, I pictured a monstrous lecher, so I'm taken aback by the frail old man I find in the courtyard sweeping up sand. He looks up at me and smiles. I take a deep breath, then utter the words I've practiced.

"I've come to ask for a blessing."

THE PRIEST'S STATUE is heavier than I anticipated.

He was a small man, but turned to stone, his body is cumbersome and ungainly as I drag him clumsily down the rocky beach and to the shore-line.

Dawn has broken across the sky by the time I reach the shore. The tide that was coming in on my way to the temple has since receded, and I suck my teeth. I'll have to push the priest's body farther out to ensure it sinks. For the first time, I'm touched by a flutter of nervousness. It took longer than I'd planned to get him down here. I'm running out of time. I continue dragging his body toward the water and exhale in relief as, at last, I feel the ocean waves around my knees. I shouldn't have to go much farther.

The sun is rising now. I know in the back of my mind that I will need to clean up and get home. Apollonia won't stay asleep for much longer. The less she knows, the better it will be for both of us. I feel a slight pang of guilt then, not for what I did, but for the lies I know I'll have to tell. She asked me to try my best to fit in here, to let go of the rage. I know she will be disappointed in me, and that truth settles like a weight on my shoulders. A wave crashes against my back, soaking my dress, and I sigh, exhausted.

I'm still in the water when I feel eyes on me, and for a moment, I wonder, *If I keep very still, will whoever's watching me decide I'm just a rock and move on?* But the gaze I feel prickling my back does not relent, so slowly, wearily, I rise, then turn.

The three boys are standing farther down the beach. My vision is better than it was before I was cursed, and I see them clearly. Their long, gangly legs and lack of facial hair tell me they teeter on the cusp of manhood without having quite crossed that threshold yet. I can tell, even at this distance, that they are of privilege and wealth—no common boys would be able to afford their richly dyed tunics, which stand out vividly in the morning light. Two of them are dark-haired, but my gaze fixes on the one in the center. He is taller, with a shock of curly golden hair that shines like afternoon sun. He might have been a beauty, but the look of repulsion on his face twists his features. I realize now what I must look like to him. My head wrap is gone, and the snakes writhe wildly about my head. I know what he sees.

He sees a monster.

We stare at each other for what feels like a century. Self-preservation tells me I should turn him and his friends to stone then and there. Make it quick and painless, then get back to the work I set out to do. But something stops me. I could kill the young man in an instant, but I don't. He looks nothing like the boy who once came to our island to kill me—the one Stheno ultimately turned to stone—but I still think of him. In an instant, the moment is over. The boy and his friends turn away from me and pelt in the opposite direction, kicking up sand in their wake.

Reason returns to me, and with it, fear.

They saw me.

There are few men who have seen my true appearance and lived to tell the tale, but now these three boys have. They are still running down the beach, the bright red of the blond one's tunic now just a pinprick against the sand. Dread builds within me. I am fast; perhaps normally I'd be fast enough to catch up, but after carrying the priest's statue all the way down from the temple, I have little energy left. As if in confirmation, my leg muscles throb.

My mind begins to spiral. The boys will undoubtedly find the authorities, report that they saw a monster. Perhaps one of them will tell the king. The king will send warriors to this beach in search of me, and when they do not find me, they will raid the entire city; they will ask its people if they have seen a woman who fits my description.

And those people will tell them about the two widows living above the tavern. They will lead them to Apollonia.

The only thing I can think to do to protect her is run. I leave the priest's stone body half obscured in the waves, and my plan solidifies as my steps quicken. Every part of my body aches in protest, but I ignore the pain as I scour the beach for what I'm looking for. Plenty of the island's fishermen store their boats on the shore. I find the biggest one I can and pull it out into the water.

The waves rise to my waist, and I shiver as a breeze kisses my wet clothes. I launch into the boat, grit my teeth, and begin to row. My biceps ache, then grow numb, but I keep rowing. By the second hour, my wet clothes have all but dried. Only then do I look back. Cyrene is still visible, but it is only a speck of red brown. For the first time, my shoulders heave with relief. Even if by now that golden-haired boy has reached the king, even if the king has already sent soldiers to the beach, they will find little but sand and a statue. Apollonia will be safe.

I once read that a person can survive for up to three days without water. By my second day, I am less sure that is true.

The sun is merciless. My lips have cracked from lack of moisture, and the skin on my shoulders has blistered. I continue to row in a direction that feels like east, like home, but there is no guarantee I'm heading in the right direction, that I am not simply subjecting myself to a slow and agonizing death.

The hallucinations begin that afternoon. At least, I *think* they are hallucinations. I have no other way to explain seeing my mother. She was always a beautiful goddess, but in her element, in the water, she is truly magnificent. I think to myself that this is how she must have been before she was my mother. At last, I meet the great and powerful Ceto.

White barnacles trace a line down her neck like a grotesque necklace; she doesn't wear clothes. And her hair—the hair she so painstakingly cared for while she was on the island—now frames her face in a dark, wild mane that glitters with droplets of salt water.

I did try. Her mouth doesn't move as she bobs among the waves, but I hear her voice clearly. *You must remember, I did try to keep you safe.*

I do not have the strength to answer her; nor do I have the strength to be alarmed when two great finned beasts rise at her summons and charge at me. They are gray-skinned, muscular, and when one of them turns, I see a mouthful of dagger-sharp teeth. I feel them underneath my boat, and then it's moving faster. It takes me a moment to understand. They are not attacking me: They are *carrying* me.

You must remember that I tried. I can't see my mother in the waves now. Her voice is distant. *I tried.*

My mother's finned monsters stay with me for the next several hours. Somewhere in that time, my body finally succumbs to the sun and fatigue, and I fall asleep, only to dream of Apollonia, red-eyed, standing on Cyrene's shoreline screaming my name. I try to answer her, but I can say nothing.

The sky is dark when I open my eyes again. The finned beasts have left me, but in the distance, I make out a familiar shape. My island. My home. I gather what little strength I have left as I row as close as I can to its shore. I didn't realize its beach has a distinct smell until it fills my lungs again.

With a cry of anguish and relief, I jump from the boat and stumble onto the sand. My body is spent; it will be hours yet before I have the strength to climb the rocky cove and find my sisters. For now, lying here seems good enough. I rest my head and close my eyes.

"I knew you would return," a low voice says. "Eventually."

My eyes open and I face Athena.

XXXV

THE GODDESS IS still as beautiful as I remember.

I imagine what I must look like to her. My snakes have not eaten in days; some lie limp around my shoulders, while the more irritable ones snap at the air and weave erratically. My peplos is torn and soiled. I reek of salt water, urine, and sweat. Meanwhile, the goddess of wisdom, warfare, and craft sits upon a large rock on the shoreline as though it were her own personal throne, as though she has been waiting there for me for days. Some part of me wonders if perhaps she has.

My knees threaten to buckle as I lift myself from the water. My peplos is soaked and heavy, but I force myself to stand tall as I approach her. A wave crashes against my back, nearly sending me tumbling forward, but I remain upright until I'm standing before her. We survey each other in perfect silence.

At last, when I can suffer it no longer, I speak. "What do you want?" I don't bother with civility, though instinct warns me I should be careful. Athena may pretend to be aloof, but I know better than most how sensitive she is to perceived slights, particularly from me.

Indeed, her gray eyes flash a moment at my insolence, and I wait for her to reprimand me. Instead, she lets the silence between us build for several more breaths before she finally speaks. "I thought of visiting sooner, you know." She pretends to examine her fingernails. "It's been some time since I've set foot on this wretched little island."

I don't know what game she's playing, so I err on the side of caution and remain silent. Athena's smile is cool, and a shiver stipples my skin.

"That was quite a performance you gave, back in Cyrene." She nods to me as though impressed. "Seducing a man of faith and then killing him, in a temple no less. How honorable of you."

"You know as well as I do that he was no true man of faith," I spit. "He was abusive. He exploited the vulnerable. What I did was—"

"Necessary?" Athena smiles again. "You've always had a propensity for necessary violence, Medusa. In truth, it's one of the reasons I was first drawn to you." She steeples her fingers. "I wonder, though, does Apollonia share your appetites? I'm not so sure she does."

Blood rushes to my face. The idea of Athena watching me and Apollonia like a voyeur at our most intimate moments sends a fresh new anger blazing through me.

"Further corrupting an already corrupted ex-acolyte," says Athena. "I suppose you'll tell me that was necessary on your part, too."

I clench my fists, but Athena has already moved on. She stands, stretches.

"You and your sisters have built quite the reputation for yourselves." She says it casually, as though we're discussing something as trivial as the color of her robes. "All around the world, great men and small ones whisper about Medusa and her sisters. *The legendary Gorgons.*" She offers a fake bow. "It is so vindicating to know I was right about you after all, to know that my instincts, old as they may be, are still good."

I know she's baiting me now. I worked in Athena's service long enough to recognize when she wants me to ask a specific question. I won't give her that satisfaction and continue to say nothing.

She sighs. "I still remember the day you came to me," she says, layering a touch of new fondness into her voice. "You were small even for a mortal, but you had the same resolve in your eyes then that you have now. I looked at you and knew at once that you were special. I was right."

I want to resist, but something in me breaks. "What do you mean?"

Athena smiles. "I asked you how it felt, when you hit Maheer, and you told me it felt good. I remember the way you attacked Kallisto when she insulted Apollonia, the way you attacked a soldier in defense of someone you perceived to be defenseless." Her eyes illuminate. "There's a rage within you. People don't like for women to have rage, but I've always found it beautiful. I've always found *your* rage beautiful."

I hate that, despite everything, I still crave her praise like a starved dog craves a morsel of meat. This time, when I don't speak, it's because there's a tightness in my throat.

Athena's expression softens. "You would have been a great priestess, Medusa," she murmurs. "What a shame you had to throw it all away with your deviance."

I thought I'd buried all the memories deep, but as soon as the words leave her mouth, I am back in the garden, the grass prickling my skin. I want to scream and cry and rage all at once.

"You really were my greatest disappointment."

"All this time, I thought you were angry with me because I failed you," I whisper, staring at my palms. "I understand now." I look up at her. "You weren't angry with me because you thought I betrayed you, and you weren't angry with Poseidon because he violated me." I shake my head. "You were only angry that Poseidon used something you thought *belonged* to you. Someone else used your tool."

"And what a tool you have become." I expected Athena to bristle at my accusation, to deny it. Instead, she cocks her head, and there is an unsettling gentleness in that look. "Look at you now, Medusa. You are strong, powerful, feared. All your life, you have looked for purpose. *I* could give you new purpose."

I can't help the doubt that crosses my face. The girl I was before Athena cursed me might have taken her words at face value.

The girl I am now doesn't dare.

"You wouldn't serve me as a priestess," Athena continues. "But you would be something greater. The sick, the vile, the horrible people of this world, the ones who deserve violence. You and I could find them, punish them. You could leave this island again, see the world, and fight for a just cause."

I cannot deny the appeal this idea holds. I hate Athena, but she knows me. She knows exactly what I've always wanted. Would it really be so hard, I wonder, to fall to my knees before the goddess of wisdom one last time?

But you would still serve, Stheno's imaginary voice in my head says, *and you would still be a tool.*

My answer is instant.

"No." I meet Athena's gaze and hold it. "I want nothing else from you."

Like that, the illusion shatters.

"You seal your own destiny, girl," Athena says coldly. "And when you die, it will be brutal."

"There are worse things than death," I say calmly. "Maybe you'll live long enough to find out."

Athena's face changes. The façade of cool indifference slips for a moment, and I catch a glimpse of what's behind it. I see fear.

"Goodbye, Athena." I turn from her and walk away. I don't look back. I know in my heart of hearts I will never lay eyes on her again.

I don't know the exact moment the air around me changes, the moment I realize I'm not alone anymore. When I turn, I'm almost unsurprised to see Maheer's lion stalking across the sand, the one the prince and his entourage brought to our island all those months ago. Once, I might have been afraid of it, but in my new form, with my new strength, I am only curious as it approaches. The creature seems to share my sentiments, because from a few feet away, it stops to look at me. The lion seems more muscled, leaner than when I left for Athens, and I imagine it is because it has had to hunt for its food. Its eyes shine like golden orbs in the evening light, and though it doesn't move, I feel power emanating from it. When I take a step closer to the beast, it doesn't snarl or shirk away, and so I take a second step, and a third. I walk until I am within an arm's length of it. I start to lift my hand to touch its black nose, but something stops me.

"You are not a monster," I murmur. I don't know if the words are for the lion or for me. "You are only what they made you."

LIFE REUNITED WITH my sisters the second time is different.

They weren't angry when they found me back in the palace, only glad I'd returned. Neither of them asked me about Apollonia, and for that, I'm grateful. I still believe what I did to protect her was the right thing, but that knowledge doesn't fill the gaping hole left by her absence. I miss so much about her, but above all things, I miss sunsets. I miss the laughter.

In the weeks that follow, men continue to come to the island. Stheno and Euryale have not changed—I can't say that I expect them to—and they still kill the men with relish. Sometimes I join them, but more often than not, I stay in the palace. Every so often, after they've gone inside, I'll walk the shoreline and find some boy or man who somehow escaped the violence. I tell them where to find the abandoned boats, and I send them off with food. I don't know how many of them make it, how many of them find their way home, but each time I watch them sail away, I hold out hope that they do.

I stay with my sisters for a month until, one night, I find them on the island's shoreline.

Euryale is playing with one of her snakes, letting it coil and uncoil around her wrist. Stheno is stiller, almost meditative as she stares out at the open sea. When they see me, they move to make room for me without saying a word, and I settle into my natural place between them. I draw my knees up to my chest as Euryale starts to hum a sweet wordless song, one whose tune I've always known. Stheno and I join her, finding its harmonies. When it's over, Euryale grabs my hand and squeezes. We stay like that until the moon rises high in the sky, casting all three of us in soft, milky light. Eventually, my eyes grow bleary and I announce I'm going to bed.

"Good night, Meddy." Euryale rises, and kisses my cheek. "We love you. I hope you always know it."

I *do* know. I kiss Stheno's cheek and then make my way up the dunes and back to the palace. By the time I walk up the stairs to my bedchamber, I'm exhausted.

I settle into my bed, pulling a warm fleece up to my chin. Around me, the serpents on my head coil and settle, their hisses quieting like the sound of cooling steam. It's a sound I've grown to find soothing, but something interrupts it. Even in the dark, I hear the echo of Athena's words.

All your life, you have looked for purpose. I could give you new purpose.

There was a time when I might have believed that, the idea that someone else can give you purpose. I'm grateful now to know the truth, that the only person who can give me purpose is myself. As the world fades, I find myself wondering if perhaps purpose is not a single thing one finds, but rather a thing one finds over and over again. I'm only eighteen, but I've already had so many purposes. I have been a mortal girl whose purpose was to marry well. I have been a priestess whose purpose was to serve. I have been a monster whose purpose was to avenge. I find that I'm excited to learn what my next purpose will be.

And that is enough.

EPILOGUE

IT'S JUST PAST dawn when the young woman climbs the steps.

Above, the sky blushes pink, the color of the woman's lips. Golden light illuminates her dark brown skin as she approaches her sister's bedchamber, humming a familiar melody that comes from deep in her throat. Euryale pays no mind to the air's unnatural stillness, nor does she heed the gulls who've found places to perch on the sills of the palace's open windows. The seabirds watch, and they wait.

She opens the bedchamber door and then she screams.

Euryale falls to her knees, throws her head back in anguish. She wails until cracks splinter through the bedchamber, until the age-old walls of the palace crumble to fine dust. She pounds her fist into the marble until every living creature within miles flees, until the island itself splits in two like a gaping wound. She whimpers and cradles her sister's limp body, letting sticky red blood soak her tunic. Through the mad haze of grief, Euryale understands that her sister Medusa is dead and that her screams will not bring life back to her corpse, nor bring back the head that's been severed from her body.

Stheno's grief is different. She does not go to see her sister's body; she hears Euryale's screams, and she knows. She has always known that her mortal sister would be taken from her eventually. She does not weep for her youngest sister, but she rages. She finds the island's remaining trees and wraps her arms around their trunks, ripping them out by their roots.

She stalks the halls of the palace, turning every slave to stone until there are none left. She glares at the sky and shouts curses in every human tongue she knows until the muscles in her throat ache and she cannot speak at all. She sees a lion stalking along the coast and thinks to kill it, but something stops her. It is the first and only time she shows true mercy.

As the sun sets on their now-broken island, Stheno and Euryale begin to plot. For the first time in all their years, they leave home. They seek out their kin first, question every god and goddess who belongs to the Sea Court. In time, a name is whispered. Stheno and Euryale learn that their sister's murderer is a favored champion of the gray-eyed bitch; he has golden hair and all his patron's cunning. Already, he has spread accounts of his triumph far and wide, and that is how they learn that it was the Olympians who helped him. It was Hades who gave him the cloak of invisibility, Hermes who clad his feet in winged sandals. Hephaestus gave him the sword he used to behead their sister, but it was Athena's gift that mattered most. It was *her* shield, forged in bronze, that the Murderer used to sneak up on Medusa while she slept. The shield reflected her gaze, so that she could not turn her murderer to stone even if she tried. Of course, she did not try; she died defenseless, in her sleep. When he tells his story at feasts, the Murderer brags that the killing was easily done. Stheno and Euryale learn that he kept their sister's head and now parades it on that same bronze shield like some obscene prize.

This, they cannot abide.

They sacrifice the last of their island's trees and build a raft from rattan wood. First, they sail along the Aithiopian coast, and when that yields them nothing, they expand their hunt. They stalk through steaming jungles full of strange and terrible creatures, march for years across scorching desert sand that blisters their feet. In their search, they turn a thousand men to stone, but they never find the one they want. When they reach the snow-covered steppes of a frigid and utterly foreign wasteland, it is Euryale who at last admits defeat and tells Stheno they must go home. They never find their sister's head.

The world changes slowly. In the end, the old gods win their battle, but lose the greater war. The mortals they thought would worship them forever keep the faith for only a few more centuries before they turn to newer, shinier gods. The older gods' strength is bled from them slowly, until they are little more than incorporeal wisps on the breeze. The minor gods—like Phorcys and Ceto—are the first to disappear, but in a matter of decades, Zeus is gone, too. There are only whispers of Athena's fate; some say she clung desperately to the last vestiges of her power until it was gone and then flung herself into the depths of Tartarus.

The two young women—who will always be young women—are unaffected by these changes. They are not goddesses, not reliant on anyone's faith, and so they enjoy a certain immunity. Their years turn to decades, which then become centuries, and somewhere in that gradual passing of time, their island disappears from the maps. Men forget the terrors of the infamous Gorgons, and they are reduced to mere myth. Euryale and Stheno do not mind this. These days, they spend much of their immortality sitting on the island's shoreline, basking in the sun. They always take care to save a place between them for their baby sister, the one men called Medusa, the one they simply called Meddy. They watch in silence as her true story is lost, as poets pen newer, more inventive ones. They listen as men give her new names—maiden, mistress, monster, legend. Stheno and Euryale understand that their sister is a myth now, and nothing at all like the girl they once knew. They do not mind.

They remember her for who she truly was, and that is enough.

AUTHOR'S NOTE

THE OLDEST STORY of Medusa appears in Hesiod's *Theogony* (c. 700 B.C.E.). She is also mentioned in works by Homer, Virgil, and Pindar, among others. In each iteration of her story, the narrative details are as varied as the poets who wrote them, under the influences of their own unique biases. This novel reimagines Medusa's story in the *Metamorphoses* (c. 8 C.E.), written by the Roman poet Ovid, a writer known for his antiauthoritarian views. It's important to remember that, despite many variations, no one version of Medusa's story can be held up as the "real" version; each retelling adds new perspective to a canon that has allowed her to remain an iconic figure for more than two thousand years.

While certain elements of Medusa's story are contested, others are less so. Medusa's parentage, for example, varies among classical poets, but many agree that she was the younger sister of Stheno and Euryale. There is no clear consensus regarding exactly where Medusa was born, where she lived, or where she died. This story sets Medusa's home on a fictional island.

In every version of Medusa's myth, she is mortal, and in every version she is murdered by a famous Greek hero through decapitation. That Greek hero's name has been excluded from the pages of this book, just as Medusa's agency was excluded from classical accounts of her story.

Medusa's relationship with Poseidon also varies in different interpretations of her myth. In some accounts, he does not appear at all; in others, he rapes Medusa, and as a result she is turned into a snake-haired monster as a punishment. There are also iterations of her myth with language that implies their relationship could have been consensual. In this novel, I chose to engage with the often-complicated nuances of rape culture, particularly when it involves perpetrators who exploit their victims using a power imbalance.

Despite modern misconceptions of ancient Athens, most historians agree that it was not a culturally, racially, or ethnically homogenous place. In fact, its coastal location ensured it was a diverse city whose economy heavily relied on foreign trade and a robust immigrant workforce. Though these metics (immigrants) were part of a class that was not entitled to the full rights and privileges of Athenian citizens, they were not necessarily enslaved people, either. Some metics would certainly have been able to carve out profitable and comfortable lives for themselves. While ancient Greeks were certainly cognizant of varying skin tones, they did not use modern concepts of race to form their identities.

When we present incomplete portrayals of antiquity, we risk erasing the legacy of those who lived in, contributed to, and shaped it. We deny some readers the opportunity to find themselves in our collective past. My aim in writing this novel was to help new communities find personal connections with Medusa, and with her story. I believe in doing so, her myth lives on, and she remains immortal.

ACKNOWLEDGMENTS

THIS BOOK WOULD not exist without the support of many talented people. Here, I'd like to thank as many of them as I can.

My first thanks is to my literary agent, Pete Knapp, who has been this story's most ardent champion from the very start. I'd also like to thank Stuti Telidevara, Emily Sweet, Andrea Mai, Kathryn Toolan, Danielle Barthel, and the entire team at Park, Fine & Brower Literary Management for always being in my corner. Thank you also to Claire Wilson at RCW Literary Agency for representing my work in the United Kingdom.

I owe many thanks to my respective editors for their guidance and encouragement: Caitlin McKenna in the United States and Melissa Cox in the United Kingdom. I'm also grateful to the publishing teams at Random House and Zaffre for their wholehearted work to bring this book to life.

At Random House: Rebecca Berlant, Maria Braeckel, Milena Brown, Madison Dettlinger, Jenna Dolan, Cara DuBois, Erica Gonzalez, Naomi Goodheart, Ben Greenberg, Will Lyman, Greg Mollica, Rachel Parker, Alison Rich, Jane Haas Sankner, Leah Sims, Kim Henze Walker, Andy Ward, and Lynn Wu.

At Zaffre: David Ettridge, Kim Evans, Kate Griffiths, Stacey Hamilton, Ella Holden, Vincent Kelleher, Leonie Lock, Georgia Marshall, Enisha Samra, Eleanor Stammeijer, and Nick Stearn.

Thank you to the artists who created this book's covers: in the United States, Will Staehle, and in the United Kingdom, Tom Roberts.

A special thanks to Dr. Sarah F. Derbew (*Untangling Blackness in Greek Antiquity*), Dr. Denise Eileen McCoskey (*Race: Antiquity & Its Legacy*), and to the late Dr. Frank M. Snowden, Jr. (*Blacks in Antiquity*), whose scholarship validated this novel's right to exist. I am indebted to Dr. Joan Breton Connelly (*Portrait of a Priestess: Women and Ritual in Ancient Greece*), whose work was integral to my understanding of religion and gender roles in Greek antiquity. I found a plethora of useful information about the material culture of ancient Athens in Dr. Philip "Maty" Matyszak's *24 Hours in Ancient Athens: A Day in the Life of the People Who Lived There* and appreciated his willingness to answer questions. Lastly, Dr. Jon D. Mikalson (*Ancient Greek Religion*) was an incredibly useful resource for Greek mythology, religious practices, and the way both shaped and influenced ancient Athens. Though I did a tremendous amount of research to understand what Athens may have looked like in antiquity, the 3D maps of the city in the classical period painstakingly constructed by Dimitris Tsalkanis were immeasurably helpful—thank you, Dimitris!

A sincere thanks to the authors who read drafts of this book and/or offered encouragement throughout the process of my writing and publishing it: Leigh Bardugo, Shannon Chakraborty, Roshani Chokshi, Natalie Crown, Saara El-Arifi, Isabel Ibañez, Rebecca Mix, Tochi Onyebuchi, Margaret Owen, Marie Rutkoski, Samantha Shannon, Sabaa Tahir, and Amélie Wen Zhao.

My foundation is my family, and I'm grateful to my parents, my brother and sister, the old friends who comprise my chosen family, my beloved pups, and my ~~grumpy~~ delightful spouse. Thank you all for your love and for always being the first to believe.

ABOUT THE AUTHOR

AYANA GRAY is the *New York Times* bestselling author of the *Beasts of Prey* trilogy. Her works have been translated into eleven languages across five continents. She currently lives and writes in Arkansas. *I, Medusa* is her adult debut.

ayanagray.com
Instagram: @ayanagray_
TikTok: @ayanagray
Facebook.com/AyanaGrayAuthor